Praise for the
Morganville Vampires N

Ghost Town

"Rachel Caine's latest Morganville Vampires thriller is awesome. . . . Young adult fans will enjoy this entry and the entire series, as this time local vampire civilization loses a primary restrictive barrier, leading to overindulgence." —Alternative Worlds

"A strong, straightforward story line featuring the residents of the Glass House facing a different kind of antagonist . . . edgy politics, petty bickering, and a sense of family add to the plot, with a sad if satisfactory conclusion that will leave readers wondering how long before something else goes terribly wrong in Morganville." —Monsters and Critics

"*Ghost Town* is rocking in every which way. . . . Caine's prose is tight, witty, and absolutely perfect in every way. Her narrator is more lively and real than ever before. After reading *Ghost Town* I can see why the Morganville Vampires is now a major force to be reckoned with. Vampire enthusiasts, eat your heart out." —YA Reads

Fade Out

"Book seven of the Morganville Vampires series won't disappoint readers, as Claire and her friends find themselves in the middle of a potential catastrophe wrought by a publicity-seeking filmmaker."

—Monsters and Critics

"Full of drama, pathos, and a touch of romance with characters larger than life, especially the teens trying to survive in a town run by vampires. . . . This is a must read for teens and adults."—The Best Reviews

Carpe Corpus

"Ms. Caine offers readers an intriguing world where vampires rule, only the strongest survive, and romance offers hope in the darkest of hours. Each character is brought to life in superb detail, with unique personality quirks and a full spectrum of emotions. *Carpe Corpus* is well-described, packed with action, and impossible to set down."

—Darque Reviews

continued . . .

"Rachel Caine has carved out a unique niche in the urban fantasy subgenre with her super young adult Morganville Vampires. The latest thriller contains plenty of action, but as always in this saga, *Carpe Corpus* is character driven by the good, the bad, and the evil."

—*Midwest Book Reviews*

"The pace is brisk and a number of loose ends are tied up as one chapter on the town of Morganville closes and a new one begins."

—Monsters and Critics

Lord of Misrule

"We'd suggest dumping Stephenie Meyer's vapid Twilight books and replacing them with these" —*SFX Magazine*

"Ms. Caine uses her dazzling storytelling skills to share the darkest chapter yet . . . an engrossing read that once begun is impossible to set down." —Darque Reviews

"Filled with delicious twists that the audience will appreciatively sink their teeth into." —Genre Go Round Reviews

Feast of Fools

"Fast-paced and filled with action. . . . Fans of the series will appreciate *Feast of Fools*." —Genre Go Round Reviews

"Thrilling . . . a fast-moving series where there's always a surprise just around every dark corner." —Darque Reviews

"Very entertaining. . . . I could not put *Feast of Fools* down. . . . There is a level of tension in the Morganville books that keeps you on the edge of your seat; even in the background scenes, you're waiting for the other shoe to drop. And it always does." —Flames Rising

"Fantastic . . . the excitement and suspense in *Feast of Fools* is thrilling, and I was fascinated reading about the town of Morganville. I greatly look forward to reading the next book." —Fresh Fiction

Midnight Alley

"A fast-paced, page-turning read packed with wonderful characters and surprising plot twists. Rachel Caine is an engaging writer; readers will be completely absorbed in this chilling story, unable to put it down until the last page." —Flamingnet

"Weaves a web of dangerous temptation, dark deceit, and loving friendships. The nonstop vampire action and delightfully sweet relationships will captivate readers and leave them craving more."—Darque Reviews

The Dead Girls' Dance

"If you love to read about characters with whom you can get deeply involved, Rachel Caine is so far a one hundred percent sure bet to satisfy that need." —The Eternal Night

"Throw in a mix of vamps and ghosts and it can't get any better than *Dead Girls' Dance*." —Dark Angel Reviews

Glass Houses

"Rachel Caine brings her brilliant ability to blend witty dialogue, engaging characters, and an intriguing plot."—Romance Reviews Today

"A rousing horror thriller that adds a new dimension to the vampire mythos . . . *Glass Houses* is an electrifying enthralling coming of age supernatural tale." —*Midwest Book Review*

"A solid paranormal mystery and action plotline that will entertain adults as well as teenagers. The story line has several twists and turns that will keep readers of any age turning the pages." —LoveVampires

THE MORGANVILLE VAMPIRES NOVELS

Glass Houses

The Dead Girls' Dance

Midnight Alley

Feast of Fools

Lord of Misrule

Carpe Corpus

Fade Out

Kiss of Death

Ghost Town

Bite Club

Last Breath

THE MORGANVILLE VAMPIRES

Last Breath

Rachel Caine

NEW AMERICAN LIBRARY

New American Library
Published by New American Library, a division of
Penguin Group (USA) Inc., 375 Hudson Street,
New York, New York 10014, USA
Penguin Group (Canada), 90 Eglinton Avenue East, Suite 700, Toronto,
Ontario M4P 2Y3, Canada (a division of Pearson Penguin Canada Inc.)
Penguin Books Ltd., 80 Strand, London WC2R 0RL, England
Penguin Ireland, 25 St. Stephen's Green, Dublin 2,
Ireland (a division of Penguin Books Ltd.)
Penguin Group (Australia), 250 Camberwell Road, Camberwell, Victoria 3124,
Australia (a division of Pearson Australia Group Pty. Ltd.)
Penguin Books India Pvt. Ltd., 11 Community Centre, Panchsheel Park,
New Delhi - 110 017, India
Penguin Group (NZ), 67 Apollo Drive, Rosedale, Auckland 0632,
New Zealand (a division of Pearson New Zealand Ltd.)
Penguin Books (South Africa) (Pty.) Ltd., 24 Sturdee Avenue,
Rosebank, Johannesburg 2196, South Africa

Penguin Books Ltd., Registered Offices:
80 Strand, London WC2R 0RL, England

Published by New American Library, a division of Penguin Group (USA) Inc. Previously published in a New American Library hardcover edition.

First New American Library Trade Paperback Printing, April 2012
10 9 8 7 6 5 4 3 2 1

REGISTERED TRADEMARK—MARCA REGISTRADA

New American Library Trade Paperback ISBN: 978-0-451-23580-0

The Library of Congress has cataloged the hardcover edition of this title as follows:

Caine, Rachel.
Last breath/Rachel Caine.
p. cm.—(The Morganville vampires)
ISBN 978-0-451-23487-2
[1. Supernatural—Fiction. 2. Vampires—Fiction. 3. Colleges and universities—Fiction. 4. Texas—Fiction.] I. Title.
PZ7.C1198Las 2011
[Fic]—dc23 2011020503

Set in Centaur MT

Printed in the United States of America

To Claire Wilkins, Griffin, and Gareth.
I know Big G will always be with you.
Love.

ACKNOWLEDGMENTS

For all their amazing encouragement:

Cat
The Pats (all three of them!)
M
Jim
ORAC
The Time Turners, collectively and separately
The lovely people at Goodreads
Joe Bonamassa
The Smart Chicks
Charlaine Harris
The Incredibly Awesome team of A.J., Wendy, & Molly
My above & beyond travel agent, Susan Godwin
Rosanne Romanello (Go Ro!)
Susie Dunlop and the A&B team
Anne Sowards, for being awesome
Lucienne Diver, for so, so much
Charles, David, & Tommy—thanks for the faith
and . . .
Breana Blan from El Paso!

AUTHOR'S NOTE

If you're new to the Morganville Vampires series, welcome! And sorry, because it's Book 11, and you may be kicking yourself right about now, but don't worry. I'll catch you up quickly once you start to read.

For those faithful Morganville Residents who've been with me the whole way, I'm trying something new this time—an extension of what I started in Book 10, *Bite Club*. So in the pages of *Last Breath*, you'll venture out of Claire's point of view (the typical way the other Morganville novels have been told), although you'll stay with her for the majority of this book as well. But you'll get to view the story from a few *other* important perspectives: those of Amelie, Shane, Michael, and Eve.

So just make sure to look at the header at the top of each chapter to know from whose perspective you're about to read. Each point of view comes with its own chapter.

Thank you for coming along on the ride, and I hope you enjoy *Last Breath*!

And yes . . . there is a Book 12.

And no, I won't tell you what happens. Yet.

Last Breath

INTRODUCTION

Welcome to Morganville. You must be new here. That's fine; we welcome new blood to our town . . . but you need to know the rules. Don't stay out after dark. Don't break our laws. And, whatever you do, don't get on the bad side of the vampires.

Yes, vampires—we said it and we meant it. They're everywhere in this town . . . and they're the people you'd least suspect. But most of them just want to live their lives in peace. Oh, there are a few troublemakers—aren't there always?—but Morganville is all about harmony and cooperation. Theoretically.

You'll probably need to find yourself a vampire Protector. That means one who'll ensure the safety of you and your family, for the low, low price of a percentage of your income and regular donations at the blood bank in his or her name.

If you don't want to go with a Protector, well, it's your funeral. Some have done it, sure. But most aren't around to endorse the practice, if you get my drift. Talk to the residents of the Glass House: Claire, Shane, Michael, and Eve. They'll tell you all about your chances of survival.

And remember: welcome to Morganville! You'll never want to leave.

And even if you want to . . . well, you can't. Sorry about that.

ONE

CLAIRE

Shane's lips felt like velvet against the nape of her neck, and Claire shivered in delight as his breath warmed the skin there. She leaned back against him with a sigh. Her boyfriend's body felt solid and safe, and his arms went around her, wrapping her in comfort. He was taller than she was, so he had to bend to rest his chin on her shoulder and whisper, "You sure about this?"

Claire nodded. "You got the overdue notice, didn't you? It's this or they come to collect. You don't want that."

"Well, you don't have to be here," he pointed out—not for the first time today. "Don't you have classes?"

"Not today," she said. "I had an oh-my-God a.m. lab, but now I'm all done."

"Okay, then, you don't have to do this because you're tax-exempt."

By *tax-exempt,* he meant that she didn't have to pay . . . in blood. Taxes in Morganville were collected three ways: the polite way, via the collection center downtown, or the not-so-polite way, when the Bloodmobile showed up like a sleek black shark at your front door, with *Men in Black*–style "technicians" to ensure you did your civic duty.

The third way was by force, in the dark, when you ventured out un-Protected and got bitten.

Vampires. A total pain in the neck—literally.

Shane was entirely right: Claire had a legal document that said she was free from the responsibility of donations. The popular wisdom—and it wasn't wrong—was that she'd already given enough blood to Morganville.

Of course, so had Shane . . . but he hadn't always been on the vampires' side, at the time.

"I know I don't *have* to do it," she said. "I want to. I'll go with."

"In case you're worried, I'm not girly-scared or anything."

"Hey!" She smacked his arm. "*I'm* a girl. What exactly are you saying? That I'm not brave or something?"

"Eeek," Shane said. "Nothing. Right, Amazon princess. I get the point."

Claire turned in his arms and kissed him, a sweet burst of heat as their lips met. The lovely joy of that released a burst of bubbles inside her, bubbles full of happiness. *God,* she loved this. Loved him. It had been a rough year, and he'd . . . stumbled, was the best way she could think of it. Shane had dark streaks, and he'd struggled with them. Was still struggling.

But he'd worked so hard to make it up—not just to her, but to everyone he felt he'd let down. Michael, his best (vampire) friend. Eve, his other (nonvampire) best friend (and Claire's best friend, too). Even Claire's parents had gotten genuine attention: he'd gone with her to see them twice, with exit permission from the vampires, and he'd been earnest and steady even under her father's stern cross-examination.

He wanted to be different. She knew that.

When the kiss finally ended, Shane had a drugged, vague look in his eyes, and he seemed to have trouble letting go of her. "You know," he said, moving her hair back from her cheek with a big, warm hand, "we could just blow this off and go home instead of letting them suck our blood. Try it tomorrow."

"Bloodmobile," she reminded him. "People holding you down. You really want that?"

He shuddered. "Hell, no. Okay, right, after you." They were standing on the sidewalk of Morganville's blood bank, with its big cheerful blood-drop character sign and scrupulously clean public entrance. Claire pecked him lightly on the cheek, escaped before he could pull her close again, and pushed the door open.

Inside, the place looked like they'd given it a makeover—more brightly, warmly lit than the last time she'd been in, and the new furniture looked comfortable and homey. They'd even installed a tank full of colorful tropical fish flitting around living coral. Nice. Clearly, the vampires were trying to put forth their best efforts to reassure the human community, for a change.

The lady sitting behind the counter looked up and smiled. She was human, and sort of motherly, and she pulled Claire's records and raised her thin, graying eyebrows. "Oh," she said. "You know, you're entirely paid up for the year. There's no need—"

"It's voluntary," Claire said. "Is that okay?"

"Voluntary?" The woman repeated the word as if it were something from a foreign language. "Well, I suppose . . ." She shook her head, clearly thinking Claire was mental, and turned her smile on Shane. "And you, honey?"

"Collins," he said. "Shane Collins."

She pulled out his card, and up went the eyebrows again. "You are definitely *not* paid up, Mr. Collins. In fact, you're sixty days behind. Again."

"I've been busy." He didn't crack a smile. Neither did she.

She stamped his card, wrote something on it, and returned it to the file, then handed them both slips of paper. "Through the door," she said. "Do you want to be in the room together or separately?"

"Together," they chorused, and looked at each other. Claire couldn't help a bit of a smirk, and Shane rolled his eyes. "She's kind of a coward," he said. "Faints at the sight of blood."

"Oh, *please,*" Claire said with a sigh. "That does describe one of us, though."

The receptionist, for all her motherly looks, clearly wasn't sympathetic. "Fine," she said briskly. "Second door on the right. There are two chairs in there. I'll get an attendant for you."

"Yeah, about that . . . Could you get us a human?" Shane asked. "It creeps me out when a guy's draining my blood and I hear his stomach rumble."

Claire punched him in the arm this time, an unmistakable *shut up,* and gave the receptionist a sunny smile as she dragged him toward the door that had been indicated. "Really," she said to him, "would it be that hard just to not say anything?"

"Kinda." He shrugged, then opened the door and held it for her. "Ladies first."

"I'm really starting to think you *are* a scaredy-cat."

"No, I'm just flawlessly polite." He gave her a sideways glance, and with a curious seriousness said, "I'd go first in any fight, for you."

Shane had always been someone who best expressed love by

being protective, but now it was deliberate, a way for him to make up for how he'd let his anger and aggression get the best of him. Even at his worst he hadn't hurt her, but he'd come close—frighteningly close—and that lingered between them like a shadow.

"Shane," she said, and paused to look him full in the face. "If it comes to that, I'd fight beside you. Not behind you."

He smiled a little, and nodded as they started moving again. "I'd still jump in front of the first bullet. Hope you're okay with that."

She shouldn't have been, really, but the thought, and the emotion behind it, gave her another little flush of warmth as she walked into the room. Like the rest of the human side of the collection center, the space felt warm and comfortable. The reclining chairs were leather, or some vinyl approximation. The speakers overhead were playing something acoustic and soft, and Claire relaxed in the chair as Shane wriggled around in his.

He went very still as the door opened and their attendant stepped inside.

"No way," Claire said. First, their attendant was a vampire. Second, it was *Oliver.* Oh, he was wearing a white lab coat and carrying a clipboard and looked vaguely official, but it was *Oliver.* "What exactly is the second in command of vampire affairs doing drawing blood?"

"Yeah, and aren't you needed pulling espresso at the coffee shop?" Shane added with a totally unnecessary edge of snark. Oliver was often found behind the counter at the coffee shop, but he wasn't *needed* there. He just liked doing it, and Shane knew that. When you were as (presumably) rich and (absolutely) powerful a vampire as Oliver, you could do whatever you damn well wanted.

"There's been flu going around," Oliver said, ignoring Shane's tone as he took out his supplies and laid them out on trays. "I understand they're short staffed today. Occasionally, I do pitch in."

Somehow that didn't quite feel like the whole story, even if it was true. Claire eyed him mistrustfully as he scooted a rolling stool up beside her and tied the tourniquet in place on her upper arm, then handed her a red rubber ball to squeeze as he prepared the needle. "I assume you're going first," he said, "given Shane's usual attitude." That was delivered with every bit as dry an edge as Shane's sarcasm, and Shane opened his mouth, then stopped himself, his lips thinning into a stubborn line. *Good,* she thought. He was trying, at least.

"Sure," she said. She managed not to wince as his cold fingers palpated her arm to feel for veins, and she focused on his face. Oliver always seemed to be older than many of the other vamps, though she couldn't quite pin down why: his hair, maybe, which was threaded with gray streaks and tied back in a hippie-style ponytail just now. There weren't many lines on his face, really, but she always just pegged him as *middle-aged,* and when she really stared, she couldn't say why he gave her that impression.

Mostly he just seemed more cynical than the others.

He was wearing a black tee under a gray sweater today, and blue jeans, very relaxed; it wasn't too different from what Shane was wearing, actually, except Shane managed to make his look edgy and fashionable.

The needle slid in with a short, hot burst, and then the pain subsided to a thin ache as Oliver taped it down and attached the tubing. He released the tourniquet and clamps, and Claire watched the dark red line of blood race down the plastic and out of sight, into a collection bag below. "Good," he said. "You have excellent flow."

"I'm . . . not sure how I feel about that, actually."

He shrugged. "It's got fine color and pressure, and the scent is quite crisp. Very nice."

Claire felt even less good once he'd said that; he described it like a wine enthusiast talking about his favorite vintage. In fact, she felt just faintly sick, and rested her head against the soft cushions while she stared at a cheerful poster tacked up on the back of the door.

Oliver moved on from her to Shane, and once she'd taken a couple of deep, calming breaths, she stopped studying the kitten picture and looked over at her boyfriend. He was tense, but trying not to seem it; she could read that in the slightly pale, set face and the way his shoulders had tightened, emphasizing the muscles under his sweater. He rolled up his sleeve without a word, and Oliver—likewise silent—put the tourniquet in place and handed him another ball to squeeze. Unlike Claire, who was barely able to dent the thing, Shane almost flattened it when he pressed. His veins were visible to her even across the room, and Oliver barely skimmed fingertips over them, not meeting Shane's eyes at all, then slipped the needle in so quickly and smoothly that Claire almost missed it. "Two pints," he told Shane. "You'll still be behind on your schedule, but I suppose we shouldn't drain you much more at once."

"You sound disappointed." Shane's voice came out faint and thready, and he put his head back against the cushions as he squeezed his eyes shut. "Damn, I hate this. I really do."

"I know," Oliver said. "Your blood reeks of it."

"If you keep that up, I'm going to punch you." Shane said it softly, but he meant it. There was a muscle as tight as a steel cable in his jaw, and his hand pumped the rubber ball in convulsive squeezes. Oliver released the tourniquet and clamps, and Shane's blood moved down the tube.

"Can I specify a user for my donation?" Claire asked. That drew Oliver's attention, and even Shane cracked an eyelid to glance at her. "Since mine's voluntary anyway."

"Yes, I suppose," Oliver said, and took out a black marker. "Name?"

"The hospital," she said. "For emergencies."

He gave her a long, measured stare, and then shrugged and put a simple cross symbol on the bag—already a quarter full—before returning it to the holder beside her chair.

Shane opened his mouth, but Oliver said, "Don't even consider saying it. Yours is already spoken for."

Shane responded to that with a gagging sound.

"Precisely why it's not earmarked for *my* account," Oliver said. "I do have standards. Now, if either of you feel any nausea or weakness, press the button. Otherwise, I'll be back in a few minutes."

He rose and walked toward the door, but hesitated with his hand on the knob. He turned back to them and said, "I received the invitation."

For a moment, Claire didn't know what he was talking about, but then she said, "Oh. The party."

"The engagement party," he said. "You should speak with your friends about the . . . political situation."

"I— What? What are you talking about?"

Oliver's eyes held hers, and she was wary of some kind of vamp compulsion, but he didn't seem to be trying at all. "I've already tried to warn Michael," he said. "This is unwise. Very unwise. The vampire community in Morganville is already . . . restless; they feel humans have been given too much freedom, too much license, in their activities of late. There was always a clearly drawn relationship of—"

"Serial killers and victims," Shane put in.

"Protector and those Protected," Oliver said, flashing a scowl at her boyfriend. "One that is of necessity free of too much emotional complication. It's an obligation that vampires can understand. This—connection between Michael and your human friend Eve is . . . raw and messy. Now that they threaten to sanction it with legal status . . . there is resistance. On both sides, from vampires and humans alike."

"Wait," Shane said. "Are you *seriously* telling us that people don't want them to get married?"

"There is a certain sense that it is not appropriate, or wise, to allow vampire-human intermarriage."

"That's racist!"

"It has nothing to do with race," Oliver said. "It has everything to do with species. Vampires and humans have a set relationship, and from the vampire standpoint, it's one of predator and prey."

"I still think you mean parasite and host."

Oliver's temper flared, which was dangerous; his face changed, literally *shifted*, as if the monster underneath was trying to get out. Then it faded, but it left a feeling in the room, a tingling shock that made even Shane shut up, at least for now. "Some don't want Michael and Eve to marry," he said. "You may take it from me that even those who are indifferent believe that it will go badly for all involved. It's unwise. I've told him this, and I've tried to tell her. Now I'm telling you to stop them."

"We can't!" Claire said, appalled. "They love each other!"

"That has exactly *nothing* to do with what I am saying," the vampire told her, and opened the door to the room. "I care nothing about their feelings. I am talking about the reality of the situation. A marriage is politically disastrous, and will ignite issues that are best left smoldering. Tell them that. Tell them it will be stopped, one way or another. Best if they stop it themselves."

"But—"

The door shut on whatever she was going to say, and anyway, Claire wasn't sure she really had any idea. She looked over at Shane, who seemed just as speechless as she was.

But he was, of course, the first to recover his voice. "Well," he said, "I told him so."

"Shane!"

"Look, vampires and humans together have *never* been a good idea. It's like cats and mice hooking up. Always ends badly for the mouse."

"It's not *vampires and humans*. It's *Eve and Michael*."

"Which is different how, exactly?"

"It—just is!"

Shane sighed and put his head back against the cushions. "Fine," he said. "But no way am I breaking Eve's heart. You get to tell her the wedding's off, courtesy of the vampire almost-boss. Just let me know so I can put my headphones on the going-deaf setting to drown out the screaming and wailing."

"You are such a coward."

"I am bleeding into a bag," he pointed out. "I think I've achieved some kind of anticoward merit badge."

She threw her red rubber ball at him.

Not that Claire hadn't secretly seen all this coming.

She hadn't wanted to believe it. She'd been involved in all the party preparations—Eve had insisted. Between the two of them, they'd planned absolutely everything, from the napkins (black) on the tablecloths (silver) to the paper color on the invitations (black, again, with silver ink). It had been fun, of course, sitting there having girl time, picking out flowers and food and party favors, setting up playlists for the music, and best of all picking out clothes.

It had been only this week, as everything got . . . well, real . . . that Claire had begun feeling that maybe it wasn't all just fairy tales and ice cream. Walking with Eve downtown had turned into a whole new experience, a shocking one; Claire was used to being ignored, or (more recently) being looked at with some weird wariness—wearing the Founder of Morganville's pin in her collar had earned her an entirely unwanted (possibly undeserved) reputation as a badass.

But this week, walking with Eve, she'd seen hate close up.

Oh, it wasn't *obvious* or anything. . . . It came in sidelong glances, in the tightening of people's lips and the clipped way people spoke to Eve, if they spoke at all. Morganville had changed somewhat, in these past couple of years, and one of the most important changes had been that people were no longer afraid to show what they felt. Claire had thought that was a positive change.

At first, Claire had figured the dissing was just isolated incidents, and then she'd thought that maybe it was just the normal small-town politics at work. Eve was a Goth, she was easily recognizable, and although she was crushingly funny, she could also piss people off who didn't get her.

This was different, though. The look people had in their eyes for Eve . . . That had been contempt. Or anger. Or disgust.

Eve hadn't seemed to notice at first, but Claire detected a weakening in her usual glossy armor of humor about midway through their last shopping trip—about the time that an unpleasant lady with church hair had walked away from the counter while Eve was checking out with a bagful of stuff for the party. As she walked away, the Church Lady had reached out to mess with a stacked display of sunglasses, and Claire had caught sight of something odd.

The woman was too old for a tattoo—at least, too old for a fresh one—but there was a design inked on her arm that was still red around the edges. Claire saw only a glimpse of it, but it looked like some kind of familiar shape.

A stake. It was a symbol of a stake.

Another, younger lady had come hustling from the back of the shop to wait on Eve, flushed and flustered. She'd avoided meeting their eyes, and had said the bare minimum to get them out of the store. Church Lady hadn't bothered to look at them at all.

Claire had waited until they were safely out of earshot of any passersby before she said, "So, did you see the tat? Freaky."

"The stake?" Eve's black-painted lips were tight, and even in sunlight, her kohl-rimmed eyes looked shadowed. Her Urban Decay makeup normally looked really cool, but in the harsh winter sunlight, Claire thought it looked a little . . . desperate. Not just crying out for attention, but *screaming* for it. "Yeah, it's the new big thing. Stake tats. Even the geezers are lining up for them. Human pride and all that crap."

"Is that why—"

"Why the bitch refused to wait on me?" Eve tossed her black-dyed shag hair back from her pale face in a defiant shake. "Yeah, probs. Because I'm a traitor."

"Not any more than *I* am!"

"No, you signed up for Protection, and you made a really good deal at it, too—they respect that. What they don't respect is sleeping with the enemy." Eve looked stubborn, but there was despair in it, too. "Being a fang-banger."

"Michael's not the enemy, and you're not—how can anybody think that?"

"There's always been this undercurrent in Morganville. Us and them, you know. The *us* doesn't have fangs."

"But—you love each other." Claire didn't know what surprised her more . . . that the Morganville folks were turning on Eve, of all people, or that she wasn't *more* surprised by that herself. People were petty and stupid sometimes, and even as fabulous as Michael was, some people just would never see him as anything but a walking pair of fangs.

True, he was no fluffy puppy; Michael was capable of really bringing the violence, but only when he absolutely had to do it. He liked avoiding fights, not causing them, and at his heart, he was loyal and kind and shy.

Hard to lump all that under the *vampire, therefore evil* label.

An old cowboy, complete with hat and boots and a sheepskin-lined jeans jacket, passed the two of them on the sidewalk. He gave Eve a bitter, narrow glare, and spat up something nasty right in front of her shiny, high-heeled, patent leather shoes.

Eve lifted her chin and kept walking.

"Hey!" Claire said, turning toward the cowboy in an outraged fury, but Eve grabbed her arm and dragged her along. "Wait—he—"

"Lesson number one in Morganville," Eve said. "Keep walking. Just keep walking."

And they had. Eve hadn't said another word about it; she'd put on bright, fragile smiles, and when Michael had come home from teaching at the music store, they'd sat together on the couch and cuddled and whispered, but Claire didn't think Eve had told him about the attitudes.

Now this thing with Oliver, telling her outright that the marriage was off, or else.

Very, very bad.

"So," she said to Shane as they walked home, arms linked, hands in their pockets to hide from the icy, whipping chill of the wind. "What am I going to say to Eve? Or, God, to Michael?"

"Nothing," Shane said.

"But you said I should—"

"I reconsidered. I'm not Oliver's messenger monkey, and neither are you. If he wants to play Lord of the Manor with those two, he can come do it himself." Shane grinned fiercely. "I would *pay* to see that. Michael does *not* like to be told he can't do something. Especially something to do with Eve."

"Do you think—" Oh, this was dangerous territory, and Claire hesitated before taking a step into it. Filled with land mines, this was. "God, I can't believe I'm asking this, but . . . do you think Michael's really serious about her? I mean, you know him better than I do. Longer, anyway. I get the sense, sometimes, that he has . . . doubts."

Shane was silent for a long moment—too long, she thought—and then he said, "You're asking if he's serious about loving her?"

"No, I know he loves her. But *marrying* her . . ."

"*Marriage* is a big word for all guys," Shane said. "You know that. It's kind of an allergy. We get itchy and sweaty just trying to spell it, much less do it."

"So you think he's nervous?"

"I think . . . I think it's a big deal. Bigger for him and Eve than for most people." Shane kept his eyes down, fixed on the sidewalk and the steps they were taking. "Look, ask him, okay? This is girl talk. I don't do girl talk."

She punched him in the shoulder. "Ass."

"That's better. I was starting to feel like we should go shoe shopping or something."

"Being a girl is *not a bad thing!*"

"No." He took his hand out of his pocket and put his arm around her shoulders, hugging her close. "If I could be half the girl you are, I'd be— Wow, I have no idea where I was going with that, and it just turned out uncomfortable, all of a sudden."

"Jackass."

"You like being a girl—that's good. I like being a guy—that's also good."

"Next you'll be all *Me, Tarzan, you, Jane!*"

"I've seen you stick arrows in vampires. Not too damn likely I'd be thumping my chest and trying to tell you I wear the loincloth around here."

"And you changed the subject. Michael. Eve."

He held up his left hand. "I swear, I have no idea what Michael's thinking. Guys don't spend all their time trying to mind-read each other."

"But—"

"Like I said. If you want to know, ask him. Michael doesn't lie worth a damn, anyway. Not to people he cares about."

That was true, or at least it always had been before. A particularly cold slash of wind cut at the exposed skin of Claire's throat and face, and she shivered and burrowed closer to Shane's warm side.

"Before you ask," Shane said, bending his head low to hers, "I love you."

"I wasn't going to ask."

"Oh, you were going there in your head. And I love you. Now it's your turn."

She couldn't help the grin that spread across her face, or the warmth that burst up inside her, a summer contrast to the winter's day. "Well, you know, I'm still *analyzing* how I feel, in my completely girly way."

"Oh, now, that's just low."

She turned, stood on her tiptoes, and kissed him. Shane's lips were chilled and a little dry, but they warmed up, and a lick of her tongue softened the kiss into silk and velvet. He tasted like coffee and caramel and a dark, spiced undertone that was all his own. A taste she craved, every day, every hour, every *minute.*

Shane made a pleased sound in the back of his throat, picked her up around the waist, and moved her backward until she felt a cold brick wall against her shoulders. Then he set about *really* kissing her—deep, sweet, hot, intent. She lost herself in it, drifting and delirious, until he finally came up for air. The look in his brown eyes was focused and dreaming at the same time, and his smile was . . . dangerous. "Are you still analyzing?" he asked.

"Hmmm," Claire said, and pressed against him. "I think I've come to a conclusion."

"Damn, I hope not. I've still got a lot of ways left to try to make my case."

Someone cleared a throat near them, and it was unexpected enough to make Shane take a giant step back and turn, putting himself between the source of that noise and Claire. Protecting her, as always. Claire shook her head in exasperation and moved to her right, standing next to him.

The throat clearing had come from Father Joe. The priest of Morganville's Catholic church was a man in his early thirties, with red hair and freckles and kind eyes, and the smile he gave them was only just a *touch* judgmental. "Don't mean to disturb you," he said, which was a lie, but maybe only a small one. "Claire, I wanted to thank you for coming to last Sunday's choir practice. You have a very nice voice."

She blushed—partly because a priest had just closely observed her thinking very impure thoughts about her boyfriend, and partly because she wasn't used to those kinds of compliments. "It's not very strong," she said. "But I like to sing, sometimes."

"You just need practice," he said. "I hope we'll see you again at mass." He raised those eyebrows at her, then nodded to Shane. "You're always invited, too."

"Thanks for asking," Shane said, almost sincerely.

"But you won't come."

"Not too damn likely, Father."

Claire continued to blush, because as Father Joe walked away, hands clasped behind his back, Shane had turned to stare at her. "Mass?" he echoed, raising his eyebrows. "Tell me you're not confessing, too."

"No, you have to be a real Catholic to do that," she said.

"So—what was the attraction?"

"Myrnin wanted to go." That said volumes, brief as it was. Claire's boss—a dangerously nuts vampire who was an utter sweetheart, most of the time, until he wasn't—was not a subject Shane really liked very much, and she hurried on as she saw his expression shift a little toward annoyance. "I went with him a couple of times as, you know, sanity control. But I'm more of a Unitarian, I guess. The church is nice, though. And so is Father Joe. Hey, did you know there's a Jewish temple in town, too, and a mosque? They're both really small, but they're here. I don't think the vamps are too welcome there, though."

"Just don't go telling him about, you know, anything personal. About us."

"Embarrassed?"

He buffed his fingernails on his coat and looked at them with an exaggerated smugness. "Me, embarrassed? Nah, I was just worried he'd feel bad about his celibacy thing."

"God, you are *such* a jackass."

"That is three times you've called me that in one walk. You need a new compliment." He tickled her, and she mock-shrieked and ran, and he chased her, and they raced each other around the block, down the street, all the way to the white fence around their not-very-attractive yard, up the walk to the big pillared porch of the peeling Victorian house. The Glass House, called that because the last (and current) owners were the Glass family—Michael being the last of that family still in residence. The rest of them were, technically, renting rooms, but over time Shane, Claire, and Eve had become Michael's family. As close as family, anyway.

As evidenced by the fact that when Shane opened the door, he yelled out, "Put your pants on, people; we are *back!*"

"Shut up!" Eve yelled from somewhere upstairs. "Jackass!"

"You know, when people say that, I just hear the word *awesome*," Shane said. "What's for lunch? Because personally I am down two pints of blood and I need food. Cookies and orange juice did not cut it."

"Hot dogs," Eve's distant voice said. "And no, I didn't make chili. You'd just criticize how I make it. But there's relish and onions and mustard!"

"You're a princess!" Shane called back on his way to the kitchen. "Okay, a lame Goth half-dead princess, but whatever!"

"Jack. *Ass!*"

Claire shook her head as she dumped her backpack on the couch. She was glowing and tingling from the run, and felt a little light-headed—probably hadn't been smart, doing that so soon after giving blood, but that was one thing you learned quick in Morganville: how to run even with blood loss. Shane wandered into the kitchen, and she heard things banging around for a few minutes. He came back with two plates, one with plain hot dogs, one with hot dogs buried under a mound of whatever that stuff was—onions, relish, mustard, probably hot sauce, too.

Claire took the plain plate. He dug a can of Coke out of his pocket and handed that over, too. "You're officially no longer a jackass," she told him, as he thumped down on the couch beside her and started shoveling food in his mouth. He mumbled something and winked at her, and she ate in slow, measured bites as she thought about what she was going to do about Eve.

Shane finished his plate first—not surprisingly—and took hers away into the kitchen, leaving her holding the second hot dog. He was gone—conveniently—when Eve came downstairs. Her poufy black net skirt brushed the wall with a strange hiss as she descended, like a snake's, and Eve did look poisonously fierce, Claire thought. A leather corset and jacket, skull-themed tights under the skirt, a black leather choker with spikes, and loads of makeup. She flung herself on the couch in Shane's deserted spot and thumped her booted feet up on the coffee table with a jingle of chrome chain.

"I can't believe you actually got him to donate without some kind of four-point restraint system," Eve said, and reached for the game controller. Not that the TV was on, but she liked to fiddle with things, and the controller was perfect. On her left hand, the diamond engagement ring twinkled softly in the light. It was a silver ring, not gold; Eve didn't do gold. But the diamond was beautiful. "You're going to be around on Saturday to decorate, right?"

"Right," Claire agreed, and took a bite of her hot dog. She was still hungry, and focused hard on the delicious taste to take her mind off what Oliver had said. "Anything you want me to get?"

Eve smiled, a happy curve of dark red lips, and dug in the pocket of her jacket. She came out with a piece of paper, which she handed over. "Thought you'd never ask, maid of honor," she said.

"I had some trouble finding the right party supplies. I was hoping maybe you'd take a look . . . ?"

"Sure," Claire said. It was a long list, and she silently mourned the loss of her day off. "Ah—Eve—?"

"Yeah?" Eve ran her hand through her shag-cut hair, fluffing it out into the appropriate puffball thickness. "Hey, do you think this is too much for meeting with Father Joe?"

Claire blinked as she tried to put the image of Eve's combat boots and stiff net skirt into the same space with Father Joe. She gave up and said, "Probably."

"Awesome. I was going for over-the-top. That way, no matter what I wear to the party, it'll be a relief."

Eve had a logic all her own, and usually it was awesomely amusing, but right now, Claire was focused on something else. Shane wasn't going to like it, and truthfully *she* didn't much enjoy it, either, but she felt like she had to speak up. That was what friends did, right? Speak up even when it was hard.

"I need to tell you something," Claire said. There must have been something serious in her voice, because Eve stopped fiddling with the controller and put it aside. She turned, putting one knee up on the couch, and faced Claire directly. Now that she had Eve's undivided attention, though, Claire felt suddenly tongue-tied, and there was a suspicious absence of Shane as backup . . . and no sound from the kitchen. He was probably lurking on the other side of the door, listening.

Chicken.

Eve saved her from the unbearable tension by saying, in a very level voice, "Oliver talked to you, didn't he?"

Claire pulled in a deep, relieved breath. "You know."

"Oh, he's been dropping hints like atomic bombs for about a

month now," Eve said. "Everything short of ordering Michael to call it off." Her dark eyes studied Claire's face, all too knowing. "He told you to tell us to call it off." Claire just nodded. Eve's lips slowly spread into a wicked smile. "See, I always wanted to turn this town upside down, and we are *so* doing that. I can just hear him now. *Back in my day, humans knew their place. What's next, marrying cattle? Dogs and cats, living together.*"

Her impersonation of Oliver's accent and impatience was so dead-on that Claire burst out laughing, a little guiltily. She heard the kitchen door swing open behind her, and when she glanced back, she saw Shane standing there, arms folded, leaning against the wall as he watched the two of them. "So," he said. "Vamp Central Command doesn't want you guys getting hitched. What are you going to do?"

"Piss them off," Eve said. "You with me?"

Shane's smile was every bit as dark and wicked as Eve's. "You know it."

"See, I knew I could count on you for quality mayhem, my man." Eve settled her focus back on Claire again. "What about you?"

"Me?"

"I know you're friends with them," Eve said. "Lots more than me or Shane. This is going to put you in the middle. I don't like that, but it's going to happen."

"Oliver already tried to put me in the middle, but as far as I'm concerned, who you marry is none of his damn business," Claire said. "I just wanted to make sure you knew what was happening."

"And what about Amelie?"

"It's none of her business, either. This *can't* be the first time a human and a vampire got married."

"It isn't."

They all jumped—Eve included—because Michael was standing at the top of the stairs, looking over the railing at them, looking casual and rumpled and fresh out of bed. His shirt was still half-unbuttoned.

"Sorry," he said. "Didn't mean to eavesdrop." He kept fastening his shirt on the way down, which was—from a purely objective point of view, Claire thought virtuously—kind of a pity. "It isn't the first time a vampire and a human have gotten married in Morganville, and that's the problem." He was a tall boy—and, oddly for a vampire, he was almost exactly as old as he looked, which was frozen somewhere around eighteen. It was a weird thought, but Shane looked just a little bit older now than when Claire had first met him, and Michael didn't. And never would.

He settled into his usual chair, the one where his guitar was lying in its case next to it. He was like Eve; he had to have something to do with his hands, and in his case, his default was the guitar. He went for it immediately, and began picking out soft chords and notes, tuning the strings as he went.

"Well?" Shane said, and sat on the arm of the sofa beside Claire. "You can't leave it like that, man."

Michael glanced at him, a flash of big blue eyes, and then set his gaze at a safe middle distance. His music face, Claire thought, the one that he put up like a shield. One place he *wasn't* looking was at Eve. At all. And that just wasn't right.

"It was before my time," he said. "Back in the sixties, I guess, a vamp named Pavel hooked up with a girl named Jenny, and it got serious. They got married."

Silence, except for the steady, relentless whisper of his fingers on the strings of the guitar. Eve was staring at him intensely, and finally said, "You haven't told me this."

That broke through his shell for a second, and he glanced over at her, an apologetic and gentle look. "Sorry," he said. "I was trying to think how to do it, because it's not a happy ending."

"Didn't think it was," she said. Eve sounded very steady, very adult. "But every story's tragic somewhere along the way. You just have to know where to stop telling the story to make it a happy ending."

"Well, this one doesn't have any happy middles, either," Michael said. "They were married for about a month, and Pavel killed her. He didn't mean to do it; he just . . . couldn't cope."

"Why?" Claire asked. Michael raised his eyebrows, just a twitch, and got a very odd look on his face, as if he was trying to think how to phrase his reply.

Finally, he said, "He wasn't used to being around humans on a daily basis. In particular, not around girls."

"And she pissed him off?" Shane asked.

"Not exactly—you really don't want to know."

"Yeah," Shane said, frowning. "I kinda do."

Michael now looked truly uncomfortable. "There are times when it's hard to be around girls when you're a vampire. Look, don't make me draw you a picture, okay?"

"I don't—" Eve's face went blank, and she looked over at Claire. "Oh. *Oh.*"

Claire shrugged, mystified for just another second, and then she got it, too.

Once a month. And vampires could smell blood.

She imagined her expression looked pretty much like Eve's.

Shane slowly sat down on the couch next to Claire. "That is . . . epically disgusting," Shane said, "and I don't think I will ever, ever get that out of my brain again, man. Thanks."

"Told you you didn't want to know," Michael said. "Anyway, Pavel didn't expect it, and he lost control and killed her. Then her family came after him and killed *him*. The vamps arrested her father and brother and executed them; some said they weren't even the ones who did it. It started the whole human underground resistance, and a bunch of them attacked the vampire districts and tried to burn them down. People and vampires got hurt; some got killed. Morganville was chaos for a while. It was bad."

They all let that sit in silence for a few seconds, and then Eve said, "And now, what? Amelie's afraid our story's going to end the same way? With her cleaning up the mess?"

"I don't want to hurt you," Michael said. He'd lowered his head while he was talking, focusing on his guitar, but now he looked up and directly at her, blue eyes clear and honest. "But we both know the risks, Eve."

"Honey, it's not the same thing at all. If you were going to snap, you'd have already done it—you've been living in a house with three heartbeats and *two* girls for how long now? You're not going to make a mistake, because you've already proved you know how to handle—this." She waved at them, the whole situation, *everything*. "You said it yourself: Pavel hardly ever came in contact with a pulse. He got overwhelmed—too much too soon. You're already used to it."

"What if I'm not?" he asked softly. "You really think about what might happen?"

She pulled in a deep breath. "All the time, Michael. I'm the one who's risking my life, after all."

Shane cleared his throat. "If you guys want to have some kind of serious convo, let me clear the hell out."

"No, you stay," Eve commanded. "Everybody stays. Everybody needs to hear this; right, Michael? If Amelie wants to come down from the mountain and tell you stop the wedding, what are you going to do about it?"

He looked—well, there was no other word for it than miserable. He looked down again, strummed a few chords, actually hit a wrong note. She saw him flinch, and he deliberately waited a few long seconds before he said, "I'd do what's right."

"That's not an answer." Eve's voice shook a little this time, and her fists clenched where they rested on her skull-patterned tights. "Michael, are you going to marry me even if Amelie tells you not to do it?"

"I don't know if I can," he said. "Amelie can influence other vampires, if she wants to. She has the power to make me do what she wants."

"Michael!"

"I'm telling you the truth!" He shouted it, and almost threw the guitar back in its case, standing up with sudden energy. His pale face was lightly flushed, and his body language rippled with tension. Claire unconsciously pressed herself back into the cushions, and felt Shane shift his weight next to her. She put a hand on his knee, and he relaxed. A little. "Dammit, Eve, *I am trying*. Don't you understand? It's not like I can just do what I want, twenty-four/seven! I'm—"

"Owned," Eve finished for him, and stood up to face him. Her fists were still clenched. "Amelie's pet. And she can make you roll over—is that it? You won't stand up to her, even for me?"

"Eve—"

"No. No, I get it." She was gulping in deep breaths now, and her eyes glittered, but she wasn't crying. Not yet. "Do you even *want* to marry me, really?"

"God," Michael whispered. He stepped forward and put his arms around her, a sudden, almost desperate move, and she was like a statue in his arms, stiff with surprise. "God, Eve, yes. I want to make you happy. I want that so much."

She went limp against him, holding on, and rested her forehead against his shoulder. "Then fight for us," she whispered. "Please."

"If I fight Amelie, I'll lose."

"Then go down fighting, you jerk!"

He kissed the top of her head. "I will." He rested his chin there where he'd kissed, and Claire realized that he was looking at Shane. She glanced up and saw Shane looking back. Whatever communication was going on there, she didn't have the playbook to read it. Shane's face was blank, his body language tense.

After a second, he got up and walked out of the room into the kitchen. Claire stuffed the rest of her hot dog in her mouth and followed him.

Shane kept walking, right to the back door, opened it, and went outside. Claire chewed fast, swallowed, and lunged out after him before the screen door flapped shut. She hopped down the concrete steps and caught up with Shane just as he sat down under the shade of the scraggly tree next to the leaning wooden garage.

"What was that look?"

Shane pulled out a pack of breath mints and took two, then passed them over. She took one. "You know what it was."

"Really don't."

"If you don't know, you don't want to know, trust me."

"It could not *possibly* be as bad as the Pavel story."

He sighed. "It's just that I'm not going to stand there while he lies to her. I'm trying to be all nonviolent and shit. And I want to punch him, and he knows it, and out here is better right now until I get myself together."

Wow. That was a *lot* of communication going on in a ten-second look. So much for guys not talking; they just did it way, way differently. "Wait. . . . He was *lying*?"

"I'm not saying he doesn't love her. He does. But—" Shane was silent for a moment. "But there's something else, too." He shrugged. "Look, it's between them, okay? We have to let them work it out."

"No, it's *not* between them—she's my best friend! I can't let her walk into this if he's not really *serious!*"

"She knows," Shane said. "Girls know, deep down."

She did, Claire realized. Eve had been focused on all the *stuff,* the party plans, the invitations, all that, instead of facing her own fears. She already knew something was wrong, and she didn't know how to fix it. "Well—she can't go through with it. She just can't."

"Hang on—half an hour ago you were saying how the vamps couldn't tear apart true love."

"If it *is.* But what if it's not, Shane? What if they're making some awful, awful mistake and they're both afraid to admit it?"

He put his arm around her shoulders, and she leaned against him, turning her face to bury it in the heavy fabric of his blue jean jacket. It was chilly out here, even in the sun, and she was grateful for the warmth of his body. The feel of his fingers stroking through her hair made some tense, anxious part of her slowly relax inside. "You can't fix everything," he told her. "Sometimes you've just got to let it fix itself, or wreck itself."

"Was it Gloriana?" she asked. Her voice was muffled, but she knew he could hear and understand. "Do you think she got to Michael?"

At the sound of the female vampire's name, Shane's muscles tightened, then deliberately loosened; it wasn't quite a flinch, but it definitely was close. Gloriana had been a horrible, manipulative, deceptive (beautiful) witch of a vamp who'd wanted . . . well, human playthings. She had definitely gotten to Shane, who'd become her toy soldier; she'd seduced the part of him that loved to fight.

She'd treated Michael differently. Still a toy, but a completely different kind.

"Maybe she did get to him," Shane acknowledged quietly. "Yeah, at least a little. She could do that, make you feel—anything she wanted. It's tough to deal with it, but at least Glory's gone in that not-coming-back way. Eve's still here."

"Is that enough?"

He didn't answer her, and Claire thought, miserably, that there really was no answer—none that the two of them could get to, anyway. He was right.

It was Eve and Michael's engagement, and Eve and Michael's problem.

If they could admit they actually had one.

The shadows got longer, and the wind got colder, and eventually not even Shane's body heat could keep Claire from freezing, so they went back inside. It was quiet, but not silent; as Claire poured herself a glass of water and grabbed an apple from the bowl on the table, she heard the creak of footsteps overhead. It had to be Eve, because from the living room drifted the quiet, contemplative sound of Michael's guitar. *Talk about "While My Guitar Gently Weeps,"* Claire thought. That was the saddest thing she'd ever heard.

Shane gave her a quick, sweet kiss and went into the living room. She stayed where she was, eating her apple, listening to the quiet, low buzz of their voices over the music (Michael was still playing), and wondering if she ought to go upstairs and see if Eve wanted to spill it out. It was a friend's duty, right? But Claire felt angry at Michael right now, righteously angry, and she wasn't sure that wouldn't boil over and complicate everything even more.

She eased over to the kitchen door and cracked it open. Shane would be kicking Michael's ass, at least verbally; she just knew it.

But he wasn't. They weren't talking about Eve or the engagement party at all.

Michael was saying, "... over it, man. If you want us to get back where we were, you have to let that crap go."

There was a short silence, and then Shane said, "I hurt Claire. Hell, man, I hurt *you*. I wanted to kill every damn vampire in the entire world, including you, single-handed." He paused for a second, and then said, very softly, "I was like my dad, only on steroids, and it felt *right*. I'm not sure that's ever going away, Mike. That's my problem. If deep down I'm an abusive, violent ass like my old man, how exactly do I pretend I don't know that?"

"You're not him." Michael kept playing, a slow and soothing tune, and his voice was quiet and deep. "Never were, never will be. You just hang on to that." He paused a second, and Claire almost heard a smile in his voice. "You still want to kill me?"

"Sometimes, yeah." Shane, on the other hand, sounded completely serious. "I love you, man, but ... it takes time for all that stuff to go away. I don't *want* to feel it."

"I know, shithead."

"If you break Eve's heart, I *will* kill you."

Michael stopped playing. "It's complicated."

"No, it's not. Stop screwing around and commit."

"Oh, so now *you're* giving me relationship advice? You can't commit to a cell phone contract, let alone—"

"I'm committed," Shane interrupted. "To her. You know I am."

"Yeah," Michael said. "Yeah, I know that. And you know if

you screw it up with Claire, I'll rip your throat out and drink you like a juice box, so you've got some incentive."

Shane laughed. "You know what? I do that, you've got permission. And you know how I feel about that whole drinking-me stuff."

It was a nice moment—one of the best she'd heard between them for a while—and then it all fell apart because there was a knock at the back door, and Claire went to answer it, and standing on the steps was a vampire. Female, wearing a hooded black jacket and gloves, very chic but also very sun-blocking. Claire couldn't really make her out beneath the giant dark glasses and the smothering garments, so she said, "Can I help you?"

"It's Claire, isn't it? Hello. You probably don't remember me," the woman said. She smiled, a little tentatively. "My name is Naomi. I met you the day that you freed us from confinement in the cells below town."

For a few seconds Claire didn't know what she was talking about, because that had happened a *long* time ago. Once she did remember, she blinked and involuntarily stepped back.

When she'd first come to Morganville, the vampires had been hiding a secret: they were sick, and getting sicker. That illness led first to forgetfulness, then to acting out, then to mindless violence . . . and finally to a motionless catatonia. The onset varied from one vampire to another; some were dangerously uncontrollable in weeks, and others were watching themselves slip slowly, day by day, year by year, toward the inevitable.

Naomi had been in the cells—one of the violent ones, confined for everybody's safety. When the cure had been distributed, those vampires had gotten better, and returned to normal—for Morganville—lives. She'd thanked Claire, back then, and seemed nice enough, if disturbingly Vampire with a Capital V.

Naomi took silence as an invitation, and stepped over the threshold into the kitchen, sighing with relief. "Thank you," she said. "I fear I don't brave the sun as much as I ought to. Even at my age, one needs to build up a tolerance, but I'm not good at forcing myself to do unpleasant things." She pulled off the glam glasses and pushed back her hood, and the face finally clicked into place for Claire. Lustrous, long blond hair, pretty, young. She looked a little like the much-loathed Gloriana, whom Claire and Shane had just been mutually hating, but Naomi was a very different person, and a very different kind of vampire—at least, from Claire's memory of her.

She smiled politely at Claire and held out a slender hand. Claire took it and shook. Naomi's felt cool and strong.

"Uh . . . it's nice to see you," Claire said, which was kind of a lie, because it was unsettling to see *any* vampire show up at your back door. "What can I do for you?"

"May we sit?" Naomi indicated the kitchen table with a very elegant gesture, and Claire couldn't shake the idea that this girl—not much older physically than she herself was now—had grown up in a time when elegance and perfect manners were survival tools, especially for girls. Especially for *royal* girls.

"Sure," Claire said, instantly marking herself as part of the unwashed rabble, definitely not throne-worthy, but she tried to sit down with at least a little bit of grace. "Can I get you any—well, anything?" They had a little extra type A in the refrigerator, not that it was Claire's to offer, but she didn't think Michael would mind. Then again, she felt weird about offering blood as if it were a cup of tea. There were limits to being social.

"I thank you, it is most generous of you, but no, I am not hungry," Naomi said. The way she sat, straight-backed and yet somehow perfectly at ease, made Claire feel sweaty and round-shouldered.

"I am very pleased to see you again. I am told you are doing very well in your studies." Her polite smile deepened a little, bringing out charming little dimples. "And that sounds as if I'm your terribly ancient maiden aunt. I am sorry. This is awkward, is it not?"

"A little bit," Claire said, and couldn't help but smile back. Naomi felt like a real person to her—someone who had lived a real life, and still remembered what it was like to have human feelings. "Things are going okay; thanks for asking. And you—how's your sister?" She scrambled to remember the name, some kind of flower. . . . "Violet?"

"I am gratified you remember. Violet is fine. She's taken up the opportunities Morganville presents with an alarming amount of enthusiasm. She's painting now." Naomi rolled her eyes. "She's not very good, but she's *very* determined. It always irked her when we were children that she was forbidden to do anything but ladylike watercolors. Every time I see her these days, she looks as if she's fallen face-first onto a paint palette."

"When we met before, you said—I think you said you were Amelie's sisters?" Meaning sisters to the town's vampire Founder, Amelie the all-powerful. Claire, looking at Naomi, could believe it; there was something about the way she held her head, the posture, even the glossy, pale hair.

So she was a little surprised when Naomi shook her head. "Oh, no, we are not sisters in the sense that we were born in the same family," she said. "Sisters in our second birth, if you will. We are both of the same generation turned by Bishop, and there are not so many of us left, so by tradition we look on each other as family. Violet is my true sister of my mortal life. Amelie is our sister of immortal life. I know it's a bit confusing."

"Oh." Claire wasn't very clear about the vampire concept of

family. . . . Apparently they traced it through who had made them vampires in the first place, so Bishop had a lot of kids, some of whom were what Claire considered good—like Amelie—and most of whom were definitely not. It mattered, but Claire wasn't really sure how much, or how it ranked against a human family relationship. Not enough to keep them from occasionally killing one another, but then, the same could be said for natural-born siblings. "I just wondered."

"At the time I met you, I wasn't used to speaking with mortals. It had been a very long time, and we were still . . . not as well as we could have been. But we're much better now." Naomi showed a full smile, and it was just a tiny bit unsettling. *My, what big teeth you have,* Claire thought. Not that Naomi had done anything wrong, not at all. She didn't even show a hint of fang. "So of course, I first want to apologize for any possible discomfort I might have caused you during our initial meeting. None was intended, believe me."

That was, in terms of what had gone on in Claire's life, a *really* long time ago, and it struck her as oddly funny. She tried not to let it show. "No, really, it was fine. I'm fine."

"Ah, you relieve me." Naomi settled back in her chair, as if she really *was* relieved, which Claire sincerely doubted. "Now that I'm reassured on that point, I can proceed to my second. I came to pay a call on my youngest relative."

Again, Claire went blank. "Um . . . excuse me?"

"Michael," Naomi said. There was something that turned warm and even sweeter in her voice when she mentioned Michael's name, and that wasn't vampire at all. . . . That was something Claire understood completely. "I have been missing him."

It was purely a girl-appreciating-a-hottie reaction.

And just like that, it all became crystal clear for Claire. There was, after all, a hidden vampire angle to what was going on with

Eve and Michael. . . . He must have been seeing *Naomi*. On the side. Without telling anyone, or at least not discussing it in front of Claire and Shane, and Claire was pretty sure that Eve wouldn't have been just *Oh, fine* about it if she'd really known.

The pretty blond reason for Michael's erratic behavior was *sitting across the table and smiling at her.*

Claire stood up, all in one rushed motion. "I'll go get him," she said. She knew it sounded rude, and saw surprise on Naomi's face, but she didn't care, not at all. "Stay here." And that was probably even ruder, that somebody with royal whatever blood was being told to stay in the kitchen like the help. *Good.*

Claire burst through the kitchen door. She must have interrupted some intense guy talk, because both Michael and Shane stopped talking and straightened up the way people did when they felt guilty. Michael hushed his guitar strings with a flat palm.

"You have a visitor," Claire said. She spat the words out flat and hard, straight at Michael, and she thought he must have been able to hear how fast her heart was beating. Maybe her face was red. It should have been; she felt hot all over. "It's *Naomi.*"

If she'd had any doubts at all about it, the sight of his face when she said the name erased them. That was the most shocked, caught-red-handed expression she'd ever seen, and God, in that moment she *hated* him.

Shane looked over at his best friend, but by the time he did, Michael had managed to wipe away all guilt from his expression and just look curious. "Oh," he said, and stood up, leaning his guitar against the arm of the chair. It seemed to her to be not just careful, but *too* careful, as if he was afraid to be seen rushing. As if he felt he had to slow down and make sure he didn't make mistakes. "Of course. Thanks, Claire."

She glared at him, and avoided him as he went past her toward the kitchen. She headed straight for the steps, prepared to run all the way up, but Shane's voice stopped her. "Hey," he said, keeping it low. "What the hell?"

"*You* go ask. You're always telling me not to try to analyze," she said, and went up, wondering if she should tell Eve, wondering if that would lead to the ultimate Glass House apocalypse. She didn't, only because she heard the shower running. Eve tended to shower when she got unhappy. There wouldn't be any hot water for anybody else, not for a while.

Claire passed up the bathroom, closed and locked her door, put her headphones on, and blocked out the world with the loudest, saddest music she could stand.

Oh, Michael, how could you?

If the knowledge hurt her, how awful was it going to be for Eve?

TWO

CLAIRE

Claire expected a blowup—daily—of the Michael/Eve relationship; Eve didn't mention Naomi, and neither did Michael, and the tension kept spinning up inside of Claire like twisting rubber bands.

Shane hadn't said much about Naomi's visit, either, though Claire could tell it troubled him. When Claire had tried to talk about it, he'd gone back to his old refrain. *Ask Michael.* Yeah, right, like she was going to get in his face and ask, when she already *knew.*

He also said *stay out of it.* And that was probably good advice. But Claire couldn't just see this all heading for the cliff and not at least *try* to turn the wheel. It might be wrong, it might be messy and crazy and a very bad idea, but she had to do it.

So she took Eve out for an ice-cream soda at Marjo's Diner, which Eve happily accepted, because there were no better ice-cream sodas available in the known universe, and Eve never turned down something ice-cream based. It was, Claire thought, a good thing Eve ran on so much nervous energy, with all that sugar craving.

As she spooned up the deliciousness, Eve couldn't put down her cell. She was scrolling through her to-do list, shaking her head. "You would not *believe* how much there is," she told Claire. "I mean, I've been doing this for weeks, and this list never gets smaller! It's insane. And I've only got a couple of days left. Oh! I need to get my appointment to get a waxing done."

"I really did not need to know that," Claire sighed. Eve threw her a wink and slurped up dessert. "Uh—I have something I need to tell you."

Eve's eyes widened, and she put both spoon and cell down. "It's Shane, isn't it? It's always Shane getting himself into some kind of crazy trouble. What vampire did he—"

"No, it's not Shane." Although Claire honestly couldn't blame her for jumping to that conclusion; Shane was trouble-prone, no doubt about that. "It's about Michael."

Eve smiled, but it looked manic and wrong. She was wearing an absolutely incredible shade of magenta lipstick, and her eye shadow matched. In the tired mid-last-century Formica and rusty chrome of the diner, she looked like a deadly, exotic flower, something imported from a place that had never seen day. Beautiful, but intimidating. And strange. "Well, at least I know *Michael's* not in jail. On the other hand, Shane just loves the gray bar hotel. Maybe it's the food or something." But there was a flash of desperation in her eyes. She didn't want to talk about Michael. Not at all.

Claire felt like something was pressing on her chest, driving all the breath out of her. "I'm not kidding," she said. "You need to hear this, Eve. About Michael." It hurt, saying this, physically *hurt,* and she felt tears tingle in her eyes. She blinked them away, fast. "I think he's seeing another girl."

Eve had picked up her spoon, and now she sat there, perfectly still, staring. She cocked her glossy black-haired head slowly over to the side, as if trying to puzzle out what Claire had just said. "Another girl," she said. "What do you mean, another girl?"

"A vampire," Claire said. "Naomi. She came to the house. I saw her. I talked to her. She asked for Michael."

Eve flinched, as if Claire had reached across the table and slapped her, and then said, "But . . . I'm sure she's just . . ."

"Just a friend?" Claire said when Eve couldn't finish. She felt like her heart was breaking. She could see the panic and horror in Eve's face, and the awkward way Eve put the spoon down. She clenched her hands together and started twisting her engagement ring. . . . "Maybe. I guess that's possible, but you should talk to him, Eve. You should ask. I don't think he wanted you to know about it. He hasn't told you, has he?"

Eve shook her head and looked down at her ice-cream soda, which was slowly melting. "He must have forgotten to mention it," she said, but there wasn't any conviction in her voice. "She came to the *house*?"

"A couple of days ago—remember when I went with Shane to give blood? She showed up after you went upstairs. I answered the door."

This time, it was *definitely* a flinch, and Eve glanced up. Her eyes were wide, and stricken. "He—he came upstairs later. We made up. He was—" She twisted the ring again, restlessly. "He was so sorry about upsetting me."

"Oh," Claire said softly. "And he didn't mention her."

"No. Not at *all*," Eve admitted. She suddenly flung her hand out across the table, and Claire grabbed it and held on, as if she were pulling Eve back from a cliff. "Oh God. I know Gloriana got inside his head, but I thought—I thought with her gone . . ."

"I know. But, Eve, I *know* he loves you. I just don't know—"

"If he loves me enough?" Eve laughed, shakily, and picked up a napkin to dab carefully at her eyes, making black blots of wet mascara on the paper. "Yeah, join the club. Well, what do you think?"

"It's not really what I think—it's what *you* do."

Eve sniffled and wiped at her nose. "This is ruining my makeup; you know that."

"You can blame me if you want."

"No. No, I don't." Eve sighed and looked up, trying for a smile but failing pretty badly. "I've known he wasn't totally—comfortable with this, you know? That he kept worrying, and thinking, and worrying . . . and I was just hoping that he'd stop, that it was cold feet, which is pretty stupid because he's a vampire and, you know, cold in general, but—I thought he'd get over it. It's just gotten worse."

"And he's not telling you about this girl."

"Apparently. Yeah." This time, Eve burst out in tears, and covered her face with the napkin. She had to use both hands, and Claire sat helplessly, wishing she could do *something,* while Eve bawled like a little girl. She finally got up and slid over to Eve's side of the booth and put her arms around her.

If the makeup had been extreme before, it was ultra-Goth now, with the dripping lines of mascara and smears. Eve started wiping it off, going through more and more napkins.

Marjo stopped by, took a look at the two of them, shook her head, and grabbed the desserts. She took them away and brought back a stack of napkins and a glass of water. "Wash that off," she said. "You look like a sad clown. Bad for my business."

For Marjo, that was all kinds of concerned and sensitive. Plus, she brought fresh cups of ice cream, for nothing.

Eve scrubbed most of her makeup off, leaving herself looking tender and raw and very young, and sucked down a deep breath and said, "I'm okay now. Here, eat your ice cream. There'll never be a better time, trust me."

The two of them ate, but Claire wondered if Eve really tasted hers at all. She kept hiccuping back sobs. "What are you going to do?" she asked Eve, finally, and her best friend shrugged without meeting her eyes.

"Well, pretending everything's just peachy hasn't really been the greatest idea," she said. "I could go full-on drama queen and scream and cry and throw things at him, I guess. I would have, a year ago. But now . . . now I think I'll just go . . . talk to him. I mean, I don't want to do that. It's going to hurt. But maybe it's the best thing for us both if we get it out in the open and . . ."

She kept talking, and Claire was listening, *really*, but the door to the diner opened behind Eve, and a man walked in, and an unnatural, weird feeling came over Claire, as if a wave of mist had washed over her. She blinked and focused on him, trying to figure out why she'd had that reaction—was it cold outside? Raining? No, it was same as it had been, winter-warm and sunny and dry.

Weird.

The newcomer wasn't so much to really notice . . . medium height, medium build, light blond hair. He was turned partly away from her, and from this angle there was nothing at all to distinguish him from a million other guys.

Then he turned to look their way, and for a second Claire saw . . . *something*. A flicker, an image, a vision. It was too short for her to really even process it, and she could easily have just imagined it, because there wasn't anything abnormal about this guy at all. He had even, regular features and eyes that at this distance looked kind of blue.

He stuck his hands in his coat pockets and walked past them to the counter, and then, without a word, went back outside, where he walked around the corner and vanished.

Claire turned to watch him go.

"Hey," Eve said. "Are you with me? Because I'm kind of in the middle of a crisis, here." She sounded annoyed, and Claire didn't blame her. She had no idea why she'd been so distracted. There wasn't any reason, none at all.

"I'm sorry," she said. "I just—thought I knew him, I guess." That wasn't it, but he'd felt somehow *wrong*. As if he didn't belong here.

"Who?" Eve twisted around. "I didn't see anybody."

Claire looked out into the parking lot. Nothing stood out there—no out-of-state plates on the cars, for certain. "Nobody, I guess. Maybe he's just passing through," she said.

"Wish I was," Eve sighed. "Anywhere else is better right now, including lava pits. Are you ready to go?"

"I— Yeah, I guess so." Claire dug cash from her pocket and paid for both of them, over Eve's halfhearted protests; Claire got a paycheck (allowance?) from the Founder's Office for her work with Myrnin, and her bank account had grown to impressive four-digit numbers recently. She didn't quite know what to do with all the money, but spending it on a heartsick best friend seemed like a good option. "Home?"

"Is there a second choice?"

"Well, we could go work on your shopping list?"

"That seems pretty dumb, considering."

Claire had to agree with that.

As they walked out of the diner, she glanced back, and saw the anonymous man was now back in the diner. He was sitting at a table, hands folded, and he was watching them as they walked to Eve's big black hearse.

The feeling of misty chill came over her again, and Claire shivered.

Shane was standing outside, in the yard, leaning against the single, ragged, winter-stripped tree, when Eve pulled up at the curb. He had his hands in his jeans pockets, and his brown hair ruffled in the breeze as if invisible hands combed through it. He was staring at the front door, and if he wasn't careful, he'd ignite it into flames by the sheer focused power of that stare.

Claire jumped out and ran to him, already anxious, with Eve right behind. "What is it?" she asked. "What's wrong?"

Shane jerked his chin at the house. "He's in there," he said. "With *her*."

"Who?" Eve asked, but it sounded as if she already knew.

"Did you tell her?" Shane asked Claire. She nodded. "The blonde. Naomi. She showed up; he told me to leave. I left."

Eve took a deep breath and walked up the steps—not running, not crying. She looked very calm and self-possessed.

Claire and Shane exchanged a look, and Shane said, "This can't be good," and they ran after her, into the house.

They found her almost immediately, standing in the front parlor of the house, the one none of them ever used; it was a stuffy sort of room, with furniture left over from the days of black-and-white television, if not older. But that was where Michael was, sitting on the stiff sofa, with a china cup of something that probably wasn't tea sitting in front of him.

And there was Naomi, sitting on the couch beside him, with her own matching cup.

The girl-vamp sat at a ladylike angle, knees together, as if she wore a dress instead of cute skinny jeans and a figure-hugging top that Claire regretfully kind of liked. Naomi's chin was up, and her gaze was level on Eve. She didn't look guilty. She looked a little defiant.

Michael, on the other hand, looked *deeply* uncomfortable. "Eve," he was saying, "it's not—"

"Like it looks?" she finished for him, very calmly. "Oh, I'm sure." Eve stepped forward, holding out her hand. "I don't think we've been introduced."

Naomi's eyebrows moved up, just a little, but she rose gracefully and shook Eve's hand, making it look as if she were a foreign dignitary performing some alien custom for the sake of diplomacy. "I am Naomi de la Tour. You must be Eve Rosser. Of course, I have seen you about town."

Eve stared straight into her face. "Sorry I can't say the same. I don't know you, and I don't appreciate your being here."

Naomi actually *blushed*, or at least, there was a hint of color in her cheeks. "I am still becoming used to human company," she said. "And I do apologize if I seemed rude toward you. I don't intend to be."

"Eve—," Michael said. She shot him a glare, and he settled back on the sofa. Busted.

"Maybe we ought to talk about what you *do* intend," Eve said, and pulled over a straight-backed chair, which she straddled, putting as strong a difference between herself and Naomi's oh-so-ladylike presence as possible. She looked over her shoulder at Shane and Claire. "Out. This could get messy."

"You're sure you don't want backup?" Shane asked.

Michael frowned. "Against *what* exactly? Me? C'mon, man."

"On second thought," Eve said, "maybe they should stay. Any reason they shouldn't, Michael?"

"Eve, don't do this."

She smiled, but it wasn't a happy kind of expression. "How long has this been going on?"

Michael said nothing. Naomi, on the other hand, leaned forward and said, very earnestly, "I've been coming here for almost two months."

"Really."

Michael shut his eyes and rubbed his temples, as if he had a monster headache. "Eve, you don't—"

"Understand? I'm sure I don't. Why don't you tell me? Because finding you all cozied up with a blood-drinking hottie on the couch *two days before our engagement party* doesn't send the wrong message at all."

"I'm not cozied up with her!"

Naomi laughed, just a little. "Indeed, he isn't," she said. "If I may explain . . . ?"

"Take your best shot," Eve said. The muscles in her jaws were tight, and she gripped the back of the chair she was straddling so hard that Claire thought she might snap it off—and then stake somebody with it.

"As I'm sure you're aware, there's discontent among some of the vampires with the idea that you and Michael should marry," Naomi said. "There is reason for this."

Eve stared at her in utter silence. Naomi waited for comment, but got nothing.

"Not only that," the girl continued, "I know that human society is not the same as it was when we were . . . among their numbers, but by our immortal standards a marriage is an *alliance,* and you, dear Eve, are allying yourself to the descendant of an ancient and important bloodline. There are many who believe that by marrying you, Michael confers upon you a great deal of... power. Implied power, if not actual. Giving this to a human is... controversial."

"Oh, so you're just giving us *advice.* I got it. Nice of you two to involve me in the discussion so thoroughly... Oh, wait."

"You think I am lying about my presence here?" Naomi's perfect eyebrows rose in disbelief. "Do not think it; I beg you. In fact, I have been acting as Michael's advocate. *Your* advocate," Naomi said. "I have standing in the vampire community, and I have been acting as peacemaker, if you will, to allow your marriage to go forward, should you still wish it. I came to tell Michael that I believe my blood-sister Amelie has been persuaded to give her blessing to the union."

Claire cleared her throat. "Oliver just told us there was no way it was going to be allowed to happen."

"Oliver is my most difficult opponent," Naomi said. "And he is persuasive, I must admit. I have spent a great many hours trying to convince him of the rightness of my cause, to no good effect. I finally decided to go directly to my blood-sister and hope for the best."

Eve was clearly still not buying it. She was staring holes in the other woman, lips compressed into a flat, angry line.

Michael said, very quietly, "You think it worked?"

"I can't be completely certain. Amelie is, first and always, a ruler, and a ruler keeps her own counsel on all things. But she was most gracious and understanding. I believe that I have convinced her of the importance of allowing this union to occur."

"Thank you," he said, and stood up. A step took him close to where Eve straddled the chair, and her head tilted to look up at him. She kept the exact same expression. "Do you really think I was screwing around on you with her?"

"Why not?" Eve asked flatly. "Vamp girls are hot. Even I can see that."

Naomi blushed again. "I am not interested in Michael in that way," she said. "I am sorry you think me capable of doing something so underhanded. And . . ." She seemed at a loss of what to say for a moment, then looked down at her clasped fingers and said, "And he is not what appeals to me, I am afraid."

"How could he *not* be your type?" Eve asked, momentarily distracted, and Claire was actually wondering the same thing because Michael was just . . . yeah.

Naomi didn't answer; she just stared hard at her lap, and Shane was the first one to get it, though how he did, Claire couldn't really tell. He said, "Because her type is more like you, idiot."

"More like—Goth?"

"More like girls."

Naomi glanced up, and Claire caught a flash of relief on her face. "In my youth it was not looked on with favor," she said. "It is still difficult for me to speak of it."

"Oh," Eve said, in an entirely different tone of voice. "*Oh.* You're *gay.*"

Naomi nodded slowly.

"I could kiss you right now," Eve said, and then immediately held out a hand. "I mean, in gratitude, you know? You're really pretty but— Oh man, I just totally screwed that up." Eve took a deep breath and turned back to Michael. "Did you know she was gay?"

"Yeah," he said. "I didn't want you to think—I knew there wasn't anything going on, but I get how it looked, meeting with her in private. I should have told you. I just didn't want you to know how much resistance there was against the wedding."

"Oh," Eve said softly. *"Oh."* Her eyes were shining now, and Michael's smile was one of the most lovely things Claire had ever seen. Free of all the burden she'd seen in him over the past few weeks. Free of the guilt. And now, there was something completely *right* in it. "You idiot. You could have told me."

"Yeah, I know." He stood up and went to her, and took her hand. "I love you. I didn't want to think that—that I could lose you over this. Over not being able to get Amelie to agree."

"Idiot," Eve repeated, but she didn't mean it. She stood up and melted into his arms, and it looked like they never intended to let go of each other, ever again. "So it's all good."

Naomi was smiling at the two of them, but now a shadow seemed to come over her face. "I hope that is true. I do worry that if the human population continues to agitate, Amelie will take the side of Oliver's cause, and not mine. But I cannot help that. Perhaps you can . . . ?"

"I'm not exactly Miss Popularity out there," Eve said. "But luckily, I've got someone everybody respects on my team . . . everybody on both sides of the blood line."

And she looked at Claire and raised her eyebrows.

"Oh, wait a minute," Claire said. Shane put his arms around her from behind. Even if she wanted to escape, he wasn't going to let her. "How exactly am I supposed to convince people it's all okay?"

"Facebook?" Shane said, straight-faced.

"Flyers on phone poles," Eve said.

"Invite them to the party," Michael said.

Claire blinked and looked at him, head cocked. "What did you say?"

"Invite them to the party. It's like if you're having a gigantic house party—invite your neighbors over, and they're not as likely to blow the whistle on you. Well, invite the humans in Morganville and give them the chance to really get to know the vampires. Show them it can work."

"Dude," Shane said seriously, "that just *cannot* end well."

"No, it could work," Naomi said. "There are precedents. And you were planning to invite both humans and vampires in any case, were you not?"

Eve nodded, still looking a little uncertain. "But—look, there are some bad feelings around here. Human pride, and all that stuff. I'm not sure it's a good idea to put vamps, humans, and alcohol all in the same place."

"Well," Naomi said cheerfully, "what's the worst that can happen?"

They were silent, considering that, because there were just so many possibilities.

But in the end, it was a better idea than Facebook.

"What's this?" The man on the other side of the counter at the camera store scowled at her mistrustfully, but he took the paper that Claire handed him. It was a nice, colorful poster, advertising the engagement party being held outside at Founder's Square.

"Could you maybe put it up in the window of your store?" she asked, and gave him her best, most confident smile. "It's going to be a great party. I know your customers would like to be there. It's free!"

He stared at her. Claire didn't know him; he was an older man, graying at the temples, and he had a square, stubborn kind of face. His sleeves were rolled back to the elbows, and she saw a fresh stake tattoo on the inside of his right forearm. "You're that girl," he said, and she was almost sure he'd continue, *The vampires' pet.* She'd heard that a few times today. "The one the Collins kid is dating."

Oh. Right. Shane had antivampire street cred. "That's right," she said. "I'm Shane's girlfriend."

"Frank said you were all right."

Great, now she had Shane's *dad* as an endorsement. . . . Well, anything that would help, she'd take it. "That was nice of him." She managed not to make it sound like an indictment on the whole Frank Collins issue. Water under the bridge, and all that stuff. "Would you mind putting it up for me?"

"You know this ain't going to end well, right?" He rattled the paper at her. "Glass and the human girl. I'm sorry the kid got turned, but he's one of them now. No coming back over that line."

She was tired of the argument. "Thanks for your time," she said. "I appreciate you thinking about it."

He grunted. "I guess I'll put it up. Don't expect me to show up, though."

"Free drinks?"

That actually earned her a smile. A small one. "Well, you drive a hard bargain, kid. Be careful out there."

"You, too."

She walked out, and Shane fell in step beside her. He had a handful of flyers, but fewer than there had been. "So, was that fun?" he asked. "Kind of an antivamp stronghold, there. Captain Obvious used to be a good friend of the manager." Captain Obvious had once been a figurehead of the antivampire underground, but he was now permanently underground, in the six-feet-under sense. Nobody had yet stepped forward to take up his masked identity, as far as Claire knew—not that she would have been in on the antivampire memo chain. "He give you any trouble?"

"Not once I pointed out there would be free booze."

"Too easy," Shane said. "How are you planning to keep the frat boys out?"

That, Claire had realized early on, was going to be a problem. . . . The Texas Prairie University campus was its own little world, a microcosm inside Morganville's strange alternate reality. And on campus, few people really knew about the vampire world outside. Keeping the frat boys on campus, instead of searching for a free drunk, was a challenge, and one that required absolute attention. There had been too many near misses already. "I talked to Chief Moses," she said. "She said the police would be checking IDs. No town resident card, you don't get into the square at all. That should keep the aspiring partyers out."

"You hope. So, who else we have left?"

They'd covered almost all of their particular sector of Morganville; Michael had taken the more vampire-centric neighborhoods this morning, and Eve had braved it with him, trying to show the vampires she could be well behaved and perfectly acceptable. By common consent, they'd all decided that Claire and Shane had the reputations to win over unwilling humans, or at least get them to listen.

They'd been about seventy percent successful, which was better than Claire had expected, but it had been a long day, and her feet hurt. "We should hit it tomorrow," she said. "I need to lay down."

He raised his eyebrows at her, and she swatted his shoulder. "Rest," she said.

"Well, we could rest *together*. I swear, I'll be good." He gave her a charming, intensely hot smile. "You can take that any way you want."

So many levels to that, she got dizzy trying to sort them out. But it warmed her, and made the walk home less of a trial . . . at least, until her cell phone rang. The ringtone was a dead giveaway, emphasis on *dead* . . . creepy organ music. She didn't even have to glance at the image of fanged bunny slippers on the screen to know who was calling. She just sighed, thumbed it on, and held it to her ear.

"Claire! I need you here *immediately*. Something's wrong with Bob." Myrnin, her mad-scientist, blood-addicted boss, sounded actually *shaken*. "I can't get him to eat his insects, and I used his favorites. He just sits there."

"Bob," she repeated, looking at Shane in wide-eyed disbelief. "Bob the *spider*."

"Just because he's a spider doesn't mean he deserves any less concern! Claire, you have a way with him. He likes you."

Just what she needed. Bob the spider *liked her*. "You do realize that he's a year old, at least. And spiders don't live that long."

"You think he's *dead*?" Myrnin sounded horrified. So wrong.

"Is he curled up?"

"No. He's just quiet."

"Well, maybe he's not hungry."

"Will you come?" Myrnin asked. He sounded calmer now, but also oddly needy. "It's been very lonely here these past few days. I'd like your company, at least for a little while." When she hesitated, he used the pity card. "Please, Claire."

"Fine," she sighed. "I'm bringing Shane."

After a second of silence, he said, flatly, "Goody," and hung up.

"You're kidding," Shane said. "Do you think I want to visit Crazy McTeeth in his lair of insanity?"

"No," Claire said, "but I'm pretty sure you won't like it if I go alone when I just kind of promised to be with you. So . . . ?"

"Right. I've been missing Nutty McFang anyway."

"Stop making up names for him."

"What about Count Crackula?"

"Just stop."

THREE

CLAIRE

Crazy or not, Myrnin was *trying.*

For one thing, he'd cleaned up the lab, meaning that he'd moved the leaning stacks of books up against the walls instead of leaving them as trip hazards between the tables. He'd even uncovered the surface of one of the marble-topped tables, and had set up . . . God, what was that? A genuine china *tea service?*

He was standing next to it, wearing his somewhat clean white lab coat with the patch on it that said EVIL GENIUS UNION LOCAL 101 on it, and there were goggles dangling around his neck. For a vampire, he was surprisingly versatile in his wardrobe, in a cracked-out way. From a purely objective viewpoint, Myrnin was a good-looking guy—frozen at the age of maybe his mid-twenties, with dark hair and a ready smile. A sharp but handsome face.

If only he didn't crazy it up all the time.

"Have you been watching *Dr. Horrible* again?" she asked him, as Myrnin poured tea into two delicate floral cups. "Not that I don't love it, but . . ."

"Thank you for coming," Myrnin said, and offered the first serving to Shane, saucer and all. Shane blinked and took it, not quite sure what to do with it; the fragile porcelain looked particularly endangered in his large hands. "It's very nice to see you both. And how have you been? Please, sit down."

"Where?" Shane asked, looking around. Myrnin looked momentarily panicked, and then just . . . disappeared, in a vibrating flash. He was back before Claire could draw in a startled breath, and he was carrying two large armchairs, one in each hand, lifting them like they were made of Styrofoam. Myrnin thumped them down on the floor and indicated them with outstretched palms.

"There," he said.

Well, he'd gone to a lot of trouble, really. Shane sat, then jumped back up with a yelp, splashing tea in a pale brown wave.

"Oh, sorry," Myrnin said, and picked up something that looked like a surgical saw from the seat. "I wondered where that had got off to."

"Should I even ask?" Claire said.

"You know I do the occasional research," he said. "And in answer to your question, quite likely you should not. Milk?"

That last was directed at Shane, who was still recovering. He slowly settled into his chair. "Dude, we live in *Texas*. Hot tea is not our thing. Iced tea, sure. I have no idea. Is milk supposed to be in there?"

"I give up trying to civilize you," Myrnin said, and turned to Claire. "Milk?"

"No, thank you."

"Much better." Myrnin set down the cream pitcher and leaned against the lab table, hands in his pockets. He'd stuck the surgical saw in there, too; Claire hoped he wouldn't slice something off accidentally. "I've thought of a few improvements to make to our system, Claire. Just a few. Nothing that will cause concern, I promise. And by our agreement, I am not making them on my own without peer review. Well, not *peer,* as I have no peers, but you do understand what I mean."

"All that, and modest, too," Shane said. "Is Frank around?"

They all three paused for a moment, waiting. Frank Collins—Shane's dad—was more or less a ghost, to all intents and purposes. In fact, he was only a little dead. . . . His brain had been saved, and wired into Myrnin's alchemical machine that ran a lot of the stranger things in Morganville. But sometimes Frank paid attention, and sometimes he just didn't want to respond. Maybe he was asleep. Brains needed sleep.

But after a long stretch of seconds, there was a flicker at the end of the lab, like an old cathode-ray tube television starting up . . . and then a slowly stabilizing image of a man walking toward them. Frank always manifested in gray scale, not color, and it was a paper-thin two-dimensional image. Limitations of the system, though Claire had never been able to figure out why. Then again, she didn't altogether understand the whole mechanism of how he projected the image at all.

Frank had chosen his avatar to look a lot like his old physical self: middle-aged (though not quite as beaten-up as Claire remembered him) with a scar on his face, and a perpetual bad-tempered scowl. He even wore the same old motorcycle leathers and stomping boots.

The scowl eased up as he saw Shane sitting in the chair. "Son," he said. "That girl's got you drinking tea now?"

Shane very deliberately took a sip of tea Claire absolutely knew he didn't want. "Hi, Frank." He was trying on this front, too; dealing with his dad alive had been a struggle, and dealing with him as a vampire had been worse. But now at least there was one thing settled between them: Frank couldn't physically abuse him. And from Shane's perspective, things were looking up. "How's living in a jar these days? Fulfilling?"

"Been better." Frank shrugged. "I see you're still together. Good. You could do worse."

"Frank," Myrnin said, and all the fussiness was gone from his voice, leaving it flat and cold. "If you wish to be insulting, I can just mute you for a few days until you learn manners. These are my guests. Granted, I don't really like your son, but I tolerate him, and you can do the same."

"I was talking to the girl. I meant *she* could do worse. Like you, for instance."

Myrnin stared at Frank's flickering image with dark, unreadable eyes for a few long, unsettling seconds. "Crawl back in your cave," he told him. "Now."

"Can't," Frank said. "You had me set to alert you if anything happened on my side of town. Well, it's happening. Somebody just tried to run the southern border of town in a van. It's disabled by the side of the road. I dispatched the cops."

"And?" Myrnin said. "What about it?"

"And someone just walked up to the eastern edge of town and is waiting there for permission to enter. Thought you'd like to know, it being daylight and all."

"Who is it?"

"I don't know, but he's a vampire. He's sitting in a pop-up tent right now."

"Well, that's odd."

"Seems so," Frank agreed. "He doesn't match any of my databases, so he's never been in Morganville. We've got us a genuine newcomer."

"A newcomer who knows enough to wait at the border for permissions," Myrnin said. "That's unusual."

"That's why I brought it up."

Myrnin tapped a finger on his lips for a moment, then suddenly whipped around to face Claire. "You could go," he said. "Ask him what he wants."

"Me? I'm not the vampire welcome wagon!"

"It's daylight," he said. "And while many of us *can* go out, we'd prefer not to risk it; wearing layers of protection in Morganville tends to mark us as . . . unusual. With the current unrest among the human population, it's safer if we send someone like you."

"Send the cops," Shane said. "That's what you own them for."

"I'd prefer to know exactly who or what we are dealing with before I involve bureaucracy," Myrnin said. "Oh, very well, since you're reluctant, I will come with you. I should get out anyway."

Claire hastily downed the rest of her tea and put the cup and saucer down; Shane gratefully dumped his out on the stone floor. Myrnin did that fast-motion thing again, and zipped back again adjusting a spectacularly badass black leather duster, a wide-brimmed leather hat, and gloves.

And a long, multicolored scarf he looped around his neck about six times.

"Too much?" he asked, pointing at the scarf. Claire didn't have the heart to tell him yes, so she shrugged.

"What about Bob?" she asked.

"Oh, Bob's fine. I think he's shedding his exoskeleton, which is why he didn't want to eat. Our Bob is a growing boy, you know."

Frank gave him an unpleasant smile and said, "You know, I think I'll call and get an exterminator in here. There's a real problem with creepy-crawlies. Present company not excepted, of course, since I consider leeches to be creepy-crawlies as much as spiders."

Frank Collins had been an ass when he was alive, and he wasn't any better dead and living in a machine. Claire didn't *like* Bob, but that didn't mean she wanted him chemically murdered, either. And referring to Myrnin as a leech . . . Well, that was just rude.

So she frowned at Frank, then turned to Myrnin and said, "I'm ready if you are."

Shane said, very quietly, "I hope you know what you're getting us into."

"Would you really rather drink more tea and chat with your dad?"

"Right," Shane said. "Let's roll."

It was bright enough outside—barely—that Claire commandeered the keys to Myrnin's sleek black car and had Shane drive. Yes, it was dangerous; vampire cars weren't meant to have human drivers, and the window tinting made it like driving at night without headlights, even in full sun. But she'd been driven by Myrnin before, and it was an experience she *really* didn't care to repeat. Shane was careful, and the roads heading to and from Morganville were, as always, relatively deserted, except for mail and delivery trucks that were just passing through.

He pulled off the road on the dusty shoulder near the LEAVING US SO SOON? sign. It had a 1950s-era sad clown painted on it that had been rendered almost a ghost by sun and time. Someone had decorated it with a spray of shotgun pellets, but it had happened long ago; the whole sign leaned and creaked in the wind, about one gust away from collapsing completely.

And in its shade was a pop-up tent, and inside the shelter sat a young man wearing a sports hoodie, with BLACKE TIGERS written across it in raised embroidery in black and red. As the three of them got out of the car, he scrambled to his feet, looking anxious; that got worse when he saw Myrnin's outfit, but Claire held up a hand to calm him down. "He's harmless," she said. "You're from Blacke?"

The boy nodded hesitantly, watching her with wary dark eyes. She didn't remember him, but she remembered Blacke *very* well. It was another little isolated town, one that had been overrun with infected vampires a few months back. With Oliver's help, Claire had managed to cure the sick ones, and a group of Morganville vampires had settled in there as a kind of satellite colony. Blacke's citizens had good cause to support them, because so many of Blacke's own people had been turned during the initial chaos caused by the sick vampires.

"How's Morley?" Claire asked, still trying to sound calm and reassuring. The boy looked like he might bolt at any moment. Morley had spearheaded the group that had left Morganville and settled in Blacke; he was definitely an old-school vampire, but he was oddly entertaining, sometimes. She respected him, a little.

"Morley sent me," he replied, looking just a little relieved she'd found the magic word—or name, anyway. "He and my aunt—Mrs. Grant. They kind of run the town now."

"I'm Claire." She stuck out her hand, and he took it and shook.

"Graham," he said. "Hey."

"Graham, this is Shane." Shane shook hands, too, and Claire finally got around to Myrnin, but she didn't need to; he stepped forward decisively, whipped off his hat, and bowed.

"I am Myrnin," he said. "I'm in charge."

Claire rolled her eyes and mouthed, behind his back, *Not really.* Graham almost smiled, but he managed not to, and gave Myrnin an awkward bow back. "Uh, hi, sir," he said. "How's it going?"

"That all depends on what you're here to convey," Myrnin said. "Did you walk all this way from Blacke?"

"No, sir," Graham said. "I ran. But mostly during the night. It's not bad. Kind of restful, actually."

That settled the question of which sport Graham had been—or still was?—part of in school before he'd been turned vampire. . . . It had to be cross-country. "So what's so important you'd run more than fifty miles over the desert, but Morley couldn't pick up a phone?" Claire asked.

In answer, Graham unzipped his hoodie and took out a sealed envelope, which he showed her. On it was written, in a spiky antique style, *For the eyes of the Founder only.* "He said what he had to say couldn't be done over the phone, that it was too sensitive. So he wanted me to run it over and put it in the hands of either the Founder, Oliver, or—well, you, I guess. Claire."

Wow. Claire blinked, amazed that Morley would have put her in that particular company. "Uh, okay," she said, and accepted the envelope. It felt light—maybe one sheet of paper inside. "Do you know what it is?"

"Not a clue, and from the look on his face when he gave it to me, I want to keep it that way," Graham said. He zipped his hoodie up again. "So, that's it. It's clouding up, probably will be overcast in the next hour. It'll only take a couple of hours to get back."

"Don't you think you should wait for dark?"

"Nah, I'm good," Graham said, and flashed her an unexpectedly flirty grin. "Morley sent me because I'm a freak, anyway. High tolerance for sunlight. He says it's unusual or something."

"Oh, it is," Myrnin said, and looked thoughtful, and interested. "Would you mind providing me a blood sample, boy? I've been conducting a study these past few hundred years of the relative immunity of younger vampires to the influence of the sun. . . ."

Graham looked alarmed, which was probably wise. "Uh, maybe later?" he said, and put his hood up. It shaded his face well, and when he pulled the sleeves down over his hands, he was as covered as Myrnin, if not quite as flamboyantly. "Thanks. See you, guys."

"Be careful!" Claire said, but she was telling it to the wind, because Graham was *fast*. She saw a flutter of motion at the edge of her vision, and sand drifting, and he was *gone*.

"Whoa," Shane said, impressed. "Boy's got some skills."

And they'd been put to a very curious use . . . because picking up the phone would have been easy for Morley, and Oliver, at least, would have taken his calls even if Amelie still held a grudge against the tattered old vampire for running away from Morganville. Still, older vamps didn't trust technology much. Maybe he just felt that paper and pen were safer.

Still, something labeled *For the eyes of the Founder only* didn't seem to bode well.

"Are you going to open it?" Myrnin asked her.

"No," she said. "It's not for me. It's for Amelie."

He looked crestfallen. "But you could accidentally open it."

"Accidentally how, exactly?"

"Tripping. A rock could—"

"It's not a glass jar, Myrnin. It's not going to just break open."

He snatched it from her hand before she could stop him, and held it up to the light. "I can almost make it out," he said. "Morley has horrible handwriting. It looks like he learned to write in the time of Charles the Second and it went downhill from there. . . . Oh."

He fell silent, and slowly lowered the envelope. He stood very still, staring after the boy's fading trail of dust, and there was something in Myrnin's expression that woke shivers of goose bumps on Claire's skin. Graham had been right about the clouds; some skidded dark across the sky, high and fast, and blocked out the sun. The wind suddenly whipped colder, stinging Claire with blown sand, and she instinctively reached out and found Shane's warm hand.

"What is it?" she asked. She wasn't sure she wanted to know.

Myrnin handed her back the unopened envelope and, without a word, jammed his hat back on his head and walked back to the car. He got into the backseat and slammed the door.

Shane looked at her and said, "What the hell is this all about?"

"No idea," Claire said, "but it really cannot be good. Not at all."

Myrnin rolled down the window and said, "We need to go. *Now.* Shane, I assume you can pilot this vehicle at higher speeds than you used to get here."

Shane lifted her fingers to his lips and kissed them, just a brief brush of his lips against her skin, but it steadied her. Then he said to Myrnin, "How fast do you want to go? And where, exactly?"

"Founder's Square," Myrnin said. "And quickly. *Quickly.*"

Shane couldn't go quite as fast as Myrnin wanted, but that was good; as it was, Claire felt she was hurtling uncontrollably down a dark tunnel, like something flung out of a slingshot. It was a deeply unsettling feeling. As short a drive as it was, she was relieved when Shane hit the brakes and slid to a stop at the Founder's Square guard post, manned by a uniformed cop. He was starting to explain when Myrnin rolled down his window and snapped, "Call Amelie and tell her I'm coming. Tell her to be waiting."

"Sir!" the cop said, and practically saluted. Not because Myrnin was so commanding, generally, but right now, he sounded very focused.

He was actually very scared, Claire thought. And that raised her personal terror scale all the way up into the red zone. "Myrnin, what's in the envelope?" she asked.

He didn't answer, but then, she didn't really expect him to. "There, take a left," Myrnin said, leaning over the seat to point.

"Get your hands out of my face, man," Shane said, but he followed the directions, and steered the car down the ramp into the parking garage beneath Founder's Square. It was crowded today, and as he looked for a parking space, Myrnin growled in impatience, opened his door in the back, and bailed.

"Hey!" Claire called. Shane found a parking spot and pulled in. They got out at the same time, and caught up with Myrnin as he punched the elevator's call button for about the hundredth time in thirty seconds. "Chill out, Myrnin; you're going to break it. Listen—it's coming."

He was practically vibrating with tension, and she couldn't understand why. She'd seen him in many bad situations, and even in the worst, even with Bishop, he hadn't been *this* freaked. When the elevator doors parted, he shoved his way in and jammed the floor button just as frantically as he had the one outside. Claire finally put herself physically between him and the control panel, out of a very real fear he was going to shove his finger through the button and short out the electronics altogether.

Myrnin took in a breath—unusual, except when he was

talking—and slumped against the back wall. He pulled off his hat and wiped his forehead with a trembling hand, as if he were sweating, though Claire was pretty sure he couldn't, physically. "It was only a matter of time," he said, but it was in a whisper, and Claire didn't think he meant for her to hear. "Inevitable."

"Myrnin, what the *hell* is going on?" She looked at Shane, and saw that he was watching her boss with a worried frown, too. He knew this was freaky, too. *"What's in the envelope?"*

"A word," he said. "Just a word."

"Must be a hell of a word," Shane said.

"It's a short one," Myrnin said. He was watching the lights climb on the elevator display, and finally, the car lurched to a stop and the doors slid open. "I'll take it to her. You two—go home. Now."

"Wait!" The elevator doors started to close after him, and Claire slapped a hand in place to stop them. "Myrnin, *what's the word*?"

He turned to look at her, and that look—that look chilled her, all the way down.

"Run," he said. "It says run. Now *go home*." And he moved, vampire speed, down the hallway.

She let go of the rubber bumper and stepped back, leaning against Shane. He put his arms around her, and reached past to push the button for the ground floor as the doors rumbled shut.

"What the hell does it mean?" she asked him. He pulled in a deep breath, then let it out.

"I don't know," he said. "But Myrnin does. And it's bad, whatever it is."

They held hands on the walk back home. It was colder now, the sun covered over with scudding dark clouds, and there was a mass on the horizon that had to be a storm. The wind felt damp, edged with ice, as if Morganville had been magically transported to a much colder, wetter place. The humidity felt incredibly high; ten percent was the norm for this area of the desert, and on a really bad day it might rise to forty. But this felt like ocean waves against her skin. Even the air seemed heavy, more like mist than the light, clean stuff she was used to here. Despite the chill, she felt as if she was sweating. As if the whole *world* was sweating, and it was all over her skin.

Morganville residents were still out on the streets, doing their daily business; some were casting anxious looks at the sky and hurrying up about it, wanting to get home before the rain arrived. Claire was starting to wish she'd brought an umbrella, but really, who needed one in this town? It rained two days a year, if that, and never for long—or if it did rain hard, the wind was so fierce an umbrella was useless. But *this* storm . . . this one looked nasty, with that green edge to the clouds that tokened real trouble.

As they passed Oliver's coffee shop, Common Grounds, Shane said, "Hey, are you cold? I'm freezing. Let's get something."

That sounded good, actually. Normal. And maybe—Claire knew he was thinking this as well—maybe Oliver would be there, and would have some kind of clue as to what was going on.

You knew things were bad when you were actually looking forward to seeing *Oliver.*

But . . . no Oliver behind the counter. Instead, Eve was there, just fastening on her tie-dyed apron over her black outfit. She looked tired, but she put on a bright smile for the two of them. It was made about five thousand watts brighter by the shade of lipstick she'd used, which was a shocking bright blue, to match the stripes in her skirt. "Hey, rooms," she said. "How'd the flyers go?"

Flyers? God, Claire had forgotten all about that. "Uh . . . okay," she said. "We got them up in a lot of places, anyway."

"That's good, because my morning? Not so fabulous." Without asking, Eve started a mocha for Claire, and a plain tall coffee for Shane. "In celebration of the fact that my occasional part-time boss just tore out of here like his ass was on fire, coffee's on the house."

"He just left? We didn't see him," Claire said. Eve jerked a thumb at the back, which had a trapdoor tunnel exit.

"He took the shady street. What crawled up his ass? Because I *know* Bishop's no longer the big, bad boogeyman. Did Amelie break a nail or need a pipe fixed or something?"

"Wish we knew," Claire said. "I was going to ask. Because he's not the only one freaking today."

"No?" Eve cocked a black eyebrow at a wicked, inquisitive angle. "Spill."

"Myrnin," Shane said, and reached over to grab the cup she shoved over toward him. "Not that the guy's stable any time, but today he's extra-crispy crazy."

Eve leaned over, resting her elbows on the counter, as the milk hissed and steamed in its pitcher, heating to the proper temperature. "You think it's because of us? Me, and Michael?"

"Look, I know that you two getting engaged is somehow worse than him turning you—and no, don't ask me to explain that; it's just popular theory—but I don't think it's creating quite this level of drama," Claire said. "And Myrnin doesn't have any opinion, anyway. He's happy you're having a party, and he doesn't care what it's for. *He* wouldn't be getting all grand mal about it."

"Shit," Eve said. She retrieved the milk and began expertly blending Claire's mocha. "I was kind of hoping it was just about us, because at least that would be stupid. Now I'm scared it's actually *smart* to be worried."

"You and me both," Shane said. "And when the two of us agree, something is definitely wrong."

Things were busy at the counter, so Eve couldn't talk longer; Claire and Shane took their drinks to an empty table and sat, savoring the warm beverages and watching the clouds flow by overhead through the big plate glass window. Wind whipped the scalloped fringe on the red awning, and Claire could feel the glass of the window humming slightly in the gusts.

"Run," she said. "What do you think that means, Shane?"

He shrugged. "Who the hell knows? Maybe it's a message from an immortal bill collector, and she forgot to pay her rent for the last two hundred years or something. Maybe someone's reminding her that exercise is important."

"You don't really think that."

"No." He took a long sip of coffee, eyes hooded and dark. "No, I guess I don't. But we can't figure this out without more intel, Claire. And whatever it is, it doesn't look like the end of the world."

"Yet," she said softly. *"Yet."*

She caught sight of something out of the corner of her eye, something that made her cringe and recoil and go weirdly dizzy inside, as if what she was looking at was so deeply wrong it made her physically ill. It was outside the window, just passing . . . but when she looked, she saw nothing out of the ordinary at all.

Just a man, walking.

She knew him, she realized, or at least recognized him; it was that guy, the one she'd seen come into Marjo's Diner. Mr. Average. He wasn't hurrying like the other people on the street; he was walking calmly, hands in the pockets of his coat.

Smiling.

It shouldn't have looked so odd, but it made the hackles rise on the back of her neck.

"What?" Shane was watching her, and he stared out the window, too, trying to see what was alarming her. "What is it?"

"Nothing," she said, finally. The man had passed out of sight. "Absolutely nothing."

Which was the weirdest thing of all, she thought.

FOUR

AMELIE

I had heard many insane things during my lifetime, and more than half of them had come from Myrnin—friend, servant, occasional enemy, chaos personified on the best of his very numerous days. Today, when he burst into my office, disregarding the warnings of my assistant, I was in no mood to tolerate him.

I turned from the candle I was lighting to face him, put on my best royal expression of anger, and said, "You do *not* have leave to barge in whenever you wish, and you know that. Go back to your—"

He strode toward me with his ridiculously heavy black leather coat flaring about him, and sailed a letter toward me with a flick of his wrist. I caught it with instinctive ease and turned it over to see the front. It was modern paper, of a smooth, bland construction, but the writing on the front reminded me of other times, other places, not all of them as pleasant as this one.

"It's from Morley," Myrnin said, and slapped his large hat down on my desk, ruffling the paperwork. "He sent a runner from Blacke."

That caught my attention, and I stared at him for a beat. "A runner," I repeated. "Has he quite forgotten we live in more modern times, or has he simply adopted the lordly attitudes he once so despised in others?"

"Read it," Myrnin said. The writing said *For the eyes of the Founder only,* and the *only* had been underlined three times. The envelope was still sealed. I slit it open with the side of a sharp fingernail and glanced at him again.

"I sense you are well aware of what it says," I told him. "What magic trick?"

"The oldest. I held it to the light."

"Ah." I slid the paper out and unfolded it—one thin sheet, and only one word on it, drawn in straight slashes of ink, spiked with an ancient style but also with alarm. If he'd written it in blood, the urgency could not have been more clear.

RUN.

For a moment I failed to understand what it meant, or perhaps I didn't wish to know; that couldn't last, and didn't. I took in a sharp, aching breath, expanding to the fullest lungs that were no longer used to the exercise—a human's reaction. The realization affected me that deeply.

"You see?" Myrnin whispered. "We both knew it would happen. We knew it was coming, however slowly. He'll be organizing things there in retreat, and we *must* begin to mount our defenses. Today. *Now.* We may already be too late."

My dear old friend. He sounded dispirited, and afraid, and I wished I had consolation to offer him, but he was most appallingly right. For whatever reason, Morley—a ragged, grubby vampire of no particular skills except a peculiar luck for survival—had stumbled over something I had missed. Something we'd all missed.

We might already be too late; Myrnin was entirely correct. I had known it would happen, eventually; I'd known things would come to this. But now, I looked helplessly around at the office, at the once-vital, suddenly meaningless paperwork, at the warm, cherished glow of the world I'd built around myself. Outside the windows, the clouds were gathering, heavy with threat, but people still walked the town square; normal life still proceeded.

But it was all a lie, a terrible and cruel lie.

I picked up the telephone and dialed, feeling lost and numbed. Myrnin was pacing on my much-cherished Persian rug, and I did not have the heart to tell him to stop. It didn't matter. None of it mattered.

I rang Oliver, and he picked up almost immediately. "Amelie," he said. "I've been meaning to speak with you again about this foolish business of the engagement party—"

"Come," I said, stopping him cold. "Whatever you're doing, drop it, and come *now*."

Even then, he hesitated for a second to say, "What's happened?"

"Not on the phone," I said, and hung up. I put my palms flat on the desk and leaned into it, suddenly feeling faint, as if I'd starved myself for months. It was shock, an ancient and unremembered reaction. "Who else knows?" I asked.

"Claire was with me," Myrnin said. "And the boy. Shane."

I closed my eyes. Heartbreak on heartbreak, glass walls crashing down. They had never protected any of us, really, for all our pretending.

"Silence them," I said.

"But—"

I lifted my head, and I knew my eyes were flaring with white power, driven by my rage, my revulsion, my desperation. "Silence them, Myrnin. You know you must."

He stared back at me for a moment in mute horror, and shook his head. "I can't," he said. "God witness me, I *cannot* do it. Not to her. The boy, yes, but not her. Amelie, there must be another way."

"*Jesu*, you think if there was, I wouldn't take it?" I shouted it at him, fists clenched against the need to strike. "You *will* do it. You *must*." And I put my will on him, pushing in a way that I so rarely did these days. That I so rarely had to do.

Tears filled his eyes, and Myrnin swayed in place. He grabbed for the back of an armchair and braced himself, but even so, his knees sagged, and I heard the sounds of pain he made as he fought to escape my influence.

"Say you will," I said. "You know we have *no choice*."

"There's always a choice, *ma belle*." His voice was soft and shaking, just a thread of sound on a dying breath. "That was what you gave us here. A *choice*. Don't take it away now. I will not do it. Not to her."

I could have crushed him, with a further exertion of will; I had done it before, to others, shattered them into mindless creatures that did my bidding no matter what the cost. It is not always pretty, what I am. What I do to others. In my position, mercy is the last option considered, not the first.

But the idea of shattering *him*, destroying the core of what made him the bright, fevered candle of brilliance he was . . . No. I could not do that, as he could not do it to the girl.

"Very well," I said, and let my will depart from him. "Not the girl. But I cannot have two of them with this knowledge, at twice the risk. You must silence the boy."

Myrnin still clenched the armchair in a death grip, like a drowning man clinging to the water-soaked remains of his salvation. The tears that he'd held in his eyes broke free when he blinked, and slid silver down his cheeks. "That will destroy her just as surely," he said. "She loves him, as much as you ever loved Sam."

Ah, Samuel, my love. I'd tried to protect us both, and in the end, it had gotten us nothing but grief and death, loss and silence. I'd knelt at his grave for months, hands buried in the ground, wishing to feel *something*. Some hint of his belief that part of the human soul continued after death, even the contaminated souls of vampires.

Someone had taken him from me, for hate. And now . . . now I would be doing the same, not from hate, but from fear.

And it wouldn't be the first time.

"Do it." I said it kindly, but I meant it.

And Myrnin slowly nodded. He picked up his hat and walked out, head down, shoulders slumped beneath the weight of all that I'd just heaped upon him.

There were no good choices. Not now.

Oliver took only another moment to arrive, slipping in the door and shutting it on my assistant's exasperated protests. He was wearing the odd and faintly ridiculous clothing that he kept to blend in with the human population, forsaking his own natural liking for dark, plain lines and fabrics. He took in my expression, my stiff back, the look in my eyes, and crossed to pick up the fallen piece of paper that Morley had sent us.

He read it and let it fall back to the floor. Without looking up at me, he said, "It's come, then."

"Yes."

Now he met my eyes. "And what will you do, Amelie? Will you retreat as you've always done?"

"It's called survival, Oliver."

"Often confused with cowardice," he said.

I shot him a hard look. "Aren't you afraid?"

He gave me a smile then, spare and warlike, and it steadied me. "Fear is the natural state of anything that dies, even us," he said. "So of course I am. But perhaps it's time to use the fear."

"To stand and fight?" I said. "That's always your answer, you know."

"That's because it works."

I shook my head slowly. "You only remember when it does. Avoiding the fight means you stay alive. And I prefer to live, Oliver. I always have."

"And I prefer to fight," he said. "And always will." He was very close to me, and beneath the camouflage of modern clothing he was the same as he'd ever been, spare and hard, lean and cold. The very opposite of Samuel's light and spirit of gentleness.

But perhaps now I needed a warrior more than I needed a saint.

That is the only reason I can think for the kiss.

I think the sudden and half-desperate attraction came as a shock to us both, but it was . . . oddly inevitable. And the kiss . . . the kiss was sweet, and commanding, and it soothed something mad and terrified that had broken its cage within me.

I could see a sudden wariness on his face when I pulled back from him; he thought he had just made a serious tactical error. In truth, I wasn't sure he hadn't, or that I hadn't, but I gently put a hand against his face, and smiled without a word.

He put his fingers over mine, staring into my eyes. "This has been a long time coming," he said. "And yet I must confess, it is something of a surprise. Why do you think that is?"

"Because we are well matched in stubbornness," I said. "And pride. And fear."

Our smiles faded, and I mourned them a bit, because seeing Oliver relaxed in this way was something radiant, and rare as a unicorn. "Perhaps it's something we should take up later," he said. "When we have leisure to explore all of those questions that have just been raised."

"Yes," I said. "We must—yes." I took in a fresh, shallow breath and said, "Claire and Shane know about the note. Myrnin did not tell them all of it, but I have no doubt he gave them enough to make them curious, and we cannot afford curiosity. Not now."

The spark went out of his eyes, and it was only the warrior general facing me now, not a man, or even the immortal shell of one. He took a physical step back, breaking the contact between us. "Then you must stop them from telling others. I don't think harsh words will suffice. We need to buy time to prepare, and if the human community suspects . . ."

"I know that," I said, irritated. "Myrnin—"

Oliver barked out a laugh. "You send *Myrnin* to do such a thing? Not that he isn't an enthusiastic little killer under the right circumstances, I will grant you that, but he's as sentimental as a dewy-eyed child about some things, and that girl is one of them."

"I've agreed he can spare the girl. We can control her, so long as the boy is gone." Even as I said it, even as the words came out of my mouth, I realized what I'd just said.

And how very, very wrong it was.

Oliver was shaking his head. "If that boy dies, she won't bend. She won't break. She'll be the perfect spark to ignite this powder keg, and we *cannot* afford the fight, not now. You know this girl, you *know*. You must call Myrnin off."

And he was right. I'd reacted foolishly, and even Myrnin, sweetly insane Myrnin, had known. He'd tried to tell me.

"Then stop him," I said. Oliver nodded and headed for the

door. "Wait. Do it quietly, and don't hurt Myrnin unless you have to."

"Sentimental," he said, and shook his head again, smiling that razor-edged smile. "I find that oddly beautiful in you, princess."

I sat down, and stared out the windows at my fatally ill town, and wondered why I always realized too late what I wanted.

And why what I wanted was never good for me.

FIVE

CLAIRE

The alarm on her phone beeped, and Claire flinched and pulled it out of her pocket. She shut it off and looked at the reminder. "Crap," she said. "I have to go. I have a meeting with a professor about my grade."

"Wait, what? Are you trying to get something higher than an A?" Shane tossed back the rest of his coffee. "Don't try to tell me you're in trouble in a class, because I won't believe it. You never met a class you could fail. You're the book whisperer."

Claire felt herself blushing furiously, and tossed a wadded-up napkin at him. "No, seriously! I blew a test off because—you know, Morganville stuff. So I wanted to make it up, and he said I couldn't, and I got a note. I have to give him the note so he'll let me take it."

"And keep your golden four point oh."

"I still want to go to MIT. Eventually. If I can't keep a four-oh at *this* school . . ." Claire's voice faded, because *obviously* MIT would never call her again if she had that humiliation on her record. She'd always, always wanted to go to MIT. The fact that she'd turned down an invitation once purely because of fascination with the crazy-dangerous-yet-brilliant stuff Morganville had to offer . . . Well, it wasn't her *final* answer.

"Let me see the note."

She dug it out of her backpack and handed it over. He whistled as he looked at the heavy cream-colored envelope, the fancy embossed gold seal on the back. "A note from *Amelie*? You don't screw around when you want an excuse, do you?" He pulled the paper out and read it, eyebrows climbing higher. "*Excused on town business.* Wow. You realize that I've lived here my whole life, and I can hardly get the Founder to remember my name. She's writing frickin' makeup notes for you."

Claire snatched it back from him and put the paper back in the envelope. "Well, I was on town business when I missed the test. I didn't make that up."

Shane was smiling at her in that warm, knowing kind of way, eyes half closed. "I know you didn't," he said, "because you just . . . don't. Which is so weird, by the way. I must have forged twenty excuse notes in my not-very-glorious school career, but I'll bet you never even tried it."

Claire's face still felt hot, so she drained the last of her mocha to stall for time. Then she stood, gathered up her things, and said, "Yes, I was boring. I've been boring all my life."

"I didn't mean that." He stood up, too, and bent and kissed her. The sweet mocha on her lips mingled with the bitter coffee on his, but that wasn't why she licked her lips when they parted, and she knew it. Shane just had that effect on her. "You are *anything* but boring, Claire Bear. Believe that."

She had no idea why he thought that, because from her perspective, Shane was the exciting one, the one with all the fire and fury. She had . . . what? A history of being sheltered, a flawless academic record, and a bad habit of trying to make everything better. Not as exciting as all that, surely.

"I'll try," she replied. "See you at home!"

"Adios," he said. "Text if you can't stand being away."

"Dork." She blew him a kiss, which he air-caught and theatrically slapped over his heart.

Claire stepped out into the chilly wind and looked up at the clouds. Dark, and getting darker. Big, wet plops of rain were already falling to darken the concrete sidewalk. She flipped up the hood of her jacket and jogged, trying to beat the storm, but it caught up with her halfway through the TPU campus. Students dashed around, covering their heads, clutching books and papers to their chests to try to protect them. It was no use. Everything was going to get soaked in this downpour; it was as bad as Claire had ever seen, a torrential silver curtain that limited her visibility to no more than a few feet. She had to cut across the big open spaces to head for the science building, and very quickly realized that leaving the path was a bad idea; it wasn't just the rapidly forming mud that sucked at her shoes, but the loss of landmarks. She couldn't tell where the sun was, and the buildings were invisible behind the thunderous curtain. A big tree loomed on her right, but she couldn't remember where it was placed in relation to anything else.

Besides, standing near a tree probably wasn't the best idea, she thought, as a brilliant stab of lightning ripped across the sky. The one advantage of that eye-burning glare was that it showed the structures in the distance, just for a second, and Claire adjusted her course to head for them, blinking away the afterimages.

She almost ran into Myrnin, who came up on her out of nowhere. He was still wearing his black leather duster, but he'd lost his hat somewhere, and his shoulder-length black hair was plastered flat around his pale, sharp face. His eyes were wide and blank, and she took a step back from him, startled and wary.

He grabbed her as she slipped, and held her at arm's length. "Where is Shane?" he asked. It wasn't quite a shout, though he'd raised his voice to be heard over the loud hiss of the storm. She was so startled by the question that she didn't answer, and Myrnin shook her, not too gently. "Where is he?"

"Why?" She found her balance and twisted out of his grip—or more likely, he let her go, because Myrnin was about a hundred times stronger than she was, and she didn't think she had Shane's skill at fighting hand to hand. "Since when do you care about Shane?"

There was something very strange about Myrnin's expression, about the way he was acting. It wasn't just the weirdness of him standing there getting soaked, as if he didn't feel it; it was the way he was watching her, with an odd mixture of fear and impatience. "I'm trying to help you!" Myrnin said. "Just tell me where he is, Claire!"

"Help me? Why, what's wrong? Is Shane in trouble?" All thoughts of meeting with her professor vanished, swept away on a torrent of anxiety. "Myrnin, tell me!"

"I have to find him," he said. "I have to find him quickly. Tell me where he is!"

"I'll come with you!"

"No," he said. Had he ever looked this pale to her before? This . . . alien? "Just tell me, Claire. I travel faster alone."

Something inside her warned her not to say, not to trust him . . . but it was *Myrnin.* For all his faults, all his oddities, he wouldn't hurt her. Or Shane.

Still, she hesitated. "Just tell me why," she said, and shivered as the rain soaked through her jacket and began to crawl cold over her skin.

"He's in danger. *Now,* Claire, before it's too late!"

She couldn't banish that tingle of doubt, but she couldn't take the chance that he was telling the truth, either. Not if Shane was really in danger. "He was at Common Grounds," she said. "I think he was headed home. . . ."

Before she finished saying it, Myrnin was a flash through the rain, a shadow . . . and gone.

Claire fumbled in her pocket, pulled out her cell phone, and bent over to protect it from the rain as she quickly texted Shane. *Get home fast,* she sent. *Something wrong. Run.*

That was all she could do. There was a gnawing, terrible fear in her now. Myrnin wasn't playing around, hadn't been since he'd seen that message out in the desert. There was something more wrong than she'd ever seen it.

She hesitated, torn, and then ran for the science building. Another flash of lightning put her back on course, and she pounded up the steps, shivering from the chill, and skidded into the relatively dry shelter of the lobby. Hers weren't the only wet footprints, but they were definitely going to be the muddiest. She wiped her shoes as best she could on the mats, threw back her sodden hood, and ran down the hall to the stairs, then up to the offices. Professor Howard's door was shut. She knocked twice, didn't wait for an answer, and opened it to see him look up from his paperwork.

"Sorry," she said. "Got caught in the storm."

"I can see that, Miss Danvers. Have a seat; the chairs are plain wood for a reason."

"I can't, sir." She let her backpack slide off her shoulder—waterproof, luckily, with the rain still beaded up on its surface—and opened up the compartment to grab the envelope inside. She passed it over, her damp fingers leaving smudges on the surface. "I have to go. I'm so sorry, but it's an emergency!"

"What, another one?" Professor Howard eyed her cynically over the top of his reading glasses, unfolded the note, and then glanced back up at her with an entirely different expression. He carefully folded it again, slipped it into the envelope, and handed it back. "I'll expect you here to take the test tomorrow at noon, Danvers. No excuses other than death—do you understand me? Hospitalization will not cut it."

"Yes, sir! Thanks!" She hastily stuffed the note back in her pack, shouldered it, and hurried out of the office. She banged the door shut behind her and nearly flew down the steps again, down the hall, and yanked her almost-useless hood back up before plunging out into the rain again.

And ran into another vampire on the sidewalk.

Oliver.

What was this, Vampires Take Strolls Day? It was way out of character for Myrnin to be on campus, and now Oliver, too? This was starting to be less weird than outright terrifying.

"Where's Shane?" Oliver demanded. "I thought he'd be with you."

Suddenly, *everyone* wanted Shane. Claire blinked as rain dripped in her eyes. Oliver hadn't bothered with a raincoat *or* a hat, so he looked about as drowned as she felt. He also looked like he wasn't going to let that—or anything else—stop him. He had that same look, like Myrnin's—focused, intense, committed. But without that edge of sadness. Oliver's was all business.

"What the *hell* is going on?" she demanded. "Myrnin said—"

Oliver stepped into her personal space, chin lowered. That was, to put it mildly, intimidating. "Myrnin found you," he said. "Of course he did. He's tasted your blood—he can always find you if he wants to. What did he say to you?"

"He said Shane was in danger and he needed to find him."

"Did you tell him?"

She slowly nodded, not taking her gaze from Oliver's eyes. They were dark and unreadable, and rain dripped from his lashes.

"Then I have to hurry if you want me to save him," he said.

"Who? Myrnin?"

"Shane. Where is he?"

"Heading home from Common Grounds." She grabbed him by the arm, suddenly terrified he was going to bolt off like Myrnin, lost in the rain before she could draw a breath. "Wait! If you're going, take me! Please!"

"Bother," Oliver sighed, but he grabbed her around the waist, and suddenly she was being lifted, thrown with bruising force over his shoulder, and then . . .

. . . Then the world smeared around her into a blur. Rain whipped her like stinging lashes, and Claire hid her face as the wind rippled her clothes under its force. *Too fast, too fast* . . . She couldn't get her breath to protest, not that Oliver would listen to it anyway. She'd always known vampires could move fast, but this was *insane*. It was like being trapped in a wind tunnel, and if it hadn't been for his iron grip holding her legs, she'd have been torn away from him like some flapping piece of paper in a tornado.

It seemed to take forever, but it couldn't have been more than a minute or two at most before Oliver slowed and stopped, and Claire's whole body lurched as they decelerated. The change in speed threw her backward, and she felt him let go, but only enough to catch her as she tumbled off. He set her on her feet, and she stumbled as she tried to get her disorientation under control. There was a brick wall within reach, so she leaned on it, gasping.

Oliver stalked forward toward . . .

Toward Myrnin, in his thick black coat, who was holding Shane against the alley's other wall with his right hand, and drawing back with his left, claws catching the light in sharp angles. He hesitated as he spotted Oliver, and froze as he saw Claire's shuddering form.

"No," he whispered, then turned a glare on Oliver. "Damn you! She shouldn't have to see this!"

"Let the boy go," Oliver said. "Now."

Myrnin turned his attention back to Shane, who was fighting for his life but failing to break Myrnin's hold on his throat. His face was turning purple. "I can't do that," he said. He sounded sad and miserable, but determined. "I made a bargain. I intend to keep it."

Oliver didn't argue about it. He hit Myrnin from the side, like a freight train, and the two vampires flew off-balance through the air, then bashed into a giant rusty Dumpster, which rang like a bell from the impact. Myrnin jumped, snarling, and his coat flared like bat wings as he leaped for Oliver.

Oliver met him in midjump, slammed him against a wall, then down flat on the flooded alley floor with a splash of gray water.

Claire staggered over to Shane, who'd slumped down to a crouch. He was gagging for breath, and she could see the red marks on his throat where Myrnin had choked him. She put her arms around him, and Shane hugged her back with a desperation that surprised her.

"Get him out of here!" Oliver shouted, trying to hold Myrnin down. "Go home and stay there! Run!"

Claire grabbed Shane's hand and pulled him up to his feet, then yanked him into a stumble. The alley had protected them from some of the rain, but as they made it out into the street, the lash of the icy downpour took her breath away. No time for questions; Oliver had sounded utterly serious, and she didn't intend to take a risk. Not with Shane's life.

It took another couple of minutes to run through the blinding rain the remaining blocks to Lot Street. She half expected someone else—Amelie, maybe?—to jump out at them before they got to the shelter of the porch, but the streets were deserted. Morganville wasn't set up for heavy rains, and the gutters were already overflowing. The street was a lake, and the water was creeping inexorably into the yard under the picket fence.

Claire's hands were shaking, but she managed to get her key in the lock, open the door, and shove Shane inside. She slammed it behind them and shot all the bolts and locks home before she slumped down on the cheerful rag rug that Eve had put in the entry hall.

Shane collapsed next to her, just as drenched, and for a moment there was nothing but the sound of their raw gasps.

Claire leaned against him, and he put his arm around her. "Are you okay?" she asked in a small voice. She saw him swallow, and it looked painfully red all around his neck now.

His voice came out raspy and deeper than normal. "Thought he was going to kill me," he said. "What the hell did I do to piss him off?"

"Nothing. I don't know." Claire chewed her lip, feeling sick inside. "He told me he had to find you, that someone was after you. I—I told him where you were. God, Shane, I trusted him! I *told him where you were!*" The enormity of Myrnin's betrayal stunned her, and she felt as if a perfectly sound floor had suddenly broken under her feet, sending her plummeting down a rabbit hole where everything was wrong. "How could he do that? *Why?*"

Shane put his arm around her and hugged her close. "It's okay," he told her hoarsely. "I'm okay. Not your fault."

It was, though. It was her fault for trusting Myrnin. Shane could have died. Claire could imagine that all too well—arriving too late, seeing Shane's blood drifting through the water in that flooding alley. Red on Myrnin's sharp fingernails. Shane's body facedown in the puddle.

And she could imagine turning on him, on all of them, because if Shane died, if the vampires *killed him,* she would hunt down every single one of them. Claire knew it wasn't rational, wasn't right, but she didn't care.

If the vampires came after Shane, they came after her, and she'd fight back any way she could.

"Something's wrong," Shane croaked. "Really wrong."

She gulped down tears, and nodded silently. She rested her head against his chest, closed her eyes, and listened to the strong, sure beat of his heart.

The one she'd almost stopped, by trusting Myrnin.

Shane stroked her wet hair, trying to comfort her, *her,* when he was the one who'd been knocked around. "It was my fault," she managed to say. "Really. I told him. . . . What did he *say?*"

"To me?" Shane asked. She nodded. "Nothing. I turned around and he was right there, and he didn't say a single word except *Sorry.*" He swallowed and winced. His voice had a raspy burr at the edges. "Look, I've fought before—you know that—but he wasn't fighting. He was there to kill me, plain and simple, no hesitation. Assassination. Like he was under orders."

"Orders," Claire repeated. And whom did Myrnin take orders from? Nobody, really. Nobody except . . . "Amelie." She said it out loud, very softly, and it sounded sad to her own ears. "Amelie ordered it." But that didn't really matter, not as an immediate thing; Claire felt the burn of outrage, but she'd never really been under any illusions about Amelie's loyalty toward her. What *really* hurt was Myrnin. After all that she'd been through for him, done for him, he'd turned on her. He'd tried to take Shane away.

Didn't he understand how that would tear her apart?

"Hey," Shane said. "*Hey*, Claire, I'm here. I'm right here." His fingers stroked her wet, cold cheek, and she struggled to focus on his face. "It's all right."

It wasn't. She clung to him fiercely, until they both stopped shivering from the cold, until she felt the warmth of their bodies drying the soaking-wet fabric of their clothes. It wasn't like Shane to just sit like this with her, not when they ought to be getting up, drying off . . . but he didn't seem to have any more will to move on than she did. Maybe, deep down, he was just as shocked and scared as she felt.

"We need to think about why they'd do this," Shane said. "I know I piss people off, but this is a little much even for vamps."

"It's something we did," Claire replied. "Something we know. Something *only* we know." But by the time she finished saying it, she'd realized what it was, and so had Shane.

"The boy, out in the desert," he said. "The letter from Blacke. So that's top secret, eyes only? If all it said was *run* . . ."

"I don't think it's so much what it said," Claire said slowly. "I think . . . I think it's because we know Amelie too well. We know how she thinks, a little. More than any other humans, anyway."

She swallowed hard. "I think she wanted to keep us from talking to anybody else about what we'd seen, or thought would happen."

"Me," Shane corrected her. "She wanted to stop *me*."

That quieted her; obviously, it was true. Myrnin had gone after Shane like an arrow; he'd had the *chance* to kill her, but he hadn't even tried. Why spare her, if both she and Shane knew the same dangerous things?

You know, some voice deep inside her whispered. *You know how Myrnin feels.*

Claire shuddered. She didn't. *Really,* she didn't. And she didn't want to know, either. But if Myrnin—if he'd refused to kill her, he wouldn't have had much problem killing Shane, for exactly the same reason.

Then why had *Oliver* stepped in to save them, of all people? It made no sense. It left Claire feeling vulnerable and shaken in ways that all her time in Morganville hadn't. If Amelie had turned on them . . .

She wrapped herself more closely around Shane. He made a faint, pleased sound in the back of his throat and pulled her over on his lap. Their lips met gently at first, then more urgently. Shane's mouth tasted of rain and the bittersweet memory of coffee, and Claire found herself whimpering a little, wanting more than this, so much more, wanting to know he was alive and *with her*. The kiss strengthened, and Shane's hands stroked fire down her skin. Suddenly, she felt stifled by the damp clothes. She wanted them *off*.

"Hey," he whispered, and grabbed her hands as she reached for the hem of her shirt to yank it off. "Wait."

She stopped and stared at him, stricken. The smile on his damp, kissable lips reassured her. So did the hungry, hot look in his eyes.

"Upstairs," he said. "Got to get you dried off and warmed up properly."

It *sounded* innocent, but oh, it wasn't. Not at all.

She climbed up to her feet and offered him her hand. He raised his eyebrows, took it, and rose to put his arms around her and kiss her, again.

"He could try it again," Claire said. "If Amelie's turned against you, I swear, Shane, I swear that I'll—"

He shook his head and kissed her, warm and sweet and full of promises. "Don't think about it now," he said in that husky whisper. "Whatever happens, we'll be ready for it, Claire. Both of us."

And then he led her upstairs, into the stillness of her room, where he promised her again. So many things.

Oliver knocked on the door two hours later. They were both up and dressed, and Claire was heating up soup for Shane—it was about the only thing he could get down his bruised throat. Claire opened the door and stared at him—glared, really—and said, "You knew what was going on. You knew about Myrnin. Was it Amelie?"

"May I come in?" Oliver asked. He didn't wait for an answer, just pushed past her and walked down the hall. Claire cursed under her breath and locked up behind him. Around her, the house's energy gathered, protective and menacing, but not quite sure who the enemy might be. It responded to her moods, even more than with the other residents. That might be useful, right about now.

Oliver had stopped at the couch, and was looking down at Shane, who was deliberately ignoring him as he stared at the flickering television. "Are you all right?" Oliver asked. Shane pointed to his throat. "Nothing permanently damaged, I trust."

Shane flipped him off.

"Ah, I see you haven't lost your sense of social decorum and excellent manners." Oliver shot a glance at Claire and raised his eyebrows very slightly. "*Is* he all right?"

"No thanks to Myrnin." She was so angry right now that she was almost vibrating with it. "What the *hell,* Oliver?"

"Not entirely Myrnin's fault, I'm sorry to say. There was a fear that having the two of you knowing . . . what you know might be too great a risk. Count your blessings. Myrnin fought to save your life."

"*My* life. Not Shane's."

Oliver just shrugged. "As you can see, he lives and breathes. No harm done."

Shane silently pointed an index finger at his neck, which was an angry dark red, heading toward purple.

"No permanent harm," Oliver amended. "Let that be an indicator of how serious this situation is, and how very serious we are about keeping even a whisper of it from the general public—and by that, I mean vampires as well as humans. *Silence,* do you hear me? You were never there, and you never saw anything. Or I promise you, your reprieves will be over."

"But we don't *know* anything!" Claire almost screamed it at him. She was so angry she wanted to attack him with her bare hands, and it was only the fact that Shane, usually the hair-trigger one, was sitting quietly on the couch that held her back. Well, that and the fact that Oliver wouldn't have had the slightest problem crushing her like a bug. "What are you all so afraid of?"

Shane looked up at that, at Oliver.

Who hesitated for a moment, and then said, "I hope you never have to know the answer to that, Claire. Don't go out tonight.

Wait until tomorrow to leave this house. I have some . . . persuading to do."

Then he left, quietly. She heard the door unlock and Oliver called back, "Lock it behind me." Then he was gone.

Claire screamed out her frustration, dashed down the hall, and slammed the locks home with so much force she bruised her hand. Then she banged her fists on the wood, and kicked it for good measure.

Shane had followed her, and he put his hands on her shoulders. She turned toward him, staring up into his face. God, that bruise looked really bad. He'd almost died.

No, he'd almost been *killed*. By *Myrnin*, of all people. How screwed up was that?

"Relax," he whispered. He moved his hands up to cup her face in warmth. "Just relax. The door didn't piss you off."

"Says the guy who punches walls."

"Yeah, well, the walls had it coming."

She had to laugh, but it came out as more of a cross between a bark and a sob. "God, *what is going on* out there? What are they not telling us?"

"Don't know," Shane said. "But for once, I vote we don't ask, because it's way out of our pay grade." He kissed her forehead, then moved down to kiss her lips. "God, you taste good."

"This is what you're thinking about? After that?"

"When I get nervous, I focus on the positive. Like you." He took her hand and led her back toward the living room, where he had her sit down on the couch as he retrieved two glasses of iced tea (Eve had taken to making it, for some reason), and put a movie into the player. She was too tense to relax, but Shane clearly wasn't; he stretched out on the sofa, and after a few moments of feeling foolish, Claire finally settled down next to him, with his warm, heavy arm around her waist, pulling her close against him.

She had no idea what the movie was, and in a matter of moments, she really didn't care, either. Shane's hot kisses on the back of her neck ensured that. So did the sneaky, wonderful moves he made with his hands.

Within an hour, they were asleep together, curled up under an afghan, while the movie played on without them.

When they woke up, it was to the sound of plates clattering in the kitchen, and the smell of pizza. Claire was the first to stir, and her yawning and stretching made Shane mumble something that sounded happy, and burrow in closer to her, but she smiled and slipped out from under his arms.

Shane cracked his eyelids open just a slit and said, "No fair, you're leaving."

"Well, there's pizza," Claire said. "Get up or I won't save you any."

Pizza was almost as magical a lure as tacos, apparently, because he was on his feet in thirty seconds, shaking his head to flop his hair back into its usual I-don't-care style.

Oh God, his neck looked horrible. No way of disguising *that.* Claire stepped close to him and whispered, "We can't tell them. You remember, right? Oliver said—"

"Right, 'cause I'm so good at taking orders from walking fangs," Shane whispered back. Even his whisper sounded raw and painful.

"Shane, you *can't!*"

"Fine. I won't. *You* explain it."

That was the best he was willing to offer, so Claire pushed

through the kitchen door, still casting him doubtful looks, and found Michael and Eve standing at the counters, filling plates with pizza from a box. There were two larges, and Shane made straight for the one with everything. He grabbed a slice and started eating it standing up.

Eve rolled her eyes and slid a plate down the countertop. "Honestly, were you raised in a pony pen or something? Plates! Learn them; love them...." Her voice trailed off, and her expression turned shocked. "What the *hell* happened to you, Shane?"

Michael looked up from preparing his own plate and saw it, too. His blue eyes widened. "Damn," he said. "You okay?"

Shane gave him a silent thumbs-up.

"Shane! What happened?"

He pointed at his throat and looked pitiful. Oh, of course. He was seriously dumping this whole thing on her, Claire realized. She had no choice but to step in. "He can't talk," she said. "Well, he can, but it hurts." All true. "He got in a fight." Also true, although it hadn't been so much *fight* as *attack*. "The good news is he won."

"Dude, someone tried to choke you. That goes a little further than most fights," Michael said. He sounded genuinely concerned. "Was it about the flyers?"

It was a perfectly good explanation, but Claire couldn't help but flinch from using it. For one thing, Michael and Eve already felt bad enough about the tension in town. "I don't think so," she said. "It was . . . personal."

"You know, you really need to stop trying to make new friends, Shane. You're not good at it. And aren't we enough for you?" Eve batted her thick eyelashes at him and smiled, but Claire could tell she was still alarmed, and worried. "Here. Have a Coke. That's good for a sore throat, right?"

"Good for everything," Shane croaked, and took the extended cold can with good grace. "Thanks."

"You owe me a dollar," Eve said. "I'll add it to the five thousand you already owe me, though."

He blew her a kiss, and she stuck her tongue out at him, and that was the end of the subject, thankfully.

They sat at the table together, eating; Michael and Eve did most of the talking. Shane, of course, stayed quiet from necessity; Claire just couldn't think what to say, because today's events had crowded out all her small-talk skills, and she was afraid of saying anything for fear of blurting the wrong thing. Oliver had made it clear enough what the penalties for that would be. *Oh God, we already told Eve that Myrnin was freaking out,* Claire remembered—they'd said it at the coffee shop, but at least they hadn't spilled anything more than that. If the breaking news was that Myrnin was acting weird, well, nobody was going to interrupt regularly scheduled programming. Hopefully.

"Earth to Claire!" Eve was snapping her fingers in front of Claire's face. She blinked, jerked back, and hastily took a bite of cooling pizza. "Wow. See what happens when you take a nap in the middle of the afternoon? Brain cells hibernate."

"Sorry. What were you saying?"

"I was asking if you planned to be around tomorrow. I may need help picking up the cake and flowers and stuff."

"I—" Claire's brain went completely blank for a second. There might have been something to Eve's brain-cell-hibernation theory. "I have to make up a test tomorrow morning," she finally remembered. "And I really ought to check in at the lab sometime."

"So that would be a no, then," Eve said, and turned to Michael.

"Teaching guitar lessons," he said. "If you need me to cancel—"

"No. Because I *know* Slacker Boy here has nothing planned. Right, Shane?"

He mimed chopping things. Eve shook her head. "Oh, no, you don't. I checked the schedule. You're not working until Monday. Don't even try."

He took a too-big bite of pizza for a reply. Michael patted him on the shoulder. "I like this plan," he said. "You and Eve, picking up cake and flowers, and you can't even say a word. Should be tons of fun."

Shane almost choked, and gave Michael a sideways glare. Michael sent him a hundred-watt smile in return—no fangs, which was probably for the best.

All in all, it wasn't a bad evening, especially when they all curled up on the sofa together for bad-movie night. It wasn't quite the same without Shane's snarky commentary, but just relaxing against him, his arm around her, made Claire feel that all might just be right with the world after all.

No, it's not, some traitorous, cold part of her brain insisted. *Nothing's right. You're in danger.*

If Amelie was freaked enough to try to kill Shane, even if it was some kind of terrible mistake, Claire's instincts were almost certainly correct.

SIX

CLAIRE

Friday morning dawned clear, all rain clouds gone; the air was crisp, dry, and icy cold, and the wind—which never really stopped out here—whipped up random gusts of blown sand as Claire, wrapped in a thick jacket, scarf, hat, and gloves, picked up her coffee from Common Grounds. Eve hated the early-morning shift, so this morning it was a girl named Christy; she was a bouncy little blonde who had probably been a Morganville High cheerleader last year, two years ago at the most. Common Grounds was doing brisk business serving up coffee delicacies to people heading off to work and students making their way to early classes. Claire had trouble finding a table, but finally spotted one crammed in close to the wall just as the previous occupant vacated it.

She was three sips into her mocha and checking e-mail on her phone when a plaid book bag thumped down on the table. Claire glanced up and saw Monica Morrell dropping into the chair across from her. Monica wasn't making any concessions to the weather. She had on white kneesocks and a plaid, pleated mini-skirt with a low-cut white top. No coat.

"Aren't you freezing?" Claire asked. "Oh, and by the way, the seat's taken by my invisible friend."

"Yes, I'm freezing—it's what you do for fashion, not that you'd know anything about that, Brainiac. And screw your invisible friend. I want my coffee, and you've got the only open chair. Not like I want to be besties or anything." Monica tossed her lustrous dark hair back over her shoulders. It had been a while since she'd changed the color, and Claire thought this one suited her best anyway. She was a tall, attractive girl with a mean, sharp edge to the pretty, but she and Claire had, over the long months, achieved something like armed truce if not friendship.

"How's Gina?" Claire asked, and took another drink. The faster she finished her coffee, the faster she could escape from Planet Princess. "I heard she's in rehab."

Gina was one of Monica's two normal wing girls, and she wasn't in the celebrity kind of rehab; no, this was physical rehab, because she'd smashed up her car in a pretty spectacular wreck. One that Claire figured was karmic in nature. She felt a little guilty about not being more concerned. The question had been purely for form's sake.

"She's walking fine," Monica said. "They're thinking about putting her into some kind of mental-therapy thing, though. Apparently she slapped a nurse."

"Well, that's Gina," Claire said. "Making friends."

"Grudge-hold much?"

"She pulled a knife on me, Monica. More than once. And she

broke Miranda's nose." Miranda was a skinny kid who'd taken way too much trauma in her short life; Gina had cold-bloodedly punched her, and just for that, Claire hoped that the rehab lasted *forever.* Well, not literally. But hopefully it was at least painful.

Monica didn't say anything to that. She hadn't, Claire knew, been all that thrilled with Gina's behavior, but she hadn't put a stop to it, either. "It's probably good they get her in to see a shrink," Monica said. "Bitch is crazy."

Three words, and she dismissed one of her most loyal followers and henchwomen. Claire didn't know whether to be impressed or disgusted. Probably both. "She's not the only one around here."

"You should know. Speaking of crazy bitches, can't wait to see what happens at the engagement party. Ought to be epic." Monica's eyes sparkled with petty delight. "I hear Wannabe Dead Girl invited half the rebel alliance of Morganville, and they're bringing their friends. I'm wearing something that blood will wash out of, just to be safe."

Of course Monica would be coming to the party; Monica never missed one, especially one where she could cause mayhem. Well, Claire figured she wouldn't be the biggest problem they had. Or even the worst behaved.

That was just sad.

"This has been fun," Claire said, and even though she had half her coffee left, she got up to leave.

Monica flung out her hand, grabbed Claire's coat sleeve, and said, "Wait. Sit. Please."

A *please* from Morganville's self-appointed crown princess? Now, that was interesting. Claire settled back down and took a sip of her mocha, waiting for the other designer shoe to drop.

"Something's going on," Monica said. She dropped her voice, and leaned across the table as she glanced around to be sure nobody was watching them. As far as Claire could tell, nobody was. "My brother got called in to some kind of closed-door meeting with Amelie yesterday and he hasn't come out yet. He doesn't answer his cell, either. Can you find out . . . ?"

Richard Morrell, Monica's brother, was the mayor of the town—young for it, but one of the most responsible people Claire had ever met. He'd gotten Monica's normal share of it, apparently. And Monica was right—closeted with Amelie all night? That didn't sound good at all.

"I can ask," Claire said. "But they probably won't tell me anything more than what you know."

"I just want to know if he's okay." Monica looked almost . . . well, human. "Richard's all I've got. You know?"

Claire nodded. "I'll see what I can find out, but I'm sure he's okay. Don't worry."

"Thanks." Monica said it grudgingly, but she did say it. That was more than a little amazing. Claire didn't want to spoil it by saying anything else, so she drank her coffee in silence, and so did Monica, and after a while, it almost felt . . . comfortable.

Compared to the other times when they'd tried to kill each other, anyway.

Claire's next stop was the TPU science building, where she found Professor Howard waiting with her test. She took it in twenty minutes, not needing the hour he'd allotted; it was an easy A, she knew that, and so did he as soon as he glanced over her answers. She got a nod of approval from him, and a stern warning not to miss any other tests.

Sadly, she wasn't sure she could accommodate him on that. Not in Morganville.

After the test, she sat on the steps in the chilly sunlight and dialed Oliver's phone. Not surprisingly, it went to his voice mail, which sharply ordered her to leave a message. "Monica Morrell's worried about her brother," she said. "She's worried enough to talk to *me,* and that means she's probably tried everybody else in town. I assume you don't want the buzz, so go calm her down. Please." The *please* was an afterthought, and halfhearted; she was still angry at him, and furious at Myrnin. And Amelie. She was *truly* furious at Amelie.

She'd given so much to the vampires, given so much to keep things stable around here, and *this* was how they paid her back? By trying to take away *Shane*?

The longer she considered it, the angrier it made her. And the more frightened. Because what it meant opened up a terrifying gulf in front of her. . . . She'd always thought that at a certain level she could trust Myrnin, and Amelie. (She'd never deluded herself about Oliver.) But if she couldn't . . . if deep down, they saw her as disposable . . . what chance did any human really have in Morganville?

None.

That was what Shane had been trying to tell her all along. *We don't mean anything to them except as a life-support system,* Claire thought. *Individually, we're nothing. Servants. No, cattle with opposable thumbs, occasionally useful.*

She clutched her phone hard, stood up, and went down the steps, two at a time. Burning in her stomach was a mixture of nerves, nausea, and a new sense of purpose.

She went straight to the camera store that she and Shane had visited; the engagement party flyer wasn't posted, but Claire hadn't really expected it to be. The man behind the counter—the same one—straightened as she entered and put both hands on the glass top. "What do you want?" he asked. The indigo dye of the stake tattoo showed against the pale skin of his forearm, peeking out from under his rolled-up shirtsleeve.

Claire pulled off her cap and gloves, jammed them in a pocket, and said, "I don't know." That was honest. She'd come here on impulse, but now that she was facing him, she wasn't sure what she wanted to ask. "What's the deal with the tattoos?"

He rolled down his sleeves, staring at her with cold suspicion. "Chicks dig them," he said. "I don't do tats. This is a camera store. You might want to check down the street."

"Captain Obvious used to be your friend."

He didn't answer that at all. He was frowning now, and she was wondering if she'd made a terrible, impulsive mistake.

"I just—" She took a deep breath and plunged on. "Shane may be in danger. Real danger. From the top. Can you protect him?"

"Sorry?" His eyebrows rose. "Don't know what you're talking about. I just run a—"

"Camera store, yeah, I heard you. *Listen.* I need to know—can you, I don't know, watch out for him? *Please?*"

"You think I'm going to fall for your innocent act? You've been in the vampires' corner since day one around here. No chance, sweetheart. And if you keep poking around here, you're going to get hurt."

"It's not for me," she said. "It's for Shane. And I think you know he's never been in the vampires' corner. So please. Just—help him if you see he's in trouble. That's all I'm asking."

"What about you?" he asked, and gave her an evil little smile. "What if *you're* in trouble?"

Claire shrugged and put her gloves and hat back on. "I guess I'm on my own. Right?"

He was still watching her, trying to figure her out, as she walked out into the weak winter sun. There were still pools of dirty water at the edges of the uneven parking lot, and the ground remained soaked.

When she looked back, the camera shop owner nodded, once.

She put her hands in her pockets and walked home.

Home was chaos, and for a moment, Claire was truly worried that something awful had happened; Eve was stomping around the house slamming things around, and Shane was saying, in a thin and raspy voice, "It's not a big deal, man; calm down."

"I'm not your *man* and I will not *calm down!*" Eve yelled, and gave a piercing, full-throated shriek of frustration.

Claire dumped her stuff in the hall and raced into the living room, expecting to see . . . Well, she didn't know what she expected to see, except disaster in some form.

What she saw was a cake sitting on the dining table that was . . . well, a disaster. In cake form.

The two-tiered dessert itself was uneven and leaning, the icing was messy, the red flowers had melted into the white and left unsettling bloodlike stains, and, worst of all, as Claire got closer, she realized that the writing on top said *MICHAEL & EVA* in a big, lopsided, amateurish outline of a heart with an arrow through it.

Eva. Not *Eve.*

Eve kicked the sofa with her Doc Martens boots and burst into tears, and really, Claire didn't blame her a bit. Shane was looking helpless as he stood there watching her, not sure what to do.

So he did, of course, the wrong thing, and said, "Look, it's just a cake. I'm sure it's still delicious."

Eve glared at him. Claire walked over and put her arms around her friend, and sent Shane an irritated look.

"What did I do?" he croaked. His throat was turning a spectacular sunset purple now, with hints of blue. "Cake! It's cake! Delicious cake!"

"Honey, it's okay, really," Claire said. "We can—fix it."

"We can't," Eve managed to gasp out between sobs. "I shouldn't have made the trim red—it's all runny. . . ."

It did look a little bit slaughterrific, actually, but Claire put on a brave face. "So we scrape it all off, get some store-bought icing, and put it on," she said. "Can't be any worse, right? And we decorate it ourselves. It'll be fun!"

"It's *horrible!*" Eve cried, and buried her face in Claire's puffy coat. "It looks like Dracula's wedding cake!"

"Which should be a plus, shouldn't it?" Shane asked. "I mean, thematically?"

"*Really* not helping, Shane!" Claire said.

"I am helping! I even carried it in!"

"Yeah, good job." Claire sighed and shook her head. "Go upstairs or something. We'll find a way to fix this. Eve—just calm down and relax, okay? Breathe. I'll get the frosting and be back in a little while."

She got Eve to sit on the couch. She'd stopped sobbing, which was good, but she was staring at the cake with a dead-eyed, horrified look. The sooner the icing was scraped and the whole cake redone, the better.

Shane said, "Want me to go with?"

Her first impulse was to say no . . . but he'd survived the morning running around with Eve, and Eve was more consumed with party planning than watching his back. Besides, it was still broad daylight. The safest he'd be, even from Amelie.

He gave her puppy-dog eyes and said, "Please?"

She could never resist the puppy-dog eyes, and he knew it. "All right," she said. "But wear a scarf. Your throat makes you look like a zombie."

"I hear zombies are hot right now," Shane said, straight-faced. "They've got their own TV show and everything. Okay. Scarf."

She supervised, making sure the scarf was looped high enough to cover up the worst of the bruising. "Just tell anyone who asks that you got a wicked new tattoo and you're still healing up," she said. She stopped and brushed her fingertips lightly over the discolored skin. "Does it hurt?"

He bent his head and lightly kissed her forehead. "Only when I laugh."

"I'll try not to be funny."

"Epic fail, beautiful." She tingled all over when he called her *beautiful*. He didn't do it often, but when he did, he said it in this tone that was . . . just so incredibly intimate. "You know I need to watch your back, right?"

"I'm buying *icing*, Shane. I'm not going on safari. Besides, you're the one with the target on his back, not me."

"Then *you* can protect *me*." He kissed her on the nose, lightly.

The idea of her—small, not-very-physical Claire—protecting big, strong, *very* physical Shane . . . Well, that was just funny, somehow, and she couldn't help but laugh.

But he kept looking at her, very warm and very serious, and after her giggles faded, he said, "I mean it, Claire. I trust you."

She put her hand on his cheek and, without speaking, led him out the door.

At the grocery store, the first thing Claire noticed was that there was some kind of a crisis . . . not a we're-out-of-milk crisis, but something bigger. Management-style. As she and Shane walked in the door, they were almost knocked down by a very agitated man with that store-manager look about him. He was on his cell phone. His tie was pulled askew, and there were sweat stains under his arms. He was saying, "Yes, I *know* you need payment for deliveries, and I'm trying to reach our owner—I've been trying for days! . . . No, I don't have another number. Look, I'm sure nothing's wrong. I'm going over there myself to see. If you can just go ahead and make the scheduled delivery . . ." His voice faded out as he kept walking, heading for the office. Claire exchanged a look with Shane, who shrugged, and then they went in search of cake supplies.

Claire could tell that the shelves were badly in need of restocking. . . . Not that there was ever a huge selection in the store, but when the cake mixes were down to one or two boxes, and entirely out in most of the really good flavors . . . well, that didn't bode well. No wonder the manager was freaking out.

Like in most businesses in town, Claire suspected the owner was a vampire. . . . They liked to keep a tight grip on the purse strings of their investments, too. So why was the manager having so much trouble getting money for his store? Not like vamps went broke, not in Morganville.

"Did he say he couldn't get in touch with the owner?" Shane asked her, very quietly. "Because that's weird."

"Very," she agreed. "You think he might have been part of Bishop's, ah, support group?" Bishop, Amelie's father, had gathered up a nice little cadre of backstabbing traitors to help him on his most recent bid for power; Amelie and Oliver had responded by basically making most of those people disappear. And Bishop had done his share of damage, too. . . . He'd grabbed some of Amelie's supporters, and they hadn't survived the experience.

Civil war among the vampires: not pretty.

"Possible," Shane said. His voice sounded rougher than before, like he was starting to really hurt. "But that should have been taken care of weeks ago. Amelie doesn't let things go like that."

He was right. This sounded recent, and pretty dire. Amelie certainly wouldn't want one of the town's main grocery stores to crater; she'd fund it first. So this had to be something happening under her radar.

Claire shook her head and checked the frosting. There was enough white available, and she found some red candy flowers, too. The red decorator writing stuff looked doubtful, though Claire grabbed some of that. "Done," she said, and turned around.

Shane was gone.

"Shane?" She clutched the stuff to her chest, suddenly feeling very cold, and turned in a circle. He wasn't at either end of the aisle. In fact, he wasn't anywhere in sight. Claire hurried up toward the registers, hoping to catch sight of him.

Nothing. Her heart sped up, painfully fast. She started walking, fast, pacing past aisle after aisle. There were a dozen or so shoppers, but no sign of her boyfriend.

And then, off to the side, she saw a flash of a blue scarf. She backed up, stared, and saw that Shane was standing close to the office door, head down, listening. He looked up and saw her, and her heartbeat slowly began to ease up. Sweet relief flooded through her. *God.* She'd thought . . . Well, she'd thought someone had taken him right behind her back. Which was ridiculous, now that she thought about it—he wasn't some defenseless kid; he was a big guy, and he'd make noise, at the very least.

No, of *course* he'd gone off on his own. Jackass.

She got in line to pay for her stuff, and he came to join her by the time she reached the register. "Jerk," she told him, without the usual lighter edge of humor. "You scared me to death!"

He helped her put her armload of supplies on the belt and nodded at the bored, overweight girl running things over the scanner. "Hey, Bettina."

"Hey, Shane." Bettina sighed.

"So, lot of drama today."

"Haven't had a delivery in two weeks," she said. "I'll be lucky if we're not closed by tomorrow. It's supposed to be payday. No sign of checks, either. This sucks."

"Hang in there," Shane said. He smiled at her, and she smiled back wearily. It occurred to Claire, with a bit of surprise, that he knew the girl, probably from his old neighborhood or school or something. "How's your brother?"

"Same jerkwad as he ever was, only now he's old enough to drink, all legal," she said. "Pretty much sucks."

"Tell me about it."

Bettina's eyes finally focused on Shane's throat, and the scarf. "Hey, is that a bruise? What happened?"

"Tattoo," he said, straight-faced. "It's hard-core."

She looked impressed. "I guess it must be."

Bettina silently bagged the groceries and handed them over, and Claire thanked her—sincerely, because it was obvious Bettina and everybody else at the Food King was going to have a pretty miserable time today—and walked with Shane back out into the cold.

"So, superspy, what did you learn hanging around the office door?" she asked him. Shane was hunched over, hands in his pockets, looking thoughtful.

"The manager called the cops," he said. "Filed a missing persons report. On a vampire."

"Seriously?"

"That's how desperate he is." Shane raised his eyebrows. "He gave them an address, if you're interested."

"*That* is not a good idea. We're supposed to stay quiet, remember?"

"We're not talking. We're just looking."

"You're going to get us killed," Claire said. "Well, yourself, anyway. Which will kill me, too, Shane. Please, let's *go home,* just this once! No poking around, no Scooby-Dooing, no taking crazy risks. I'm scared, and I think the less we have to do with whatever's going on, the better."

He shot a look over at her, a smile playing hide-and-seek with his lips. "Who are you, and what did you do with Claire?"

"I'm serious."

"I can see that." He sucked in a deep breath, as if playing for time, and after a moment, he said, "Claire, Myrnin's a few sandwiches short of a picnic, but he's got no reason to come after me. I could tell it wasn't his idea. He actually apologized to me before he choked the crap out of me. So . . . who gives Myrnin orders?"

"Shane—"

"C'mon. Help me out."

Claire sighed, and her breath puffed white in the fierce, cold wind that stung her skin. "Only one person."

"Yeah. Her. And then Oliver comes racing to stop him. Again, who gives Oliver orders, when he bothers to listen?"

"Amelie."

"And you think that by keeping our heads down, we're really going to get out of this? You want to believe in Santa and the Easter Bunny while we're at it?"

Claire jumped over a broken part of the sidewalk, which Shane's longer legs carried him effortlessly over. "Hey, you're the one who says the Easter Bunny is actually evil."

"Granted, but you're avoiding the point."

"I've thought about it," she said. "And I'm angry, Shane. I'm really angry. After everything we've done, everything we've risked, we're *expendable.* And it hurts. Believe me."

He stopped and looked at her for a moment, then put his arms around her. The street was empty except for a few passing cars, and it felt like they were all alone, against the world. That wasn't true, but in that moment, Claire was feeling particularly vulnerable.

Shane kissed her on the top of the head and said, "Welcome to Morganville. We grew up knowing that. You're just now realizing it."

She hid her face in the warm, rough weave of his jacket. Her voice came out muffled. "How do you stand it?"

"We get mean," Shane said. "And we get cynical. And we stick together. Always. Because first, last, and always, we rely on each other."

They stood there together, holding each other, until finally the wind got so cold Claire shivered even in his embrace.

Shane put his arm around her and walked her the rest of the way home. She forced herself to forget all they'd seen and said, and throw herself into salvaging Eve's engagement cake. It was actually fun, and three tubs of frosting later, they'd made it look, if not professional, presentable. The cakes were level, and the decoration was even; the red flowers looked sweet and just a bit in-your-face. Claire had decided to make the most of the amateurish clumsiness of the squeeze decorator stuff, so there was a funny lopsided heart with a childish arrow through it, and the initials MG and ER.

Simple, but fun.

Eve hugged her, hard. "It's beautiful," she said. "What happened to the old frosting?"

Shane, sitting at the table, raised his hand. "Took one for the team."

"Jesus, you *ate it*? All of it?"

"Nah." He held up the bowl that was sitting in front of him. There was still about half a cup left. "Couldn't finish it all."

Eve blinked and looked at Claire, who shrugged and said, "I always thought he was sweet."

The next day, they were all up early—hideously early, according to Eve, who looked hollow-eyed and desperate as she glugged down three cups of coffee before heading up to hog the bathroom for an hour and a half. Claire had wisely done all her showering and getting ready before Eve was even up.

She hadn't seen Michael at all yet, but Shane was up, yawning and looking almost as out of it as Eve. "Why are we doing this again?" he asked. "And where are all those doughnut things I bought?"

"Eaten," Claire said. "Besides, you ate about a pound of frosting last night. No sugar for you."

This time *she* got the finger, which was amusing; he never, ever shot it at her. She gave it right back, which made him smile. "So wrong. So what's Slave Driver Eve got us doing today?"

"We have to take the cake and flowers over to the ballroom," Claire said, ticking it off on her fingers. "Decorate the tables. Put out the plates and forks. Get the punch ready and set up the plasma table . . ."

"You cannot be serious."

"Relax—we're not *managing* the plasma table. The blood bank is doing that."

"Great. My two pints are going to be party food."

"Stay on target, Shane. What are you wearing?"

"Relax, Fashion Police. I'm dressing up. I've got a tuxedo T-shirt and everything." When her mouth opened in horror, he grinned. "Kidding. I'll look okay. Oh, and I'm wearing a turtleneck, so don't get on to me about the bruises not going with my shoes or anything." The bruises were, Claire had to admit, spectacular today, though his voice sounded more normal. "I promise, no lime green suits." He yawned. "I guess I'd better go bang on Michael's door. Dude's going to be late to his own party, and Eve would stake him right through the heart. Messy."

He took his coffee and ambled away, and Claire found herself standing there smiling like an idiot. She didn't know when it had happened, but something had changed in Shane—something important. It wasn't a big shift, from most perspectives, but he seemed . . . more responsible now. Less the rebel slacker and more someone who liked being thought of that way.

Progress.

She sucked down the rest of her coffee, fast, and washed up the mugs in the sink. She was wrist-deep in warm, soapy water when Shane's voice came from behind her, calling her name. She looked around, and saw him standing in the doorway, holding it open. He looked . . .

Odd was her first thought, but in the next second, she amended it to *scared*. She hadn't seen him scared very often.

"Shane?" She left everything where it was and reached for a towel to wipe her hands.

"You'd better come out here," he said. "We've got visitors."

"Who . . . ?" It wasn't even eight a.m. and someone had come calling? So not right.

"Sheriff Moses and Dick Morrell," Shane said. "They've got Michael with him. He never came home last night."

"Oh God," Claire breathed. "Is he okay?"

"Depends," he said. "Come on."

She threw the towel at the counter and didn't care where it landed as she followed him out, down the hall, and into the parlor room at the front, where Hannah Moses and Morganville's mayor, Richard Morrell, were waiting. Hannah was dressed in her crisp blue police uniform, holding the peaked cap under her arm; she was a tall African-American woman with a scar on her face that she'd earned in Afghanistan combat, and she was one of the most capable and practical people Claire knew. Richard Morrell was wearing a suit and tie, but the tie was pulled loose and it seemed like yesterday's clothing, from the wrinkles and the dark circles beneath his eyes. He and Hannah were both kind of young—under thirty, at least—and even though Shane had never gotten over Richard being Monica's brother, Claire thought he was sort of all right.

They both nodded at Claire as she came into the room.

Michael didn't. He was sitting down in one of the chairs, elbows on his knees, hunched over. Like Richard, he didn't look like he'd changed out of the jeans and dark blue shirt he'd been wearing yesterday. He raised his head to glance at Claire, then returned to studying the carpet.

"What's wrong?" she asked breathlessly. She'd expected it was something to do with Michael, but he didn't seem to be in custody, exactly. Besides, handcuffs were more Shane's style.

Eve came in right behind her, still in a black silk kimono robe embroidered with cranes; her hair was up under a towel turban. She went to Michael and touched him on the shoulder. He looked up and smiled wanly, put his paler hand over hers, and straightened up in the chair.

Hannah cleared her throat. "I need to ask you all some questions," she said. "About a missing vampire."

Claire saw Shane's reaction, and imagined she'd made the same half-guilty start. Someone must have seen him snooping, or heard them talking . . . but they hadn't gotten involved. They hadn't! *Great, now we're guilty even when we didn't do anything.*

"We don't know anything about it," Claire said, before Hannah could continue. "We overheard it at the grocery store, that's all. The only thing we know is that whoever the vampire is, he's been missing for two weeks and the checks aren't getting signed."

Richard Morrell frowned at her. So did Hannah, just a little. "What grocery store?"

"The . . . Food King?" Too late, Claire realized that she'd gone entirely the wrong direction. "Oh. So . . . not him?"

"Separate case," Hannah said, "but similar circumstances, as it happens. We're looking into Mr. Barrett's disappearance, but we have a more pressing issue now. He was the fourth vampire to go missing in the last three weeks, and now there's a fifth."

"It's Naomi," Michael said. "Nobody's seen her since she visited us here. We're the last people who saw her." He didn't say *alive,* but Claire understood what he meant. It was possible that Naomi, like the other four vampires, had been killed.

No wonder Hannah was tense, and Richard was losing sleep. Dead vampires in Morganville were a very, very serious problem—for humans.

"I need you each to tell me exactly where you've been since then," Hannah said, and took out a pad and pen. "Eve. Go first."

Eve clutched her robe closed, even though it was tightly tied, and her dark eyes widened. "You think *I*—"

"I don't think anything, except that you need to establish your movements so I can eliminate you, fast. You know that if something is going on, Amelie will come down hard on whoever is responsible. Let's make sure you're not on that list."

"But I didn't—we wouldn't—"

"Just tell her where you've been," Michael said. "Eve. It's going to be okay. I promise."

But looking at him, at the tense set of his body and the worried look in his blue eyes . . . Claire wasn't so sure.

SEVEN

CLAIRE

☽

The interrogation—because that was what it was, no matter what anyone said—took about an hour. One by one, Eve, Claire, and Shane told Hannah where they'd been and what they'd done, hour by hour, since they'd last seen Naomi sitting here in the parlor.

Hannah had made notes, but her face had remained impassive; she didn't give any hints about what she thought about the whole thing, none at all. She asked more questions of Eve than she did of Shane or Claire, and after she'd left, Eve collapsed on the sofa, buried her face in her hands, and said, "They think I did it."

"No, they don't," Michael said. He sat beside her and put his arm around her. "It's just that you—you were pretty angry about her."

"They suspect all of us," Shane said. His voice was flat, his expression so tense that his jaw looked sharp. "Us in particular, I mean. But after us, everybody else with a pulse. Maybe that's why—" He shut his mouth with a snap, eyes widening, and Claire bit her lip. He'd *almost* blurted it out.

As it was, Michael said, "Why what?"

"Why they're nervous," Claire put in quickly. Probably too quickly. "About the wedding, I mean."

Michael stared at her, and she suddenly knew he knew she was lying. Her pulse was too fast, for one thing. He'd once told her that he could tell when she was lying, and even if he'd been kidding her, he had an instinct for these things. A killer instinct. "Something's going on with you two, and don't tell me I'm imagining it," he said. "First Shane shows up choked half to death—"

"Dude, it's not that bad!"

"—and now this. You know something. You're hiding something."

Even Eve was looking at Claire now, not quite ready to believe but obviously wondering. "She wouldn't do that," she told Michael. "Would you, CB?"

"She's not hiding anything," Shane said. That was a relief, because Shane was a *much* better liar. "She's just worried. The vamps are acting weird. Trust me, being worried is a survival instinct right about now. Go on, tell me I'm wrong, Mikey."

Michael was quiet for a moment, then shook his head. "I can't," he admitted. "Something's going on there, too. What, I don't know; they don't exactly keep me in the loop. But whatever it is, they're closing ranks." He fidgeted with the end of Eve's satin belt. "I'm worried, guys. I'm worried about you. I'm worried about *us*."

Shane sat down in the armchair Michael had vacated, but he mirrored his best friend's posture almost exactly—elbows on knees, leaning forward. Intense. "Okay, I need to know something. Seriously."

Michael raised his eyebrows and nodded.

"I need to know you're going to stand with us if it comes to a fight. Me and Claire and Eve. I need you to say it, right now, because my feeling is that this is going to go real bad, real fast. I can't be worrying about whether or not you've got our backs."

Michael stood up. It was a vampire move, sudden and shocking, and in the blink of an eye, he was looming over Shane, and he had Shane's T-shirt bunched in his fist, lifting him half out of the chair. "You've got to be fucking *kidding me,* Shane! Have I *ever* not had your back? I had your back when you tried to kill me. I had your back when you were locked in a cage. I've had your back *every single time.* What do I have to do to make you believe I'm on your side, be an asshole like your dad? Well, I can do that. Maybe if I punch you a few times, you'll be convinced."

He let Shane drop back down in his chair, and walked out, back stiff. Furious.

Shane sat, stunned, hands clutching at the armrests. He exchanged a look with Eve, and they both stood up at once. "No," Shane said. "I did it. Let me fix it."

He went off after Michael. Eve chewed her lip and said, "Well, we're either going to see half the house destroyed, or their bromance is going to go all the way." She gave a shaky laugh, one that was dangerously close to hysteria. "God. What is *happening*? Claire—"

Claire hugged her. It was instinctive, and it was the right thing to do; Eve's tension slowly relaxed, and she hugged her back, fiercely. "It's going to be okay," Claire said, very quietly. "I don't know how, but it will. Just—trust me. Please. Because Michael's right—there are things I can't tell you, but it wouldn't help if you knew them. You have to trust me."

Eve pulled back, looked at her, and said, simply, "I always have."

It was odd, Claire thought, how it was the boys who were full of drama about this, while Eve, the acknowledged Drama Empress of Morganville, was the calmest.

The house didn't come apart, although they heard raised voices from upstairs, and a few thumps. Finally, Shane appeared at the parlor doorway and said, "We're okay."

Eve lifted her chin and said frostily, "Well, of *course* we are. You're the only one who doubted it. As always."

Ouch. Yet, Claire thought, Shane really had that one coming.

And he acknowledged it with a nod. "Shouldn't you be getting ready?" he asked. Eve looked at the clock in the corner, made a panicked squeaking sound, and dashed past him, robe fluttering.

"Shouldn't you?" Claire asked.

"I'm showered," he said. "Taking my stuff to change. I'm not decorating crap in fancy clothes. And I'm not admitting to decorating at all, by the way."

She had to laugh. "Yeah," she said. "I kind of knew that."

Shane had been granted the keys to Eve's hearse for the day, to transport all the stuff, so the rest of the morning was occupied with loading, unloading, checking in with the guards at Founder's Square, setting up the tables in the big, empty ballroom (which still, to Claire's eyes, had a funeral parlor elegance, but that was mostly because of all her bad experiences), putting on tablecloths, streamers, flowers. . . .

It was a lot of work, and Shane had been right: wearing regular jeans and shirts helped, because it would have been twice as bad in formal wear.

By the time the (human) blood bank attendants arrived with their punch bowls, coolers, and cups (crystal, because vampires didn't drink out of plastic if they could help it), the tables were decorated in black cloth and silver streamers, and Shane had, at great personal risk, hung the Eve-required disco ball from the majestic crystal chandelier looming over the room. The dj—one of Eve's friends, apparently, although Claire had never met her—arrived with her own table, her computer, and a massive sound system that she assembled near the open area designated as the dance floor.

Claire put the centerpieces on the tables and checked the time. Just barely enough.

She grabbed Shane and dragged him off from playing with the remote that turned the disco ball's motor on and off. "Get dressed," she said, and pressed the hanger with his clothes on it into his hands. "We have to be ready to greet people!"

"Yeah, that'll be super fun!" he said, with utterly fake enthusiasm.

"Just go already!"

He kissed her, quickly, and disappeared into the men's bathroom. Claire took her own dress and shoes into the women's room, which was really nice but—again—more or less funeral-homey, with all the subdued velvet and gilt. Dressed, she examined herself critically in the mirror. It was a nice, flattering dress of white trimmed in red, and the shoes (Eve had found them) were awesome. Claire finger-fluffed her shoulder-length hair—more red now than brown, thanks again to Eve—and headed out for the ballroom. Shane, of course, was already there, slouching on a straight-backed chair. He stood up when she walked in.

"You're beautiful," he said, very spontaneously, which warmed her all over.

"You're pretty fantastic, too," she said, and meant it. He'd put on dark pants and a dark turtleneck that *almost* hid all the bruises, and a really nice jacket. He looked . . . adult.

The dj started up with a song, testing the volume levels, and it broke the moment completely. In fact, it almost shattered the chandelier, considering the loudness. The dj dialed it back, but not before Claire's ears were ringing as if she'd been in a club. "Wow," she said. "This is going to rock. Probably in all the wrong ways."

And that prediction was way, way too correct.

First to show were friends from high school—nobody Claire knew, but Shane greeted them with easy familiarity. There were about ten of them, and they arrived in a pack, probably for safety; the girls seemed too boring-normal to be friends of Eve's, so Claire assumed these were Michael's circle. Some had brought gifts, and Claire pointed them to the table set up to deposit those.

Miranda, the skinny teen psychic, arrived dramatically alone, wearing a peculiar, mismatched skirt and top that were too big for her. She was (technically) Eve's friend, although she was younger and still in high school; as always, she seemed to be walking in a dream state, not really noticing where she was or who was around her. Eve liked to be thought of as strange; Miranda was the real deal. Nothing like creepy future predictions to put a chill on fun.

But she was an odd little thing, and Claire felt bad for her. She seemed to be always on her own.

"Hey, Mir," she greeted her, and handed her a white carnation.

Miranda looked at it as if she couldn't quite figure out what it was for. "Is it food?" she asked.

Shane mouthed, over Miranda's head, *Please say yes,* but Claire scowled at him and said, "No, it's just pretty." Miranda nodded wisely and tucked it behind her ear, with the long stem sticking back at a dangerous angle for anyone behind her. "Uh—there's food over there, and punch. Don't cut the cake, though. That's for Eve and Michael."

"Okay," Miranda said. She got a couple of steps into the room, then turned and looked back at Claire. "It's too bad you wore white. But maybe it will wash out."

Oh *crap.* If only Miranda had a sense of humor, Claire would have been sure she was just messing with her, but knowing that the girl had never joked, she thought of several interpretations and none of them was good. The best Claire could think of was that she'd get punch spilled on her.

Unfortunately, the best-case scenario never seemed to arrive.

"Easy," Shane said. "Sometimes she's wrong." He knew what Claire was thinking, because (she assumed) he was thinking it, too.

"Not often." And never on important things, although Claire truthfully couldn't judge whether that had been, in Miranda's mind, *important.* Difficult to say. She had a chaos-theory view of life, so what was important to normal people wasn't necessarily the same thing to her. And sometimes the most minuscule things were the most urgent.

Claire didn't have time to brood about it, because just then the first vampires arrived, cold and icily polite. Claire handed carnations to the ladies, who accepted them with disdainful grace as they glided in, heading straight for the plasma refreshments. Next came a group of cautious-looking townies, dressed in ill-fitting fancy dresses and suits, all prominently wearing their bracelets of Protection. These weren't the rebel underground; these were the humans with a vested stake (no pun intended) in the status quo, and they had a certain beaten look to them that made Claire's heart ache. She'd tried to use her influence with Amelie—such as it was—to make things better for them, but she couldn't counteract lifetimes of oppression in a couple of years.

"Claire," Shane said quietly. When she looked around, there was a vampire standing right in front of her, wearing an elaborate black satin coat with enormous long tails that reached to his heels, a red brocade vest, a ruffled white shirt. . . .

Myrnin.

He looked deeply worried and very uncomfortable. "My dear girl, I really feel I need to—"

"Go away," she said. Not loudly, but she meant it. "Don't talk to me. Not ever again."

"But—"

She pushed him back, hard. *"Never!"* She didn't shout it, although she felt like screaming it; the fury that boiled up inside her made her shake and see red. "Don't you ever come near me or Shane again!"

He couldn't have looked more heartbroken, but she didn't care. She *didn't.* Her eyes filled with tears, but she made herself believe that they were tears of anger, not sadness. Not disappointment.

Myrnin bowed from the waist, old-fashioned and very correct, and said, "As you wish, Claire." Then he turned toward Shane and gave another bow, not quite as deep. "I regret the necessity of my actions." He didn't wait for Shane to say anything, not that Shane would have, anyway; he was busy watching Claire as she hastily wiped the tears from her eyes.

Myrnin walked away. He looked . . . small, somehow. And defeated, although he tried to keep his head upright. And even though she was angry—she *was*—it still hurt to see him like that. And deep down, she felt lost thinking that she'd never see him again. Never roll her eyes at his insane leaps of conversation. Never see those stupid bunny slippers again.

He did it. Not me.

Then why was it so *awful*?

She couldn't dwell on it, because more people were arriving, a *lot* more, and she had all she could do forcing smiles and saying polite things and handing out carnations to the ladies. This influx was a mixture of townies and a few wary, tense people she was sure were in Morganville but not of it—the resistance, maybe, come to scope out the situation. Shane recognized a few, and she saw him exchange some quick words with a couple.

There was a brief lull in arrivals, and Claire caught her breath and checked her carnation supply—getting low. Then again, the ballroom was now teeming with people—more than a hundred, for sure. Quite a crowd, in this town.

More vampires this time, at least twenty of them. One of the women accepted a flower with a charming, graceful smile; another lifted her chin and glided right by, refusing to even acknowledge Claire's existence.

So much fun.

"I believe that's for me," said a low, cool voice, and Claire jerked her attention back front and center just as Amelie plucked the carnation from her hand. "Do forgive Mathilde. She's not been the same since the French Revolution."

"You came," Claire blurted.

Amelie raised a single eyebrow in a sharp curve. "Why would I not? I was invited. It's only polite to attend."

"I thought you weren't in favor of—this."

"It would be hypocritical of me to say that it pleases me. But it suits my purposes to be here." Amelie nodded her good-byes and started to move on.

Claire took in a breath and asked, "Did you order Myrnin to kill Shane?"

Amelie stood there silently with the white carnation turning in her cool, long fingers, then turned and took Oliver's offered elbow as he entered the room, looking very much *not* himself in a suit that was almost as beautiful as what Michael was wearing. "Ah. There you are. Shall we proceed?"

"I suppose we must," he said. He didn't seem happy about it.

Claire said, "Wait! You didn't answer—"

Amelie turned back to Claire just for a moment, and said, "What I do for this town, I do without regard to my own feelings, much less yours. Is that clear?" Her voice was cold, low, and very clear, and then she was gone, the queen walking off to greet her subjects.

So, it hadn't really been Myrnin's choice. No wonder he was so wounded; he'd been ordered, and he'd obeyed, and Claire had dumped the blame on him (well, he *was* to blame—he could have refused!), but Amelie was definitely the puppet master pulling his strings. As hurtful as Myrnin's betrayal was, it didn't scare her nearly as much now.

Amelie had told her long ago that she would do anything, sacrifice anyone, for the safety of Morganville, but it still felt like betrayal.

Eve peeked around the door and gestured at Claire, who moved closer. "Is everybody here?" she asked. She looked terrified and excited all at once. "Is it ready?"

"Ready," Claire said. "Everyone's waiting on you."

Eve took a deep breath, closed her eyes, and whispered something to herself, then disappeared behind the edge of the door again. Thirty seconds later, she swept in on Michael's arm.

Claire thought that she had never seen them look better, especially together; Eve's dramatic long red dress clung to her figure and made her look even taller, while Michael had put on a really great suit. His blond hair blazed in the light, and was the perfect counterpoint to Eve's black.

They looked at each other, and Eve smiled a slow, delighted smile that Michael echoed.

Claire stepped forward and pinned on Eve's corsage, and then the two swept on into the crowd, full of people murmuring and whispering. Everyone watched them, and Claire moved back to grip Shane's hand tightly. It was Eve and Michael's party, but somehow, it felt like a test.

Nobody spoke to them directly as they made their way across the room, until Myrnin stepped into their path. He was silent for a few seconds, then reached for Eve's hand. He raised it to his lips and bent over it, and Claire could hear him say, even where she stood by the door, "Congratulations to you both, my dear. May your happiness last forever."

"I'll drink to that!" someone said, and a number of people laughed, and the spell was broken. People mixed and mingled. More came up to shake Michael's hand and offer Eve a hug or a smile.

It was going to be all right.

"Uh-oh," Shane said. He jerked his chin toward the far edge of the crowd. "She's not joining in." By *she* he meant Amelie, who stood in regal isolation with Oliver. They were talking together, ignoring what was going on in the center of the room. It looked intense. "I don't like the look of that."

"She practically admitted she ordered—" Claire didn't dare

say more, not in a room full of vampire ears, so she touched the soft fabric of his turtleneck, and he nodded. "I don't know if we can count on her help."

"I never have," he said. "Or anybody else's, except yours, Eve's, and . . ." He hesitated, but he smiled and finished anyway. "Michael's. Safer that way, CB. You get wrapped up in the politics of this town and you get dragged under."

Richard Morrell arrived late, and he brought his sister. Monica Morrell took the very last carnation Claire had, made a face, and handed it to her brother. "Cheap," she said. "I should have known they wouldn't have *orchids,* but I expected something better than that." As if Claire weren't standing right there. "Ugh, I'll bet they don't even have an open bar."

"How exactly would that matter to you, since you can't drink legally?" Richard asked. He sounded worn-out and sharp, and Monica fell into a pout. She wore a low-cut, thigh-high shimmering blue dress that emphasized her long legs, and had probably cost more than Claire had saved for her college fund. "You wanted to come, and you promised you'd be civil. If you're not, you go home. No arguments."

"Oh, try not to sound so much like Mom—you don't have the ovaries," Monica said. She threw Claire a nasty smile as she strode past them, tossing the carnation to the floor and crushing it beneath her fancy stiletto-heeled shoes. "Isn't there supposed to be dancing? Knowing Eve, it'll probably be that crappy death metal and emo ballads, but I came to *dance.*"

"Shut up and put the gift on the table, Monica," Richard said. He handed her a nicely wrapped box, which she held at arm's length as if it held live cockroaches. Claire pointed her to the gift table, already loaded up with presents. Monica stalked over and dropped it on the pile, then turned a dazzling smile and hair-flip on the nearest man.

"God," Richard sighed. "I'd apologize, but you know by now that you can't expect anything else out of her."

"In a weird sort of way, it's comforting," Shane said. "Nice to know some things never change. Plagues, death, taxes, Monica."

"I guess we can stop playing greeters," Claire said. "I'm all out of flowers." She picked up the one Monica had trampled and tossed it back in the box, which she shoved under a handy table. "I need punch."

"May I escort you to get it?" Richard asked, and offered her his arm. She blinked and looked at Shane, who shrugged.

"I'd be honored," she said.

It felt weird, being led around by the mayor. . . . People talked to him freely, and gave her odd looks; she was well aware of Shane moving along behind them, and wondered if she should have done this, after all. Morganville was a gossip hotbed. Next thing, she'd probably find out she'd dumped her boyfriend for Richard, which was *so* not going to happen; Richard was nice enough, but not when compared with Shane. Besides, that meant getting Monica as a relative. Terrifying.

Richard steered her to the punch, released her, and went off to talk to constituents; Claire filled two cups and handed one to Shane, who took a long drink, then winced and touched his throat.

"Hurts?"

He nodded. "Burns," he said. "Somebody spiked the punch, FYI. Maybe you should stick to water—that tastes like Everclear."

"Ugh." Claire put her punch down, untasted, and went for bottled water instead. Safer, anyway; she hadn't forgotten Miranda's words about her dress. Her throat was dry, and the water tasted cool and sweet. She nibbled a bell-shaped cookie and eyed the cake, which looked considerably better than it had when the bakers had shoved it on Eve as professional work; she was, in fact, kind of proud of it. "Should we do something about the punch?"

"Don't take all the fun out of things," Shane said. "Besides, I'm not lugging that all the way to the kitchen." He was right—the punch bowl was enormous, and full. Not much that *could* be done about it.

She was still worrying about it when a fight broke out, somewhere near the middle of the room.

Where Michael and Eve were.

The first warning was a shout of alarm, then a woman's scream, and the crowd between Claire and whatever was happening closed ranks. Shane, who was taller, gazed in that direction and said, "Crap."

"What?"

"Stay here!"

He took off, shoving his way through the crowd.

No way was she staying behind. Where he went, she went. Claire squirmed through the close-packed bodies of humans (on this side of the room) and suddenly was in the open area, which held Eve, Michael, the newly arrived Shane, and two men.

The two men—part of that not-quite-townie crew Claire had wondered about earlier—had ganged up on Michael. The fight was already over; one was down flat on his back, and Eve's sharp high heel was planted in the center of his chest, holding him down (although he looked unconscious, and not likely to give anybody trouble). As Claire arrived and skidded to a halt, the second man that Michael was fighting stabbed in with a stake aimed at Michael's heart.

Michael easily slapped it out of his hand and shoved him backward. His attacker tripped over the downed body of his partner, and Michael loomed over him, beautiful as an avenging angel, practically glowing in the lights. His fangs were down.

"Don't you *ever* raise a hand to Eve again!" he said, and bent down to grab the man's tie. With a single, effortless yank, Michael raised him back to his feet and shook him like a rag doll. "Don't you even *look* at her!"

Shane yelled, "Behind you!" and threw himself into a full tackle, just as a woman lunged out of the onlookers with another stake aiming for Michael's back. He knocked her down, and the stake went flying. Shane bounced back upright and grabbed up the length of sharpened wood. "Hey! Sorry, lady, but nobody's staking anybody at this party! I hung a disco ball for this!"

Michael looked over at him.

"Yo," Shane said, and nodded toward the man Michael was dangling. "He's turning kinda purple. I think you made the point."

Michael dropped him. His fangs disappeared, and he held out his hand to Eve. She left her own fallen attacker and took it.

Claire left the safety of the crowd and went to join Shane. The four of them, surrounded.

"Anybody got anything to say now?" Shane said. "Any crap about mixed marriages? The floor's open; say your piece!"

The vampires, Claire realized, hadn't come rushing to Michael's defense. In fact, they were standing in a clump next to the blood supply, sipping from crystal cups, looking utterly uninvolved. She looked around for Oliver and Amelie and Myrnin. Myrnin was sitting down at a table, running his fingernails slowly over the cloth, shredding it into fluff.

Amelie and Oliver were still standing at the edge of the crowd, watching.

"All right." A woman pushed through the crowd—a townie. Claire recognized her. The older clerk who'd refused to wait on Eve at the party supply store. She looked even stiffer and less fun today, in her boxy pastel blue dress and lacquered hair. "I'll say something. I know you invited us here, and I think that was brave, but you know this is wrong. *He's* one of *them*. No offense to *them*, but we keep ourselves to ourselves. Always have."

"As much as I hate to stand in agreement, she's correct," drawled a well-dressed vampire, who sipped at his blood with perfect calm. "A master doesn't *marry* the livestock. That's simply perverse."

Monica Morrell pushed her way through the crowd, teetering on heels that were even higher and thinner than Eve's. "Hey! Who are you calling *livestock*, freak?" Her brother grabbed her by the shoulder to haul her back, but she shook him off. "I am not your *cow*."

"I wasn't talking to you," the vampire said, and brushed imaginary dirt from his wine red velvet lapel. "You seem to have forgotten your place. And if you won't be a cow, perhaps being a pig is more acceptable."

That woke dry, sharp laughter from the vampire contingent, like the clatter of breaking crystal.

"Pig?" Monica yelped, and tried to twist free of Richard. "Let *go*. That asshole called me a *pig!* I'm not a nobody like *her*, you know!" She jerked her chin at Eve. "I'm a Morrell!"

"Excuse me, then," the vampire said. "You are therefore a *prize* pig."

Monica lurched forward on those high heels, scooped up the fallen knife from the floor, and stood next to Eve. A few steps away, but approximately next, anyway. "I have a Protector!" she snapped. "Hello? Protect me already!"

"From what?" Oliver's voice echoed through the ballroom. "Insults? I'm not obliged to defend your dignity. Provided you have any. Stop this, all of you." *He* didn't have to push through the crowd; people got out of the way for him.

Amelie, Claire noticed, did not come with him. She stayed where she was, remote and cold.

"Enough of this. Look at you, squabbling like spoiled children," Oliver said. He leveled a finger at the vampire in the dark red coat. "*You* will be respectful. And *you*—" The finger turned to point at Monica. "*You* will learn to hold your tongue."

"Like a good little pet?" she asked acidly. "Oink."

"If you don't want my Protection, feel free to take off the bracelet," Oliver said, and stared at her with fierce eyes. "Go ahead, Monica. See how it feels to be naked in the cold."

Claire thought for a second she would actually do it. Monica lifted her wrist and ran a finger over the silver bracelet she wore, the one with Oliver's sigil on it. . . .

. . . And then she stepped back, head bowed. Richard pushed her behind him.

"Better," Oliver said. He pointed at the vampire again. "More from you, Jean?" He gave it the French pronunciation, *Zhon*. Jean shrugged and sipped his blood. "Now. We are going to behave like civilized individuals." He snapped his fingers and pointed at the two men on the ground. Two of Amelie's ever-present bodyguards walked through the hole he'd made in the crowd, gathered them up, and dragged them off. "I do hope nobody else here has any other surprises planned, because if you so much as *think* about harming one another, I will oblige them. This is neutral ground. Violators will be gruesomely and violently shown the error of their ways. Clear?"

Nobody said a word. Not even Eve, which was surprising.

And then Amelie walked forward, moving through the parted crowd like an iceberg through dark seas—gleaming with cutting edges.

Oliver turned as she approached behind him, and Claire saw the look on his face. The dread, quickly stamped out into an even, expressionless mask.

"The Founder will speak," he said, and stepped back to give her the floor.

"I come today at the request of two Morganville residents," Amelie said. She stood in the very center of the room, facing Michael and Eve, who still had their hands clasped tightly together. "I come to deliver judgment on whether this planned union may proceed."

"But—," Eve whispered. "But I thought—"

Amelie stopped her cold. "I have heard the pleas of human residents to allow you to proceed. I have listened to others who insisted you be stopped. My own people are likewise divided, and equally persuasive." Her silver eyes glittered like frozen coins. "I come to tell you what will be done in the best interests of Morganville, and my will rules here. Not Oliver's, not yours. Mine." Her eyes were turning white now, and Claire felt power stirring in the room, like currents of wild electricity. "And I say that this is not the time. Not for this."

"Wait," Michael said. "*Wait!* You can't—"

"I can," Amelie said softly. "And I will. And I must. No wedding will take place, not between human and vampire. Not until I am willing to let it be so." Her eyes were pure white now, and Claire felt the crushing pulse of power. It wasn't directed at her, she realized, or at Eve, or any human. . . . It was a vampire power, directed at the vamps in the room.

Who were falling to their knees now. Some willingly, some

grudgingly. Some stayed on their feet for a while, but eventually, they caved, too.

Leaving only Oliver, swaying and resisting her . . . and Michael, who was holding on to Eve for support.

"No," Michael said, through tightly gritted teeth. "No, this is *my* life. *Mine.*"

"Your life has always been mine, bloodchild." Amelie extended her hand toward him, and closed her fist. "Submit."

Michael screamed, and his eyes turned white. So did his face, dead white, *dead.* Claire took an involuntary step toward him, horrified, but Shane did more than that.

He stepped up to Michael's side and put his arm under Michael's, supporting his weight.

"You'll thank me later, bro," he said, and turned his gaze on Amelie. "Step off. Now."

Her fangs were out. Amelie had never looked more alien to Claire, or more beautiful, or horribly dangerous. She was *terrifying,* and the other humans of Morganville were backing off now, heading for the door. The vampires were pinned in place.

Claire moved in to help brace Michael. Her head felt black with the buzzing power around her, and she knew it must be killing Michael; the color was gone out of him now. He could have been made out of marble, and it was scary, so very scary to touch his ice-cold skin. . . .

Eve let go of Michael, leaving Claire and Shane to support him, and walked in front of Amelie.

She took off the pin that was on her red dress and threw it at her. "Go to *hell* and take that with you!" She shouted it right in Amelie's face. Eve was an exotic blaze of color against Amelie's white fury.

And then she *slapped the Founder in the face.*

Amelie took a step backward, stunned, and the crush of power in the room faltered.

Oliver lunged out and grabbed Eve by the waist, slinging her out of the way as Amelie went for her. He grabbed the Founder and wrapped her in his arms, then yelled at Claire, "Get them out! Now! Go home, and *hurry*! Do it now!"

Amelie's fury jumped into the other vampires, and one by one, they shot to their feet, hissing. One threw a crystal glass of blood at Eve, but got Claire instead, splattering her white dress.

She looked down at the mess with a startled gasp, and thought, *Damn, Miranda was right. Again.*

"Ahh . . . maybe we should be going," Shane said. "Ditch the shoes, Eve. We'll be running now."

"I love these shoes!"

"More than your circulatory system?"

Eve silently kicked off the stilettos and backed up. Shane and Claire got Michael moving, weakly at least, and headed for the door. Eve acted as rearguard, not that she had anything to fight with other than the shoes she'd grabbed up.

The vampire in the red velvet coat headed for her, fangs out. She got the stiletto heel up, ready to strike, but something grabbed him in midleap and slammed him up, straight into the chandelier. Crystal shattered, and the disco ball spun wildly, throwing drunken sparkles over the room.

At the far end of the room, the fleeing dj hit a button on her system, and thundering techno music started up, shivering the air and thumping beats into Claire's body like kicks. *Way* too loud.

Myrnin, who'd intercepted the attacking vamp, turned and looked at them.

At Claire.

His lips shaped words, but Claire couldn't hear them. He made a shooing motion and smiled at her, one of those fragile and half-crazy things, and her heart just broke all over again.

She shook her head, and Eve slammed the ballroom door, cutting off the rush of vampires heading their way. She jammed a chair under the handle.

They ran for the elevator. Shane punched the button about sixteen times before the doors opened, and he dragged Michael inside as Claire held it for Eve. "They're breaking out!" Eve gasped. "That chair's not going to hold!"

"Close close close!" Shane yelled at the buttons, punching the one for the garage. Claire heard wood splintering, and then a crash as the ballroom door shattered off its hinges.

One vampire appeared in front of the elevator—a vampire with shoulder-length dark hair and ridiculously long tails on his black brocade coat.

Myrnin, again.

"I'm sorry," he said, and turned to face a horde of oncoming attackers. "I'll buy you time. Oh, nice party, by the way!"

The doors closed before Claire could thank him, and the elevator lurched and started inching its way slowly down.

"Michael?" Shane shook him, still holding him upright with an arm under his shoulders. "Hey, man, you with us?"

Michael nodded. He looked better. Not good, but not as statue-pale now. His eyes were fading back to blue again, slowly. "You had my back." He sounded surprised.

"Always," Shane said. "Thought you knew that."

Eve put her arms around his neck and kissed him, on the lips. Shane did a funny little wiggle, trying to squirm away while not dumping Michael on his ass, but she kept it brief. "Sorry, but I had to do that," she said. "You rock."

"Yeah, well, you don't have to brand me with lipstick," Shane said, and wiped it off. "My girl's standing right there."

"Your girl doesn't mind," Claire said. She was still scared, but somehow also elated. Free. Reborn. "I'd kiss you, too, if I was closer."

"I wouldn't," Michael said. "I don't love you that way."

"That's not what you said last time."

"Ass." Michael almost smiled, but it faded as the movement of the cabin stopped with a jerk. "We're here. Stay alert; we're not clear yet."

Claire got out, watching the angles, but the garage seemed deserted. She gestured for the others to hustle after her, which they did, quickly. Shane had the keys to the hearse, which he tossed to her, and Claire quickly unlocked the back. They loaded Michael and Eve inside, in the vampire-shaded area, and got in the front. "Lock it," Shane said. Claire nodded and hit the control, just as a white-faced vampire popped up at her window and tried the door. She shrieked and jumped, but got control and jammed the hearse into gear. *Too fast, too fast . . .* the thing was like a luxury liner, and she had to make several fast back-and-forth moves to rock it free of obstructions. The vampire jumped on top, and punched fingernails through the roof.

"Go go go!" Shane yelled, and Claire finally had a clear lane. She jammed the gas down, and the hearse roared up the ramp, around the curve, and out into full sun.

The vampire on top hung on for a moment, and then the claws disappeared. She heard him tumbling across the length of the roof, and saw him drop off, land on his feet, and dash for the shade as he left a trail of greasy smoke behind. Claire whooped and pumped her fist, and Shane bumped knuckles with her.

"Combat-driving merit badge," he said. "With bonus vampire clusters. Now all you have to do is get us home."

"No." Eve slid back the divider between the front and the rear, and leaned in. "Michael and I decided. Take us to the church."

"What?" Claire and Shane blurted it out at the same time, in perfect chorus.

"They'll stop us if they can. We have to do this now if we're going to do it," Eve said. "We're getting married. Right now."

Claire almost drove off the road. "But—wait, now? Like, *right now*?"

"You're not serious," Shane said. "You can't do it now."

"Why not?"

"You're wearing red," Shane said.

"I have blood on my dress," Claire put in.

"You, Shaggy, shut up," Eve said, giving Shane a scornful look. "Claire, cold water in the bathroom. There. Fixed." She slammed the portal shut.

Claire drove on in silence for a moment, and then said, "So."

"So," Shane repeated. "Yeah."

She took the right turn, toward the church.

Nobody was in the church. Nobody. Not Father Joe, not a parishioner, not a cleaning crew. It was deserted, and Claire knocked on the office door and found it empty, too. Nobody in the vesting chamber. She walked out into the main chapel and held up her hands in helpless surrender, as Eve put on her high heels, balancing on first one foot, then the other.

"You're kidding," Eve said. "He's gone?"

"He was at the party," Shane put in. He was sitting with Michael on a pew. "I'm not so sure this is a good idea right now, Eve. Oliver said—"

"I know what Oliver said. Damn if I am taking another order from another vampire in this town, ever!" Eve finished strapping on the heels and stood there looking tall and strong. "We'll wait."

Shane looked at Michael doubtfully. "I don't know, man—"

"We wait," Michael said. "She's right. Look, if you want to take Claire home—"

"No," Shane said. "I'm not leaving you two here alone. We stick together."

"I'm still not kissing you," Michael said.

"Tease."

Michael started to retort, but the hollow *boom* of the church door cut him off. He and Shane both came to their feet—Michael faster—and Claire looked around for something antivampire she could improvise, but none of it was necessary, because striding into the chapel was Father Joe, red hair blazing in the multicolored light from the rose window overhead. He slowed when he saw them, then sighed and came forward toward where they were waiting.

Eve opened her mouth to say something, but he held up his hand. "No," he said. "I have a good idea why you're here. And the answer is no."

"What? You can't just say *no!*" Eve said. "Why would you say that?"

Father Joe stopped and turned as he reached the steps to the altar, and instead of being a harried young man, he seemed to change into a grave, composed person with no doubts about what he was about to do. He held up both hands for calm, and Eve subsided, not very willingly.

"You don't have the Founder's permission," he said. "Without the Founder's signature on the marriage license, no marriages conducted inside this church are legal in the eyes of the town. You won't accomplish what you're trying to do, and from what I saw back in that ballroom, you will never get her permission. You'll be lucky to escape a jail sentence, Eve."

"She could change her mind," Claire said.

"She won't. You shamed her, you publicly defied her, and Eve slapped her. As Amelie, she might forgive, and she might quietly shift her opinions. You called her out as the Founder of Morganville, and the Founder can't let it pass, whatever her personal feelings might be. Whatever you do here, it doesn't matter beyond that door. Not to the Founder."

There was a heavy silence, as Eve and Michael looked at each other. He came to stand next to her, and their fingers slowly intertwined.

Michael looked at Father Joe and said, "Would you do it anyway?"

Father Joe cocked his head to one side, watching the two of them, and clasped his hands in front of him. A slow smile warmed his serious expression, and he said, "In the eyes of God, do you come before the altar to be married?"

"Yes, Father," he said.

Father Joe turned his focus to Eve. "And you?"

"Yes, Father. More than anything."

"I see you have witnesses," he said. Claire and Shane moved to stand near them, and Claire realized that she was short of breath now, and trembling. She could see that Eve was shaking, too. Michael squeezed her hand a little and smiled at her, and she smiled back. "Do you have the ring?"

Eve looked at Michael with panic, and he seemed blank, too,

until Shane said, "Can you use her engagement ring? I mean, just for the ceremony?"

"I can," Father Joe agreed. "Generally people prefer double-ring ceremonies these days, but a single one will work just as well. Now, I ask again: are you sure of what you're about to do? Marriage is not a state to be entered into lightly."

"We're sure," Michael said. "Please. Go ahead."

The chapel door boomed shut at the other end.

Claire turned, blinking back tears that were threatening to form, and saw that a whole lot of people had appeared in the back of the church. Some were throwing back hoods and taking off hats, but not the one in front, dressed in cool white, with her pale hair worn up, like a crown. She hadn't bothered with sun protection.

Amelie walked down the church's aisle toward them, and behind her followed Oliver, Myrnin, and a half dozen other vampires. More than they could fight. More than *anyone* could fight.

Father Joe froze, watching them. Michael and Eve turned to look, too, and then Michael said, "Go ahead, Father. We're ready."

"No one will be married here today," Amelie's cool voice said, ringing out with authority. "You serve here at my sufferance, Father. I do not wish to disrespect the church, or your autonomy, but I have made my pronouncement, and these two have no permission. Now, please go. I have things to discuss with these four."

He hesitated, looking at the two standing in front of him, and then bowed his head. "I'm sorry. She won't hurt you, not here. The church is neutral ground. You're safe inside."

"Wait—" Eve reached out for him, but he stepped back, went up the steps, and knelt down to pray at the altar. Eve shut her eyes and swayed, and only Michael's arm around her kept her on her feet.

They all turned to face the vampires.

Amelie continued toward them, but made a silent gesture that caused almost all those following her to stop and take seats in the pews. Only Oliver and Myrnin stayed with her the rest of the way.

Four to three, but not exactly even odds. Michael could hold his own, maybe, but Claire knew the rest of them had the chance of a rabbit caught in a wolves' den.

Amelie let a cold moment pass before she said, "You're simply intent on defying my wishes, apparently."

"We want to get married. That's not anyone else's business," Michael said. He sounded angry, dangerously so. "Why are you doing this to us?"

"I'm trying to keep the peace," she said. "And the peace will not be kept this way. You have many years to take this step; a few more will not matter if your love is as strong as you claim. However, a few more years may make all the difference in achieving a lasting peace in Morganville."

"You've had about a hundred years to try to make that happen, and it hasn't," Eve said. "What makes you think another couple of years will change anything?"

Amelie studied her with a remote, cold intensity that made Claire shudder. "I have only been physically struck by two others before. Neither of them still live, and both were *vampires*. I suggest you allow me some time to consider how I feel about *you*."

"Amelie," Claire said, drawing the vampire's attention; she immediately wished she hadn't. There was something tight and furious inside there, completely unlike the Amelie she normally saw. "I know Eve's sorry about that. But you shamed *her*, right in front of half the town. In front of people she knows and has to face every day. All she wanted was to be with the one she loved. You know how that feels."

Something flickered in Amelie's gray eyes. Surprise, and hurt, and almost immediately anger. She didn't like being reminded of the love she'd lost, or that the four humans standing in front of her had once seen her at her most vulnerable as she mourned.

"Sam wouldn't want this," Claire said. It was the last, and only, card she could play. "Sam would want you to let them be together." Sam Glass had been Michael's grandfather, a vampire Claire had known only a little, but he'd been the kindest, most caring one of them all.

And now he was gone, and Amelie—Amelie still hurt inside.

The problem was, pain could sometimes make people turn cold and savage.

Like now, Claire realized, as the icy silence deepened. When Amelie spoke again, it was in a fatally quiet voice. "Do not invoke Samuel to me," she said. "We *waited.*"

"You waited until your chance was gone to be happy," Claire said, even though every instinct screamed at her to shut up. "Do you want the same thing for Eve and Michael? Really?"

Amelie said nothing this time, just stared at her. It was possible—remotely—that she was thinking it over.

Oliver cleared his throat and said, "We don't have time for your drama, children. We have things to attend to. Urgently." That last was directly at Amelie, Claire realized, not toward them at all, and Amelie stirred and glanced at him, then nodded. "Myrnin's going to escort the four of you home. He'll take the portal from there."

"No!" Claire blurted, but Amelie was already turning and walking away, and so was Oliver. Her opinion didn't matter, clearly. She looked mutely at Shane, who shook his head and shrugged.

"I'll be on my best behavior," Myrnin said. He looked cautious and hurt, which made her angrier; what right did *he* have to feel wounded in all this? He'd totally betrayed her trust. She was *not* going to feel guilty about taking that to heart. "Shall we?"

Amelie's entourage filed in behind her, and the doors boomed shut again behind them. At the altar, Father Joe crossed himself and walked down again to join them.

"Way to stand up, Father," Michael said.

"I can't be in the business of martyrdom," the priest said. "Not now, and not here. I have a duty to my parishioners, and I'm not denying you the sacrament of marriage; I'm merely postponing it. Come back in a week, bring your witnesses and rings, and I will do exactly as you wish. But not today. You need to go home with your escort." He inclined his head to Myrnin, who bowed back. All of a sudden, Father Joe's stiff posture relaxed, and he held out his hand to Michael, who reluctantly took it. "I'm sorry about this. I know how hard the two of you have worked to overcome the barriers between you. I won't be another; I promise that. Give me one week, and I will give you what you want."

"I'm holding you to it," Michael said. "We'll be back."

"I will see you then. Go in peace. I'll be praying for you all."

He walked up the steps and through a door near the altar.

They all looked at one another, and then Myrnin said cheerfully, "Shall I drive?"

"No," they said as one, and walked out toward the hearse.

After letting Myrnin in the house, it turned out to be almost impossible to get rid of him.

Partly it was because of what happened when they *did* let him in, or tried to. Michael and Eve went in first, then Shane, and Claire last, with Myrnin right behind her—and without any conscious direction from her at all, the front door tried to slam right on his face.

Claire hadn't even touched it.

"My," Myrnin said, slamming his hand against it and, despite vampire strength, being driven back a few inches before he got his balance and pushed it open. "This *is* interesting." He stepped over the threshold, and the door banged shut behind him with unnecessary force. Glass rattled in the overhead fixture, and the windows of the parlor. The temperature of the house dropped fast into refrigerator territory, and Claire saw her breath fog the cold air of the hallway. Eve yelped from where she was in the living room, and said, "Damn, the AC is broken! It's like a morgue in here!"

"It wasn't a second ago," Shane said. He was standing at the end of the hallway, looking back at Claire, and Myrnin. His eyebrows were raised. "Claire?"

"I'm fine," she said. Myrnin had forgotten all about her. He was pressing his hands against the wood paneling, looking fascinated.

"I can actually *feel* it resisting me!" he said. "How marvelous. I know it can do such things, but to really have it directed at me—it must draw power from the very air. That's the cause for the temperature change, I would imagine. Claire, are you doing this?"

"No," she snapped, and walked away. She probably was, on some level; the house had grown really attuned to her moods, and she could not have wanted Myrnin gone more—well, maybe she could have, because if it had really been an emergency, the house could have thrown him completely out. It was just trying to strongly discourage him.

"I honestly think this house has accumulated more power than the other Founder Houses over the years," Myrnin said. "It's a side effect of the portals, you know, and the alchemical processes we used to lay the foundations, but this is the only house that has been continuously occupied since it was built. Even the Day House remained empty for several years at the turn of the last century, after that unfortunate business with the Langers . . . Well. In any case, this house has attained something like an independent consciousness. A soul, if you will. It's fascinating!"

It was, a little, and normally Claire would have been jumping right in, talking about the physics and alchemical theories that made something like that possible, but right now, she just wanted him *out*. Badly. "Isn't there something you have to do somewhere else?" she said. "Because you got us home. Fine. Now go away."

Eve had come back to stand next to Shane, eyes wide. She'd shed the high heels, but she still looked like an exotic ghost from the early 1920s, even in bright red. "Wow," she said. "I didn't even know you *could* put that tone in your voice, Claire. You haven't forgotten, this is *Myrnin*, right? As in, your boss? As in, the guy who just covered our asses at the party?"

"Thank you, Eve," he said, and gave her a very warm smile. "I was happy to do it." The smile became more tentative when he directed it at Claire. "I do apologize for any wrongs I have done you. Truly, I do. It was—not my first choice, believe me." He nodded at Shane. "And that goes for you as well."

"Wrongs?" Eve asked, mystified. "What wrongs? What—"

And then she caught sight of the bruise around the collar of Shane's turtleneck. It was now one *hell* of a bruise—dark purple, red, blue at the edges. Almost black in the center. *God.* You could see the actual outlines of Myrnin's fingers. Claire saw Eve's mind working, and then said, "You did it. Shane said he'd been in a fight, but it was *you*. That's why she's so angry."

Myrnin looked even *more* kicked-puppy sad. "I am sorry for

my actions. As I said. I can't remove bruises, but happily he is recovering fully."

Now Michael was in on it, too. "Wait a minute—what? *Myrnin* choked you?"

"Dude, it's over. Done."

"He tried to kill you!"

"If I'd really tried," Myrnin said helpfully, "I'm sure I would have succeeded."

The crazy thing was he actually thought that would be it. That Claire would forget about it—and if he'd come after *her,* she realized, she probably would have done just that. She had forgiven him for all kinds of crazy stuff before.

But this was a cold, calculated attack on Shane, and he'd gotten her to tell him where to find him.

No. Not this.

Myrnin was happily babbling on, oblivious to the mood of the four of them—and the house, whose internal temperature was falling so fast Eve was shuddering in her thin red dress. "The thing is, this house, this *house!* It's developing, you see. It's growing stronger. I've always suspected that there was something special here—obviously, it saved you once, Michael—and now it seems to be reacting quite strongly. . . ."

Michael took off his coat and put it around Eve's shoulders, hugging her close. The four of them were aware now of what Myrnin had done. And united in their anger.

And something *changed.*

Myrnin's cheerful blather ended in a yelp as the hallway floor literally *rolled* under his feet, a clatter of boards, and sent him reeling forward, toward Shane, Eve, and Michael, who quickly got out of the way. Claire braced herself against the wall, but she could tell this attack wasn't directed at her, or her friends.

Only at Myrnin, who board-surfed the ripple in the floor, fighting to stay upright, until it ended in a sudden upward rise that snapped him into the air, flinging him—

Toward the wall where Myrnin's mystical portal lay hidden.

It took time to open the thing—well, normally—but Myrnin had powers that Claire would never possess in that area, and by the time his outstretched arms reached the wall, the wall melted into a swirl of black, and Myrnin fell straight through it.

Gone, except for his shouted plea of "Claire, please listen—"

And then the portal snapped shut, the dark mist faded, and it was just a wall, again.

Claire walked over and put her hand over the surface. Paint, plaster, boards. Nothing magical about it, at least not that she could detect. "House," she said. She rarely addressed it directly; none of them liked to acknowledge that they were living inside something that had actual consciousness, because that made their privacy iffy, at best. "I need you to keep him out. Lock this portal. Don't let him inside through the doors, either."

She felt an odd, deep throb rise up through her feet, and out through the palm of her hand, and although she couldn't really detect a change, she knew it was done.

Myrnin was locked out.

Her cell phone rang. Claire pulled it from her coat pocket and looked at the screen, which showed a picture of Myrnin's bunny slippers. She thumbed the connection open and said, "Don't try coming through again."

"Claire, listen to me. I need to speak to you privately. There's something very odd going on, and I need your input to understand exactly what—"

"I quit," she said. "I thought we were clear on that."

"The house. Listen to me, the house could be your salvation, in an emergency. I need you all to stay in that house as much as you possibly can. Claire—"

She hung up on him. Myrnin would never tell her what was going on, not in any way that made sense; neither would Amelie, obviously. And Oliver seemed to have come down firmly on the opposite side, too.

She couldn't trust any of them. Not anymore.

Shane put his arms around her. "Sorry," he said. "I know this hurts."

"You're the one with the bruises," she said, and turned around to hug him back. "And you're the one I care about."

Michael cleared his throat. "Sorry to break the mood, but can we please talk about *what the hell is going on*?"

Claire took in a deep breath. "I guess we should."

Because no matter what Amelie wanted, Claire couldn't protect her friends if they didn't know.

EIGHT

CLAIRE

Staying in the house was possible for only a day or two before they began running out of important survival supplies, like Coke, hot dogs, and toilet paper. Michael insisted on making the supply run the first time, but on the second, Claire and Eve held a whispered meeting upstairs, and declared that they would be going on their own.

"No way," Michael said. "You heard what Myrnin said, and besides, if Eve wasn't the most popular girl in Morganville before, she's on the blacklist now. They'll lock up when they see you coming, babe. Amelie's not happy at all."

"Maybe she should go ahead and arrest me," Eve said. "Because I'm *not* hiding in this house for the rest of my life. First, I need a haircut. Second—"

"There's no second," Shane interrupted her. "You're not going, girls. Things are getting weird out there."

"Says who?"

"Me," Michael said. "The Food King is closed down and locked. They just put an out-of-business sign on Marjo's Diner, too."

"What?" Shane blurted. Marjo's was his favorite place in Morganville, and hey, Claire was pretty fond of it, too. "It might be a cockroach factory, but it's been around for what, fifty years? Never closed?"

"Well, it's closed now," Michael said.

Shane shook his head. He was sitting on the couch, game controller in his hands, but he'd forgotten all about it now. On the TV screen, zombies were ripping his avatar apart. "That's insane. You know about my job, right?"

"What about it?" Claire asked.

"Fired," he said. "Well, laid off—they called this morning. They're closing for renovations, or so they said. Pretty soon, we're not going to have anyplace open around here. What is up with this crap?"

"What about Common Grounds?" Eve asked anxiously. "I mean, Oliver let me take the week off, but . . ."

"Still open," Michael confirmed. "So far, anyway. But that's just the tip of the iceberg. This isn't just some financial problem. There's more to it." He hesitated, then said, "And more vampires have gone missing."

"More? How many more?"

"According to the gossip this morning, at least ten. Naomi hasn't been seen again. Neither have the others."

"Well," Eve was saying, "we still *have* to go to the store. And *we're* going, not either of you."

"Why?" Michael asked. He'd folded his arms, and was frowning at her, but not in an angry way. He looked concerned.

Eve sighed. She ticked things off on her fingers. "I need fingernail polish, and neither of you can tell decent lacquer from rubbing alcohol. Next, Claire has a prescription she needs to pick up from the pharmacy, which neither of you really ought to be doing on her behalf, since it's personal. Last, speaking of personal, there are intimate feminine products that I promise you neither one of you want to be taking up to a register, manly men."

Shane actually flinched. Michael looked uncomfortable.

Eve grinned. "In case that wasn't clear, I'm talking about *tampons*."

"Yeah, pretty clear," Shane said. "And okay, yeah, maybe you should go. Considering."

"Damn right," Eve said. She was in Action Eve mode today, dressed in black jeans, heavy combat boots, and tight-fitting tee with a massive silk-screened Gothic skull wrapped around it. Big spiked bracelets. A leather collar. All her Goth makeup was firmly in place, right down to jet-black lipstick and eye makeup the color of bruises. "Trust me. We've got this. Plus, I'm going armed." She opened a leather pouch hanging from her spiked belt, and pulled out a bottle of silver nitrate, as well as a silver-coated stake. "We'll be fine. In and out in thirty minutes."

"Maybe I should go and just wait in the car," Shane said.

"Maybe you should stop treating us like fragile china dolls," Eve shot back, and spun the stake expertly in her fingers. "What do you say, CB?"

Claire was smiling, she realized. Unlike Eve, she wasn't dressed to aggress; she was wearing plain jeans and a simple blue blouse, but she had her backpack, and inside it (instead of books) were a small, compact crossbow, bolts, silver nitrate, *and* stakes.

Plus her wallet, of course. She wasn't planning on holding the place up.

"We'll be fine," Claire said, and held Shane's eyes. "Trust me."

He nodded, still frowning. "I don't like it."

"Yeah, I know," she said. "But we can't hide for the rest of our lives. This is our town, too."

The drive to the other store was a little bit longer, but Eve livened it up by blaring death metal and driving with the windows down, which made people not only turn and look, but glare. Oh, Eve was in a *mood*. It was fun.

Eve pulled the hearse up in front of the pharmacy and put it in park. "Don't get out," Claire shouted over the music. "I'll be right back, okay?"

"Five minutes!" Eve shouted back. "Five minutes and I come to kick ass. That is not a metaphor!"

Claire made an OK sign with her fingers, because it was impossible to yell loud enough to be heard as Eve cranked it up another notch; she escaped from the vibrating hearse, dashed across the empty space, and into the relative silence of Goode's Drugs (known locally, she had learned from Shane, as Good Drugs, because the pharmacist was known to sell some not-quite-legal stuff under the counter from time to time). The thumping bass from the hearse rattled the glass, but other than that, it seemed deserted.

Claire walked past racks of cold medicines, pain relievers, mouthwash, and foot powders to reach the actual pharmacy counter at the back. No one was in sight at the window, so she rang the bell. It made a clear, silvery note in the air.

Silence.

"Hello?" Claire said, and then louder, leaning over the counter, "Hello? Anybody?"

She caught sight of someone right at the corner of her vision, and turned to look. There, standing behind the counter at the end of a long set of shelves, was a man. Not Mr. Rooney, who ran the pharmacy; not the vampire Claire had seen in there a few times, who probably owned the place. No, this was—

This was the man she'd seen outside Common Grounds. The quiet, nondescript one.

"Hello?" she asked, looking right at him. "Do you work here?" She leaned farther over the counter, trying to get a clearer angle, but when she blinked . . .

. . . He was gone.

"Mr. Rooney?" She yelled it this time. "Mr. Rooney, there's somebody behind the counter! I don't think he's supposed to be there! Mr. Rooney, are you all right?" Nothing. Claire felt her mouth dry up and her palms get sweaty. She took her phone out of her pocket and dialed 911. "Hello, I'm at Goode's Drugs, and I think there's something wrong—the pharmacist isn't here, and I saw somebody in the back. Yes. I'll wait."

The emergency operator told her a car was on the way; in Morganville, that wouldn't be a long wait at all. Claire considered going back outside to wait in the hearse with Eve, and in fact was retreating back from the service window when Mr. Rooney suddenly popped up out of *nowhere* behind her and said, "Can I help you?"

Claire yelped, jumped, and almost overbalanced as she banged into a shelf. She steadied herself and said, "Where were you?"

"Me?" Rooney frowned, his kindly old-man face turning surly. "Taking out the trash. Why do you care what I was doing, missy? What do you want?"

"My prescription," Claire said. She got her breathing under

control as Mr. Rooney entered some numbers on a door keypad and buzzed through to the back. He appeared at the service window a second later.

"ID," he said, and combed through a plastic bin while she got it out. "Danvers, Claire. Yes, right here. Twenty-seven fifty." He eyed her license, frowning. "You're a little young to be taking these birth control pills, aren't you?"

"I don't think that's any of your business," Claire said, blushing. "You don't lecture the seventeen-year-old *guys* who buy condoms, do you?"

"That's different," he said.

"No, it's really not." Claire put the money on the counter—exact change—and grabbed the bag. She almost walked away, but then turned to say, "I called the police. There was somebody behind your counter back there."

"Nobody's back here," Rooney said.

"Look around. There is!"

"I'm telling you there's nobody," he said sharply. "You go tell your friend out there to turn that noise down or I'll get the police on *you!*"

He watched her go. Claire glanced back once, just as the door swung shut, and saw the face of that man again.

This time, he was in the store itself. She had no idea how he could have gotten out there; he was standing next to the old-fashioned water fountain, and the electronic door definitely hadn't opened and closed.

She had a split-second impression of something that couldn't be right, something she couldn't even process, before the face came into focus.

And then the door shut.

She yanked it open again, but he was gone.

"What?" Rooney snapped. "In or out, missy. In or out!"

She let it close.

Claire walked back to the hearse, thinking hard; a siren Doplered closer, and a Morganville cruiser swung into the parking lot and slid to a stop behind Eve's car, blocking it in.

Eve turned down the music. "Oh crap," she said, and looked at Claire as she walked over. "I guess Grandpa Grumpy got his Depends in a twist."

"It's not for you," Claire said. "I called."

"What—"

She didn't have time to tell her, because a Morganville cop had exited the vehicle and was walking closer. He wasn't someone she recognized, but then, she was glad not to be on a first-name basis with the entire MPD. "You called 911?" the cop asked.

"Yes, sir. It might be a mistake. Mr. Rooney's there now, but I swear, there was someone behind the counter before he got there. A stranger. I thought it might be a robbery."

"Can you describe this stranger?"

"No need to bother with that," said Mr. Rooney; he'd come out of his store and stood on the porch in his white lab coat. He had on his grandfatherly face again, and a warm smile. "The girl just got confused, is all. There's nobody but me behind that counter." His smile thinned, just a little. "In fact, she got so confused she forgot to pay me for those pills she has."

Claire blinked. "I didn't—"

The cop turned toward her. "Is that true?" Before she could answer, he plucked the sack from her hand and looked into it. "No receipt. You didn't pay for these?"

"I did! In cash!"

Mr. Rooney was shaking his head sadly. "No, I'm sorry, but that's just not true. She didn't pay. She ran out of here and straight for her friend's car. I think she might have been planning to take off while you were talking to me."

It made it sound like Claire had called in a false alarm, just to steal the pills. "No, that's *not true!* I paid him for it! Twenty-seven fifty! And there was someone in the store, behind the counter. I saw him!"

"Can you describe him?"

She struggled to remember. Average, average, average. No matter how much she tried to find something detailed, it all faded into . . . gray. He just wasn't *memorable*. "He was average height," she said. "And . . . had blond hair. Fair skin, I think. Maybe blue eyes."

"Average, blond, fair skinned, blue eyes," the cop summed up. "Miss, that describes a lot of men in Morganville, including me—you realize that?"

"I know."

"What was he wearing?"

And that, Claire realized, was a complete blank. Clothes, obviously, but she couldn't remember a color of shirt, or pants, or patterns. Nothing.

The cop read her face and shook his head. "Pay the man for the pills, miss."

"But—"

"Pay him or we settle this downtown." He was polite, but hard underneath, and Claire gritted her teeth and dug out her wallet again. Twenty-seven fifty. She had thirty dollars left, and Mr. Rooney folded it up and put it in his pocket. "I'll get your change for you next time," he said. "I'm sure it's just a plain misunderstanding, Officer. No problem."

"All right." The cop touched the brim of his hat. "You-all have a nicer day." He gave Claire a lingering look, as if *she* were the villain of the day, and walked back to his cruiser.

Claire glared at Mr. Rooney. He was smirking, and he turned and went into his store before the policeman pulled away. She didn't dare follow.

"Rooney got you, huh?" Eve was smiling, but her eyes were hard. "Don't sweat it, CB. He tries to shake down girls all the time if they're getting birth control. Some kind of personal thing with him. You're lucky you got off just getting charged twice. He's put girls in jail for it before, claiming they stole from him." She sounded like she spoke from personal experience. "He is a prime grade-A jackhole, believe me. And if there was anywhere else . . ."

But as usual, in Morganville, there wasn't.

Claire no longer cared about her average-looking stranger, but as she started to get back in the car, she saw him again. The policeman had pulled out and was halfway down the block, Rooney was in his store happily counting his ill-gotten gains, and that man, that *stranger*, was standing at the corner of the building, watching her.

Claire paused and stared back.

He stepped out of sight.

Not again.

Claire bailed and took off running, pulling her cell phone as she ran. She didn't mean to follow him; she just wanted to get close enough to snap his picture. Then she could prove what she was talking about. Photo evidence.

"Claire, *wait!*" Eve called from behind her. She cursed, and Claire heard her getting out of the car, but she didn't slow down. She couldn't. She'd seen how fast this—this *thing* could move. She no longer thought of it as a man, she realized; there was something fundamentally wrong about it. It wasn't a vampire, or she didn't think it was, but it was . . . something else.

Maybe something worse.

She skidded to a stop as she rounded the corner, eyes wide, because behind the building sat a wide, empty field. A block away, at least, were some dilapidated houses turned a dull gray by the relentless sun.

But no sign of her mysterious stranger. None at all.

"Claire! Do *not* go running off like that!" Eve shouted from behind her. She skidded to a stop, running into Claire, then grabbed her and shook her. "What the *hell*? I am not going to be telling Shane that you're—"

"He's gone," Claire said. She pulled free of Eve's hold and looked around, really *looked*. There were some puddles on the ground from the recent rain, and a drainage grate. Maybe he'd gone down that? But it was heavily rusted, and would have made a hell of a lot of noise if he'd moved it.

She hadn't heard a thing.

"He? What he? He who?"

"The—" It didn't matter. Claire shook her head. "Never mind."

"Yeah, good. Let's go, dummy—hanging out in deserted vacant lots around here is a prime way to get yourself dead. Haven't I taught you anything?" Eve hustled her around the building again, and back to the hearse. "I promised the boys we'd be back in thirty. We've got to move it."

Claire got in the passenger seat and strapped in. As Eve made the ponderous giant circle that was required to turn the hearse around, Claire stared at the edge of the building where she'd last seen her mysterious visitor.

And there he was, stepping out of nowhere, staring at her. Mr. Average.

"Stop!" Claire yelled. She threw the door open, but instead of chasing him this time, she grabbed her cell and took a picture. Eve slammed on the brakes, yelling inarticulately, but before she could manage to protest, Claire had already slammed the door shut again. "Go!"

"Make up your mind, traffic light!" Eve said, and accelerated again. "I'm afraid to ask, but what was that?"

Claire opened up her photo album on the phone. There, captured in a rush of digitized light, was the rough brick wall of Goode's Drugs, and a dark figure. Except it looked almost... translucent. And there were no details to it, just shadows. *It's a bad camera,* she thought, but that wasn't it, not completely.

Her visitor was there, and not there. Schrödinger's cat, come to life—neither dead nor alive, existing nor missing.

"Eve," Claire said, and showed her the phone. "What do you see?"

Eve took a fast glance at the picture, then went back to piloting the hearse. "Side of the building," she said. "What?"

"Nothing else?"

"Look, this isn't the time to play a hidden-object game." Eve looked again, and shook her head. "Nothing."

"Not even a shadow?"

"No!"

Claire clicked the phone off and settled back in her seat, thinking furiously. *Why can I see him when Eve can't?* It wasn't just Eve. Mr. Rooney *might* have been lying, but he could have just been unable to spot the stranger, too.

Very, very odd.

The other grocery store on the far side of town was like the Food King, only with less variety. They were, at least, still stocked up. Claire and Eve retrieved their necessary items, and then Eve vanished toward the candy aisle while Claire gathered up chili ingredients. Shane hadn't asked for them, but he would, probably just as soon as they got back home.

She was getting garlic when she saw her mysterious stranger again through the windows outside the store. This time, he wasn't watching her.

He was talking to someone else, but she couldn't see who it was. *Well, at least someone else in this town can actually see him,* Claire thought, and put the garlic in her basket as she slowly walked at an angle toward the front, trying to see who Mr. Shadow's friend might be.

It was *Oliver.*

Claire instinctively took a step back, then quickly turned her back and began looking over a selection of pies.

When she risked another glance over her shoulder, the two of them weren't talking anymore. Oliver was standing there, staring off into space, and as she watched, the stranger leaned forward, touched his fingertips to Oliver's broad pale forehead . . .

And Oliver didn't move. Didn't blink.

Something was wrong.

Claire found a display of hand mirrors and grabbed one, which she angled up to see what was happening outside the store. For a second she thought she'd taken too long, but then she focused her mirror on the right place, and saw that the stranger was walking away, toward the corner of the building.

Oliver was following.

It's Oliver. He can take care of himself. But she couldn't get past the sight of the stranger's fingers touching Oliver's forehead, and Oliver's total lack of reaction. There was no way that was normal.

Claire looked around for Eve, but she wasn't anywhere visible, still lost in the candy aisle. Claire dumped her basket of stuff and got her phone out as she headed for the door. Eve picked up on the first ring. "Don't yell," Claire said, first thing. She felt short of breath, and her heart was pounding hard. "I'm going outside."

"What? No, you're not! Where are you?"

"Outside," Claire said, as she stepped through the doors and out into the whipping winter wind. Puddles of water shivered on the ground in the blast, edged with ice. The air felt heavy and humid: more rain on the way, probably. "I won't go out of sight of the front windows, I promise."

"Jesus, CB, you're killing me here. Fine, I won't get any candy. Just get back *inside*!"

She could see Oliver at the edge of the building, heading north. Claire hurried that way, keeping the phone on. "I'm following Oliver," she said. "Something's wrong."

"Even *better* reason to get your ass inside," Eve said. "Okay, I'm here. I can see you." She sounded calmer. Claire looked over, and saw Eve standing pressed against the glass, stuffed shopping basket in one hand and her phone to her ear.

"I'm just going to the corner," Claire said. "I'm trying to see if they get in a car." It was overcast, but most vamps knew better than to go out for a stroll without light protection, and Oliver was more cautious than most—yet he wasn't wearing a hat. The big, black coat looked large enough to pull over his head, though.

Claire made it to the corner in time to see the stranger bend over and yank up a drainage grate, which tipped up in a rusty metallic groan. Oliver didn't pause. He walked right into the open hole and dropped. Disappeared.

She expected the stranger to go with him, but instead, he let the drainage grate slam shut, stood on it, and . . .

And then he turned and looked at her. His skin was gray, and it looked *dead*—not pale, like vampires, but a slick, decaying shade like something rotting in the shadows. His eyes weren't eyes. His mouth, as it opened, wasn't a mouth.

She didn't know what it was. Her brain refused to put it into a pattern.

And then the creature *melted,* and flowed in a rush of liquid down the drain.

Claire gasped, eyes wide, and felt sick, *really* sick. She didn't know why; it was wrong, sure, but not nearly as wrong as many things she'd seen in Morganville. Something inside her was screaming, as if she'd seen something entirely different from what she *thought* she'd seen.

Eve's tinny voice was coming out of the phone. Claire raised it back to her ear, moving slowly. She still wasn't sure if she needed to sit down or not. Nothing seemed right now. Nothing. She squeezed her eyes shut and could almost, almost see . . .

See what?

"I'm okay," she whispered. "I'm—"

Claire felt the world tilt and go dim, and with a distant feeling of surprise, she realized that she was going to fall down.

It didn't hurt at all.

She woke up with her head cradled in Eve's lap, and a circle of half-interested bystanders surrounding her. Eve was fanning her face with a folded piece of paper, and as soon as Claire's eyes opened, she cried out in relief. "Oh, thank God," she said. "You scared the *crap* out of me! What happened? Did someone hit you?"

"No." Claire felt deeply weird, as if her brain was working at one-quarter speed. "I fell." But *why*? "I tripped." That made more sense than anything else. She'd seen . . . something. She just couldn't imagine what it was, because her brain refused to even try.

Gray. Something gray.

Eve was pulling her to her feet. "Enough of the detective shit," she said. "We are going home."

"But—"

"No buts. You get in the car. I'm going in to buy the stuff and I'm coming *right back.* I will not take my eyes off you. You do *not move.*" Eve looked really scared. Claire thought she should be scared, too, but something in her had just . . . switched off. Burned out.

She felt so *wrong.*

Eve put her in the hearse and locked the doors, bent down, and mouthed, *Don't move!* before she dashed back inside to grab up their two baskets and rush to a register.

Claire leaned against the cold window glass and dialed her phone. Myrnin's number. He didn't answer. She felt oddly short of breath, as if she were drowning on dry land.

"Please," she whispered. She'd been angry at Myrnin, she remembered, but none of that mattered now. "Please answer me. I need you."

"Claire?" That wasn't Myrnin's voice, and technically, the phone was still ringing. "Claire, it's Frank. What's wrong?"

"I saw something."

"You don't sound good. What was it?"

"I don't know." She was so tired now. So tired. "I saw something that shouldn't be."

"You mean shouldn't be here?"

"Yes. No. Shouldn't be at all." She struggled to make sense of things. The day looked so gray and misty. Rain. The rain had started again. She could see the bright front windows of the store, see Eve in there buying their purchases, but none of it had any real meaning. That part of her was . . . gone. Burned. "Frank, tell Myrnin—tell him Oliver—I think Oliver is—"

"Is what? Claire? Where are you—are you in the hearse? In the parking lot? I have a surveillance camera—I can see you." Frank Collins was concerned. That made her smile, a little, because that was just wrong, too. He didn't exist. He was a brain in a jar, watching through mechanical eyes, hearing through mechanical ears, and he was *concerned.*

"Cameras," she said. "Can you run it back?"

"Back to what?"

"To before I fell. Can you see what I saw?"

"Hold on."

Myrnin's cell phone stopped ringing, and his voice mail picked up, but it was her cheery voice telling people to leave a message. She was talking to herself. That seemed odd.

Frank was gone.

"Frank?"

"Right here," his voice said, this time from the hearse's stereo speakers. Claire dropped her phone in her lap; it felt too heavy to hold. "I see you coming out of the store. You're following Oliver."

"Just Oliver?"

"Yeah, just him."

"You don't see anybody else?"

"No. Oliver walks around the corner. He drops into a drain. You fall down. What am I missing?"

"I don't know," Claire said honestly. "Except that you are."

"I'm running the recording through filters. I'll get back to you." With a click, Frank disconnected from both the phone and the car's stereo.

Claire listened to the hesitant tap of rain on the roof, but the tap became a pounding, then a roar. Silvery sheets of water veiled the store windows.

She felt very alone. Floating.

The driver's-side door suddenly popped open, and Eve threw grocery bags at her, jumped in, and slammed it behind her. She was drenched and shivering. "Damn, that was *freezing!*" She turned the key and got the hearse started, then looked over at Claire. "Are you okay?"

Claire smiled a little and made an OK symbol with her fingers. She wasn't, but Eve couldn't help.

The rain hissed and roared, and Eve drove slowly through the downpour. Around them, Morganville had turned into an alien world. None of the landmarks looked right. The streets were rushing rivers. What lights showed were thin and watery, smeared all out of recognition.

How Eve figured out the streets and got them home, Claire had no idea.

"Damn," Eve said as she parked the hearse. "I guess we'll have to make a run for it. Can you do that?"

Claire nodded. She felt distant and floating, but not weak. There just didn't seem to be any urgency to anything now. Or any emotion. If Eve told her to run, she'd run, but it was just physical movement.

She took hold of one of the grocery sacks, opened the door, and stepped out into the rain.

It was breathtakingly cold, lashing at her like whips of water, and Claire stood there, face upturned to the downpour. It felt . . . soothing.

Then her eyes opened, and images flashed across her brain in a vivid, incomprehensible flow, and Claire *screamed*. She couldn't help it. Whatever wall her brain had built between her and what she'd seen came down hard, and adrenaline flooded back into her body, kick-starting her heart.

Eve was running for the front door; Claire's scream had been lost in a roar of thunder overhead.

In the flash of lightning, Claire saw a gray shape standing next to the car. It was a man, and it wasn't.

Not at all.

She ran for the house.

Eve was already inside, shaking off water, when Claire lunged through the door, slammed the door, and locked it with trembling hands. Somehow, she'd held on to the groceries, but she had no idea how. Her teeth were chattering from the chill, and she sluiced water in silver streams to the already-drenched rug.

"God, we're both soaked," Eve said. "Guys? Hey, guys, we're back!" She headed down the hall, paused to look at the clock, and sighed. "Oh God. We're thirty minutes late. What do you want to bet Shane overreacted? Yep, here's the note—they're out driving to the store. Good job, guys, now you'll get soaked, too. Hey, has he been blowing up your cell or what? Oh, damn, Michael's been hitting mine. I'll let him know we're home. Wait here—I'll get you a towel." Eve headed for the stairs, phone to her ear. "Michael? Yeah, relax, emergency's over. We're home. Claire passed out at the store. I think she has low blood sugar—she seems really tired. I'll get some candy in her and see if she feels better. . . ." Her voice faded as she disappeared up toward the bathroom.

Don't go, Claire wanted to say. She managed to croak something out, but Eve was already gone.

Claire dropped the groceries and staggered into the living room. It felt like the water was turning to ice on her skin, and the cold was sinking deeper and deeper. . . .

I have to tell Amelie what I saw. What I know.

Eve's indistinct voice was still talking upstairs. The house seemed warm around her, as if it were fighting to make her feel better. Feel safer.

But she wasn't safe, and Claire knew that. Nobody was safe.

She turned, and the gray man was standing right here.

Her body threatened to collapse again, and Claire braced herself against the wall. He was just standing there, staring at her with eyes that weren't eyes. She couldn't think of anything now except drowning, drowning alone.

"Shhh," he said, and his voice sounded like the rain outside. Like water coming out of the faucets. "Shhh. It's over now." He tilted his head to the side, as if his neck had no bones. "Curious that you see me. I'm not ready to be seen. Why?"

"I don't know." She wanted to cry, scream, run, but none of those was possible now. "I don't know why I can see you." She swallowed and said, "Who are you?" Because even now, she couldn't let her questions go. "*What* are you?"

That face that wasn't a face smiled. It was the most horrible thing she'd seen, ever. "Magnus," he said. "I'm the end."

Then he reached out and wrapped those cold, damp hands around her neck, and she felt the house's energy scream and rush around her, but it was as if it couldn't help, not this time.

"Shhh," he said again. In the last instant, Claire thought, *Oh no, Shane, I'm sorry. I'm so sorry people keep leaving you. I love you. . . .*

Magnus snapped her neck, and everything went star white. It hurt.

But it hurt for only a moment, and then the world shrank down to a bright pinpoint of light, racing away from her. Leaving her behind.

And then it was gone, and she was gone.

NINE

AMELIE

"As of last report," Mayor Morrell said, "there are now at least twenty vampires missing. All just disappeared in the course of their normal activities, and most vanished during the day." He stood in my office, looking exhausted and worried, as well he should; I had made it clear that sleep was a luxury none of us could afford now. With him was his chief of police, Hannah Moses, who seemed almost as tired but a great deal less rumpled.

"Here's the report on what we know," Moses said, and passed me a sheaf of papers. "Detailed information on where and when each one disappeared, as far as we can track it. Some vanished right in public, but nobody seems to have seen anything. What the hell is going on, Founder?"

I stared down at the papers, but the ink formed meaningless

patterns. It was all meaningless now. All useless. I had waited too long, allowed myself to be swayed by sentiment and argument. I had denied my own instincts.

And now it was too late.

Instead of answering her, I pressed the intercom button to alert my assistant outside of the door. "Bizzie, get Oliver," I said. "Get him now. I will hold."

"Ma'am," Bizzie said, efficient as always. There was a short delay, and then she said, "He's not answering his phone, Founder."

"Keep trying."

Not Oliver. No, most likely he was simply out of contact for another reason. I had to believe so, at least. To lose Oliver now would be . . . catastrophic.

Chief Moses was repeating her question, more stridently. I lifted my head and met her eyes, and she went quiet. So did Morrell.

I stood and clasped my hands behind my back as I walked to the windows. The curtains were drawn against the day, but now I opened them. There was no light. Rain was falling, torrential rain that would wash away the world.

It was my fault.

I stared out into the cold silver downpour and said, "What do you know of our origins?"

In the reflection on the glass, I saw them exchange a look, and then Morrell said, "The origins of Morganville?"

That was not what I meant, but it would serve. "Have you never wondered why I founded this town here, in the desert? So far from the comforts of cities, rivers, lakes, *water*? In the baking sun, when sun is so toxic to younger vampires?" I didn't wait for his answer; of course he had wondered. Everyone had wondered, and only three of us now living knew that answer: Oliver, Myrnin, and me. "I chose this place because the rains came so rarely, and when they came, the land soaked up the water so quickly. No lakes. No rivers. Not even creeks."

"I—don't think I understand," he said.

"No. No, you wouldn't." I pulled in a breath and let it slowly out, a memory of the need for air. Vampire blood did not pound in the veins the way human blood did; it glided, cool and serene, never troubled by spurts of emotion. I missed that, betimes. "We have enemies. And those enemies are a kind of vampire, one that needs water to live. In the old tongue we are both called *draug,* vampire; my kind ruled the land, and theirs ruled the sea, and we were never, never at peace. I brought us here to be safe. Now the sea draug have found us. They're here. They're picking us off, like a pack of circling wolves. We have only one option if we wish to survive."

I turned from the windows and faced them, these two most burdened with responsibility for the safety of the humans of Morganville. "The vampires must run," I told them. "Far and fast. We cannot wait, and we cannot rescue those already taken. We must get out, because there is no fighting the sea draug. We did, once, in a war that shook the world. And they destroyed us."

I saw the greedy spark of light in Hannah Moses's eyes, quickly hidden; it was better concealed in Mayor Morrell, but still recognizable. *Freedom,* they were thinking. And they were right in this, but not in the way they understood. "So . . . you're leaving Morganville," Morrell repeated slowly. "All of you. When?"

"As soon as possible," I told him. "We've lingered too long already." I crossed back to the desk and pressed the intercom button again. "Oliver?"

"Nothing, ma'am," Bizzie said. "His phone rings, but it goes to voice mail. I checked at Common Grounds and his home. There's no sign of him anywhere."

I felt the universe waver around me, and sank slowly into my chair. I tasted salt and ashes. Oliver would never turn his phone off, not now. He would never fail to answer. He would never drop out of sight, not of his own accord.

He was gone. Another possibility taken from me, another piece of my world removed. The draug would take it from me bit by bit until there was nothing left but these humans, staring at me with the fatal glow of hope in their eyes.

I was alone now. Vulnerable.

"Ma'am?" I had left the intercom open. "Ma'am?"

"Myrnin," I said. "Find Myrnin. Tell him *not* to leave his lab. Tell him to get what he needs together in preparation for departure. Bizzie—in your desk you will find a black binder. Break the seal and follow the instructions. On no account will you leave your desk until it is all done. Do you understand?"

"Yes, ma'am." She sounded curious, but not shaken. Not yet. The intercom clicked off.

It was done, then. I had released the brake, and now the train would roll relentlessly on, no matter what might happen.

I had almost forgotten Morrell and Moses, but they were still standing there, watching me. I hated them in that moment for their humanity, their pulses, their *safety*. For the hope in them. For the way their fingers twined together, a secret promise of love that they thought no one could see.

So much lost now. So much.

"What do you need us to do?" Richard Morrell said. Fourth of his family to hold that office, and in many ways, he was the best of them. His family had rotten roots, but against all odds, it had produced this strong, healthy branch.

And Hannah Moses . . . a long history of her family here as well, a proud one. She had gone away to fight a distant war, and returned to us. She had strength, courage, loyalty, and cleverness.

I mourned for that.

I took a shallow breath, just enough to fill my lungs to speak. "I need you to get word to the humans of Morganville," I said. "Bring them to Founder's Square tomorrow at dusk. I will give you your freedom then, as we leave."

I could not look at them now. Instead, I focused on the papers Hannah had given me, the meaningless reports, the world that was already gone.

They murmured their good-byes, and I did not look up to see them go.

I heard the door close, and I was alone.

So very, very alone.

TEN

CLAIRE

☽

The world was gone, but there was something holding her. It felt like a rope, a thin, invisible rope; she bobbed against it like a balloon on a string, lost in a night sky. *I'm dead.* The thought came to her, but she didn't really know what that meant anymore. If you were dead, you shouldn't *know* you were dead. You just were, or were not, like Schrödinger's cat.

I'm the cat in the box, with poison. The cat might be alive. The cat might be dead. You can't tell until you open the box. Indeterminacy.

Funny how physics didn't go away when you were murdered.

Claire thought she shouldn't be feeling anything, but she felt . . . warm. Cradled, as if in someone's arms. Safe.

The utter darkness was lifting a little, to a dark gray, and then to a pale shadow. There were things in the shadow that blurred, sharpened, became real as she concentrated. It was like watching an old black-and-white television, only she was in the television.

She was standing in the Glass House living room, and simultaneously, she was lying down on the floor, with her head turned to the side, hands flung out to either side. Her hair was covering her face. Her eyes were open.

That was the old Claire. Old Claire was lying there dead.

New Claire was standing over her, feeling a little odd about the whole thing, but not . . . not sad. Not afraid. Just interested. *The cat in the box,* she thought. *I'm both things at once. Myrnin would be fascinated.*

Now she was hearing something. A faint buzz, like electricity . . . no, a vibration. Claire concentrated on it, and realized it was a voice.

It was Eve's voice, becoming audible as she descended the stairs. Muffled, because she was rubbing her head with a towel. ". . . really pouring out there," she was saying. Eve's voice sounded different from before, but still recognizable. It rang and echoed here in this not-place Claire inhabited. "I don't think it's letting up anytime soon. The boys should be back in a couple of minutes—they hadn't gotten very far." She reached the bottom of the stairs and let the towel slip down to hang around her neck. She was carrying another one, neatly folded. "Claire? Are you in the kitchen? Get me a Coke!"

Eve started to walk that direction, and Claire thought, *I'm so sorry.* This was going to be hard. Very hard.

At first she thought Eve was going to walk right past her; Claire's body was behind the sofa, visible really only at an angle. But there was a thin trail of water running from Old Claire's soaked clothes, like a miniature stream, and Eve slipped in it, caught her balance, and, as she bent to wipe it up, was at just the right angle to see Claire's foot.

Eve came slowly upright. "CB?" She sounded quiet and breathless. "Oh God, you passed out again. I *knew* I should have taken you to the hospital. Damn damn damn . . ." She fumbled in the bag on the table and pulled out a candy bar. "I have sugar—it's just low blood sugar; you'll be okay. . . ."

Eve shoved a chair aside and knelt down at Old Claire's side with the candy bar. She started to move her, and as she did, Claire's head rolled a little—wrong, all wrong.

Eve saw her open eyes. Her blank, open eyes.

She froze. "Claire?"

New Claire crouched down, on a level with Eve. *I'm here,* she said. *Don't be afraid.*

Eve couldn't hear her at all, and her gaze remained riveted on Old Claire's body. Horrified. Disbelieving. "Claire?" It came out small and pathetic this time, trembling with terror. Eve felt for a pulse. "Claire!" This time, it was a scream, a full and awful scream.

Stop, Claire said, but it was no good; she wasn't going to be able to tell Eve it was all right. It wasn't, really; that *was* her body lying there. She'd died. No, she'd been murdered, silently, without a witness. And now she had to watch helplessly while Eve realized all that.

Eve gasped, paper-white under the Goth makeup, and then steadied herself. She straightened out Claire's body, opened her mouth, and breathed into her body. Claire watched her old chest inflate, then deflate. Eve feverishly counted ribs and put the heel of her hand on Claire's chest, topped it with her other hand, and began pushing, five sharp, hard movements. Then another breath. Then five more pumps. Breath.

Stop, Claire said. *Eve, please! Stop!*

She couldn't make Eve hear her. Couldn't make her understand that it was useless.

"Claire! Claire, come back! You *bitch,* come back!" Eve was sobbing now, trembling with effort. It wasn't doing any good, but she kept on trying. And trying.

There was a rattling sound from the hall. Keys in the lock.

Claire stood up and drifted that way, unconsciously moving around Eve even though it no longer really mattered. *Why don't I go through the floor?* she wondered, but even as she did, it felt like the floor softened under her feet, and she realized that she *could* go through the floor if she wanted. Or the ceiling. The only thing that was stopping her was the Old Claire viewpoint.

The locks gave way, and the door swung open, and Michael and Shane came inside. Shane shut the door and locked it, shaking water off his coat and throwing back his hood.

She wanted to freeze him like this, in this one moment, where everything was still okay for him. Where he was smiling a little, and calling her name, because he expected her to be there for him.

Then from the living room, Eve screamed, "Help me!" There was a tortured panic in her voice, and the single instant of peace and normal life shattered, gone.

Michael and Shane lunged forward, through New Claire's insubstantial body. Shane didn't pause. Michael faltered, half turned, and then kept running.

She didn't want to watch this. She didn't.

But New Claire, Ghost Claire, The Only Claire . . . really couldn't turn her back on it, either. She drifted there in the room, watching as Michael thumped down on his knees next to Eve, lips parting in horror.

Shane skidded to a halt, face gone utterly still and blank.

Eve sat back, sobbing inarticulately now. Michael moved her out of the way and put his palm flat over Claire's heart, then touched her neck.

Then, after a long, hard second, he reached up and closed her blank, open eyes, and grabbed Eve as she tried to lunge forward again. "No," he whispered. "No. It's no good. Eve, she's gone. *She's gone."*

Eve fought him for a few seconds, and then collapsed in his arms. Michael rocked her, and then looked up. There were tears rolling down his cheeks, and Claire didn't think she'd ever seen him look so . . . human.

He held out a hand toward Shane—to help, to hold him back, Claire wasn't sure, and she didn't think Michael was, either.

She drifted closer to Shane. Closer. *I'm still with you,* she said. *I'm not leaving.*

He wasn't moving at all. It was as if Shane had shut down, as if he was as gone as she was. She looked around, somehow expecting to see the *other* Shane here, where she was, but it wasn't like that.

Whatever was dying in Shane, it wasn't coming here.

"Her neck is broken." He said it quietly, in an awful, still monotone. "She didn't just fall. Someone killed her." He was staring at Claire's body with so much intensity, but his eyes seemed dark and dead. "I know who did it."

Michael slowly lowered his hand. "What?"

"I know who killed her," Shane said.

He couldn't. He'd never seen Magnus, as far as Claire knew. . . . What could he be thinking?

There were no tears for Shane. There was no breakdown. He was nothing but ice and steel. She'd never seen him like this, not even when he'd been at his worst and most violent. This was . . . empty, and yet still full of something she couldn't really understand.

"Shane, what are you—" Michael kissed Eve's forehead and slowly stood up. He wiped the tears from his face. "You're in shock."

"Yeah," Shane said. He still had that distant, terrible flatness to his voice. "Yeah, probably. It's probably better than what's coming later."

"Bro—"

Shane tore his gaze from Claire's body and looked Michael in the eyes.

And Michael *stepped back.*

"Don't get in my way," he said. "I'll kill you. I'll kill anybody who gets between me and him."

Eve stumbled up to her feet, clinging to Michael's arm. "She's *dead,* Shane! God, this isn't about—"

"I mean it," he said. "Don't move her until I come back. And don't get in my way."

Shane, what are you doing? Claire shouted. She tried moving through him, but if he felt a chill, it didn't register. He was too cold inside for it to matter. *Stop! Don't leave!*

He went into the kitchen, pulled open a cabinet door, and took one of their black ready-bags that Eve kept stocked for any fang-related emergencies. Claire drifted after him, aching for him, wanting to stop him, but there was nothing at all she could do as she watched him unzip the bag, inventory the water bottles of silver nitrate, the stakes, the crossbows.

Michael followed, at a careful distance. "Shane, at least tell me where you're going. Please, bro. Please."

Shane zipped the bag, hefted the strap to his shoulder, and looked back at him. Those dark eyes—they were pits of utter blackness. "I'll be back," he said. "Don't let them take her away."

He headed for the front door. Michael came as far as the hallway, and Eve joined him; he put his arms around her, but they were both staring at Shane. He looked back, once, but didn't say anything else as he left.

Claire tried to follow him. The closed door didn't really matter, and she passed through the wood easily enough; the thick grain floated past her vision, disorientingly real, but then she came up against a barrier. It wasn't solid, more like . . . plastic. She pushed, and it stretched.

Then it broke as she pushed harder, and she drifted a little beyond the threshold.

There was a silver curtain of rain out there, and Shane had plunged out into it, hood up, running. She wanted to follow him, but the more she drifted from the doorway, the more—tenuous she felt. Stretched. Faded.

This is what Michael meant, about not being able to leave the house, she thought. When she'd first met Michael, he'd been a ghost, invisible during the daylight hours, physical at night.

Saved by the house.

It's the house, she thought. *I'm like what Michael was. I have to stay inside.*

It was harder getting back in, as if she'd been caught in some unseen undertow, but Claire managed to struggle through the barrier again, then drift through the door and back into the hall.

It was so quiet. Michael was still standing there, staring, and for a moment she thought he could actually see her . . . but he was just looking into the distance, a total blank stare.

"Where would he go?" he asked. "I don't understand what—"

Eve did. She was wiping her face with a towel now, but her eyes were red and the tears seemed to keep coming. "He's going to find Myrnin," she said. "Shane thinks he did it. Because he was the one who came after them in the first place."

Michael looked down at her, then back at the closed door. "God," he whispered. "He could be right."

No, Claire thought, appalled. *Oh no.*

Shane would kill Myrnin, or Myrnin would kill Shane, and it was all for nothing. *Nothing.*

Claire stood in the center of the black-and-white living room, a ghost in a ghostly landscape, and screamed. It came out of the very core of her, a bloody and horrible nightmare of a scream, full of anguish and despair.

Eve and Michael didn't seem to hear her. Not even then.

Claire collapsed to the floor, utterly drained.

Don't, she thought. *Please don't.*

ELEVEN

SHANE

☽

Claire was gone, and the worst part was that I couldn't *feel it*. I stood there staring at her on the floor, at the peaceful way Michael had straightened her body and closed her eyes, at the silent, pale face and the soft, limp hands that would never touch me again, and I should have felt torn apart. I should have been crying, like Eve. Hell, even *Michael*.

But I couldn't. I couldn't feel.

Well, not *that*. What I *could* feel was a dull, crushing pressure, and one pure, vivid thing. . . .

Rage.

I could see the marks on her throat, faint but there. The marks of fingers, just like the ones around my own neck. I'd survived, because she'd been there to save me.

But this time, I hadn't been there for her. No one had. He'd come in here, waited for her, grabbed her by the throat, and snapped her neck.

At least he hadn't choked her to death. At least he'd spared her that much.

There were only three vampires with easy access to our house: Michael was out, because he'd been in the car with me. Amelie . . . I couldn't see Amelie getting her own pale, strong hands dirty. No, it was the one who'd betrayed us already.

Myrnin.

I needed to do the things they expected me to do—get down there next to Claire, hold her, cry, let out all the awful pressure inside me . . . but not yet. Not yet.

No, first . . . first I had to make sure someone paid for it.

I didn't think about anything else as I grabbed the vamp bag, checked it, and left the house. As the cold, cold rain hit me, I half expected something else to hit me, too—the real impact of what I'd just seen.

But the pressure inside me crowded out everything else except that harsh, desperate ache to avenge her.

I ran. I couldn't see through the rain well, and made some wrong turns, but by the time the downpour started to let up, I got my bearings and headed for the Day House a few blocks away. The water in the streets was rushing at curb level, every street a river; trash and debris were rolling along with the flood. These were the kind of gully washers that killed people in this part of the country; get caught in an arroyo out there in the desert and you could be swept for miles, body torn apart by a torrent that disappeared into the sand an hour later.

But not here. Not in town. Here, you'd just get your shoes and pants soaked through as you waded the currents.

The Day House appeared through the still-falling rain, a

weird kind of déjà vu; the Day House and Glass House looked almost exactly alike, except that Gramma Day kept hers in better repair, and there were warm golden lights shining in the windows.

Claire liked—*had liked*—the old lady. I stared at the deserted front porch for a moment, then turned and jogged down the high-fenced alley between the Day House and its closest neighbor. No lights here, and with the unnatural gloom of the storm, it felt more claustrophobic than usual. The rain had washed it clean, but not of the sense that someone, some*thing,* was watching. Waiting to pounce.

I didn't care. Let him pounce. I couldn't fucking *wait.*

If Myrnin was watching me, he let me get all the way to the shack. Claire had some way in that didn't involve the chained-up front door, but I didn't bother to look for it. A heavy kick knocked the thing right off its rotten hinges.

I unzipped the bag and found a heavy steel-cased flashlight, which I turned on. It lit the junked-up room, and I kicked a couple of boxes aside to uncover the staircase that led down. The first few steps were dusty, but then the concrete turned to a sleek, polished marble, and the tunnel widened out as I descended.

There were lights on in the lab, and I clicked off the flashlight by the time I was halfway down. I didn't bother to be stealthy. It wouldn't matter; if Myrnin was here, and *God,* I hoped he was, then he'd know I was coming.

He was packing.

There was a massive old trunk, and he was sorting through books—discarding some, dumping others in. The place was a mess, worse than it usually was; Claire would be—*would have been*—beside herself at the idea of cleaning it up.

Myrnin was standing there paying no attention at all to me as he scowled at the titles and spines of his precious books, but he knew I was there.

"To what do I owe this unexpected—well, I can't call it a pleasure, I suppose—" He kept talking, but it was just a smear of sound. I didn't hear the meaning.

"We found her," I interrupted him. "Just where you left her." I dropped the bag at my feet. I was dripping all over his floor, making a little lake of rainwater around me; the canvas bag was soaked through, too. Didn't matter. I unzipped it and took out a crossbow.

He could have moved. Could have tried to attack, or run, or defend himself.

He didn't. He just stood there, Claire's sad, crazy, manic boss with his handsome pale face and lunatic eyes and stupid damn bunny slippers that had always made her smile. . . .

She would never smile again.

. . . And I lifted the crossbow. It was already cocked and loaded, the silver-tipped arrow a special one, with barbs sticking out so it wouldn't be easy to pull free.

I wanted this to hurt.

He still didn't move. His dark eyes had gone wide, his body very still. Vampires could do that—go so quiet you'd think they were statues. One of the many creepy things I hated about them.

"Tell me why," I said. My voice sounded flat and hard, but it didn't sound like me, really. Not the me that Claire had known, but then, I wasn't that person now. I'd never be him again. "Was it Amelie? Did she tell you to clean up her loose ends?"

"What are you talking about?" Myrnin asked, and put down the book he was holding. That was stupid, because he might have been able to use it to block the bolt I was about to shoot through his dead heart, but hey, I didn't mind. "Shane, what's happened?"

He sounded sincere. He sounded . . . worried.

My finger tightened on the trigger. I wouldn't miss, not this time. I'd put it right through his chest, into his heart, and he'd die right here, in agony, the way he *ought* to die for what he'd done.

Except that there was fear in his face now, real fear, and he said, softly, "Did something happen to Claire?"

The cry tore its way out of me, and it didn't sound like anything human. It was full of rage and fury and all the things that I'd pushed down, locked out, frozen.

I knew that sound way too well. It was the same scream I'd heard when I'd seen my home burning, with Alyssa still inside. The same one that had echoed around that dirty motel bathroom where I'd found my mom.

Myrnin must have known it, too. His eyes filled with tears and he said, "No. *No.*"

And all of a sudden, I knew he hadn't done it.

I *hated* that I knew it. I *wanted* to shoot him, and I wanted to do it anyway, because I needed to do *something* and he was easy, he'd been so close to Claire, and I needed—needed—

Needed to make him hurt like I hurt.

He braced himself on the table with both arms, head down, and chanted, very softly, *no no no no* as he rocked back and forth.

I waited until he looked up again and saw I was still aiming the crossbow at him.

"Shoot!" He screamed it at me. It was shocking and sudden, and it sounded wild and dark underneath. "Go ahead! What difference does it make?" He slammed his hands into the teetering stacks of books around him, sending them flying. He grabbed one and shredded it, just ripped it to pieces, all the paper fluttering around him like dying birds. "Go ahead, do it! Make us both feel better!"

I almost did. My finger pressed the trigger, and I felt the tension; another tiny increase, and I could have killed him.

Instead, I slowly lowered the crossbow. "It wasn't you," I said.

"No. My God, *no.*" He gathered up a handful of torn pages and crushed them in his hand, as if he had to hold on to something. "Not me."

"Then who?" The anger was gone inside me, and that was bad; it left a vacuum, and Claire had taught me enough about science to know that a vacuum had to be filled. I knew what was going to come in place of the rage, and I didn't want it. I didn't want to feel that, not ever. The longer I managed to avoid it, the less gone she would be. "Did Amelie send somebody else to take us out?"

"How did she—"

"Broken neck," I said. As I said it, the world tilted around me, and I thought I might have to sit down, but I managed to stay upright. *Not like Claire, lying there so fragile and helpless on the floor . . .* "Someone broke her neck."

And just like that, it hit me.

The grief and shock fell on me like a concrete block, smashed me down to my knees. I heard the crossbow clatter to the stone floor. I know falling down hurt—objectively—but the pain inside was so great that I couldn't even begin to care about that.

I wrapped both arms around my body, to try to hold it in, but I couldn't. I couldn't.

I knew he was coming closer. I knew I ought to grab a stake, be ready for anything, but some black, dead part of me no longer cared if he finished the job. I wished he'd killed me days ago, so I wouldn't have to know this, see this, feel this.

Her eyes had been open, and so blank, and God, *I hadn't even dared to touch her.*

I'd walked away.

Myrnin's hand touched my shoulder. I was distantly aware of that, of him saying something, but I couldn't focus. I didn't want to hear all his platitudes, his sympathy, *his* pain. She was mine, and she was gone.

It hurt worse than any pain I'd ever felt. Not even losing my sister had been this bad. Not even my mother.

I couldn't understand why my heart was still beating.

"Shane," Myrnin was saying. He shook my shoulder, hard enough to break through the continuing waves of agony I felt. "*Shane!* Listen to me—it's important!"

I gagged in a breath, then another. My insides ached as if I'd gone a dozen rounds in the ring, and been pummeled for all twelve. I felt like I was bleeding inside. Bleeding out.

Nothing was important now that she was gone.

"Shane!" He grabbed me by *both* shoulders, crouched down, and shook me hard enough to rattle my teeth. His dark eyes were wounded and desperate, with a tint of red glowing far back in their centers. "Damn you, boy, *listen*! Where? *Where* did she die?"

How fast it had all changed. Opening the front door, I was still whole, still alive, still sane. Ten steps later, I was . . . "Home," I said. It came out in a raw, ragged whisper. "She's at home."

"God defend me, *you idiot!*" Myrnin bounced to his feet, and dragged me with him. Literally, dragged. I stumbled to my feet after being pulled like a toy for a couple of feet, and had to run to keep up as he darted forward, kicking books and chairs out of his way with shattering force. He took the most direct route to where he was going, which meant ripping an entire lab table up out of the floor and tossing it end over end across the room to smash against the far wall.

We stopped in front of a door set in the wall. It was locked. Myrnin stared at the padlock for only a single second, then reached out and ripped it off.

Then he ripped the entire door off its hinges.

The blackness beyond was a portal. I knew that, and I knew it could go directly to our house. Claire had fallen right in front of it, probably trying to make it out.

Oh God, I couldn't help but replay that in my mind . . . her realizing her danger, running for the portal, being caught before she could go through. . . .

Dying.

Myrnin went still, and concentrated. There was a ripple of color over the dark, but it quickly faded. He tried again, and again.

Nothing happened.

"You think you can save her," I said. I felt dull and heavy inside with grief, beaten down with it. And I knew it was only going to get worse. "You can't. She's gone, Myrnin."

"The *house,* you idiot, the *house* has saved her. It's done it before, and with the four of you living inside it, it's grown more powerful than ever. . . . It *must* have tried!"

Michael. The house had saved Michael, once. I felt a wild, crazy, painful spike of hope, like a shaft of sunlight hitting eyes that had never seen day, but it was gone almost immediately. Burned-out. "Michael's body disappeared," I said. "When the house saved him, his body vanished—he told me that. Hers is still there. If the house tried, it didn't work." And I would have known. I would have felt something if she'd still been there, trapped. I would have *known,* because what did it say about me if I couldn't feel that?

Myrnin wasn't listening. He was muttering under his breath, something in a language I didn't know, but from the sound of it, he was cursing like a drunken sailor as he stared murderously at the black portal. Then he switched to English. "All right," he said. "Kill me, then, you faithless pile of lumber and nails. Kill me if you have to, but I am *coming through*."

I'd thought he was talking to me, but he wasn't. He was talking to the Glass House.

He lunged forward into the dark portal. Even I knew that wasn't a good idea; Claire had been really clear about that. He hit the blackness, and it swallowed him up like a pool of ink. Ripples of color spread and faded.

Nothing else.

I stared, waiting, but I didn't see anything. Maybe he was just . . . gone. Dead. Maybe we were all going to die today. I didn't really see any downside with that, except that I seemed to be the one left behind. Always.

That just couldn't keep happening. It couldn't.

I was sensible enough to go back, pick up my vampire kit, and *then* jump blindly into the dark. I had one thing in my mind as I did.

Please let me see Claire one more time.

Because that was all I wanted now, before the end.

TWELVE

CLAIRE

☽

The portal suddenly swelled out of the wall like a black balloon, and Claire heard Eve's startled cry as she saw it happen.

She felt the door opening like a strange pressure blowing through the house; the whole world seemed to shudder as if it were a pond into which a rock had been dropped, and then there was a sharp, cracking sound, like a bell breaking in half.

And Myrnin came tumbling out of the portal.

He overbalanced and fell flat, landing right next to Old Claire's body. He raised himself up and froze, staring right into that still, silent face. New Claire, floating close by, saw the look that came over him, and realized something she never really, truly had let herself know before.

Myrnin cared about her. Really, really cared. That wasn't the kind of expression someone had for the death of a person who was unimportant, replaceable, just another warm body in a lab coat. That was genuine grief.

It broke her heart, just a little.

Myrnin had just risen to his feet when *Shane* came crashing through, pale and coated with a layer of frost; he collapsed in a heap, panting and shivering. Eve cried out and went to him.

Michael was busy watching Myrnin, wary and ready for anything. There was a red glow in his eyes, a predatory warning.

"Shane—?" Michael asked, without taking his gaze off the other vamp. "You okay, bro?"

Shane didn't answer him. Eve reached down to help him up, but he avoided her reaching hands and crawled—*crawled*—to Old Claire's empty body.

He sat up and carefully, so carefully, lifted her up in his arms. When her head lolled in an awful sort of way, he gasped and braced her, holding her against him.

Rocking slowly back and forth.

No, Claire said. *No, don't. I'm here; please don't do that, please don't feel so bad*— She tried touching him, but her hands passed straight through. He looked so horribly lost and desperate now, and she didn't know how to help him.

Let me go! She screamed it at the house, and battered ineffectually at the walls. Her fists passed right through them, too. *God, please, just let me go to him!*

Eve choked and turned away, hands curling into fists. She was struggling not to cry, again.

But Myrnin—Myrnin was staring off into space, not watching Shane at all. He turned in a slow circle, hand outstretched.

Claire drifted closer, and held her own hand out. His passed right through it.

He kept moving. Searching.

He couldn't feel her, either.

Frustrated, Claire moved her incorporeal body forward, right into the middle of Myrnin's. Weird didn't cover *that*; she could see *inside* him, the layers of flesh and bone and muscle, the odd pale veins, a heart that looked gray and still. . . .

She was way too creeped out to stay there, and quickly moved away. If she'd been capable of shaking, she would have done it.

But it *worked*. Myrnin stopped moving and stood very, very still. He closed his eyes. "Claire?"

Michael's mouth opened, then closed, and the red glare disappeared from his eyes. He looked as if someone had sucker punched him in the face—too shocked to react immediately. And then a new expression came over him. A new tension.

"Oh God," he breathed. "I didn't think—but her body's still here. Why would it still be here if she—?"

"Shhh," Myrnin said. "Claire, if you can hear me, do that again."

She didn't like it, but any chance at communication was better than nothing. She moved forward and stayed there, trying *not* to think about all of Myrnin's innards she was inhabiting. She managed to hold herself there for almost a full minute before instinct drove her away. Letting go of him was a total relief.

And it didn't work.

Myrnin stayed where he was, waiting tensely, until he finally relaxed. She'd never seen him look so . . . devastated. "I thought—I thought for a moment that she—but she *must* be here. She *must* be! Perhaps she's weaker than I'd thought, perhaps if I had some instruments to magnify—"

"Go away," Shane said, his voice muffled and dull. "Get out."

"But it's possible that she's still—"

Shane finally did look up, and oh *God,* the numb hurt on his face, the loss, the *loneliness.* "She's dead," he said. "Now go away. Stop pretending you can fix this. You can't."

Myrnin didn't seem to know what to say now. He kept turning, seeking, and it seemed frantic now. "But I *know* she must be here. She's not one to give up, you see? She would hold on, whatever the cost. You believe that, don't you? She's strong, our Claire. Very strong."

Michael's head slowly bent, and he took a deep breath, then walked away as he pulled out his cell phone. Claire followed, drifting in his wake, as he moved to stand in the middle of the parlor. He dialed and waited as he stared blankly out the window at the falling rain. "Amelie," he said. "It's Michael. Something—something bad has happened. To Claire." His voice failed, and for a moment, he held the phone against his chest. Then he raised it again and continued. "She's dead," he said. "Shane's—I don't know, he's pretty bad off." He listened, then sank down on the sofa. "What do you mean, *leave*? I can't leave. Did you hear what I said? *Claire is dead!* She's dead on our floor!"

Silence. Michael listened and finally said, "No." It was simple, and final, and then he hung up the call and sat there, still staring at the blank screen.

Then he called 911. "There's been a murder," he said. "At 716 Lot Street. The Glass House. Please send somebody. We need—we need help."

Then he dropped his phone to the carpet, put his face in his hands, and sat in bitter silence.

Hannah Moses came herself, with a police detective Claire didn't recognize; an ambulance came, too, but the paramedics waited outside in their truck while the police took photos, measurements, talked with Michael and Eve and Shane. Shane wouldn't let go until Hannah herself crouched down and talked to him in a low, soothing voice. She knew what that horror felt like, Claire realized. She'd been through it, maybe during the war, or even here in Morganville.

Anyway, she got Shane to lay Claire's body down again, and took him to the parlor to sit down. Someone made coffee, and she pressed a warm mug into Shane's hand. He didn't drink. He didn't seem to notice it was there.

"I should go back," he said. "I shouldn't leave her alone." He tried to get up, but Hannah managed to settle him down again. "It wasn't Myrnin who did it. I thought it was him, but it wasn't. Someone else came in here, in our *house*."

Myrnin, Claire realized, was being taken away, under protest, by two black-suited men in sunglasses. Amelie's guards. She must have sent them. "Wait!" He was shouting it, digging in his heels as he shouted at Shane. "Wait—*listen*—she's here. I know she must be. I can help—Claire, if you can hear me, don't despair. I'll help! I'll find a way!"

"Get him out of here!" Hannah said sharply, and the bodyguards physically picked Myrnin up and carried him, still shouting and struggling. The noise faded, and the house seemed appallingly quiet now. Michael and Eve were somewhere else—kitchen, Claire realized; she could sense where people were in the house, just as if it was a part of herself. *Wow. I'm like Frank, only instead of being a brain in a jar, I'm a soul in a house.* Floating and trapped.

Just as Michael had been. Only Michael couldn't seem to sense her, and neither could any of the others. As trapped as he'd been, her prison sentence was much, much worse.

Hannah was talking to Shane in a low, soothing voice, but he wasn't responding. He seemed to be trapped again in that dark, lightless place without any hope or help, and there was nothing Claire could do to make him understand.

She couldn't just watch him suffer; it was too awful. She drifted away, through the kitchen door, and found Michael and Eve sitting at the kitchen table, hunched over steaming mugs of some kind of hot drink. Without color to shade things, and—she realized—without a sense of smell, she couldn't really tell whether it was coffee or a really dark tea.

Come on, Michael, she thought, and stretched out her hand to pass it through his body, again and again. *Come on, you know I'm here; you have to know! This was you once!*

As if she'd heard Claire's thoughts, Eve said, "You don't think—what Myrnin said, you don't think that the house could have, you know, saved her? Like it saved you?"

Michael didn't look up. "I'm a Glass," he said. "She's not. I don't think it could do that for her, but even if it could, do you feel anything? Any sign that she's really still here?"

"Like what?"

"Cold spots," he said. "We'd feel cold spots where she was standing. And you know Claire; she wouldn't be just standing around. She'd be in our faces, telling us she's here."

He was right. Claire was, in fact, jumping in and out of his body, screaming at the top of her lungs, all through that speech. Michael didn't feel it.

Not at *all.*

"Maybe she's just not, you know, as strong as you were," Eve said. "But if she's really still here—"

He stretched out his hand across the table and took hers. He squeezed. "Sweetheart, she's gone. I'm sorry."

Eve sucked in a deep, uncontrolled breath in a gasp, and said miserably, "But I was *here.* I was upstairs, getting towels. I used the bathroom and I dried my hair and I— Michael, I was *here when it happened!*" She grabbed her mug and took a gulping drink; liquid slopped over messily on the table as she set it down. "This can't be how it ends. I can't deal. I really can't."

Michael looked up at her and said softly, "If you can't, how do you think Shane feels?"

Eve shook her head. Her eyes were full of tears, again. "What are we going to *do*?"

"I don't know." He stared at her for a second, then seemed to come to a decision. "Eve, Amelie told me to report to Founder's Square tomorrow night, and to bring you all with me. It was an order, not a request."

"But—"

"The vampires are going to leave," he said. "All of them. She's handing over control of Morganville to the humans."

"Wait—what?" Eve wiped her eyes with the back of her hand. "What are you talking about? She can't— The vampires can't just *leave.* That's insane!"

"I'm telling you what she said. The vampires are leaving, and they're not coming back."

"Why?"

He shook his head. "I don't know, but whatever it is, it's worse than Bishop, and that's—about as bad as it gets."

Eve finally connected the dots. "And—if the vampires are leaving—what about you?"

He waited for a breath, then shook his head. "They won't let me take you with us," he said. "So I'm staying."

"But you'll be alone if you stay—I mean, *all* of them are going?"

"All but me. That means no blood bank, no help, and nothing but a town full of pissed-off humans. I'll be the one vampire left they can take it out on." Michael tried to smile. "But I'm not leaving you, Eve. Whatever happens. Especially not after— I can't lose you."

She slid out of her chair and into his lap, and he cradled her close, and it was really sweet and sad and private, and Claire felt like a voyeur, suddenly.

She drifted away. Looking at her own body was horrifying; it seemed only more and more empty while the minutes passed and the cops took more pictures. They were getting ready to take her out, she saw; there were paramedics waiting with a stretcher. *Good,* she thought. *Maybe once the body's gone, I can make them feel that I'm here.*

"You can't," a voice said. It was a faint voice, soft and featureless, and it seemed to come out of the air around her. Claire looked around the room. The police detective was there, and the bored and waiting paramedics. Her own corpse. Nobody else. "You can't make them feel you. You're too weak, and however fond of you it may be, the house is not connected to you by blood."

"And who are you?" Claire asked.

She saw a ripple out of the corner of her eye, like heat off a summer pavement, and turned that direction as a body formed out of thin air.

He was a nondescript little man, only a bit taller than she was, with thinning light-colored hair and a round face. He was wearing an old-fashioned vest and a high-collared white shirt, just like out of old Western movies. Some kind of banker or something.

"I'm Hiram Glass," he said. "And this is my house."

"*Your* house."

He shrugged and crossed his arms. "Well, my bones are buried in the foundation, and my blood was mixed with the mortar. Yes, my house. And the house of my family. *You* were never meant to be here. It's Claire, isn't it?"

"I . . . Yes." She was still unable to process the whole idea that there was a *dead man* in the basement. "What do you mean, I'm too weak?"

He smiled faintly. "You've got grit, but you're not a Glass. Michael brought you in, and that makes you part of the family, but not of the blood. The house likes you, and it tried to save you, but it can only do so much. It won't be like Michael. He had a chance at life, even after death, because he could draw on his connection with me. You don't have one."

"He never said anything about you," Claire said. She would have remembered that, if Michael had actually mentioned an ancestral ghost showing up during his off-hours.

"Well, he couldn't." The ghost shrugged. "Seeing as how I never spoke to him. There was no need. He was getting along just fine. Not like you, screaming and waking the dead, if you'll pardon the expression. Now, you just settle. You won't be able to get their attention, only mine, and I assure you, you don't want more of mine. You're an intruder here."

There was a slight dark edge to that last part. The edges of his image rippled, and Claire realized he was about to leave. "Wait!" She drifted closer to him. "Wait, please—what about at night? Michael said he was weaker in the day, stronger at night. Strong enough to actually have a real body. Can I—"

He was shaking his head now. "See that flesh and bone over there?" He pointed at her body, which was being lifted and put onto the stretcher. Claire had tried not to notice that. She felt a little sick, at least mentally—she couldn't be nauseated without having a stomach. "You're not a Glass. The house might have saved you, but that's *all* it can do, without my cooperation. You have no way to manifest yourself, night or day. *This* is what you have, or will ever have. Be grateful I allow you to stay. *Quietly.*"

And even though she yelled at him to wait, again, Hiram Glass shivered like vibrating glass, and vanished in a grayscale ripple.

I'm trapped, Claire realized with dawning horror. *Trapped alone. Just . . . observing.*

A real, genuine ghost.

She couldn't imagine how it could get any worse, really.

THIRTEEN

CLAIRE

☽

By the time the sun started to set, all the strangers were gone from the house. It was Michael, Shane, and Eve, and Claire, who hovered silently nearby—unseen and eternally separated.

Better if I'd died, she thought miserably. She'd never felt more alone. More completely useless.

"We have to call," Shane finally said in a voice as colorless and gray as Claire felt. She turned to see him holding his cell phone in both hands as he stared at the screen. "We have to tell her parents."

He didn't dial, not immediately. He just sat there as if he couldn't remember how to work the phone.

"Maybe Hannah's calling them," Eve said. "Maybe we should let her handle it—I mean, the police, they know how—"

"It's my responsibility." That was Michael, who stood up and took the phone out of Shane's hands. "I'm the one who let her stay here. I'm the one who told them I'd keep her safe." He sounded hoarse, but steady, and before Shane could object, he brought up the address book and hit a key. Shane slumped. Claire couldn't tell if he felt relieved, or just defeated.

But Michael frowned, checked the phone, and dialed again. Then a third time. "It's not going through," he said. "I'm getting a circuits-busy message. Hang on. I'm going to call Oliver." He did, then hung up. "Circuits busy."

Eve stood and picked up the house's old landline phone, big and clunky, hardwired into the wall. Claire could hear the discordant tones from where she drifted a few feet away. "This one's out, too," Eve said. "What's going on?"

"Check the Internet," Michael said, and Eve went upstairs. She was gone only a moment before she came down again.

"Out," she said. "No connection. They've cut us off."

"They?" Shane asked blankly. "They, who?"

Michael took out his own cell and tried it, then shook his head. "It's not just you—it's me as well, and mine's on the vampire system. Cell phones, landlines, and Internet—it's all down."

"Why would they do that?"

"At a guess, they're getting ready to leave Morganville, and they don't want anyone to be making plans for trouble," Michael said. He dropped his useless cell phone on the table. "It's probably wrong that I feel relieved right now."

They all froze as a knock came at the front door. After a silent exchange of looks, Michael went to answer it, and Claire went with him, just because it was something to do.

Outside the door was a vampire policeman, dressed in a big raincoat, and his police cap protected by a rain bonnet. It was still pouring, Claire saw. The yard outside was a sea of muddy water.

"You need to bring your charges to the meeting tomorrow night, Mr. Glass," he said. "We're going house to house to remind everyone, and we'll be checking all buildings tomorrow to ensure full compliance. Everyone at Founder's Square at dusk tomorrow."

"What if we don't want to go?" Michael asked. "Our friend died today."

The cop gave him a long look, and said, "Nobody stays away. I'm sorry for your loss, but if you don't show, we'll come and get you. Orders of the Founder."

He tapped the front of his hat with a finger in an abbreviated salute, and walked away, heading for the next house.

"This is not good," Michael murmured. "Not good at all."

Claire had to agree with him, for all the use it was; she didn't want them to leave the house. Especially, she didn't want them to leave her alone. What if they never came back? What if she was trapped here all alone with just Hiram Glass for company, forever? That seemed selfish, but she was terrified at the very thought.

Michael shut the door and locked it, and stayed there a moment, head down. Then he whispered, very quietly, "Claire, if you *are* here, please tell us. Please. God, I hope you are, because I'm scared. I'm scared for all of us."

Michael was scared. God.

That made her even more panicked.

Think, she ordered herself. Clearly, she couldn't expect any help from the head ghost of the Glass House, who was actually kind of an ass; she was going to have to find a way out of this herself. As she thought about it, she drifted back down the hall, into the living room, past the couch where Shane and Eve sat together, silently holding hands . . . and then to the spot where her body had fallen. *Come on,* she told herself. *Think.*

She felt a warm surge of power condense around her, like an

insubstantial hug. The house. Hiram had said the house liked her; clearly, the house and Hiram had different opinions. It was trying to tell her something.

It shoved her a little, pushing her toward the wall.

The portal.

No, I can't do it. It's impossible.

But if it was, what did it hurt to try?

Claire focused on the blank wall—on the textured paint, on the gray color, on every flaw and imperfection.

Come on. Come on. . . .

She sensed a flicker of power, almost a sense of surprise, and then the portal responded.

And when it gradually misted open, she smiled, just a little, even though nobody could really see it.

She looked around. Eve was facing away, and Michael was still in the other room. Shane sat slumped on the couch, facing the silent TV. Nobody was looking at the portal, which was too bad, because at least they'd know *something* was odd.

This may not work, she told herself. *You may not come out of this.*

But really . . . would it matter? She was already gone, as far as those she loved were concerned.

If the physics of the portals had been complicated before, she'd be *years* working out how the potential energy of a dead soul could possibly travel through wormholes. *Well, if nothing else, it'll keep me occupied with calculations for as long as I live.*

And then Claire, ghost of a dead girl, stepped through the portal and was lost in the dark.

She opened her eyes, and she was in Myrnin's lab. It was deserted, and it was *trashed*. . . . Someone had scattered books everywhere, ripped some up, and an entire lab table had been thrown all the way across the room, smashing the marble top into pieces.

So, pretty normal, then.

"Frank!" she said. She felt thinner here, almost fading, and realized that she was still connected to the house, through the portal. If the portal failed . . .

. . . She'd be gone along with it.

"Frank Collins! Can you hear me?"

She felt a sudden buzz of power, and Frank's image formed in front of her, one grayscale pixel at a time. He blinked. "Anybody there?"

Oh. He couldn't see her. Great. "Frank, can you hear me?" She yelled it, loud as she could, and Frank's image flickered, as if interference had ripped it apart for a moment.

"Jesus, Claire, turn it down," he said. "Where are you?"

"Right here!" She was so happy to be communicating she felt like kissing him—only that wouldn't work, on so many levels. "I'm right here, in front of you. I'm sort of—"

"Dead?" he asked. "I heard the chatter. Guess saying I'm sorry seems a little redundant, since you're actually talking to me."

"I need your help."

"Nothing I can do for you, cupcake. Dead is dead, although I have to admit, pretty big achievement since you're audible."

"Not for me," Claire said. "There's a gathering at Founder's Square tomorrow night. Why?"

"Can't say," Frank Collins said. His image flickered again. "Move back; you're screwing up my projection."

She floated back, just a little. "Can't say, or won't say?"

"What did I just tell you?"

"So you've been told not to talk about it." He didn't answer, which she supposed was answer enough. "Frank . . . Amelie once told me that if she ever decided that the Morganville experiment was over, she would take it all down. Is that what we're talking about?" More silence. She felt thinner and more faded, as if pieces of her were slowly streaming away into the dark. "*Frank!* Is she going to destroy the town?"

"She's setting the humans free, and the vampires are leaving town," he said. "Upside: Myrnin's going to turn me off, and I can get on with dying the right way, finally. Downside—well, there's always a downside."

Talking to Frank was like talking in circles. "Where's Myrnin?"

He shrugged. "He tore ass out of here to see *you*. Hasn't come back."

"Don't pretend you don't know. I know you've got surveillance everywhere."

Frank raised his eyebrows, and smiled crookedly. "All right. He's at Founder's Square, with the Big Cheese. I don't have eyes inside her offices, but they frog-marched him straight there and he hasn't come out."

That . . . wasn't good. Myrnin was the only real hope she had. "Frank, when you see him, I need you to tell him that I'm still here. Hanging on. That he wasn't wrong. Do you understand? He said he might be able to help me. Tell him I really, really need him now." She swallowed. "Can you call Shane? Tell him . . . tell him I'm still in the house?"

He shook his head. "Can't, sweetheart. I would if I could, but the comm system is screwed right now. They pulled fuses at the source, cut connections. I can't activate the speaker on his phone unless he comes here. I'm limited, too."

She was getting stretched too thin; she could feel the pull from the Glass House getting more tenuous. If it broke, she'd vanish like a puff of smoke on the wind.

"Frank! Please, you have to help me!"

He slowly shook his head. "You haven't thought this through," he said. "I guess that's understandable, all things considered; it's been a big day for you. Suppose Myrnin gets the message that you're still around. Suppose he comes and works some kind of crazy magic and makes contact with you. You're still trapped. Only way Michael got free of that place was to turn vampire." His rippling image stared through the air, not quite focused on her. "You ready to be a vamp, Claire? Full-on bloodsucking freak? Because I can tell you, it was the worst damn thing that ever happened to me, in a lifetime of bad things. And I don't want that for you. Or for my son. Better he lose you now. Better he not get false hope."

"But—" She really, *really* couldn't stay. Claire began drifting back to the portal, already worried that the cord connecting her to the Glass House was so thin. Or that Frank just might decide to cut it by slamming the door himself. "It doesn't have to be that way. . . ."

"I believe it does. Think about it," he said, as she fell backward into the dark. "Do the right thing."

"But—please tell Myrnin; tell *someone!*"

He shook his head, again. "It's better this way, Claire. Trust me. Just . . . let go."

Claire snapped out of the portal and into the Glass House's monochromatic living room, and energy rushed back into her. She felt an overwhelming relief, and a follow-on fear, because she hadn't realized just how weak she'd let herself become, through the looking glass.

Whether Frank was going to help her or not . . . that was anyone's guess. He probably didn't even know himself.

But as last hopes went, it was shaky, at best.

It got late. Eve made sandwiches, which the three living housemates ate in silence—or rather, Michael and Eve ate them. Shane just picked at his, and then left the table without a word. Michael and Eve watched him go, silently asking each other what to do, and then Michael said, "Better let him go."

Claire wasn't so sure that was the right thing.

She drifted upstairs—easy, since all she had to do was concentrate on going up, and suddenly she was passing between floors and seeing all the old wood and wiring and rat droppings and spiders hidden in the walls, and ugh, that wasn't the best trip ever. She was relieved to be floating in the silent upstairs hallway. *We need an exterminator,* she thought, but that really wasn't the biggest problem any of them had at the moment, truthfully.

Shane's door was open, and he wasn't inside. She looked in, checking the other side of the bed, and even drifting into the closet, but unless he was hiding under the leaning pile of laundry, he hadn't come here for his solitude.

The bathroom was empty. She didn't bother with Eve's room, or Michael's; she knew where he was, after she thought for a second.

She drifted through the closed door of her own bedroom, the one at the end of the hall, and found herself standing in twilight stillness. Outside, the sun was setting; this side of the house was already facing the night, and the sky beyond the window was a deep, dark blue.

Shane was sitting on the floor with his back against the bedroom door, in the dark. His knees were drawn up to his chest, and his head was back, resting against the hard wood. Somehow, she expected him to be crying, but he wasn't, not even silently; he was just sitting, eyes open and dry, staring off into the darkness. She hadn't made her bed, she realized; it was still a mess, sheets and blankets twisted from the last time she'd bounced up from it. Stupid to be embarrassed about that now, or about the laundry sitting in the corner, or about the nightgown she'd left flung on the floor when she'd gotten dressed.

"Shane?" she said. She didn't try to scream it; she knew that wouldn't get her anywhere except in Hiram Glass's bad books, again. "I'm so sorry. I wish I could do something to let you know that I'm here. I didn't want to leave you like this; it was stupid and—"

She froze, because his head had turned, and he was staring right at her. Joy bolted through her, but then it turned gray and faded as she realized he wasn't looking *at* her but *through* her.

At the nightgown lying on the floor.

He got up and grabbed it. For some bizarre reason she expected him to fold it up, maybe put it on the bed, but instead, he returned to the door, sank down in exactly the same spot, and held her nightgown in both hands.

He put it to his face and drew in a deep, shaking breath. "Help me. Please. I can't do this anymore. I can't. God, Claire, please." She'd never heard Shane like this before. He sounded . . . broken. Worse than when his father had died, worse than when he'd discovered what use Myrnin had made Frank into for the lab.

It didn't sound like Shane at all.

She settled in next to him, wishing she could touch him, hold him, make it right.

Finally, Shane sighed, as if he'd made some decision, and took something out of his jacket pocket. She didn't see what it was, not at first; it was just an angular shape in the dark.

And then, as he raised it to look at it, the shape turned into a *gun*. A semiautomatic pistol.

"Shane, where did you get a gun?" she blurted, and realized that was *so* not the question; his dad would have had them, and probably supplied him with an arsenal back in the bad old days. He'd always had a surprising amount of weaponry, but she'd never seen the gun before.

The problem wasn't where he'd gotten the gun.

The problem was that Shane was sitting in the dark, with a gun, and he was holding her nightgown to his chest.

"No!" She bolted upright, as much as an insubstantial ghost could, and faced him straight on. "No, you *listen to me,* Shane Collins, you can't do this. *You can't.* You hear me? This is not you. You're a *fighter*!"

He was staring at the gun, turning it to catch the dim light as if it were some beautiful jewel. There was no particular expression on his face, but she could sense the suffering inside him. This was real. As real as it got. He wasn't trying to get attention and sympathy; it wasn't some cry for help.

It was despair.

"I'm tired," he murmured. "I'm tired of fighting. And I want to see you again."

It *sounded* like he was replying to her. She knew he wasn't, but she couldn't stop herself from trying. Her whole insubstantial form was vibrating with terror and panic. "I know; I know you are. You've fought for all of us, for so long, and you keep losing us; I *know*. But you can't do this. I'm still here, Shane. I'm still here for you and I will always be here—*please*. . . ."

"You're not," he said. This time, there was absolutely no doubt that he was replying to her, although he didn't *know* he was—it was as if he was talking to himself.

He thought he was *imagining her.*

"You're not here, and you'll never be here again," he was saying in that dull, empty voice. He checked the clip on the handgun, racked the slide with a harsh metallic click, and then sat quietly with it held in his hand. "You're just in my head."

"I'm not." She knelt down facing him and concentrated on making him feel her presence. Believe her. "I'm here, Shane. I'm trapped in the house. Please tell me you can hear me."

"It's a bullshit lie. Just because Myrnin said it doesn't make it true."

"No, it *is* true, and as long as there's even a chance that I'm here, that I can come back, you can't do this, understand? You *can't.*"

"Claire." A very faint curve of a smile touched his lips, and his eyes shone—not with happiness, she realized, but with tears. "You got in my head, you really did. And my heart. And I'm sorry."

He raised the gun.

"No!" She screamed it, and lunged at him, *into* him. "No, Shane, *don't!*"

She felt a surge of white-hot power ripple through her, felt the same world-ending snap of lightning that had ended her life, and suddenly—

Suddenly she was sitting in Shane's lap, holding on to his hand with both of hers, forcing the gun up and away from his head.

Sunset. It was sunset, and she had just . . . for a moment . . . become real again.

Shane yelled, and his hand opened. He dropped the gun, which bounced away on the carpet, and for a frozen second he just stared at her.

She let go of his arm, and he slowly lowered it, still staring.

And then his arms went around her.

Or tried to.

They went right through her.

She was fading again.

"No—" He grabbed for her. "Claire! Claire!"

"I'm still here," she shouted. It came out as a thin whisper of sound, but she knew he heard it; she saw the flare of life and hope in his eyes. "Don't give up!"

He reached out again, and she reached, too. Their fingers caressed. Hers looked like a faint outline in smoke. "God," he breathed. "You are here. The crazy fool was right; you *are* here. Claire, if you can hear me, I'm going to get you back. *We're* going to get you back. I swear."

He lunged to his feet and realized he was still holding her nightgown. He kissed the fabric and put it on the bed, laid his hand there in the hollow where she'd slept, and then grabbed the gun up from where it had fallen on the floor.

He pulled the clip, racked the slide, and caught the bullet as it ejected. Then he opened the top drawer of her bureau, moved some things, and put all three things—gun, clip, and bullet—inside.

He shut the drawer and said, "You saw all that, didn't you? Sorry. I'm sorry. I just— Claire, if you can hear me, can you do something? Make a noise?"

She concentrated. Maybe it was the fact that the sun was down that had changed things, but by working really hard, she managed to bump a small china cat that was sitting on her nightstand, a ridiculous yellow thing with a fake feather tail that Eve had bought her at a garage sale. It tipped over and rolled.

Shane turned that direction, and his fierce smile flashed like a blade. "Damn," he said. "You really are here. I didn't just make that up."

She drifted closer to him, close enough that if she'd been flesh and blood, they would have been embracing.

And he shivered. The smile didn't waver. "Oh God, Claire, I wish I could hold you. *God.* Look, I just—it was too much, with my dad and my mom and my sister. I felt—I just couldn't—"

"I know," she said. She wanted more than anything to be solid again, to hold him and kiss him and give him the hope he so desperately needed. "Can you hear me?"

"I—think so. It's like I'm imagining you. Not words, exactly, but I hear you." He laughed shakily. "Michael had this down, but I guess he had practice, right? You're learning on the job."

"You can't live for me," she said, and meant it. "It's important, Shane. You can't live just for me, and you can't die because you lost me. I need you to be stronger than that. Do you understand?"

He was silent for a moment, and she wasn't sure she'd gotten it across at all. There was a strange expression in his eyes, and his smile had faded to a memory.

"I know," he finally said. "I'm sorry. I got tired of being strong, Claire. I don't want to be alone."

"You're not alone. Michael and Eve are here, too."

He nodded and took a deep breath. "And you're here," he said. "Somehow. You're here."

"I'm not leaving you."

"Then that's enough. We're going to get you back." He was silent for a beat, then said, "You—won't tell them what I tried to do, will you?"

"Not unless you try it again."

"I won't," he said. He looked down, just as he would have if he could have actually seen her pressed close. "You're right there, aren't you?"

"Yes."

His arms slowly came up and around where her body would have been, holding her.

Holding air.

"Then I'm not letting go," he said.

And despite everything that had happened in the past twenty-four hours, that felt . . . peaceful.

Convincing Michael and Eve of her continued existence was more difficult than Claire had expected.

"Oh, come *on,* dude, you were a ghost when I moved in here!" Shane said. They were standing downstairs in the dusty parlor, with Claire floating unseen in the corner (which, by the way, really needed vacuuming). "Totally missing during the day. And you *don't believe* that I just saw her?"

"Shane—" Eve stepped forward, hands outstretched, looking distressed but determined. "Sweetie, you really have to understand that you're under a lot of stress—"

"Oh, you didn't just call me *sweetie.* Eve, it's me. Shane. You've called me a lot of things, but *sweetie*? Knock it off." He swung around toward Michael again, who had his arms folded, head down. "Seriously, can you not just believe me? Because it's true. I can *hear* her!"

"I don't hear her. And it's after sunset. If she's been saved by the house, why isn't she here?"

Shane took in a deep, calming breath. "She *is,*" he said. "Claire, help me out, here. Say something. *Do* something."

"They can't hear me," she said. She'd been trying everything, but whatever power had zipped for her at sunset had been temporary; she couldn't make them understand, and even with all her concentration she couldn't touch physical objects anymore, much less tip something over. "I don't have enough power, I guess. But you can hear me, and that's what's important. Keep believing, Shane. Please."

Michael was talking over her. "Look, man, I want to believe you. I do. I'd be happy if there was *anything* left of her, even a ghost . . . but she's not here. It's my house. I'd know."

"Bullshit!" Claire shouted, and Shane laughed.

"She just called bullshit," he said, when Eve and Michael both gave him worried looks. "Honest. She did."

"I'm—really spooked about you, honey," Eve said slowly. "Seriously, you can't hear her. You can't."

"Because she's dead? Don't call me honey, or baby, or sweetie, or chocolate-covered marshmallow doughnuts, or whatever the code-word-for-crazy phrase of the day is, because I am *not making this up!*" Shane shouted it this time. "She stopped me—" He paused, course-corrected, and said, "She knocked over that damn yellow cat thing in her room. I asked her to do it, and she did."

"Maybe you should get some rest," Michael said.

"Maybe *you* should stop treating me like I have brain damage! Look, for once, just *trust me*. You know how much it makes me want to vomit to say this, but Myrnin was right. The house saved her—it's just that she's not as strong as you were, or the connection's not there, or something. I *know* she's here."

Michael stared at him, a frown forming on his forehead, and as Eve started to say something, he reached out and silenced her with a hand on her arm. "Wait," he said. "What time was this?"

"I can hear her *now*, man."

"When you saw her. When she knocked over the cat."

Shane thought about it a moment, then said, "Sunset. Around then. It was already dark in her room."

"Sunset," Michael repeated. "You're sure."

Shane shrugged. "I wasn't exactly watching the clock, but yeah, I think so."

"What?" Eve asked. She sank down into one of the faded parlor chairs and stared up at him with a mixture of dread and hope. "What is it?"

"Sunset was when I manifested in physical form," Michael said. "Maybe—if he's right—that's when Claire can make herself known. A little. Shane, you're sure—"

"If you ask me if I'm imagining it again, I'm going to punch you out, Dead Man Walking."

Michael raised his eyebrows and glanced at Eve. "He doesn't sound crazy."

"Er," she clarified, "crazier. He sounds like he's back to normal, which is baseline crazy."

"Says the girl dressed up in formal Goth mourning," Shane said. "Seriously, who buys a black lace veil? You keep that on hand for special occasions, like prom and kids' birthdays?"

Claire felt a laugh bubbling up. This . . . this was what she'd wanted. Life. Normal life, even if she wasn't connected the way she had been.

That's next. I'll make it back. I have to make it back.

Eve swept back the filmy net covering that had been over her face. "Excuse me, but my best friend just *died*, right here in our house! And you're mocking me?"

"She's not gone, Eve. And that is one cracked-out fashion statement, even for you."

Michael wasn't getting sidetracked, Claire realized. He was still watching Shane, and even if he believed, he was still wary. "You said she stopped you. From doing what?"

Shane's body language changed. His shoulders squared, and

hunched forward a little, as if he was protecting himself from an attack. "Nothing."

Michael knew; Claire could see it. He'd known Shane a long time; he'd seen him hit bottom even before Claire had met the boy. He'd been there when Shane had been dragged out of his burning house, screaming for his sister.

If anybody could guess what Shane had been about to do, it was Michael, and from his expression, Shane knew that, too.

"You're not going to do nothing again, are you?" Michael asked. "Because if you are, come talk to me. Please."

Shane nodded, one short jerk.

"What?" Eve asked, mystified.

Shane changed the subject, fast. "Claire? Look, can you try again? See if you can make some noise. Anything."

It was almost midnight, and Claire was heartily sick of trying, but she concentrated, again, and pushed at the dusty vase sitting on the even-dustier table nearby.

It shivered, just a little.

Just enough to make a soft scraping sound.

Eve cried out and jumped out of her chair, staring at the vase; she'd been the closest to it. "Did you hear it?" she asked. She picked up the vase and put it back down. "It moved. I heard it!"

"Eve, chill," Michael said. "If she did move it, that wasn't much. It means she's really weak, if that's the best she can do even at night."

"And?" Shane asked. He took a step forward. "What?"

Michael shook his head. He picked up the vase, ran his fingers over the dusty surface, and put it back down. "Claire, if you can hear me, do it again. Try."

She concentrated so hard it felt like she might collapse into a tiny white dot, like a dying star, and the vase shivered and rocked. It wasn't much, but it was enough.

Michael steadied it, and smiled. A real, warm smile of relief. He closed his eyes for a few seconds, then opened them and said, "Thank you."

"I was right, wasn't I?" Eve suddenly shrieked and jumped like a cheerleader, waving her hands in the air. The black mourning veil floated in the air behind her like a cloud. "Yes! Yes! Yes!"

"Excuse me, *you* were right? I've been yelling at you guys for half an hour while you gave me the sad eyes and counseling!" Shane shouted back, but he was grinning now. He ran at Michael and hugged him fiercely, then Eve, catching her in midair as she squealed in delight. He spun her around. "She's here. *She's really here!*"

Claire wanted to collapse on the couch, but being insubstantial, collapsing was sort of theoretical. She settled for hovering close to it, and moved quickly as Shane threw himself in a relieved, boneless slouch on that end of the cushions. He covered his face with his hands for a moment. When he looked up again, his eyes were bright with tears. "She's here," he said again, more softly. "Thank you, God."

"Claire? Do it again, with the vase," Eve said. She knelt down and stared intently at it. "Go on, do it!"

She reached deep again, but there wasn't anything left, really . . . and then she felt a dim, whispered trickle of power. *Of course.* The house had power, loads of it. She might not be a Glass, but she was something to it—it had saved her. And if she was careful, maybe she could siphon off just a little. . . .

She could actually *see* the power running through the boards and beams now, a close-knit cage of light. There, right in the middle, was a particularly bright, pulsing thread, like . . . well, like a blood vessel.

She touched it and got a shock, a small one, not the kind that hurt, but a feeling of stability and warmth.

Then her fingers sank into the flow of power, and the vase *flew* off the table and bashed into the wall and shattered into pieces, and Eve gasped and fell back, staring. She shot to her feet and did a victory dance. "Yes! Yes, that's my girl!"

Claire felt a ripple of power, and when she looked back, Hiram Glass was standing behind her. "Stop," he said. "Take your hands *off that. Now.*"

She did, and the sudden removal of that surge of energy left her feeling even weaker and less real than before. Claire felt all the joy in her melt away, even while her Glass House family was celebrating.

Hiram was *angry*.

"You stupid, stupid creature," he hissed. "Don't *ever* touch my lifeblood again. Do you understand? You are *not* a Glass. You don't *belong* here, no matter what the house thinks. It's a dumb beast. A pet. It has no intelligence. *I* say who lives and dies, not the house, and I don't choose to help *you*."

"I'm sorry," she said. She hoped Shane couldn't hear her now—or hear the dread in her voice. There was something awful about Hiram now, something cold and black and violent. "I didn't mean—"

Hiram gave her a vicious, dry smile. "You won't last," he said. "You're already beginning to feel it. You're like the afterimage of the sun—a ghost, burned in for a moment, but after a few blinks it's gone. The house might have saved you temporarily, but you're just a memory without my help. And memories fade, Claire. They fade."

No, that couldn't be true. It couldn't. She looked at Shane, laughing, knuckle-bumping Michael. Eve was twirling in delight, catching Michael in her arms and kissing him.

This couldn't be temporary. It just couldn't.

Hiram gave her another bitter little smile when she said it, shrugged, and rippled into nothing.

He didn't even bother to convince her.

That, more than anything else, made her sickly sure he wasn't lying.

Nobody slept. Claire couldn't move objects anymore, no matter how hard she tried, and the effort exhausted her—but ghosts, apparently, didn't need unconsciousness like humans did. She stayed awake, drifting, watching as her friends broke out the cherished stash of Shiner and each had a beer in celebration.

"This is weird," Shane said, swigging one as Michael popped the cap on his own. "I mean, seriously. She died today. We should be—"

"She's not dead," Michael said. "And we'll get her back. You convinced me, man." He held up his hand, and Shane high-fived it. "But we need Myrnin. He's the one who said he could do it."

"I have his cell number," Eve volunteered. "Claire gave it to me. We could call?"

"Phones are out," Michael reminded her. She looked crushed. "I'll have to go get him."

"What about the portal thingie? Can you go through—Wait." Eve turned to Shane, frowning. "*You* went through, didn't you? How'd you do that?"

Shane shrugged. "Don't know exactly. I'm not sure I could do it again."

"Okay, Michael?"

He shook his head. "I don't have the right stuff, I guess. I've tried. Even if I get it to open, it's just black. Congrats, butthead; you can do something I can't."

"I'll add it to the list," Shane said loftily. "So, you want me to give it a shot?"

"It won't do any good," Claire said. She had to concentrate harder than before, and she wasn't sure Shane heard her, so she repeated it. He jerked and looked off into empty air, not remotely close to where she was floating. "Myrnin's not there. Amelie has him at Founder's Square."

"Say that again," Shane said. "Something about Myrnin?"

She composed herself and tried again. It *was* getting harder. Maybe that was just because Hiram had spooked her so hard, but she didn't think so. "Myrnin's at Founder's Square," she said again, very distinctly. She looked at the hot, burning lattice of power that ran through the walls of the Glass House with real longing, but she didn't dare try to touch it again. Hiram would know.

"Founder's Square." Shane had shut his eyes to listen, and now he opened them and looked over at Michael. "Claire says he's at Founder's Square."

Michael tipped the bottle and drank about half of it in three long gulps, then put it down. "I can't take the easy way," he said. "I have to go in person, get him, and bring him back."

"But—what if he won't come?" Eve said, wide-eyed, as she anxiously turned her unsipped beer in her hands. "Michael, what if Amelie won't let *you* come back, either? Don't go. I have a wicked bad feeling."

"I'll come back," he promised her. "How could I leave you?" He kissed her, long and sweet. It left her breathless, with splashes of color high in her pale cheeks.

"Maybe we should go along," Shane said. "Strength in numbers, man."

Michael smiled at Eve and shook his head. "After she bitch-slapped the Founder? Not a good idea. The two of you don't just have baggage with the vampires—you've got baggage trains. I go alone, and I come back with Myrnin."

He went into the kitchen, where he picked up his keys, and then he looked around and said, "Claire? Are you here?"

She tried doing the cold-spot thing, but clearly, she wasn't powerful enough now to pull it off. Even moving through him didn't work.

"I didn't want to tell them, but—if I don't come back, Claire, you have to find a way to stay with Shane. Somehow. Understand? And take care of Eve. I need you to promise me."

He wasn't confident now, not like he'd been in front of the others. He knew it was dangerous, going out there. Deadly dangerous.

"I will," she said. He still couldn't hear her. Even though it was not a good idea, she reached out and touched the house's power line, soaking up energy. She heard her voice actually ring and echo here in the black-and-white world as she said, "I'll do everything I can, Michael. I love you. Take care."

He heard her. She saw the relief wash over him, and he smiled, and then he was gone.

Claire let go of the pulsing latticework of power, and immediately felt exhausted. Thin. *Faded.*

She saw a flash of color—*color,* in this black-and-white world—and pirouetted in midair to face it.

Leaning against the closed kitchen door, cutting her off from Shane and Eve, was Hiram. The color came from the red brocade vest he was wearing, and the gold gleam of a watch chain. He looked almost real, almost *more* real than her live friends in their black-and-white world.

"I warned you," he said. "I warned you not to touch that again."

"Michael needed to hear me."

"He's running off on a fool's errand, and if he dies out there, I can't save him again," Hiram said. "That's your fault, girl. He's hell-bent on saving something that ain't even real anymore."

"I'm real!" she snapped. "More real than you."

He looked down at himself, in all the glorious Technicolor, and Claire felt stupid saying it. Of *course* he was more real, or at least had more power. "I said it before: the house likes you. Doesn't mean *I* have to like you. It's all instinct. I'm the brain, Claire. And I've decided you're dangerous. You keep blundering about, touching things you're not allowed to handle. You're a toddler in a room full of glass."

"Don't you mean I'm dangerous to *you*?" she asked.

Hiram smiled, but it was a terribly cold kind of thing. "I should have ripped you up and thrown you out when you first crossed over."

Claire backed off instinctively. There was something real about him, even though he was a ghost, just like her. Hiram had *power.* More than she'd thought. What had he said? Something about his bones in the foundations and his blood in the mortar . . . ugh. But that would make him *very* strong, she guessed. And very territorial. He was part of the house, but the house was still something else, with its own will. The house had saved her, and Hiram didn't agree.

Dangerous.

He was drifting in her direction, even though he wasn't seeming to move. Claire hesitated for a second, and as she did, he rushed at her. She had the absolute certainty that if he touched her, got hold of her with those strong, grabbing hands, he would rip her to pieces.

Claire shrieked and dropped straight through the floor. It was all she could think of . . . and suddenly she was falling through wood, dirty pipes, a totally startled rat, a freak-out number of cockroaches, and into the dark, creepy basement, which, with the lights out, was *super-awful* creepy.

It was also dangerous. She heard Hiram's soft, bodiless laugh. "I'm in the *foundations,* girl. You think you can fight me better down here?"

Claire wasn't actually sure she could fight him at all, but he was absolutely right: this was the *last* place she wanted to try. Instead, she arrowed herself up, fast, blurring through the floor, through the parlor, up again into the second floor, and . . .

. . . Into the secret room, which was directly overhead but on the attic level. This was Amelie's retreat, from when the house had originally been built (Hiram, she guessed, had been around even then). It had always been Claire's special retreat when things got intense, and now she hesitated there, trembling, waiting for Hiram to come screaming through the walls after her.

But he didn't. She listened, she extended her new and very awkward senses (this being-dead thing took work), and she sensed . . . nothing. It was as if this room existed in a different house altogether. It even *felt* different . . . and, she realized with a sudden shock, it definitely looked different, because the lights were on, and she could see the dusty red velvet of the sofa, and the brown wood, and the colored jewellike glass of the Tiffany lamps.

Color.

When she closed her eyes, she could actually feel Hiram, but he was outside the room. He'd hit the floor and bounced off, and now he was circling around like a shark, looking for a way inside.

Somehow, Amelie's influence made this a refuge not just on the physical level but on this level, too.

She was safe, as long as she stayed here.

Not only that, but she could actually see herself, like a very faint transparent image, and when she tried sitting down on the couch, she actually felt gravity.

It was as close to real as she'd been all day, it seemed, and she curled up on velvet she could *almost* feel, and closed her eyes.

Michael will be back, she told herself. *Soon. And Myrnin will be with him.*

She was going to get out of this.

She *had* to get out of this.

Claire didn't sleep, exactly, but the stillness and soft peace of the room made her . . . drift. When she heard the snap of the lock on the door, though, she came bolt upright on the couch in terror.

Hiram had a way in.

Only . . . he didn't. It wasn't Hiram at all. She heard footsteps on the stairs, and then Shane was standing there in the room, saying, "Claire?" He sounded anxious. "Claire, are you here?"

"Yes," she said.

His head snapped around, and his eyes widened. *He heard me. No, he sees me!*

"Claire," Shane said, and the relief in his voice was intense. He hesitated for a second, then pointed at her. "Don't move." He clumped down the stairs and yelled, "I found her! She's in here!"

"Okay!" Eve yelled back. "Um, do you want me to come up, or—?"

"No," he said. "Not right now."

"I'm taking a shower, then."

Eve, Claire thought with a smile, always showered when she was nervous and worried. She was probably *very* worried about Michael.

Shane closed the door to the hall and said, "There goes the hot water." He walked back up the steps and looked at the couch, at *her.* "I can see you," he said.

"Really? I'm solid?" She looked down at herself. She wasn't, really, at least to her own eyes. More like a genuine ghost—there, not there.

Shane reached out slowly and touched her arm, and where he touched . . . where he touched, it felt real. Looked real. "Yeah," he said. It sounded very soft, and not very steady. "Solid." He sat down on the couch and, before she could even think about moving, grabbed her and hugged her close. Where he touched her, where her body pressed against his, everything felt right again, as if he was anchoring her back into the world. He kissed her, and it was just exactly right, all the sensations, all the tastes, the warm velvety feel of his lips . . . so amazing.

She didn't exactly know how it had happened, but he was stretched out on the couch, and she was lying on top of him, and it was so delicious and sweet and wonderful. His fingers stroked through her hair, and it swept down to brush his face.

"You make me real," she said, in wonder. "It's you."

He didn't say anything. Not with words. It was all just a blur after that, beautiful and strange and perfect, and she didn't want to let go of him, not ever.

But when she finally opened her eyes again and looked, she realized that there was something wrong. Shane was asleep next to her, curled tight against her, but he was . . . faded. The colors of his skin, his hair, they were pale now. Almost as black-and-white as they had been downstairs, *out* of this room.

And she was brighter. More vivid.

She'd taken it from him.

Claire stood up and backed away from the couch. Shane mumbled and reached for her, but she stayed where she was, at arm's length. "I can't," she whispered. "It's—the room, it's *Amelie's* room; it's doing something to us. . . ."

"It's making you real," he said. "It's okay."

"No, no, it's not. You're fading, Shane. And I can't do this."

She looked real now, and felt real, but not at this cost. Not ever.

"Claire . . ." Shane tried to get up, but he was weak, and he almost fell. He sank back on the couch, looking pale. "Whoa. Dizzy."

"You have to go," she said. "You have to leave me here. I'll be okay until Myrnin comes. Please, Shane. You can't stay."

"I'll go," he said. "But only if you give me one last kiss."

She didn't want to, but she couldn't help herself, either. He stood up, braced himself, and walked toward her. She backed away, but the wall behind her stopped her; if she went beyond it, Hiram was there, waiting.

Shane kissed her. It was hot and lovely and full of promises, and then he stepped back, smiling.

But he looked even more faded.

"Go," she whispered. "Go *now,* Shane. Please. I love you, and *you have to go.*"

He picked up his jeans and stepped into them, grabbed his shirt, and threw it on as well. "I'm not losing you," he said. "I'm telling you that. I'm not."

She smiled at him, and watched him go.

Then she stretched out on the velvet couch, in the ghost of his warmth, and just for a while, she closed her eyes and dreamed.

FOURTEEN

MICHAEL

The thing most people forget, when they start talking about being a vampire, is that it's lonely. It's *supposed* to be lonely. Vampires are predators. They're more like tigers roaming territories than they are wolves, who hunt together in a cooperative group. Tigers don't form packs. They're alone, and they're supposed to be.

Morganville had always felt forced and artificial to me when I was a breathing human, but now . . . now I realized how forced and artificial it was on the night side of the equation, too. Having so many vampires pressed this close together, and close to their natural prey, and then hemming it all in with rules and social behaviors . . . I don't think any of the humans, not even the ones who were closest to us, suspected how hard that really was.

I'd adjusted better than most because I'd started out my supernatural life as a ghost, trapped in my own house. I'd become a vampire only out of necessity, because it was the only way to regain my freedom—even a part of it. And by that time, I'd gotten used to having the heartbeats and lives of my friends around me.

I'd adjusted to Eve being so close, so alive, so *willing*. Mostly, at least.

But it wasn't easy. It was never, ever that. Still, I'd thought I'd known what I was getting into. I'd thought that all this was a stable, manageable existence. Morganville, where the vamps had forced themselves to be civilized.

But when I got to Founder's Square, I began to realize that it was all bullshit.

All of it.

There were vampires present—always were—and they were shutting down their stores. Many of these had been open all night, catering to hard-core adventurous people with pulses, and those without, but every building I saw was shuttered. The vampires were locking doors, clearing out valuables and cash, and getting ready for the orderly shutdown of our entire town.

I stopped a vampire I knew slightly—Breana—and said, "No humans around?"

She gave me a look, as if I were mentally handicapped. "No," she said. "Of course not. They're confined to their homes until we're gone." She reached up and grabbed a metal accordion gate and pulled it down in a shriek of cranky metal. It banged in place on the pavement, shedding flakes of orange rust, and she secured it in place with a thick padlock. "Do you have your seat assignment? No? Go to Amelie's office. Her assistant is giving out passes. You'll need one for the evacuation." Breana pocketed the keys and walked away carrying a metal case, probably containing all of the most valuable items from her jewelry store. Vampires tended to travel light, and invest in tangible wealth, something easily traded.

The lights in her store went out, but I could still read the sign she'd put up in the window.

CLOSED PERMANENTLY.

I headed for Amelie's office. I'd told Shane I'd bring Myrnin back, but I knew this was going to be a test . . . a big one. A test of exactly where I stood in Morganville, and with Amelie, and it was going to take every ounce of inherited respect that I got from being the grandson of Samuel Glass, and the last child of one of the first human families in town, to even get her to open the door.

My chances of being able to actually bring Myrnin home with me? Small. So were my chances of being able to leave myself. But I had to try, for Shane, and for all of us. We needed Claire. I hadn't realized how much she held us all together until I'd seen her lying there, still and pale . . . until she was gone, and I felt everything we had collapsing. Shane couldn't make it, not without hope.

Claire was his hope. I guess in a way she was mine, too, and Eve's; she was the one who was always quietly going about the business of getting things done, even when the rest of us thought the things were impossible.

And that got her killed, some part of my brain insisted on telling me. I didn't even know why someone had wanted her dead; Shane and Eve had pieces of the puzzle, but not enough.

I needed to know that even more than I needed to get Myrnin.

Getting in to see the Founder normally was no big deal for me; I had that Glass family season pass, after all. But today, I could see it wasn't going to be easy, or fast. There were a *lot* of vampires in the hallway, all with fierce, tense body language that spoke more than snarls and bared teeth of the need to enforce their territorial boundaries. Jamming this many this close together was a bad idea.

There was no way I could force my way through. There were maybe thirty vampires filling the space, and every single one of them was at least a hundred years older than I was. They also weren't nearly as inclined to patience, since they'd probably survived centuries by virtue of being rich and powerful and ruthless.

It took an hour for the line to move forward until I could actually see the open door of the Founder's office. The hallway was a long one, with deep carpets and glossy portraits on the walls, but just now I swore I could smell desperation in the air.

Two vampires ahead of me in the line got into a shouting match over which of them had been closer to some forgotten throne or other. I didn't care. I was imagining Eve and Shane back at the house, and what might happen if Claire's killer came back for more.

I grabbed one of the two—the taller one, dressed in an antique business suit—and propelled him inside. "Sorry," I said to the surprised shorter one. "This goes faster if you don't measure your family trees. Just shut up."

He gave me a classic *Don't you know who I am?* stare, and was on the verge of opening his mouth to tell me—not that I cared at all—when all of a sudden the Founder herself was standing in the doorway facing the two of us.

Amelie didn't look like the Founder I'd grown up with. She'd always seemed icy and perfect and royal, and although I'd seen her show emotion from time to time, I'd never thought of her as weak.

Now she looked . . . fragile. And tense enough to shatter. And she'd lost the careful edge of distance.

She gave the other vampire a look that utterly silenced him, and pointed at me. "Come with me," she said, and vanished. I squeezed by Prince Whatever of Who Cares before he could protest how he'd been slighted, and saw the other, taller Prince Whatever taking a sheet of paper from the hands of Amelie's assistant, Bizzie. It had a number bold-printed at the top.

"Now," Bizzie was telling him, "this is your seat assignment and car number. You'll carry only what you see on the sheet. Nothing else. You may not take pets, either animal or human. No personal snacks will be allowed. . . ."

I didn't hear the rest, because Amelie had walked into her private office, and I had to follow quickly.

"Shut the door," she said as I hesitated. I did, and heard a lock automatically engage. "Sit."

"I came to get Myrnin," I said. "I need him."

She didn't even glance my way as she walked to the windows and looked out on the evening. There were fewer lights than usual. Even the moon was dark, hidden behind the clouds. A few fitful drops of rain rattled the glass like machine gun bullets, driven by a gust of wind.

"You can't have him," she said. "I've put him to work on important things. Critical things."

"Amelie—"

"Don't," she said, very quietly. "Don't presume on my friendship toward your family, or my personal fondness for your grandfather, or even for you. Sentimentality has weighed us down here, made us complacent and stupid. No more."

"Amelie, *what happened*? Just tell me. Explain."

"I'm no longer explaining myself, Michael." She turned, and there was something about her face, her eyes, her body language, that made me take a long step back. "I allowed you to see me so I could make this abundantly clear. You cannot choose to remain with the girl you love. You cannot choose to stay with your friends. That time is past, for all of us. You will take your evacuation instructions and wait downstairs, or I will order my guards to take you to a room and lock you up."

I'd expected—well, a lot of things, but I'd never actually imagined she'd go this far.

"What killed Claire?" I asked. Not *who* killed her—I was already realizing that was irrelevant.

"The inevitable," she said. "She knew too much, it appears, more than he could afford. And if he dared act so openly, then even the preparations I've made will not save all of us. Some will be lost. Some will be foolish, and make themselves ready victims. But not you, Michael. You've been foolish enough already, coming here alone."

"I'm not going to leave Eve behind," I said. "I love her. I'm not just going to—"

She turned away from me toward the outer door. I hadn't heard anything, but she must have; she pressed a button on her desk, and the lock clicked over.

Myrnin walked in.

He looked . . . well, different. Sane, for one thing. The pupils of his eyes were wide and dilated, and I wondered if she'd drugged him, or he'd done it himself. Either could have been true. He closed the door without being asked and stood there, hands clasped behind his back, like a schoolboy reporting to the teacher. "It's done," he said. "Frank has been programmed with all the necessary sequences. He'll initiate it and shut himself down once it's confirmed. Then the countdown will start. It's all set to begin at dusk tomorrow."

Dusk tomorrow. I'd been told that all Morganville human residents had to be present in Founder's Square. "Countdown for what?" I asked. If Myrnin had set Frank to some kind of suicide mode, it was dire. *Really* dire.

Amelie and Myrnin both ignored me. "I will need you to help me trace Oliver's last movements," she said. "I realize there is no way to track Magnus directly, but we know that Oliver vanished within a short window of time. Perhaps there are clues to be seen, even now."

Myrnin frowned at her and rocked uncomfortably back and forth. "You mean to go after him? It's—not wise."

"I don't intend to stage a rescue," she said. "I can't. Oliver's lost, as are the rest. But if we know where the draug are gathering those they've taken, we can isolate it. Perhaps we can contain them and buy ourselves some time."

"Unlikely. You know how easily they could—"

"I know," she interrupted, and waved him off. "No more talk. Go."

Myrnin put a hand to his chest and bowed, just a little. As he did, he shot a look at me. This one was knife sharp. Amelie turned her back toward the window, and as Myrnin straightened, he mouthed one word to me.

Follow.

I let him leave, and heard the click of the lock engage behind him. Amelie waited, as silent as the grave, until I said, "You say I don't have a choice, but I do. I can either cooperate or get dragged along. Right?"

"Yes," she said. "I regret that they are the only options I can offer. Leave the humans behind now, Michael; tomorrow it will only be harder. Do you understand?"

"You can really do it that easily. Just . . . end things."

"Yes," she said. She sounded tired now, and sad. "Unfortunately, I can. And I will. And so will you. So which is it? Go downstairs voluntarily, or under a guard, to a locked room? You can't leave. That much is absolutely guaranteed."

"Then I'll go on my own," I said. "But this isn't over. Trust me."

She didn't bother to point out to me how useless that was to say. She just pressed the button on her desk, and waved me off. I had no doubt that she had people watching me, ready to pounce, but Myrnin had been definite.

And that meant Myrnin had a plan. A crazy plan, sure, but right now, I'd take anything at all.

I walked out of the outer office and into the hallway, then looked right. Nothing showing that direction. It was entirely blank and bland.

To the left was a solid block of vampires, all impatiently waiting their turns at Bizzie's desk.

And beyond them, I saw Myrnin standing at the end of the hall. He waited until I'd caught sight of him, then took off in the opposite direction from the elevators.

I shoved past the waiting vamps, most of whom shot me poisonous looks or flashed fangs. I managed not to get bitten somehow. When I achieved relatively free space, I moved faster. Myrnin hadn't been dawdling, and while I didn't dare run, I couldn't exactly stroll.

I looked back. Two of Amelie's best and brightest goons had come out of a doorway only about fifteen feet behind me, and they were falling in on my trail. I turned the corner, heading the exact wrong way, and knew they'd be on me in seconds.

I ran, hard, and the walls blurred around me. I couldn't see Myrnin ahead, just more endless hallway. . . .

. . . And then something tripped me, and I was falling.

Only a hand grabbed me out of the air by the arm and yanked, and in the next microsecond a door slammed, and I was on the floor being held down with a cold hand pressed over my mouth.

Myrnin. I rolled my eyes to look around, and from what I could dimly see, I thought we were in some kind of janitorial closet. It was tiny, cramped, and stank of cleaning products.

He looked down at me after about five seconds, and said, "We have less than a minute until they find us. Is Claire alive?"

"I thought you said—"

"I was hopeful, but you wouldn't be here if you hadn't seen proof," he said. "And now we have forty-five seconds."

"I need you," I said. "She needs you. Come with me."

"I can't," Myrnin said. "It's impossible. She'll never allow me to leave." He dug in the pocket of his vest, dropped a handful of old movie tickets, a foil-wrapped stick of gum, and something that looked like an ancient piece of candy to the carpet. "Where is it— Oh, bother— Wait—" He slapped pockets. I thought about reminding him of his own countdown, but honestly, it wouldn't do much good. Myrnin, Claire had always insisted, ran on Standard Crazy Time, not the regular clock.

He found a folded sheet of paper in his breast pocket, glanced at it, and handed it over to me. "Here," he said. "I'll need these things. Get them for me, before morning comes. Oh, and I'll need her body."

I was trying to read the list, but that stopped me cold. I looked up. "Her *what*?"

"Body," he repeated. "Corpse. Remains. Mortal shell. *Her body*, lackwit, get it to the house, and now we're out of time, for heaven's sake—*go!*"

"Go where?" I wondered how Claire dealt with this, the crazy talk, the sudden insanity, the demands—and then Myrnin spun me around, put a hand in the center of my back, and shoved. Hard.

I stumbled forward and brought up my arms, because I was going to hit the blank wall . . .

. . . And then the wall vanished into a well of black, a confusion of color, and the rest of my fall went through a freezing void and then out again into a cold, whipping wind, pellets of rain on my face, and the hard, scraping impact of my hands on pavement.

I was outside a brick wall, in a part of town I didn't recognize at first glance, until I found the distant lights of Founder's Square and spotted the darkened sign for Marjo's Diner, no longer open twenty-four/seven.

I was halfway to the edge of town, in the entirely wrong direction from home . . . but the right side of town for Morganville's one and only mortuary, run by a strange, stiff vampire called Mr. Ransom.

I was close to a single, flickering streetlight, and I took the piece of paper and angled it to catch the glow. It was a list. A crazy list.

And the first thing on it was *CLAIRE—BODY.*

He's nuts, I told myself. We all knew it, even Claire; Myrnin was a few pints short of a gallon at his best, and I wasn't exactly sure this was his best. He was medicated, for sure. That *might* be a good thing, of course. Amelie wouldn't want him to be scattered, so she might have made sure he was ruthlessly focused. In which case, the nutty list I was holding might actually make sense, in whatever universe Myrnin and Claire inhabited that the rest of us didn't.

I didn't really have a choice. He'd given me orders, and a list, and if I wanted to save Claire, or have any chance of it, I needed to get moving.

At the very least, Amelie was going to have a hell of a time finding me.

And that made me grin, before I took off running toward the mortuary.

The mortuary was deserted when I broke the door open and went inside. Ransom had already abandoned the place. I checked the viewing rooms, but they were all empty of coffins and bodies; I supposed he'd actually had the decency to make sure all the other deceased had burials.

At least, I hoped that was what he'd done with them.

I found Claire zipped in a body bag in a large walk-in refrigerator downstairs. Frost had formed on the ridges of the bag, and the fastener was stiff, but I unzipped it far enough to see her pale, still face. It wasn't just pale anymore. It was an eerie blue-white, and the marks on her neck had turned black.

I closed it up and wondered what I was going to do. She'd been gone for hours, and I knew enough about the dead to understand that she was probably going to be stiff.

I honestly wasn't sure I could stand to pick her up. There was something horribly wrong about even trying, but Myrnin had been insistent.

Man up, Mikey, I told myself. Shane would have done it.

I had to do it for him.

I slid my arms under her shoulders and thighs, and lifted her. She wasn't heavy, and she also wasn't stiff. Not at all. I almost dropped her as she sagged in my arms, and had to hug her close to my chest to balance her out.

I couldn't leave her in the body bag. It just felt so wrong.

I unzipped the plastic all the way. She was still wearing the clothes she'd died in, which was a relief. I picked her up again, carefully, like a sleeping girl instead of a dead body, and braced her against me.

"Claire?" I said, ridiculously somehow expecting her to open her eyes and talk to me, because she felt . . . almost living. Her color was wrong, and she was cold, but still . . . and it was probably better that she didn't answer me, because that would have been too weird even for a vampire to contend with.

I carried her out of the refrigerator, through the lab room, up the stairs, and out through the broken front door. Outside it was still raining, in chilly little fits, as if the sky were shivering in the cold. I bowed my head over her, somehow not wanting her to get wet, and ran for home.

I made it only as far as the end of the block before a police cruiser turned the corner, and its blue and red lights suddenly popped on and flashed. It nosed in to the curb, and a bright light focused on me.

"Hold up," called a familiar voice. I squinted against the light, and it was redirected to glow on my feet instead of my eyes.

Hannah Moses closed her car door and walked toward me, settling her nightstick in its loop on her belt. "Michael Glass," she said. "You planning on explaining to me why you're stealing a dead girl out of the mortuary?"

"To tell you the truth," I said, "I'm not exactly sure I know why I'm doing it."

She was staring at me—no, she was looking at Claire, with grim sadness grooving lines on her face around the prominent scar. "Never thought I'd see her go down," she said. "I honestly didn't."

"The thing is, she may not be gone."

Her eyebrows rose, then fell. "The house."

"You know?"

"I've got relatives in the Day House, Michael. And I spent time there. There's something not quite right about those things. Ghosts. I heard them growing up."

"I think Claire's still in there," I said. "And we're going to get her back."

"Just you."

"Myrnin," I said. "And me, yeah. And Eve, and Shane. So you have to let me go. You have to let me *try*."

She looked tired, and the sadness wasn't all for Claire. She seemed . . . beaten down. "This whole town's dying," she said. "Did you know that? It's our home, and it's being taken apart around us. What difference does one girl make, against all that?"

"I don't know. Maybe none at all. But she matters, Chief. She matters to *us*."

Hannah was silent again, for a long moment, and then she sighed and said, "Put her in the back and get in there with her. I'll drive you home."

"Uh, I'm not exactly supposed to be doing this—"

"Amelie gave orders to grab you on sight, stun you, and drag you back to Founder's Square by any means necessary," she told me. "I'm not supposed to be doing this, either. But I'm damned tired of doing what people tell me."

"Me, too," I said. "Thanks."

She drove fast, but carefully. We passed a few cruising police cars, and she told me to get down, but nobody tried to stop us. Why would they? She was chief of police, and as far as anyone could tell, the back of the car was empty. A fugitive vampire wasn't likely to be escaping in a police car.

Claire's body felt loose and relaxed where it rested on my knees. I was holding her neck and head still. In the passing flashes of streetlights—where they were still working—she looked not so much peaceful as just . . . vacant. She still had that fragile look to her, that pretty shape to her face, but everything that had been Claire was missing now. She could have been anybody.

"They'll be watching your house," Hannah said. "I'll park, pop your door, and go to the front to talk to Shane. They'll watch me do it. You take her and go around back." She put on her cap with its plastic covering and looked at me in the rearview mirror. "Stay out of sight of the windows once you're in there. Amelie will be checking the house as soon as she realizes you aren't in any of the other spots. I'll try to warn you if I can."

"Thank you," I said.

She shrugged. "Tomorrow I'm out of a job," she said. "Might as well go out flipping the bird to the powers that be killing us."

It occurred to me to wonder what she meant by that, but then she was out of the car, and my back door was open just a crack, and I had to get moving, fast, with Claire balanced in my arms. Good thing I was a vampire. Running with a second person's weight while in a crouch, keeping to the shadows, wasn't a job for a human.

I made the back door and got inside. I could hear Hannah saying something, and then the front door closed while I locked the back behind me.

I paused for a moment. Eve and Shane were talking out in the hallway, and I realized that there was no way around it: this was going to come as a shock.

Better, I thought, to get it over with fast.

I expected Eve to scream when I stepped out with Claire's body in my arms, but she just stared at me, eyes gone wide and strange, and then she turned and looked at Shane, lips parting.

He froze, and I saw all the color drain out of his face. He braced himself by slapping a hand against the wall, and blurted, "What in the *hell* are you doing?"

I couldn't tell him, because I didn't know. "Draw the shades," I told Eve. "Go. All of them. We can't let anyone see me."

"Where's Myrnin?"

"He's coming," I said, and hoped like hell I was right. "Help me put her on the couch in the living room."

Shane ran on ahead, tossing pillows and game controllers to the floor, and then he took a deep breath and helped guide her legs as I eased her down. "Why did you do this?" He sounded shaken. I'd have been surprised if he wasn't, honestly. "They took her away."

"Myrnin gave me a list. She was on it." I took one of the afghans Eve kept draped on the back of the couch and put it over Claire, then folded it carefully up to conceal her face. "Just leave her where she is. I have to go get the rest of what he wrote down. I'll be back."

"Wait!" Shane grabbed my arm as I started to head for the back door again. "Amelie's guys were just here. They tossed the place looking for you."

"Good. Then they won't be looking here again for a while."

Eve was standing off to the side. She hadn't said a word until now. "Michael—they told us we had to call when you came back. If we don't, they said—" She darted a look at Shane. "They said they'd come back and kill us all. I think they meant it."

"They did seem pretty serious about their mayhem," Shane said. "Screw it. Go, Mike. If they want to give it a try, they'll get a fight. I'm not ready to give it up, not as long as there's a chance we get her back."

I nodded. "Have you seen her again?"

"Yeah," he said, and cleared his throat. "She's okay." Shane wasn't, I realized. He looked . . . really tired. Dark circles under his eyes, an unhealthy color to his skin.

"I hope so," I said. *Hope.* I'd thought of Claire before as Shane's hope, and here I was, carrying corpses in the hope that Myrnin—

professional lunatic—would show up and work some kind of weird magic and bring my friend back to life. That was, all things considered, a pretty good definition of hope, too. "Take care of them. I'll be back."

"Wait. Give me half the list. I can help." Shane had real passion in him now—a purpose. I knew it was dangerous. Then again, from the few hints Amelie had dropped back in her office, being a vampire was no longer any protection against the perils of the night, either.

I folded the paper in half, tore it, and handed him his portion. "Three items on there," I said. "One hour. Understood?"

"Got it," he said. "Watch your back, bro."

"You, too," I said.

"Wait," Eve said, and stepped forward. "Seriously, you two are *not* going out in the middle of the night and leaving me here with—" She didn't look directly at Claire's body, lying covered on the couch. Instead, she took a deep breath and plunged gamely on. "With the possibility of those vamp assholes coming back to kill us—"

She was right about that. "No," I said. "You go with Shane. Nobody should be here alone."

"Claire's alone," Shane said. He'd pulled an olive green canvas bag out from under a cabinet on the other side of the room and unzipped it, and was checking the contents. "I hope she understands why we have to do this." He looked up. "Stay strong, Claire. We'll be back for you. I promise."

"I'd like to go with you," Eve said to me, in a close whisper.

"I know." I took her hands and kissed them, then her lips. She could always bewitch me that way, just with a kiss, all over again, and it was hard to break away from the taste of raspberries and chocolate and the sweet, delicious, spicy flavor that was all Eve. "I'm going to be moving fast, and on foot. You and Shane get the hearse. Meet you back here in one hour. If you're late, I'll find you."

She smiled, and a dimple formed in her cheek. I wanted to kiss it, but there wasn't time. Especially not time for all the parts of her I wanted to kiss.

"You be careful," she told me. "I *am* marrying you, you know."

"I know." I gave in to temptation and kissed her nose. "Same here."

I waited to be sure that the house was tightly locked and Shane and Eve were safely in the big, black tank of a hearse before I took off running. My portion of Myrnin's list required things from his lab, and I was far better qualified to be in that part of town after dark—and Myrnin was prone to setting little traps for visitors, too. Better me than my friends.

The Day House next to the alley had all its lights ablaze, and I paused before I entered to look up at the second-floor corner window. The lace curtains parted, and the ancient, seamed face of Gramma Day looked out at me. She saluted me and raised a shotgun. I waved back.

We had an understanding, me and Gramma. I wondered if her granddaughter Lisa was back; if she was, she'd be heavily armed, too. The Days could tell things were changing, and not for the better.

Good. That meant they stood a good chance of not being victims.

I raced the rest of the way, dodging standing puddles of water—the rain had ceased, at least for a while—and trash cans as I went. The alley narrowed at the end, funneling directly to the shack that concealed Myrnin's lab entrance.

Someone had helpfully busted open the door, and I didn't even slow down as I jumped the stairs, landed flat-footed on the stone floor, and took a moment to look at the jumble that was in front of me.

Holy crap. Someone had definitely had a tantrum, or a fight. Knowing Myrnin, I'd put my money on the first thing.

I shoved books out of the way—there were a *lot* of books—and heard the crash of glass somewhere underneath the pile. I knew what I was looking for, but it was anybody's guess as to whether he'd have kept it where he'd had it the last time I'd visited. Myrnin liked to redecorate. Forcefully.

Bob the Spider was still doing fine, sitting in his web in the fish tank near Myrnin's battered leather armchair; he'd grown to almost the size of a tarantula by now. I wondered what Myrnin fed him, but that wasn't my concern, not today. I edged by the tank, while eight beady eyes watched me, and opened the chemical cabinet that Claire had insisted be installed for things that might actually sear flesh or cause horrible death.

Inside, the bottles were all intact, and neatly labeled in Claire's careful printing. I paused for a second to stare at that, because it felt as if she were right here, standing with me; but that was illusion, not fact. The real Claire was trapped in the house, just as I'd been once.

This was just . . . an afterimage. Wishful thinking.

I looked at the list and grabbed two bottles. Claire had left a shopping bag in the corner, and I started filling it up. The chemicals were only part of what Myrnin wanted; he also needed a piece of equipment that looked like some kind of defibrillator. He'd drawn a sketch in his sloppy, yet oddly accurate, hand, and I held it up as I stared at each steampunked-out machine in view.

There, on the fifth table, sat a match to what he'd drawn. I grabbed it up.

The last thing, though, wasn't in view, and I spent long, frustrating minutes opening cabinets and pulling out crap to try to find it. A black leather bag, like an old-fashioned doctor's kit.

It was nowhere.

"I'd ask if you were looking for something, but that seems pretty obvious," said a gravelly voice from behind me. I hadn't felt anybody approach, but I knew the voice, all right, and there was nobody *to* sense behind it.

Just a picture, flat and grayscale, of Shane's dad.

I tried not to show it too much around Shane, but I hated his father. *Hated* him, more than any human being or creature or whatever on the face of the planet. It wasn't from any one thing, although he'd done horrible stuff to me; I could get over that, bad as it was. No, it was what he'd put Shane through, day after day, all his life. It was bad enough when he was just a mean drunk, pushing his son to be a bully like him; it had gotten ten thousand times worse after Shane's sister and mother had died, and Frank's obsession with destroying the Morganville vampires had taken over whatever good he had left inside.

Shane had a big dark streak inside him, but honestly, I'd always been surprised that he had anything *but* the dark, after what he'd been through.

Because of his dad.

So, without turning around, I said, "Fuck off, Frank, before I find your jar and smash your brain like a boiled tomato."

"Aw, that's cute. Who grew up and got all butch? Doesn't suit you, Glass. You're the sensitive musician type, remember?" The bitter mockery in his voice was about as subtle as a rock to the head.

One thing about me—I *am* a musician, but I grew up in Morganville, and here, sensitive types don't last long unless they have steel underneath. So I was never the weak pushover Shane's dad had always assumed I was. Shane had known that, but his dad had always wanted him to make friends with *real* guys.

Honestly, smashing his brain would solve *so* many problems right now, for all of us, because the idea of Frank Collins continuing to throw his weight around when Claire was lying dead in our house . . . it really reeked of irony.

I turned around and said, "Black leather bag. Where is it?"

Collins had upgraded his image a little; he seemed younger, and he'd made himself look more badass at the same time. Sad. "Feel free to look around," he said.

"Myrnin needs it."

"You think that cuts any ice with me, Goldilocks? He didn't exactly ask me before he wired me into his Frankenmachine. I don't run his errands."

I kept opening cabinets and pulling drawers. The clock was ticking away on me, and I was well aware that I still had to get back to the house before the deadline with Shane and Eve. If Amelie's search team showed up here, I'd be screwed.

"Warmer," Frank said. "Oooh, nope, wrong, cooler."

"Shut up."

"Tell me one thing and I will."

"Or I could go pull your tubes—that'd work, too."

"What do you think would happen if I told Shane about you and Claire?"

I froze. It was like a two-by-four hitting me in the head, and for a few seconds I couldn't even organize a response . . . and then I had to fight back the red splash of rage that flooded over me.

I turned to look at him. Pretty sure my eyes were glowing a bright, angry crimson. *"You fucking liar."*

He laughed. "Oh, come on, Michael. She's a pretty girl; she's living in your house. . . . Are you telling me you never even *thought* about it? You think Shane would believe that, either? If I told him?"

It was a lie, a complete and total bullshit lie, but he was right about one thing: I *had* thought about it. Not after Shane had started falling for her, but before, a little. Just a little.

One thing about Frank, he'd always known how to see the cracks in your armor, and just where to hit. My friendship with Shane would always be strong, and it would always be fragile, too; he didn't trust vampires, but he trusted me, and all that noise in his head over that made it harder than it should have been.

Any hint about Claire and me . . . that would shatter it all over again.

"What do you want, Frank?" I slammed one drawer and opened another one. Damn, I was getting hungry, spurred on by all the anger he was pulling out of me. I had a sports bottle at home filled with type O that I'd chug down, but it was distracting, feeling that jittery need at a time like this. I wondered where Myrnin kept his snacks. Then again, knowing Myrnin's general whackitude, I wouldn't have tried anything out of his refrigerator anyway.

"I want you to stop Amelie," Frank said.

That made me turn around. All the bullying was gone now, all the crap, and *this* was the real Frank Collins. The one who still had a streak of—well, I wouldn't call it humanity, exactly—*honor* left in him.

"Stop her from doing what, exactly?"

"Destroying this town and everybody in it."

"Not the vampires," I said. "And she said she's handing over power to the humans."

Frank laughed, a tangle of electronic noise from the speakers across the room. "You really believe she'd ever do that? Even at the end? She's one of those who'd kill you to save you. Vampires get to leave. Humans get to die, all together, right in Founder's Square—just like scientists humanely get rid of lab animals when they're done with the experiment. And I'm the one who has to pull the pin."

Part of me insisted that he was lying, again, because that was Frank's deal. He lied. He bullied. He manipulated people to do what he wanted.

But the other part warned me that he just *might* be telling the truth. I'd heard Amelie and Myrnin talking. What he'd just said fit with what I knew from the two of them—although they'd left out the part about humans dying.

Of course.

"Tell me where the bag is," I said.

"Only if you tell me you're going to stop this thing."

I opened another drawer and slammed it so hard the wood splintered. "Don't be an ass—of *course* I'm going to stop it. Do you really think I'd let Amelie do a thing like that?"

"Maybe. Vampires are all about self-preservation."

"All right, then suck on this: I'm staying here. I'm not going with the others. So she'd have to kill me, too." I threw a stack of books out of the way and uncovered another set of drawers built into the bottom of the lab table I was searching.

And inside was a dusty black leather bag. Exactly like what I was searching for.

I pulled it out and opened it. Medical equipment. Things I didn't recognize, but it looked like what Myrnin would want.

"Told you that you were getting warm," Frank said.

"Game's over, Frank." I snapped the catches shut again and picked up the bag, along with the shopping bag of chemicals. "You lose."

His voice came out of my cell phone speaker as I climbed the steps, heading out. "Do we have a deal?"

"No," I said. "I don't make deals with you."

But that didn't mean I wouldn't be stopping the massacre. If he hadn't been lying about that, too.

Frank said, "What if I told you Claire was still alive in your house?"

And how Frank Collins it was, to save that as his *last* bargaining chip.

I held up the phone and said, very clearly, "I already know, dipshit. And we're going to get her back without any help from you."

There was silence for a second, and then Frank said, "You know what, kid? I really hope you can. But the thing is, even if you do . . . you're all going to die. Because I'm going to kill you. I've got no choice."

We'd have to see about that.

But after Claire.

I made it home in an hour and three minutes, unlocked the back door, and raced inside to put my stuff on the table.

The house was silent, except for the dry ticking of the clock in the parlor. Claire's body still lay motionless on the couch, covered with Eve's knit afghan.

I went to the front and carefully checked the window. No sign of the hearse out front.

They were late. Later than me, and that was *late.*

I waited as the clock ticked, every second winding my nerves tighter. *Dammit, Shane, if you got yourself into it . . . If Eve . . .* I couldn't finish the thoughts; my brain kept yanking away from it like a hand from a hot stove.

What if Frank wasn't lying about the meeting at Founder's Square? What if Amelie meant to end the Morganville experiment in a blaze of glory? I couldn't understand that, but it all fit. She was scared of something, *very* scared. And scared people do insane things.

Ten minutes passed, then fifteen, and I couldn't wait anymore. The hearse wouldn't be tough to spot. If they needed help, every minute would count.

I left the way I'd come in, through the back, and took shortcuts through neighbors' yards until I was sure it was safe to be on the street.

I was two blocks from Lot Street, passing the shuttered and locked gates of Variety Liquor, when the rain began to fall again. I didn't have a coat, but it didn't matter. I kept moving.

Ahead, someone stepped out of the hissing darkness, and I saw a blur of water, teeth, something *wrong,* so very wrong, and then there was something in my head, drowning me alive. I felt cold.

The thing facing me looked like a man, but he was all wrong, too. So was his awful slicing smile as he whispered, "Come with me," and I had no choice but to follow him into the dark.

Into the cold.

Drowning.

Dark.

FIFTEEN

EVE

☽

"Dammit," Shane said. He'd been saying that for about five minutes straight, like some kind of mantra. "Hand me the wrench. *Dammit!*"

I crouched down and handed him the tool out of the box in the back of the hearse. Even Shane's strength was having trouble with the bolts on the tire.

The flat one.

So not my fault.

"You know—*dammit!*—if you actually got these things changed out before the tread is showing—"

"Zip it right there," I told him. "Really not the time to lecture me about my car-maintenance habits. Just get it changed."

"Yeah, working on it," he said. "Dammit. We're late already. Michael's going to freak."

"Hey, good, because if he shows up, we can have this fixed in thirty seconds," I said.

Shane sent me a glare from under his rain-drenched hair, which was ratted around his face. He needed a shave, I thought. And a tranquilizer. "I don't need help," he snapped. He stood up and stamped on the wrench, and the bolt turned with a horrible metallic shriek. Now that he had it started, he was able to muscle it off and start the next one.

At this rate, we'd be thirty minutes in the freezing downpour. Sitting ducks for any passing vamp with a plasma craving.

Or worse, whatever worse was this week in Morganville. One thing was certain: it was not safe to be out with a flat tire after dark, even on the town's best day ever. Which this most assuredly wasn't.

I was trying to be the old Eve. I really was; I'd even zinged Shane a couple of times with wisecracks, but nothing felt the same. I kept seeing flashes in front of me, vivid as camera shots, of how Claire had looked lying there on the floor, her eyes open, head turned to the side.

Of how I'd known, even before I'd touched her, that she was gone.

Nothing was the same now. The rain was all wrong for Morganville; it *never* poured like this, especially not this time of year. The streets were flooding, again, and even under the hooded jacket I was wearing I felt chilled and soaked. And so many stores were shut—not just closed for the night, *closed*, with whited-out windows and notices on the doors.

It felt like the whole population was suddenly deciding Morganville was no longer safe.

Which, *duh*.

I shivered again and stamped my feet, which was a bad idea. I sent splashes of freezing water up my legs.

Shane had moved on from *dammit* up the cursing food chain as he struggled with the third bolt. Stomping on the wrench wasn't cutting it, but he was doing it with so much enthusiasm I wouldn't have been surprised to hear a bone break. Finally, the bolt creaked over, and Shane collapsed to his knees again to unscrew it.

Three down, three to go, and we really were *very* late. Michael would be out looking for us, but in this rain, it'd be hard for him.

A bolt of lightning ripped the sky in half, and a couple of blocks down, I saw someone watching us. The flash gave me only impressions—human-shaped, pale, nothing special. But anybody who would be standing idly around in *this* weather deserved special alarm.

"Speed it up," I told Shane. "Seriously. Go faster."

"Hey, princess, don't make me break a nail."

"I'm not kidding."

He glanced up at me, shook hair out of his eyes, and said, "Yeah, I know. I'm moving it. Get the tire ready."

I didn't like the idea of leaving him alone to go to the back of the hearse and drag the spare out of its compartment, but I really didn't have much of a choice; it would speed things up, and I'd just been ragging on him to count seconds. I waited until the next jagged flash of lightning.

The corner where I'd seen the man standing was empty. Good news? Probably not.

It took thirty seconds to unlatch the compartment, grab the spare, and haul it out. Shane was still unscrewing the last bolt when I rolled it over. He lifted the flat clear and passed it to me, then took the replacement and slotted it on with speed a NASCAR pit crew would have envied. "Five minutes," he shouted.

"Less would be better!"

"Just watch our backs."

I was, even while I threw the flat tire into the back of the hearse. The street looked deserted. We'd lucked out in being able to pull under an actual working streetlamp to fix the tire, but that also made us about as obvious as the last pork chop at the all-you-can-eat buffet. I had been given watchdog duty over Shane's precious canvas bag, and now I grabbed out my two favorite weapons—a silver stake, and my slightly upgraded fencing épée, which had a coating of silver on it, too. My coat pockets had two squirt bottles full of silver nitrate.

"Trouble?" he asked me without looking up from screwing on bolts. He was working fast. "Four more minutes."

"I don't know," I told him. "It's just real exposed out here."

"Yeah." He tightened bolt two and went on to three. "Believe me, I'm feeling it."

Lightning stabbed again, so bright it practically sizzled my eyeballs. Close, too, real close. It must have struck a transformer about a block away; I saw something flare up in hot blue sparks.

Our streetlight went dead with a sad little fizzle and zap.

"Shit," Shane said. "Can't see a thing! Flashlight!"

I grabbed one from the back, but that meant dropping one of my two weapons. I debated, then left the stake on the seat. The flashlight worked, at least, and I focused it so he could continue bolt three.

By bolt five, I was feeling pretty good. We were almost back on the road. Yes, we were—*yikes*—half an hour late, but at least we were in one piece. . . .

I felt something brush past me.

The wind was blowing, and rain was thrashing, and the feeling was so subtle, I shouldn't have been able to pick it out of the general chaos around us, but there was something about that touch. Something very bad.

I spun around, throwing the light all directions, but I didn't see a thing.

"Sorry," I said, and turned back toward the car, and Shane, who was—against all character points—waiting patiently for me to stop freaking out.

Only he wasn't waiting.

He was standing up. The light hit his face, and it was pale, dead pale, his brown eyes almost all pupil.

I yelped and scuttled back, and the light slipped and lit up someone standing behind him.

My mind fried, just like the streetlight, as if it couldn't make that work, couldn't process, couldn't deal. It was like a shadow, but—

"Hey!" I shook it off, mostly by refusing to look at whoever that was behind Shane. "Shane, get out of the way. What the hell are you doing?"

He just stared at me. It was as if he was gone, like Claire had been gone, only he was still standing there.

Then he turned and started to walk away. He passed the shadow, which rippled black like a standing-up puddle of oil, and I felt something horrible and cold well up inside me.

Whatever this thing was, it had Shane, and now it was taking me, too.

Hell with this.

I yelled, closed my eyes, and lunged.

It was a *perfect* lunge, the fencing move of a lifetime—razor-straight extension, weight balanced, every bit of my reach forward into the silver-coated steel of the sword.

And it caught the thing dead center.

Problem was, it didn't *feel* like I'd punctured anything *real*. It was more as if I'd hit a balloon, one filled with gelatin and water.

The give was way too easy, way too wrong, and I snapped my head up to see the thing—because it damn sure wasn't a man, and wasn't a vampire—collapsing in on itself.

Whatever was inside it splashed to the wet ground a second before the thin, empty oil-black skin collapsed.

I shrieked and scrambled backward, shaking my sword free of the ick. There was no sign of blood on there, or anything I could see in the dim light from my fallen flashlight.

The black stuff was flooding away in the water.

Shane had fallen face-first to the street, as if he'd just been turned completely off. I gave that dead skin a wide margin of respect as I ran for him and grabbed his arm. "Shane! *Shane!*" God, flashbacks, I couldn't lose him, too. I couldn't. . . .

And I didn't, because in the next instant he coughed, spraying water, and rolled up to his feet. He almost went down again, so I steadied him. "What the *hell* was that?" He vomited, and way too much water came out of him. It was as if he'd been drowning, which he couldn't have been, could he? No way.

"I don't know what that was," I said. "But I like it like cancer. Come on, we *have* to get out of here!"

Shane definitely didn't argue. I dragged the skin-heap over to the side, well away from us, using only the point of my épée. That was more sickening than your average vomit-inducing event. Seriously, I would rather kiss Monica, or lick a toilet bowl, than ever, ever do that again.

Shane tightened the fifth bolt and got the sixth in and tightened in less than a minute, hit the release on the jack, and thumped the car back to the pavement, fast. He grabbed all the tools and tossed them in the back, yelled, "Go!" and I didn't wait for a second opinion. I was in and starting up the hearse before his door was closed.

And now I could hear something. It sounded like—singing? Confused, I fiddled with the stereo, but it was off. Nothing coming out of it.

I realized, as I accelerated, that Shane was *trying to get out of the car.* Holy floating Moses, that was—insane. I grabbed him by the hair and pulled, hard, and he yelped and slammed his door again and turned to glare at me. "What?"

"You were *leaving!*" I shouted back. He looked utterly lost for a second, then nodded, as if he'd just realized something. "God, what is going on? Because even for Morganville, this is totally whacked!"

Shane, ever practical, reached in the glove compartment, pulled out some tissues, and tore them into strips. "Can you hear it? The music?"

I nodded. I could, and it was making me sweat. Hard to keep my hands on the wheel, my foot on the gas. I was feeling more and more—relaxed. Distracted.

"Here," Shane said. He was jamming rolled-up pieces of tissue in his ears, and handing me some. I didn't really want it, but I took one and stuffed it in on the left.

I instantly felt better. Sharper. And much, much more scared. I grabbed the other piece and got it in my right ear, pressed the accelerator, and *ripped* through the red light at top speed. Bill me for the ticket, Morganville, because I knew that stopping right now was an insane idea.

Shane was breathing easier now, too, but he looked pale and wild-eyed. We didn't talk—well, considering we'd just jammed up our ears, it probably wouldn't have been productive, either. I drove too fast for the heavy rain, but the streets seemed deserted, and anyway, I was way too freaked-out to slow down.

Lot Street showed up suddenly, and I swerved into a left turn, tossing Shane into the passenger's door (but not, thankfully, out of it). When I slithered the hearse to a stop in front of the house, we looked at each other, and Shane pointed from me to the bag in the back, then from his chest to the items scattered on the backseat. I nodded and did a silent three count.

I hit the back, grabbed the weapons bag, threw the stake inside, and raced through the gate and up the walk. I fished for my keys as I ran, and had them out and ready. The door swung open right on cue as Shane pounded up the steps behind me carrying his load, and we rushed inside, slammed the door, and locked it, hard.

We stood there breathing hard for a few seconds; then Shane yanked tissue out of his ears and turned away. When I got mine out, I heard him yelling for Michael as he carried his items toward the living room.

There was a black doctor's bag and two bottles of liquid sitting there, and damp footprints on the carpet—but no Michael. "Michael!" I yelled up the stairs, adding to Shane's voice as he checked the kitchen. "Michael, we're back—"

No answer. I tried not to look directly at Claire's still form as I headed to the kitchen. I met Shane as he came out.

"Nothing," he said. "He's not here."

"He went out after us."

"Yeah."

"Well—we should—"

"Nothing," Shane said. "We should do nothing but wait. Eve, it's really freaking nuts out there. He'll have to get back on his own. Look, he'll be fine; you know Michael. He's tough."

I nodded, but I felt short of breath. We were more than thirty minutes late. Even if he'd gone out, surely he should be back soon.

But he wasn't. The minutes slid by, greasy and way too fast, and with each one, my panic got a little stronger. I kept wanting to fiddle with my cell phone, but there was no point; the lines were still out. The TV stations were dark. What I could pick up on the radio were ghostly out-of-town signals, nothing local.

It had been an hour when Shane said, very quietly, "I think we have to assume something happened."

I was trying very hard not to lose it. "Then what are we going to do?" I asked him. "Please. Tell me. We can't call for help. It's too dangerous to go out there. *What the hell do we do?* Jesus, Claire is—Claire is right there on the couch. What are we *doing, Shane*?" That last tipped over from distress into real terror, and Shane grabbed me and held on for both our lives. He was scared, too. Really scared.

There was a knock at the back door.

We sprang apart like we'd been caught doing something totally illegal, and I felt a surge of relief so intense it was like being soaked in a hot bath. "Michael," I said, and raced to let him in.

Rationality caught up one step later, as did Shane, who said, "Michael has keys."

I hit the reality wall face-first, and skidded to a stop.

Shane eased the curtain aside. I saw his shoulders stiffen, then slump. He unlocked the door and stepped aside.

And Myrnin swept in, all giant leather swirling coat and dramatic swooping hat. Rain fell off both in a miniature fountain as he shook himself, then took it all off. Despite all that cover, he still looked half-drowned. "We don't have much time," he said. "They're looking for me. Did you get everything?"

"I don't know," Shane said. "It's in here."

He led the way back and indicated the stuff piled on the dining table. Myrnin pushed him out of the way and, with quick, able gestures, opened the doctor's bag and pulled out all kinds of tubing, needles, some kind of pump . . . and made a little *aha!* sound as he grabbed a gear-studded machine covered with brass. He plugged the end of one tube into it, and the other into the pump.

I watched as he set up a complicated, inexplicable device there on our dining room table, mixed chemicals together into a test tube, and poured the result into a funnel on the brass machine.

It started up with a barely perceptive hum.

"Where is Michael?" Myrnin asked, as he fitted a needle on the end of one of the tubes. "He should be here. I will need his help."

"He—" Shane cleared his throat, and didn't look at me. "He didn't make it back. We don't know where he is."

Myrnin's hands stilled for a second, and then he nodded. "Very well," he said. "I have a blood connection to Claire, but none to the house; this will be trickier without that. You two are residents, so you have *some* standing. I'll need vials of your blood." He grabbed syringes and those rubbery tie things, which he pitched to each of us. "It's best if you draw it yourself."

I held the capped needle—at least he was using a *modern* syringe—and the tourniquet and glared at him. "I'm sorry? *What?*"

"Apparently I have not made myself clear," he said, speaking the way vampires did when they thought you were drunk, stupid, or just deeply worthy of a smack. "If I do not have the blood of someone attuned to this house, then all this is busywork and window dressing. So please, stop following your usual extremely useless agenda of jabbering questions and *put the needle in your arm!*"

"Are you high?" I blurted it out spontaneously, because the light had caught his eyes, and they looked seriously weird, in a medically induced kind of way.

Myrnin blinked. "Amelie thought it best to calm me," he said. "Given my distress." His gaze darted toward Claire's body on the couch, and suddenly I *did* understand. Of course he'd been distressed—too rattled to work. So Amelie had given him happy pills.

Lovely.

I wanted to catch Shane's attention and get some solidarity going on this, but he had quietly, without fuss, dropped his coat and rolled up his sleeve, and was fastening a tourniquet around his arm.

"Here," I said. "Let me help."

"Got it," he said, and tightened the rubber strap with his teeth in a way that made me wonder if that was actually the first time he'd tried it. Probably not. Shane had done some bad things out there on the road with his dad. "Let me do yours."

I didn't want to—*boy,* did I not want to—but I stripped off my coat, sat down in a chair, and shivered while he rolled up my sleeve, fastened the tourniquet, and told me to work my fist. I have good veins—not a major plus, in Vamptown—and it took only about half a minute for him to find one, slip the needle in, and fill up the tube. "Just one?" he asked Myrnin, without looking up.

"Two would be better," Myrnin said. "Three would be extremely nice."

Shane silently pulled the crimson-sloshing tube from the syringe and slotted another one in. It hurt, and he touched my hand in silent apology as the blood bubbled up. He was better on the third vial, and then we were done.

Myrnin reached in the bag and found a couple of premoistened antiseptic swabs and cotton balls. Shane finished me up and sat down next to me. His arm was turning red from the tourniquet, and it must have hurt, but he didn't seem to mind. I could see the veins standing out in the bend of his elbow from three feet away.

"Need me to—"

"No," he interrupted me, which was a relief, because I was even more squeamish about putting needles into people than I was watching them stick into my own skin. He rested his forearm on the table, palm up, and did the whole thing with his left hand, including changing tubes, which was . . . scary impressive, really.

He smiled a little, while he was doing it.

"What?" I asked him. "You're freaking me out now."

"Claire," he said. "She had to come with me to the blood bank so I wouldn't freak out and leave. And here I am, drawing my own blood and handing it to a vamp. She'd appreciate the crazy."

Myrnin was waiting impatiently on us, and when Shane handed him the blood, he gave us a quick nod, ripped the plastic diaphragms off the ends of the tubes, and poured them one by one into his weird little spinning machine.

The house took on an absolutely horrible smell that burned my eyes and made me cough. Shane, too.

Then Myrnin took a syringe and vials and—without bothering with a tourniquet—drew some paler-than-normal blood out of his own veins. He put two vials of it into the machine, but kept the third attached to the syringe, which he capped and put in his pocket.

"Right," Myrnin said. "Sit her up."

Shane gave me a confused look.

"Not her, *her*! Idiot. Never mind." Myrnin stalked to the couch, pulled the afghan away, and . . . stopped. Just for a second. His back was to us, so I couldn't see his expression, but I didn't really need that to understand what he was feeling. I felt the same thing every time I so much as glanced toward her body—the black, horrible knotting inside, dread and anxiety and grief and horror all tied up together.

He picked Claire up and moved her limp form into a sitting position on the couch. Her head tried to roll off to the side, and he carefully, gently adjusted it. Then he took one of the tubes, the one he'd fitted the needle to, and deftly inserted it into her forearm, like an IV. He flicked a switch on the machine on the table, and a sickly greenish liquid began flowing through the tubes, and into her arm.

Nothing happened.

"All right," he said. "What I'm about to attempt is—dangerous. Very dangerous, not only for me and for the two of you, but also for Claire. If her spirit has been trapped by the house, it's as if the house is a filter, but the pressure on her spirit remains, trying to pull her free and out to—whatever comes beyond this. We have to break the filter, and grab her spirit as it flies, and pull it back into her body. It will not be easy."

"But—" I licked my lips and risked a quick look at Claire's silent body. God, she looked so *pale.* "Her neck. What about her neck?"

"What about it?"

"It's *broken.*"

"Ah, that," Myrnin said. "Yes. Well, I can fix that. You won't like how that occurs, but I don't think we have much of a choice." He took the syringe out of his pocket and held it up. The pale, watery blood glimmered in the light. "This will heal her physical damage, and it will also strengthen the bonds between the two of us. It will allow me to try to pull her back."

"Wait, hang on a second," Shane said. "You're putting *your* blood into Claire? Isn't that how you make someone a vampire?"

"Yes." Myrnin uncapped the needle. "It's exactly how I would make a vampire. The process is the same; those who cross over die, and only their vampire maker can lead them back across that line, back to their bodies. This will let me try to do the same for Claire."

Shane lunged out of his chair and grabbed Myrnin's arm as he positioned the needle over Claire's neck, right where she had two faint, faded scars from where Myrnin had once bitten her. "No! You are *not* making her into—"

Myrnin shoved him, and Shane went down. It was a gentle push, for a vampire. He didn't even hit a wall. "Do you want her back or not?" Myrnin almost spat it at him. "If there's any chance to reclaim her, *any* chance, don't you want to take it?"

"No!"

"Oh, you'd rather she was dead and gone forever?"

Shane was chalk white now, as if he'd taken up the Goth lifestyle. He didn't try to get up. It was as if he didn't have the strength, all of a sudden.

He didn't answer.

"That's what I thought," Myrnin said, and plunged the needle home in Claire's neck. I expected a flinch, but of course she didn't move, didn't react at all. I watched the pale blood press into her neck.

No reaction. None at all.

Myrnin knelt down and put his hands on her forehead. "Eve," he said, in a careful, controlled, calm voice. "Please press the button on the side of the machine now."

"Don't," Shane whispered. He was looking at a nightmare, I realized. He loved Claire, and he wanted her back, but the idea of having her back as a vampire . . . that had to rip him apart, right at the core.

He shut his eyes.

I reached out and pressed the button.

SIXTEEN

CLAIRE

Claire could feel Hiram out there, testing the walls, looking for weaknesses. It felt exactly like being in a glass-walled shark tank while the great white prowled around waiting for lunch. The house itself was protecting her—she knew that—but it was conflicted. Hiram was there first, after all. And Hiram at least *thought* he was in charge.

I can't stay here, she thought. She had no idea how much time had passed. This room was strange that way; it felt frozen, as if time didn't really affect it . . . or passed much more slowly than in other places. That was possible, of course; quantum physics allowed for the possibility that time was variable, but that was usually at the subatomic level, not in the visible world. . . . Interesting problem, though. Maybe it had something to do with the way the portals worked, also at the subatomic level.

And I'm distracting myself with physics. Well, some people recited baseball scores or movie lines; physics was a perfectly valid hobby. Besides, if she got really desperate, she could recite the periodic tables.

I can't spend the rest of my—eternity sitting on my ghostly butt up here. Alone.

But she didn't dare try to leave, either.

A ripple of raw power suddenly ran through the house. It was so strong that it seemed to break everything apart into jagged, glittering, spinning pieces—the furniture, the room, the *house.* It all flew apart in a sudden, confusing explosion, turning and falling and rising all at once.

And then she felt the pull.

It wasn't like she'd felt when she'd gone through the portal—that had been a kind of pull, too, but it was as if she'd been anchored and had to unravel herself into strings to move away. This felt more as if she were being pressed *together,* and a great, vast vacuum was dragging her away into the unknown.

Claire screamed and flailed, trying to grab onto something, anything, but it was all shattered, all cutting edges and confusion—

And then something seized her in powerful hands.

Hiram Glass.

He was still mostly whole, but there were pieces coming off him, bits chipping away and flying into the darkness. "You!" he shouted, and bared his teeth at her, right in her face. "You *vandal!* You've destroyed everything!"

"No, I didn't—" He wasn't listening. That mouth opened, impossibly wide, and Claire knew he was going to bite her and rip her apart before the dark could take her. . . .

With the strength of desperation and panic, Claire pushed, as hard as she could.

And broke his hold.

Hiram looked comically surprised as his hands slipped free, and he spun off into the black void, screaming as he broke apart into tiny, glittering pieces.

Gone.

I'll be next, Claire thought. She was weirdly calm. There was no way she could resist that pull. It was like a black hole, and she was standing on the event horizon.

Claire.

It was a whisper in the hurricane that roared around her, but she recognized the sound. *Myrnin.* That was Myrnin's voice.

"Here!" she screamed, as the void pulled her away. "Myrnin, help me! *Help!*"

The spinning pieces of reality around her seemed to slow down. She saw herself reflected in one side of a jagged shard, and then it turned, and she saw Myrnin's face in it. He looked worried, and there were lines of effort around his mouth that she'd never seen before.

His hand reached out to her, but it was as if he was trapped behind the glass; his hand slapped against it, and then the spinning shard turned again, and she lost him.

Claire twisted. There, in another piece, she saw him again, reaching out.

Take it, he was trying to tell her. It wasn't a voice—it was something else, a kind of whisper moving inside her, like blood in her veins. Only she no longer had blood, or veins. This was coming out of her very core, the thing that had survived her body.

Her soul.

Take my hand.

She couldn't. He was on the other side of that glass, and the pieces were moving, and she was being dragged inch by inch into the dark.

Then she saw Shane in one of the spinning, glittering shards. He was on his back, propped up, staring out of the shred of reality, and he looked so agonizingly *alone.*

Take my hand, Claire—do it now! Myrnin's whisper sounded desperate now. Anguished. This was hurting him, too.

She kept her gaze on Shane's face, but she lunged for Myrnin's hand as another piece of reality slid past her.

Her fingers broke through the cold, icy surface, and touched his.

And reality came back together. She could still see the cracks, hear the awful noise of the darkness beyond that, but Myrnin's hand twisted and closed around her wrist in an unbreakable hold, and she fell, and fell, and fell. . . .

And took a breath.

A real breath.

It hurt.

Her first thought was *This can't happen,* and the second was blotted out by a wave of pain so intense that she wanted to vomit, but couldn't. She couldn't move. The pain was in her neck, and she remembered the terrible snap, the darkness, the moment when everything had . . .

I'm breathing, she thought. *How can I be breathing? I can feel my heart beating. I can feel . . .*

I can feel.

The pain was fading now, but there was something else, something almost worse . . . something moving through her veins, like an ice-cold poison. Like death, but slower. Relentless.

She felt freezing hands on her forehead, and Myrnin's voice was inside her head, *inside.*

You have to choose, he told her. *If you want to live as you did before, you must fight. This is your choice. I brought you back, but now you must choose.*

She was confused, and scared, and hurting. *Choose what?*

Human life, he said. *Or the endless possibilities I have to offer. But you can't change your mind once you've made that choice.*

Having Myrnin in her head was like being Alice down the rabbit hole. He sounded sane enough, but in the background rushed images, feelings, an utterly mad jittering landscape of too much color, too much pain, too much love, too much hunger, too much everything. This was what Myrnin *was.*

And he scared her, and charmed her, and made her want to cry.

The ice in her veins had something wonderful about it, because it felt like peace. Like stillness. Not like death, but with something of death in it, and something of life. It had the fierce, sharp clarity of eternity.

Her heart was struggling to keep beating against it, and the struggle hurt. Life hurt. Everything about it brought pain, even the best things.

Then let go, Myrnin whispered. *I'll catch you. But understand—you have to let go of everything when you fall. Even him.*

Shane.

There was something about the uneven beat of her heart that reminded Claire of him—of the way he fought, every day, against something, even if it was only himself. Of the way he went still and peaceful when they were lying in bed together, on the edge of sleep. Of the taste of his kiss and the way he smiled at her and the way he had dared her to *live.*

There was cold, rational survival in the ice running through her body, and an end to pain, but Myrnin had reminded her of something else, too: that pain was life, and life could be beautiful, with all its scars and flaws.

It wasn't just Shane that was pulling her back. It was Eve, and Michael, and her parents; it was Richard and Hannah and so many others, even Monica, because in the end, they shared that experience of *life.* Of risking everything, every day, with every breath.

And she wasn't ready to give that up. There was so much more to learn.

She did it, in the end, for herself. For her own distant, uncertain future.

The cold intensified, and she struggled to reject it, fought so hard she thought she should be weeping, but her body was a prison, and she couldn't move it . . . and then she took in another, halting breath, and another, and the ice receded, warmed, melted, and was gone.

Myrnin's whisper said, *Good girl,* and she felt his sadness and loss, but then it was all gone, like the cobwebs of a dream swept away by a morning breeze.

And she opened her eyes and said, "Ow."

As first words went, it was weak, whispery, and not very inspiring, but Eve shrieked and clapped her hands over her mouth, and Shane lunged up as if someone had pushed him straight off the floor.

And Myrnin stepped back, staggered, and fell.

Shane hesitated, glancing at him, then completed his rush to grab Claire and pull her into his arms. "Ow," she repeated, and blinked. "Shane." Her whole vocabulary had been reduced to single words. "Eve."

Eve blew her frantic kisses, then went to lean over Myrnin, who was lying on the floor with his eyes wide-open. "Hey," she said. "Uh—are you okay?" She prodded him tentatively with a fingertip, and he did one of those vampire-quick grabs to get hold of her arm. Eve tried to pull back, but Claire knew that wasn't likely to happen.

"Eve," Claire whispered. Shane was holding her as if she might break, and also as if he never intended to let go, but she pushed weakly at his shoulder and jerked her chin toward the action. "Eve!"

Shane sighed and let her go. "Don't you move," he ordered, and turned to face the two of them. Eve was crouched down now, trying to pry his cold fingers off her skin. "Come on, man. Let her go."

Myrnin opened his mouth, and his fangs came out. Shane moved fast, planted his knee on the vampire's chest, and helped Eve in her frantic struggle to get herself free. Together, they were able to pry enough fingers loose to let her break the hold, and she stumbled backward, rubbing what was sure to be a monster bruise.

"Go get him blood. I think Michael's got some stashed in the fridge," Shane said. Myrnin was trying to grab him, too, but Shane batted it away, careful to keep his center of gravity over Myrnin's to hold him in place. Claire realized that her boss's eyes had gone red. Very dark red. "Better make it two pints."

Eve ran for the kitchen and came back with two sports bottles, both labeled with Michael's name. "Here." She passed over the first one, and Shane aimed the straw at Myrnin's open mouth and squeezed a fine red spray into it.

Myrnin froze, swallowed, opened his mouth again. Shane stuck the flexible straw in. "Drink up," he said. "I'm not letting you go until you can form actual words."

It didn't take long for Myrnin to drain the first bottle, and go through half the second, but by then his eyes had faded to a muddy brown, and he looked more—himself. "Sorry," he managed to say, and Shane grunted noncommittally. His expression changed as he took another pull on the straw. "Ugh. Is this AB? I hate AB! Don't you have anything else?"

"Shut up and take it," Shane said. "We're not the freaking dispensary." He hesitated, then shifted his weight and stood up, giving Myrnin room to get up on his own. "And thank you. For her."

"It was her choice," Myrnin said. He looked past Shane as he climbed up, and caught Claire's gaze. She got a flash again of sadness and longing, disappointment, pride . . . all complicated, all blazing through a mind she could only distantly understand. "She's made it." He sighed, and his shoulders rounded. "I'm tired. And there's so much to do. I'm sorry; I can't stay. As it is, Amelie's men will be searching. They may well come here looking. If they do, don't lie; tell them you don't know where I'm going, because it's the truth. I don't honestly know myself."

"Wait," Claire said. She couldn't really move, not yet; her body was still aching and struggling to come to terms with being alive again. She supposed that Myrnin's blood had done that much—repaired things, made it all work again in preparation for turning her vamp. There was a needle in her arm, and even as she realized that, Myrnin flipped a switch on the machine sitting on the table, hissing and chugging away, and the gears that had been spinning slowed, then stopped.

He slid the needle out of her arm. Claire felt a rush of heat, then cold, then sick nausea, but she almost immediately felt better. Her heartbeat steadied down from its frantic pounding.

"Wait," she said again, more strongly. Myrnin didn't pause as he coiled up tubing, and shoved things into a black leather bag. "Myrnin. Thank you. Thank you for letting me go." Because it had been as much his will as hers, she realized—he'd let her make the choice, once he knew she wanted it. Not all vampires would have done that. Or could have.

He nodded sharply, long hair veiling his face. He picked up the sports bottle, drained it, made a sound of disgust deep in his throat, and said, "Tastes like raspberries. I *hate* raspberries. Disgusting things." He snapped his bag shut. "Keep her still and quiet for a bit. The healing's done, but her body's in shock. She'll be cold. Get her water now, food in an hour, but not too much of either." He managed to turn and smile, but there was something broken about it. "I must be off."

"And you must be leaving," Eve said. It was trying to be a joke, but didn't quite make it. "Sorry. Is there anything we can do to—?"

"No," he said. "Stay here. Whatever happens, you must not go out again, even in daylight."

"Wait. Michael's not back, and he's supposed to be. Can you look for him? Please?"

Myrnin stared at Eve for a few long seconds, then took her hands in his and gravely said, "If he hasn't returned to you, you must accept that he never will. What's out there now is death to vampires as much as to humans—more so, because we're the real targets. Michael took a terrible risk. He knew that."

Past tense. Myrnin was talking about Michael in *past tense.* Claire felt Shane sink down beside her, and his warm arm went around her to hold her close. He spread the afghan over them both.

"He can't be gone," Claire said. "Not now. Not when I—" *Not when I came back.*

Eve looked blankly terrified as she held Myrnin's gaze. "Please," she said again. "He can't be gone. Please bring him back!"

He kissed her hands, first one, then the other, and stepped away. "We are all trying to do our best," he said. "And I will not forget him."

That, Claire thought, was very far from a promise.

Eve looked shattered, but she didn't cry. She stood and watched as Myrnin walked to the blank wall of the living room, opened up a portal, and stepped through. Claire expected him to look back.

But he didn't.

"Eve," Claire said. Her voice sounded stronger, and her friend turned her head, just a little, in her direction. "Please. Come sit."

Eve did, at last, curling up on the couch on Claire's other side and putting her arms around her. The three of them stayed under the blanket, huddling close, as the chill settled inside the house, and rain pounded the windows.

"Something's strange," Eve said. "Things feel different. Not you, but—this. The house."

She was right, Claire realized. She didn't have the sense of the house's emotions, or anxieties; it didn't respond when she reached out to it.

It was just bricks and mortar and wood now.

Myrnin had broken the Glass House to set her free.

The first hint that something strange was going on with her was after she'd consumed the food and water that Myrnin had directed, and risen off the couch under her own power. Shane was hovering around her, obviously worried she was going to drop at any moment, but she felt . . . good. Steady. Even better than that, really.

"Seriously, you should sit," he said to her. "An hour ago you were—"

"Dead," Claire said, and rubbed the back of her neck. Something clicked in there, but not in a bad way. More like a relieving-tension way. She shook her head experimentally. Everything held together. "I know. And I'm so sorry, Shane. I know how hard it was for you. I saw." He knew she was talking about the gun, about that desperate moment as he sat with his back to her door, when it seemed like he had nothing left. "Don't you *ever* do that again. Promise me."

"I won't," he said, and put his arms around her. He felt so good to her, so real and warm and perfect, as if they were made to fit together. "Don't you ever leave me again, though."

She kissed the soft, warm skin beneath his ear and whispered, "You have to make the same promise, you know."

"I do," he whispered back, and hugged her hard enough to drive her newly recovered breath away. "What are we going to do about Michael?"

"I don't know." She was miserably aware that for Myrnin, and probably for all the rest of the vampires, if you were missing now, you were presumed dead; that meant Naomi, Oliver, Michael, and all the rest wouldn't be coming back even if they were still alive—not if rescue was left up to Amelie. "It's worse than that. I can't be sure but I think—I think Amelie's not really planning to set us all free when the vampires leave."

He pushed her back to arm's length. "What are you talking about?"

Claire swallowed hard, and said, "I think she's going to kill us. All of us. I think she's going to take the vampires out of here, and destroy the entire town to be damn sure her enemies die here, too."

Eve said numbly, "Nuke the site from orbit. It's the only way to be sure."

That old movie line usually made them all smile, but not now. Not this time.

Because this time, it was actually *true*.

Shane let go of Claire and ran his hands through his shaggy hair in a distracted, anxious gesture. "They can't do that. Myrnin—why did he bring you back if you were just going to die all over again? Why would he?"

Claire hated to say it, but she knew the answer, in her heart. "Because he feels something for me, and he wanted to give me a chance to live. Like him. *With* him. But I refused."

Shane turned and looked at her, a blank expression on his face that turned quickly into . . . something else. Claire was glad Myrnin had gotten out while he still could. "Great," he said. "I knew it."

"It's not like that. He's—" She shook her head in frustration. "It's not like he's in love with me or anything; it's more complicated than that. I don't even think he understands it, exactly."

"Yeah, he only loves you for your mind," Shane said, and smacked his palm down on top of the dining table.

One of the empty but still-blood-smeared vials tipped off the edge of the table.

Claire was at least five feet away, but without even thinking about it, she stepped forward, reached out, and . . .

. . . And suddenly she was holding the vial, and it had dropped only about two inches.

She'd crossed five feet and caught something with perfect coordination in less than a second.

What the *hell* . . . ?

Shane and Eve had both started babbling at her. She held up her other hand for silence, put the vial down, and tipped it off the table again. She waited as it fell, then willed herself to catch it before it hit the ground.

And then it was in her hand, one inch from the floor.

Nobody could have caught that.

Nobody *human.*

But she *was* human—she had blood rushing through her veins, her heart was pumping, she was breathing . . . and she felt more alive than she could remember.

Shane licked his lips and said, "It's the blood."

"What?"

"Vamp blood. It's like the stuff they gave me to drink when I was at the gym, fighting—it's got an effect on you. Makes you faster and stronger, at least for a little while. But when you crash, you crash hard. I know what you're thinking, Claire, and it's not a good idea. Not at all."

"What?" Eve asked anxiously. "What are you thinking? Why is it not good? Please, don't do anything not good—it's been a really awful day, Claire, and honestly, I don't think I can take one more trauma right now." Her voice was trembling, and she looked chalk-pale. "Unless it's about Michael. If it's about Michael, it's a *very* good idea."

"I can try to find him," Claire said. "Look, what choice do we have? Amelie's not looking for Michael, or for any of them. She's going to pack up and run with however many of her people are left. If we just wait here, we're sitting ducks for the big Morganville apocalypse anyway. Maybe I can find out where they are, and I can get Michael, and Oliver, and Oliver can stop this. He'd rather fight than retreat. He can convince Amelie."

"That's true," Eve said. "He's not really the giving-up type." She blinked back tears and grabbed Claire's hand, vial and all. "Do you really think you can find Michael?"

"Wait a second. Think about it," Shane said. "Eve, that thing that almost got us—that's probably what got Michael, if the vamps are so scared. You want Claire to go one-on-one with it?"

"I won't," Claire said. She already had, and it hadn't ended well. "All I'm going to do is try to find where they're keeping the ones they take. Then once I know where they are, we can get help. I can call—"

Shane was shaking his head. "Phones are dead. Hell, for all I know, she's downed carrier pigeons, too. There's no way for us to find you if things go wrong, Claire, and I can't—I *won't* let you take that risk."

She put her hands on his face. He looked so serious now, and she ached for him, really, but there was no way that she could hide here. Hiding would get them all killed.

Sometimes, you had to risk everything, and she knew, beyond any shadow of a doubt, that this was the time.

"You will, because you love me," she told him, and kissed him. It was a gentle, sweet, wrenching kiss, and it made her want to cry at the thought of leaving him. "Shane, I'll come back. Be ready when I do, because this is going to get dangerous."

He closed his eyes and pressed his forehead to hers for a long few seconds, then stepped back.

"You're not seriously letting her go!" Eve said. "Did Myrnin give you the crazy? Because this is *not safe!*"

"I know." He let go of Claire's hand. "And she's not going alone. I'm going with her."

Well, Claire couldn't honestly say that she hadn't expected that, but she'd been dreading it. "You can't," she said. "Shane, I'm going to be on foot."

"Even more reason for me to go. Hey, don't worry. I'll carry the heavy weapons."

She didn't *want* him to come with her. For good reason—she was scared of losing him, and she knew, *knew,* that what was out there waiting was capable of . . . anything. He'd survived terrifying experiences, she knew that, but this—this was different.

She also knew that there was no way he'd take no for an answer. Just no way at all. He'd follow on his own if she tried to leave him, and that would only put him in even more danger.

Finally, she shook her head and sighed. "Then get the stuff and hurry. We probably don't have long before Myrnin's blood wears off."

"Wait," he told her. "Seriously. Do not move until I get back."

Claire nodded. She thought about bolting while his back was turned, but that wouldn't do any good. He came back in less than a minute, anyway, wearing his jacket with the pockets loaded down.

He handed her a set of blue squishy earplugs. "What?" She stared at them, confused, as he shoved a set in his own ears.

"Trust me," he said. "You may need them."

She pressed them in. They made her own heartbeat sound insanely loud, but blocked out voices pretty well; she had to read his lips to make out that he said, *Good to go.*

"Eve, we'll be back," she said. "Lock the doors!"

Eve nodded. She looked stressed and anxious, but she had her long fencing épée in one hand, and a silver stake in the other. *I'll be fine,* she said, or Claire thought she did, anyway.

Claire rushed to her and hugged her, hard. She kissed her on the cheek and said, "Love you, Eve."

"Love you, too," Eve said. Claire heard it, just barely, through the muffling sound barriers.

Then she and Shane set off into the dark of a Morganville they no longer knew.

There were things out there, and Claire realized why Shane had given her the earplugs by the time they reached the area around Common Grounds; there was a *sound* in the air, something like singing. She couldn't hear much of it, but it made her distracted, anxious, and it made her want to take the earplugs out to listen.

She didn't, only because when she reached for them, Shane grabbed her hand and held on to it, shaking his head.

Right. Whatever these things are out here, the sound is a trap.

Shane dragged her into the shadows next to the awning of Common Grounds, which was closed and shuttered; in the red and green glow of the neon coffee cup in the window, Claire saw a human figure standing on the street corner, under a flickering light.

In between the flickers, she thought it was black, an oily kind of darkness, but in the light, she saw a man. Pale, nondescript, anonymous.

She knew him, and drew in her breath sharply as she pushed back against Shane's warm, steady strength. His arms went around her.

Magnus. That was the man who'd killed her.

He stood on the corner for a few long moments, then turned and walked away into the darkness, heading south. Claire gripped Shane's hand tightly and led him out of the shadows. He pulled her to a stop again. *Wait,* he mouthed. *What?*

Follow him!

Shane shook his head. *Dangerous.*

Of course it was. But she knew, *knew* that Magnus was the key to all this. He'd killed her for a reason; she just didn't fully understand what it was.

She dragged Shane insistently on, to the corner. They hugged the brick wall, and Claire peeked around it to see where he was.

Magnus stopped just as she looked. He was standing over a rusty iron grating set in the concrete of the sidewalk—a drain into the sewers. Claire had a flash of memory, of a grate just like that—where had she seen it?

Behind Goode's Drugs. When she'd followed Magnus the first time.

Magnus seemed to . . . collapse. There was no other word for it; he broke into wet splashing drops, and in a second, maybe two, he was *gone.*

Like he was made out of water. It was sickening and wrong on so many levels, and it made her feel dizzy and hot, despite the cold rain pouring down on the hood of her coat.

That was how he'd gotten away from her behind the drugstore, and at the grocery store; he'd just flushed himself down the drain, and left her standing there confused, looking in all the wrong places. The idea that he'd been down there, looking up at her, watching her—that made her shudder all the way to her spine.

He knew I'd seen him, Claire thought. *He couldn't take the chance I'd known where he'd gone. So he killed me rather than risk it.*

There was no sign of anyone—or any*thing*—else on the street. Claire gulped to force down her nausea, then tugged Shane forward, to stand next to the grate.

She pointed at it.

He gave her an odd look.

She pointed again, reached down, and grabbed hold. It was *way* too heavy for her to lift, even though she pulled until her muscles trembled and spasmed.

Shane shook his head, sending spray flying, and bent over to put his back into it as well. With his help, she got it to creak up at a rusty forty-five-degree angle.

The flood of water on the streets was roaring into the gutters and drainage openings, and this one was no different; it was a waterfall leading down into a black pit.

Shane dug a flashlight from his pocket, switched it on, and lit up the darkness.

It was like a vision of hell, if hell was made of water; thick, brown currents raced below them, carrying shreds of trash, tangles of metal, branches, the debris of everything that had washed in from the streets. She caught sight of rats swimming for their lives. They were swept along at a terrifying rate.

Shane put a hand on her shoulder and shook his head, again. It was too dangerous; he was right. Going into a storm drain was suicidal in this rain; they'd be swept away and mashed up against a grating and drowned, at best.

Besides, apparently Magnus could turn himself into some kind of *liquid*. How could she possibly track that?

Think. Surely, with all this rain, Magnus wasn't actually living in the sewers; maybe it was his version of a highway. But obviously he was comfortable in the water. . . .

The singing was starting up again, high and sweet at the edges of her awareness, and she unconsciously reached for her earplugs, then stopped herself.

The singing.

Like the old stories of the sirens, in Greek mythology. Or the mermaids.

Singing, to lure people to their deaths.

All she had to do was follow the sound.

Shane pushed the grating down and spread his hands in a questioning gesture.

She grabbed his arm, and towed him on, through the rain, in the direction that the creature who'd killed her wanted his prey to go. Toward the singing.

They had two advantages, she figured; one, they were at least partly protected against the sound of that music. And two, they were coming into it knowing the risks.

The singing seemed stronger as they walked south, into one of the less-populated areas of town; there were abandoned houses here, and old shuttered buildings that had once been stores. There were still a few homes being lived in. A thick knot of dread formed in Claire's chest when she saw that some with lights on had open doors, as if the inhabitants had simply walked out and left them as they were.

She caught sight of a woman ahead of her in the rain. No coat. She was wearing light house shoes that flapped wetly in the icy stream running down the sidewalk, and her clothing was plastered flat against her body. Claire pointed, and she and Shane ran forward to catch up with her.

The woman—a vampire?—didn't seem to notice them at all. She was staring straight ahead, and her wet face was blank as she struggled on, one step at a time. She was shuddering with the cold in her thin clothing.

Shane grabbed her and pulled her to a stop. She tried to yank free, but not as if she was alarmed by getting surprised on a dark street; it was more impatience, as if he was an obstacle she had to overcome to get where she needed to be.

After a few seconds of silent struggle, the woman suddenly turned toward him and swiped her fingernails at his face. Definitely a vampire: her eyes were muddy red, and her fangs flashed sharp in the dim light. Shane let go as he ducked, and she stumbled on, at the same relentless pace.

Can't stop her, Shane said. *Want me to . . .* He mimed knocking someone out. Claire shook her head. She hated to do it, but the woman was leading them where they needed to go.

They followed behind at a careful distance, but it didn't seem like there was any reason to worry about being spotted; nobody else was around at all, and certainly the woman didn't care if they were behind her, as long as they didn't get in her way.

She slowed and turned, finally, and shuffle-splashed her way up a set of steps toward a big, old building with windows soaped opaque. Shane played his flashlight over the name over the door.

MORGANVILLE CIVIC POOL.

Whatever it was, it had been closed for ages; the building looked old and sagging, and the paint had peeled from the brick to leave it looking diseased and rotten. The big white door had been locked, Claire saw, but the hasp was broken off now, and the rusted lock lay on the stairs.

The woman went to the door, swung it open, and disappeared inside. This close, the singing was soaking through the earplugs, making Claire feel sick and shaky with the need to take the soundproofing out and *listen*, really *listen*. The message was important, and she could almost understand. . . .

Shane reached up for his, and she grabbed his hand and shook her head. He took a deep breath and nodded, and together, they went up the steps to the white door.

Ready? She mouthed it to him, and got a flash of a smile in response.

Not really, he said. *But let's do it.*

She had the urge to move fast, but held back; Shane couldn't move at vampire speeds, and leaving him behind, *here,* wasn't even an option. Not with that *sound* pressing down, dragging and piercing right through the soundproofing now, digging into her brain. *Closer,* it was singing. *Come and rest. Come and rest.*

She didn't want to rest, but she couldn't stop herself from moving forward, slowly, with Shane's hand clutched tight in hers.

The room she walked into was dark, and smelled of mold. The carpet was ancient and filthy, and overhead, the ceiling had cracked and split. Paint had peeled off in elaborate curls, like ribbons, and she ducked to avoid them. There was an old desk, and a wrinkled cardboard sign that read, when Shane turned his flashlight on it,

MEMBER SIGN-IN SHEET. The clipboard was still there, dangling from a silver chain, but the papers were long gone.

The entire place reeked of damp and rot.

Closer, the music whispered. *Peace and stillness. Closer.*

There was a hallway beyond the entry hall, and it glimmered with fairyland lights and reflections.

Shane pulled at her hand, shaking his head frantically. He pointed at the door leading back outside, into the cleaner night air.

But she had to see. Just to be sure.

Claire edged forward down the hall, still gripping his hand. She tried not to touch the walls, which were black with mold. The carpet was gone now, and there were two doors off the hall, one labeled MEN'S LOCKER ROOM, the other WOMEN'S. The texture of the floor changed to tile, and it was slick and slippery.

The hall opened into a giant open concrete space with a rusty lacework of iron overhead. The floor was cracked white tiles, and on the walls there was more tile, in patterns Claire was sure used to be beautiful, before they were discolored with time and more of the ever-present mold.

In the center was a big square pool, and it was full of glimmering blue-green water, lit from below. It glowed like a jewel, and it was beautiful and mesmerizing and the singing was coming from *there,* right there. . . .

The woman they'd followed was in the pool. In the shallow end, but walking forward.

And she kept walking as the water reached her hips, then her waist, up to her chest, her neck. . . .

. . . And she went under.

She didn't come back up.

In the deep end of the pool, Claire saw . . .

. . . Bodies.

Claire lunged forward and ran to the edge of the pool. Shane tried to stop her, but she couldn't let him, not now, *not now!*

There were bodies in the pool. Standing there, upright, six feet below the surface at least. They were anchored on the bottom, she thought, because she could see their arms floating. One woman's long hair drifted lazily in the water, veiling her face, but as it wafted out of the way, Claire recognized her.

Naomi.

The vampire was still and silent, eyes wide. She looked dead.

Oliver was down there, anchored nearby.

And there was *Michael. Right there, staring up at her.*

And he blinked.

He was alive. They were all *alive.*

She wanted to scream. Shane was dragging her frantically backward from the edge, and she realized that even as she'd been adjusting to the horrible reality of what she was seeing, she'd been thinking about taking one more step, just one, and sinking into that warm, still water, so calm and peaceful. . . .

He spun her around and screamed in her face, "Claire, we have to go!"

He grabbed her hand and pulled her toward the hallway.

Then stopped.

Because there was a pale-faced man standing there, staring at them. Claire blinked, and he wasn't there anymore—it was a black *thing,* but she could see his human disguise at the same time, like a skin stretched over the reality.

Magnus.

"You shouldn't be here," he said. "I killed you, girl."

Shane dug silver-coated stakes out of his pocket. He passed one to Claire, then took out what looked like a . . . sports bottle.

One had a snap-down top, and he thumbed that off, aimed, and squirted a silvery stream out of it to splash on the thing in their way.

Magnus screamed, and it was like that singing sound, only a million times worse, and Shane dropped the bottle and the stake and staggered, then went down to one knee. Claire came close; it hammered at her in waves of relentless sound, but she could see that the silver nitrate had hurt the thing, burned away some of his human-skin disguise, and melted part of him into a bubbling, seething mass that ran off in a black current to the tiles.

Claire took a firmer grip on the silver stake, summoned up all the speed and strength Myrnin had granted her, and raced forward in a blur.

She buried the silver stake where, in a human, a heart would have been. It was like pushing it into Jell-O, nothing like staking a vampire at all. Sickening. She could feel the cold ooze on her fingers.

Magnus's mouth opened, revealing razor-sharp rows of teeth, and he lunged at her. She yelped and rolled away, still vamp-fast, and Magnus yanked the stake out and flung it away. The wound it had left was another bubbling leak of black fluid, but he wasn't down. Not by half.

Shane staggered up, grabbed her hand, and ran for the door he'd left unguarded. Black streamers of ooze were coming across the tile at them, and Claire had the awful, sickening feeling that if they stepped in it, they'd never get free. The ick on her fingers felt like it was squeezing them white, and she felt horrible pinpricks all over the skin where it touched. She dragged her hand against her jeans as they ran.

There were more of them in the entry hall, black oily shadows with fake human faces, and they were *all* Magnus. Shane sprayed the rest of the bottle at them, and Claire grabbed a silver-coated knife from his belt loop. She slashed at the one who came for him, and heard that shriek again, an angry, pile-driving pressure like the whole ocean descending on them . . . but the creature went down, splashing into silvery black fragments that rolled aimlessly over the carpet, and Claire grabbed Shane's arm and dragged him forward for the clear air outside. He was staggering, and in the wan, flickering glow of the streetlight outside, she saw that his nose was bleeding, and his eyes were red.

She was bleeding, too, she realized, from both her nose and her hand. It looked as if it had been stung by a jellyfish. It was covered with little beads of blood.

It was biting me, she thought, and shuddered in revulsion.

"Come on!" she screamed, and Shane coughed, bent over, and vomited out a stream of *water.*

But they hadn't even gotten into the pool.

Magnus was in the doorway, and his eyes were silver white, like moonlight on water, and he was smiling at them.

They weren't going to make it.

Claire screamed again, in pure agonizing frustration, and without even thinking about it, she grabbed Shane and threw him over her shoulder.

That shouldn't have been possible, not at all; he was so much bigger and heavier than she was, but she felt like her veins were on fire, and she wanted to fight, *now,* fight this thing that had hurt her and come after Shane and come after Michael and Oliver and her *town.*

But she also knew she couldn't do that. Shane would die.

So she balanced his weight, held on to his legs, and ran for her life, and his.

It took four long blocks for the adrenaline and whatever boost Myrnin's blood had given her to wear completely off. She began to gasp and stagger, and then went down, hard, and Shane went down with her. Her whole body felt like it was coming apart. Shane had warned her that there was a crash, but this wasn't a crash; it was more like being ripped apart and put back together again, and *God,* it hurt.

Shane had made it to his knees, looking pale and out of it, but the rain on his face seemed to bring him back. He met Claire's eyes and held out his hand, and she took it.

Run, he mouthed, and she nodded. She wasn't sure she could, but he was right.

It was their only real hope.

They were racing flat-out past Common Grounds when Magnus—or his clone—stepped out from behind the building into their path. Claire shrieked and managed to avoid him, twisting out of the way of his grasping hand; Shane ran straight into him. He made it work for him; he got his shoulder around and rammed into the creature. He knocked it back. Whatever it was, it wasn't completely gelatinous; there was some kind of weird strength inside of it, and that made it vulnerable to a physical attack. It staggered a few feet, and Shane made a perfect spinning turn, grabbed Claire, and pulled her into a dead sprint.

But ahead, Claire could see more of them, more of those human disguises in that generic nothing form, and behind them . . . something monstrous. They were coming up out of the rain gutters, dripping out of faucets . . . at least four of them, with more coming behind.

She slowed down and exchanged a fast, panicked look with Shane.

They weren't going to make it.

He put his arm around her, but she shook it off and stood back-to-back with him. They circled, watching as the predators closed in. Claire wasn't sure what was waiting in the Morganville Civic Pool, but whatever it was, she knew it was awful. Living death.

The earplugs made the fast, rasping sound of her breathing into its own horror-show sound track, along with the rapid thump of her heartbeat. She tasted blood; her nose was still dripping, and always, there was singing, singing, that high, clear, perfect music trying to draw her back.

She heard the roaring engine only at the last possible second before the hood of the hearse plowed through the row of creatures closing in from the front. One bounced off and rolled; the other three hit with too much force, and splashed into a thick black film over the windshield, hood, and grille.

The hearse skidded sideways, and Claire saw Eve's white, shocked face in the driver's side. Eve screamed something at them, but it didn't matter what the message was; Shane was already throwing himself into a slide over the hood to the passenger door, and Claire scrambled after him.

Something caught her by the hood of her jacket.

She turned, pulled the silver knife, and slashed blindly. One of them shrieked that awful cry as it was hurt, and she managed to drive herself forward. Shane met her halfway and dragged her to the open door, shoved her inside, and yelled, "Go!" across to Eve as he got the door slammed shut.

She gunned it.

Claire felt a horrible bubbling pressure in her lungs, and coughed. Water sprayed out, tasting like rancid mold. She bent over and coughed until her lungs ached.

Shane pounded her back, not that it really helped, and put his arms around her when she came upright again. Eve looked seriously terrified. Claire said, "How did you know?" but Eve pointed to her ears. Claire saw a flash of blue.

Earplugs.

She didn't turn back toward the house; instead, she drove straight for City Hall, where it looked like half the cars in Morganville were parked. There was a full-scale panic under way, Claire saw: families carrying suitcases, hurrying toward the building, police officers out directing traffic.

Chaos.

Eve pulled her earplugs out as she parked, and Claire and Shane did the same. Everybody started talking at once, but Eve shouted the other two of them down. "The cops came to the house!" she said. "Everybody from Walnut Street to Garden had to get the hell out and come here. No exceptions. I figured I'd better go looking for you. Oh God, those things—I hit them. And they splashed. *Gross.* I wore the earplugs because, you know, last time, the music . . . Did you find Michael?" Eve was bouncing from subject to subject like a crazed meth fiend, but it wasn't drugs driving her, just panic. "Please tell me you found him!"

Shane said, "We found where they have him." That was all he said, and that was probably a really good thing; Eve lit up with a smile. "We need reinforcements before we can even think about getting him out."

"But he's alive?"

"Yes," Claire said. She couldn't smile back; she just couldn't. What she'd seen was too . . . grimly awful. "Yes, he's alive. So's Oliver, and Naomi, and a bunch of others. I have to get to Amelie. She has to *understand*."

"Well, you need to do it soon, because she's already started moving vampires out of town," Eve said. "I saw buses leaving.

They have blacked-out windows, like those rock star kind of things. Probably hot and cold running-blood taps, and I just totally skeeved myself out by saying that. I guess those are the first-class passengers. I heard from Hannah Moses that some were being put into semi tractor-trailer trucks, too. I guess that would explain the sudden Wal-Mart invasion."

"Wal-Mart?" Shane repeated.

"I guess they grabbed whatever trucks they could get. Wal-Mart, grocery trucks, mail trucks . . . It looks like one of those disaster movies, with the people crawling over each other to get on the last helicopter." Eve had lost her smile, and she looked . . . adult. And suddenly grim. "I think this town is done for, guys. It feels like it's dying all around us."

It felt that way to Claire, too. "Will you take us to Founder's Square?" she asked. "Please? It's not safe to try to get there on foot, not anymore. I know they told you to come here, but . . ."

"Sure," Eve said. "Like I ever followed anybody's rules anyway. Hey, try the seat belts. I hear they save lives and crap. We may be doing some seriously defensive driving."

She turned the key, and the engine made an awful grinding sound. Eve frowned and tried it again. It sounded horrible, and it definitely didn't sound like an engine was supposed to sound.

"Dammit," she said, and unbuckled as she got out. Shane joined her at the hood, but instead of lifting it, they both stood there, staring.

Claire scrambled out to take a look, too. "What is it?"

The front grille of the hearse looked *melted*. There was black, wet gunk oozing out of it, and when Eve reached out to pop the hood release, Shane stopped her. "Don't," he said. "Don't touch that stuff. Get the work gloves—I left them in the bag in the back."

Once she'd gotten them, Shane tugged the thick, heavy gloves on, took a deep breath, and reached under the grille to pop the latch. It came free with a sticky, wet sound, and as he raised the hood, there was a thin film of goo that came up with it.

The engine was fouled with the stuff, and it was *bubbling.* It looked, Claire thought sickly, like a cross between slime and seaweed, and it gave off a wet, thick smell of decay.

"Oh my God," Eve said. It came out muffled, since she was pinching her nose shut and backing away. "Oh my God, my poor baby—what *is that*?"

Shane slammed the hood and stripped off the gloves. They were smeared with the same stuff, and he kicked them under the hearse. "Whatever it is, you're not driving us anywhere," he said. "So what are we going to do?"

"Find another car," Claire said, and just at that moment, she spotted one pulling up. It was rocking pop music at an earsplitting volume, which cut off abruptly as the driver pulled the key and got out.

Monica Morrell didn't look like she was planning on getting out of town. In fact, she looked like she'd been pulled out of an after-hours club, and as she stalked up the sidewalk, stiletto heels tapping out an impatient rhythm, Claire had to give her style points. Everybody else had a mismatched refugee look, but not Monica. She had on a glittery, figure-hugging minidress, one that showed off her long tanned legs and curves and cleavage. Even her long, straightened dark hair blew in the wind like a supermodel's.

She slowed down as she caught sight of them, and rolled her eyes. "Oh, perfect," she said. "*You* guys." Claire wondered if she'd heard about her death; obviously not, because Monica skipped right over her presence. Or just massively didn't care either way.

Monica tried to go around them, but Eve stepped directly in her way. "Bitch, please!" Monica tried to shove her, but Shane's timing was perfect; he moved Eve out of the way, and Monica's flattened palm hit his chest instead. "Oh. Well, hello, delicious." She batted her eyes at him. "Looking for something a little less pasty and junior-sized?"

"Keys," he said, and looked down at her hand on his chest. "You're touching me, Monica. That's a bad thing."

"Keys," she repeated, and slowly stepped back. "What do you mean, *keys*?"

"As in, give. Now." Shane had that look—hard, and no bullshit. "We don't have time for your drama, Monica. Nobody does."

She got serious. It looked very odd on her, Claire thought. "My brother told me not to go out," she said. "He wasn't wrong, was he? Something's happening. They shut down the club and told us all to leave." Shane nodded slowly, and Monica turned her attention to Claire. "Why do you need my keys, exactly?"

"To get to Amelie," Claire said. "We need a ride. Eve's is toast."

"That's true," Eve said. "I'm in mourning."

"Really? How can anybody tell?" Monica tossed her car keys in her hand and gave them a brilliant smile. "Tell you what, losers: I drive. Nobody touches the baby but me. Besides, if I'm semisafe here with my brother, I'll be *much* safer with the Founder."

Claire doubted that, really, but she wasn't about to tell Monica that.

Eve, for once, *didn't* call shotgun, and neither did Shane. She just got in the back, behind Monica. Claire quickly rock-paper-scissored with Shane on the way to a decision, and Claire lost. She was up front, with Monica, and Shane piled in the back, along with a canvas bag of stuff that he'd dragged out of the back of the hearse.

"Seriously," Shane said as they settled in and Monica turned the key. "You live in a town full of *vampires*. Is a convertible really the best option?"

"I didn't know you cared," Monica said, and the pop music started up in midsong. It was off Monica's iPod, Claire guessed, and she was apparently a big Britney Spears fan.

"Toxic."

That was actually weirdly appropriate.

SEVENTEEN

CLAIRE

By the time they were halfway to Founder's Square, Claire wished the shotgun seat actually came *with* a shotgun, because Monica was killing her slowly, with her incessant chatter. That was funny, because Monica normally wasn't talkative, at least not to them, but it seemed like her shut-up circuit had fried.

". . . I went to DeeDee's to pick up my new dress, and it was *closed*. Not even a note in the window. I was so pissed off! I actually had to wear *this* thing. . . ." Monica plucked at the fabric of what she was nearly wearing in disgust. Claire didn't see how that was really possible, since it fit like skin. ". . . Which all the guys have seen about a dozen times now, not to mention Janis Taylor was there and wearing *her* new dress, which was skanky, and I know she was talking about me recycling the look—"

Shane, from the back, said, "I'm really trying to swear off the random fighting, Monica, but I swear to God that if you don't shut up, I'm going to go back to Step Zero on my twelve-step program. We don't give a shit about your dress or your club or Janis Taylor. Michael's in trouble."

Monica sent him a hard look in the rearview mirror, and said, "And when is one of you losers *not* in trouble, anyway? Not that Michael is a total waste of genetics; I'll give you that. So . . . what's happening? You seem to always know."

Claire said, "There's something new in town, and it's bad. It's taking vampires *and* humans and—" What was it doing, exactly? She didn't know, but whatever it was, there was no doubt it was pure evil. "Amelie's scared enough to shut up the town and run."

"Shut up the town?" Monica's glossy lips pressed flat. "Are you *kidding me*? I put a lot of work into living here. I have *roots*."

"Here I thought you stopped dyeing your hair," Shane said. Monica flipped him off.

"Shouldn't that be Eve's line?" she shot back. "Or has Goth Princess finally learned to shut up?"

Eve leaned forward. As Claire looked back at her, she felt a little shocked at her friend's set, serious expression. "I've learned a lot of things, Monica," she said, just loud enough to be heard over the roar of the wind and the music. "Michael is missing. He may be dying. I am *not in the mood* for your shallow bullshit right now. If you get in my way, I will *cut you*, because you are nothing but a speed bump on my way to saving him. Are we clear?"

Monica's lips parted, and she stared straight ahead for a few silent seconds before she said, "Clear." That was all. She shifted the car into a higher gear, and the engine growled hard. "I know you won't believe this, but I do care. He's not bad, your boyfriend. And we have a drastic shortage of hotties in this town. Can't really afford to waste one."

Eve eased back into her seat without another word. She stared off to the side, at the darkened streets, the empty stores and houses.

The Morganville that was.

Shane said, "It's about to rain again. You should put the top up."

"I have to slow down to do that," Monica said. "You want that?"

"Good point. I don't mind getting wet if you don't."

"Oh, I *mind,* hot pants; you think all this didn't take work?" She indicated, well, all of herself.

"Hot pants?" Claire said, choking on a sudden and inappropriate laugh, because she just knew what Shane's face would look like without having to turn around. "Do you have any survival instinct at all?"

Monica smiled, one of those cruel, evil smiles that had always heralded trouble. "What do you think?" she almost purred, and shook her long hair back over her shoulders, where it snapped like a flag in the wind. "I'm still alive. And I'm still *fabulous.* Unlike, well, everybody else in this car." Her smile faded, and she downshifted. "Company."

The convertible took a corner hard, tires squealing, and ahead Claire saw the glow of flashing police-car lights. They'd blocked off the street—and probably every approach to Founder's Square.

"Look, I've done my bit, but I'm not running roadblocks for you," Monica said, and slowed the convertible to an easy rumble.

"Try another route."

"Don't be stupid—they're *all* blocked. If you want to get in, you're going to have to get stealthy, and trust me, my shiny red four-wheeled baby is many things, but stealthy she is not."

That was true, and Monica wasn't exactly subtle, either. Claire nodded grudgingly. Monica pulled the convertible over to the curb, and the three of them unbuckled and got out.

"Here," Monica said, and reached under her driver's-side seat. She pulled out some kind of designer bag—Claire had no idea how to tell one from another—and opened it up, and pulled out . . .

. . . A handgun. Not an automatic, like the one Shane had held while sitting on her bedroom floor. . . . This was a classic revolver.

For a wild second, Claire thought that Monica might actually shoot her; she wouldn't have been all that surprised, really. There was a lazy, cruel pleasure in Monica's eyes as she held the gun, and one eyebrow went up. . . .

. . . And then she swung it around and held it butt out toward Claire.

Shane intercepted it, frowned, and said, "Okay, how come you're carrying around a thirty-eight?"

"It's Texas," Monica said. "I have rights. Oh, and check the bullets." She pressed a button on the dash with a slender, perfectly manicured finger, and checked her windblown hair as the black canvas top began to rise up with a whine. "Ciao, losers."

She pulled a U-turn and hit the gas.

Shane broke open the cylinder on the gun and whistled. "Okay, interesting . . . hollow points, filled with silver. All the punch, none of the problems. My dad had some of these."

"Did they work?" Eve asked.

He snapped the cylinder back in with a flick of his wrist, and put the small gun in the pocket of his coat. "Hell yeah, they work. But you'd better mean it, because it'll kill what you're shooting at, human or vamp."

"Will it kill those . . . things?" Eve asked.

"It's just a guess, but probably not. The caliber is a thirty-eight, which means it's a lower-velocity round, but plenty enough to punch through one of those—sacks of skin—front to back without bouncing around inside. I'm not sure how much damage it'll do to them, really. Your knife worked better. And your sword." He tapped his pocket. "But if any vampire wants to take us on, it'll be a pretty good deterrent."

She nodded and shouldered the strap on the equipment bag. "Then let's go."

"Wait," Claire said. "We need a plan. We can't just walk straight up to the police line and say, *Hello, let us in, please. We're heavily armed and desperate!*"

"Why not?" Claire really didn't like the gleam in Eve's eyes, or her stiff body language. "Amelie doesn't mind dumping Michael and running away. She's leaving him to die, right? Well, if she needs a reminder of why that's a *very bad idea,* I'm happy to be her wake-up call."

"Take a breath, Eve. Let's do this smart, okay? There's a lot of muscle standing between us and Amelie, and some of it's human cops who don't know what's going on. We need to find a way that doesn't involve grievous bodily harm."

"All right," Eve said. "We'll try it your way. Once." She looked over at Shane, and got a small, unwilling nod from him. "Then we do it *our* way. The Morganville way."

Maybe her ears were supersensitive now, courtesy of either Myrnin's blood exchange or the lingering fear of that high-pitched, seductive music, but Claire heard something in the distance. A rumble. It sounded like a whole lot of cars or trucks, and it was coming closer.

Voices, too. Shouts.

She turned, trying to find the direction, and realized it was coming from around the corner, the same way Monica had gone in her getaway.

It wasn't Monica.

What came around the corner was a streetwide growling wall of pickups, cars, delivery vans . . . all kinds of vehicles. And behind them was a crowd of people, maybe a hundred or so.

"Ah," Shane said, "maybe we should . . . ?"

Claire's eyes fixed on a man who was standing up in the bed of one of the lead pickups. He was facing toward the cops. It took her a second, but she recognized him—the man from the camera store, the one with the stake tattoo.

"Crap," Shane said. "Captain Obvious."

"What? Captain Obvious is dead!" Eve said.

"Long live Captain Obvious. He's the replacement. He's the one who's been getting people to sign on."

"The tattoos," Claire put in. "The resistance symbol. He's leading the charge."

"Yep. Don't know if this is a good time, but he's decided to go for it," Shane said. "Like I said, maybe we should hang back, Claire. . . . Claire!"

He grabbed for her, but she still had at least *some* residue of vampire speed, and it was enough to leap off the curb, race at an angle toward the trucks, and leap up into the bed of the one holding Captain Obvious. Shane was running after her, and so was Eve, but her attention was fixed on the man in the truck, who was turning toward her like he intended to throw her back.

She held up her hand, palm out, and said, "Wait. I just want to talk."

Captain Obvious, the new leader of the human resistance in Morganville, laughed. He had a knife. It was held at his side, but she saw the edge glittering in a passing streetlight. "Amelie's little pet wants to talk? How stupid do you think we are?"

"I know you don't believe me, but believe this: it isn't the right time for fighting back. Even if you win, you lose. You're not going to have a revolution. You're not going to have a town. You're not going to be *alive!*"

"I'm willing to die to set people free," he said. "Are you?" He raised the knife. What was in his eyes was a little bit crazy, and very serious.

"Do you know what's out there?" Claire asked, and pointed out toward the edge of town. Toward the nightmare. "Because it's worse than Amelie. Way, way worse. I've seen it."

"If it scares the vamps, I'm all for it," he said.

"It's taking humans, too," Claire said. "And you need to help them, not waste your time with this. If you want to fight, fight what's really going to kill this town." She pointed again. "It's out there, at the Morganville Civic Pool. Stock up on earplugs and silver-coated weapons, and if you hear the music, don't give in. You'll be dead if you do."

"What in the hell are you trying to sell me, kid? You really think I'm believing any of this?"

She shook her head. "You're wasting your time here. All you're doing is getting your people hurt, for nothing. Turn around. If you want a fight, the pool is where you'll find it!"

He hesitated, frowning, and for a second she thought he might actually believe her . . . and then he said flatly, "Get off or get hurt. Your choice."

He wasn't going to listen, not to her. No matter what she said. Claire stepped to the back of the open bed of the truck, and jumped down as he advanced, looking as if he very much wanted to bury that knife in her.

Shane caught her, grabbed her hand, and dragged her off to the side before the yelling crowd caught up and swept past them. "Well," he said, "I think we've found our way in. We just wait until they're duking it out, but trust me, these Humans First types don't have a lot of staying power or they'd have been at the gym with me before. I doubt Grandma Kent there is going to do a lot of damage." He pointed at a gray-haired, hunched lady in a shawl, carrying what looked like a gardening tool. "It's like Plants Versus Zombies, and I'm not rooting for the zombies, weirdly enough."

Eve came off the curb and joined them, hefting the heavy equipment bag. "So let's go," she said. "Enough with the talking."

And that, from Eve, was a sign of just how serious this had gotten.

The mob attacked the police line, and it wasn't—as Shane had guessed—much of a fight, really. The cops shot the engines out of the trucks, and when the crowd swarmed in, they were met with nonlethal Tasers and some kind of beanbag guns. It looked painful, but Claire didn't pause to watch, because Shane led them to a weak spot in the police line, and they got down and crawled under one of the SUVs, coming out on the other side behind the lines.

Then it was just a matter of sprinting for the town square.

Avoiding vampires was easy, because there weren't any. Not a one out on the streets, or, once they'd climbed the closed wrought-iron fence, out on the gracious sidewalks of Founder's Square. All of the square's businesses were shuttered and dark. Even the streetlights seemed faint, as if they were in a power-saving mode.

There were still lights on in the big main building, with its giant marble columns and sweeping steps, and they headed that way.

"Okay," Claire said as they stopped in the shadows of the trees, staring up at it. "Let me do the talking, please. And try not to do any fighting unless we have to."

"Who, me?" Shane said, with a bitter twist to his smile. "I'm a lover, not a fighter."

"I don't think the two are exactly mutually exclusive as far as you're concerned," Claire said. "Promise?"

"I promise not to pound anybody who doesn't need pounding," Shane said. "That's about the best you're going to get out of me today. It's been tough enough."

Eve said quietly, "If somebody tells me we're not going to get Michael out of this, then *I'll* pound them. I mean it."

"I know," Claire said. "And I don't mean to hold you back, but the less of that we do up front, the better. Amelie's wired tight right now. Let's not push too hard. We need her."

"Need her for what?" said a cold, quiet voice from behind them.

Claire whipped around, and so did her friends, and there, standing in the shadows not five feet away, was Amelie.

She wasn't sporting her usual entourage of guards, or hangers-on; she wasn't even wearing one of her usual retro-sixties pale suits. She was dressed in a plain pair of blue jeans and a black shirt, and her soft golden hair was down and tied back in a ponytail.

She looked even younger than Claire.

"You were looking for me," Amelie said. "Congratulations on your initiative; you've found me."

"What are you doing out here?" Claire blurted; she hadn't expected this, and wasn't prepared. Shane was busy searching the darkness for approaching vampires; Amelie basically never went anywhere without some kind of überprotection, and this was . . . just strange.

Amelie wasn't even listening to her, anyway. She was staring off into the distance. "Can you hear it?" she asked softly. "The singing. Always, they sing to us." Shane and Claire exchanged glances, and he silently held out his earplugs toward Amelie. She snapped back into focus, and smiled. It was a bitter, sad thing. "That is neither sanitary nor useful, but I thank you for the gesture. We can't resist the call, once it becomes loud enough; I have seen vampires pierce their eardrums to try to fight it, but it is only partly sound. The other part sings inside us, and we can't rip that away so easily."

"Amelie—we found them. We know where they are. Where they're keeping the ones they take." Claire expected that to spark . . . well, something. Some hint of actual *interest.*

But Amelie just went back to staring into the distance, with that calm, neutral expression on her face. "We can always find them, Claire. That isn't the issue. When their numbers are great enough, they sing, and we are called. It always starts slowly, with only one or two, but they grow in numbers the more they feed. Soon, their call will be so strong no one can resist if they remain here. Not even the humans. They prefer us, because we last longer, but humans are food to them as well."

"So that's it?" Shane said, and stepped forward. Amelie's attention snapped back to him, although she didn't move. "You're just giving up? Letting them have this town? Have *us*? What about Michael? What about Oliver and the others? You just . . . walk away?"

"No," she said. "No, I *run,* boy, and if you have a brain in your thick head, you will run as well. Stay here, and they will have you. I've fought the draug before. The vampires fought them for centuries, and lost, and lost, as the draug spread like a disease. They live in the seas, the rivers, the streams, the lakes. Why do you think we moved *here,* where there is so little chance for them to survive?" Overhead, the thick clouds gave out a rumble of thunder, and Amelie looked up and laughed. It sounded wild and uncontrolled. "But now they have adapted, and found their own way to travel. They came with the rain. And where can we go now, that the rain doesn't find us?"

Eve said, "If they're everywhere, why don't they prey on humans? Why haven't we heard of them?"

"You have, in the stories of mermaids and sirens luring the unwary and drowning them," Amelie said. She walked over to a nearby tree and put her back against it. "But human blood can't sustain them completely. When their real prey disappears, the draug die off, you see, except for one, the master, who will go in search. Once he finds vampires to hunt, he will create others of his kind. They need water to breed, but that's easily found. Even here, in this dry place." She sat down, folded her knees up close to her chest, and leaned back against the sturdy, thick bark. "Living things need water. We prey on the living. And the draug in turn prey on us, all too well." She paused, watching them with those cool gray eyes, still pale even in the dim light. "You think I'm a coward."

"I think if you love something, you fight for it," Shane said. "It's always been my theory, anyway."

"And you think I love Morganville."

"You've put a lot of time into it," Claire said. "And you care. I know you care, not just about the vampires but about the humans, too." She took a deep breath and made a gamble. "And you care about Oliver."

Those cool eyes narrowed, just a little. "Why should I? He's been a thorn in my side for several hundred years, and a relentless critic of everything I do here."

Claire shrugged. "I never said it made sense. But you care. I saw him, Amelie. I saw him down in that water. I saw *Michael*. . . ." Her voice shook, and she had to stop, because the memory was too awful, too personal. "I went into that place so I could come back and tell you that they're still alive. That you can still save them."

"You think too well of me." The vampire Founder of Morganville stood up suddenly, the way vampires do. "You can destroy the draug easily enough; they have little strength on their own, until they capture your mind with theirs. But you can never defeat their master. He's survived longer than vampire memory can stretch. And he always, always comes back. What would you have me do? All the vampires left in the world are in danger! Should I risk them to save a few?"

"Yeah," Shane said. "Because that's how it works. You save the people you love, no matter what it costs you. If you don't—" And at his pause, Claire knew he was thinking about his mom, his sister, his father. "If you don't, you never forgive yourself. You said it yourself—the draug keep coming back. When are you going to throw it down and stop running?"

"When I can win," Amelie said. "And that is not here, and it is not now. A good general knows when to avoid a battle as much as wage one."

Claire gave her a long, steady look, and said, "Then never mind. I thought you were serious about saving people, but you're not. You're weak. And you're a loser already. There's no point in avoiding the battle because it's already over." She turned her back on Amelie and slapped Shane and Eve on the shoulders. "Come on. This is a total waste of time. At least the humans around here are spoiling for a fight. Let's go talk to Captain Obvious." She glanced back at Amelie, who hadn't moved. It had been a last shot, and not too likely to work, but Claire still felt bad that she'd missed.

Amelie really wasn't going to do *anything* to stop this.

The three of them made it almost ten feet before Amelie said, in a quietly resigned voice, "Maybe it is the time. Maybe there's no point now in running. So few of us will make it, and the world—the world is much harder, today. Humans more powerful. We are hemmed in by enemies. Maybe it's time to fight, after all."

The relief was so intense that Claire almost stumbled. She got hold of herself and slowly turned around. Amelie was on her feet again, hands behind her back. Not exactly Action Figure Amelie, but at least she wasn't just . . . sitting.

"You said the draug are feeding on those they take. I'm just guessing, but it isn't like vampires, right? They don't make their victims like themselves?" *Please tell me Michael isn't becoming one of . . . those things.*

"Draug biology, if you can stretch science that far, works differently," Amelie said. "They draw the blood and life from their victims, and it fuels their reproduction, which is more akin to bacteria than to what either of our kind do. A master draug splits himself into two, and then those two may do the same, given enough nourishment."

"And the ones in the pool?" Shane asked. "They're not dead, right?"

"No. Draug prefer their prey living. Water weighs us down, saps us of strength, and it is their stronghold. They will feed on a trapped vampire for weeks, if not months, before they discard him. Humans don't last so long." She was silent for a moment before she asked, "How many did you see in this place?"

"Vampires? Maybe twenty in the pool," Shane said. "A few humans but—I don't think they were alive down there."

"Twenty vampires means that he has spawned at least a hundred of his own."

"Well, if it helps, we killed—" Eve consulted with Shane, whispering fast, and then said, "Maybe ten?"

"A good start, but hardly enough." Amelie suddenly smiled, and turned her head slightly to the right. "You may come out now, if you have anything useful to add."

Claire hadn't had any idea another vampire had been watching them, until Myrnin moved; he'd blended completely into the shadows, which was really odd, because he was wearing a Hawaiian shirt with surfers on it, a pair of ragged blue jeans, and flip-flops.

And sunglasses. Shiny wraparound sunglasses.

"You've described the problem accurately enough," Myrnin said.

"And did you bring what I asked?"

"I'm insane, not forgetful." Myrnin took off the glasses and stuck them up on top of his head. "I thought you were leaving."

"I don't believe that I'm quite ready yet," Amelie replied. She was looking at him very oddly. "What, pray, are you wearing?"

"I thought I might go to the pool," he said. "And I thought I would wear something appropriate. What are *you* wearing?"

"You knew," Claire said. "You already knew about the pool."

"I suspected," Myrnin said. "I measured their singing and found the largest likely source of water they could use at its center. It is excellent to have a confirmation before I proceeded."

"You," Amelie said. "*You* were going. Alone."

"I would have asked you before I did," Myrnin said. "But I'm done with running, Amelie. And I'm quite fond of my lab. I'm not willing to leave it. Besides, Bob's still in his tank. I can't just abandon him."

"You were going to fight them." Amelie couldn't seem to wrap her head around it. "You."

He shrugged. "It would be a logical thing to do; taking his food supply of those trapped will stop the reproductive cycle. It will slow him down, and we *need* to slow him down. He's gotten much too powerful, too fast, for us to make a safe evacuation. That's become all too clear."

"You shame me," Amelie said quietly. "You all do."

Myrnin bowed to her, just slightly. "I'm ever at your service, dear lady. But from time to time, I think you value our lives a bit too much. It's time to stand. I think you see it now."

"Myrnin—Amelie said you couldn't resist the call of the draug," Claire said. "How do you plan on getting close to them?"

Myrnin reached back into the shadows and pulled out a backpack. It looked, Claire thought, familiar, like—"Wait!" she blurted. "Is that mine?"

"Don't worry, I took your books out first," Myrnin said. "Very useful, these backpacker things."

"Backpacks."

He shrugged. "In any case." He smiled at her, a genuine expression of warmth, and said, "I'm very glad you're all right, Claire."

"Yeah," Shane said coldly. "Thanks for helping us get her back. What's in the pack?"

Myrnin pulled out a device, something small but, from the way he handled it, heavy; he flipped a switch, and Claire heard a distant howling rise up on the night air. "Oops, wrong setting," he said, and quickly turned a dial. "There."

Amelie took in a sudden, deep breath, and closed her eyes. "Oh," she murmured. "Oh, that is good. So good. You're certain it will work as we get closer?"

"It will work," Myrnin said, "and I'm frankly offended you should ask such a thing, Amelie. Have I ever—" He thought better of asking *that* question, Claire saw. "Well. In any case, it will work. My word."

"Your life," she corrected him. "Words will not protect us. That must, at all costs."

"Um . . . what is it?" Eve asked.

"Blessed silence," Amelie said.

"Noise cancellation," Myrnin said at the same time. "To block out their calls."

"Awesome," Claire said. "Weapons?"

For answer, Myrnin took out a pair of black leather gloves, which he put on, and tossed another to Amelie. She frowned at them, then pulled them on.

He tossed her a . . . "Shotgun?" Claire asked. "Okay, I'm not sure that will actually . . ."

"It's a sawed-off shotgun, my dear, loaded with silver pellets," Myrnin said, "and it took me most of the day to acquire the materials, cast them, and load the cartridges. It works best when you stand at least ten feet away to fire. Maximum spread." He dug in his backpack and pulled out a black leather belt with loops. Each loop was filled with a red shotgun cartridge. He tossed it to Amelie, and she put the gun down and fastened it low on her hips, gunfighter-style. Myrnin tossed his over his shoulder, took out his own sawed-off, which he pumped with unsettling enthusiasm. "Let's go hunting, shall we?"

Shane nudged Claire and said, under his breath, "Is this terrifying, or is it just me? Because it might just be me."

"It's not," she whispered back. "God, we're all going to die."

"Well," Myrnin said, just as if they'd said it out loud, "at least we'll go out together, my friends." He rested the shotgun on his shoulder and made an *after you* bow to Amelie. "I also secured us transportation. I hope you'll like it."

"Oh, this is good," Eve said. "I'm putting down a bet that it's a parade float."

"Not taking that one," Shane said. "Hey, do we get cool shotguns?"

"No," Amelie said, and made a sharp, military gesture. "With me. And stay close."

EIGHTEEN

AMELIE

☽

There is a certain freedom in giving up all hope. One is no longer bound by the cords of dread or fear; you simply move toward the inevitable without thinking on the consequences.

I knew that we would not escape the draug; that much, history had taught me. I'd seen entire vampire clans vanish—drawn, drowned, drained. I'd seen the mightiest and most clever of our kind brought to ruin; the more vampires fought, the more draug swarmed, until all was lost.

So why was I driving toward what was certainly going to be my doom? Perhaps only to stop running from it. It had been following me a long time—all my life—like a dark and lengthy shadow, and perhaps Claire had been right from the beginning: perhaps it was time to stop and draw a line, and hold it.

Even if there was no chance of winning.

I had lost so many whom I cared for, over the years; losing was the natural state of existence for one like me. But Morganville . . . Morganville was a special thing, a creation unlike anything in the rest of the world, and I did not think I had the strength, nor the courage, to build it again, somewhere else, only to see it fall and shatter again.

I was the Founder of Morganville, and maybe it was fit that I should end my days here, after all.

"Left," Claire said. She pointed, and I turned the wheel of the Bloodmobile in that direction. Myrnin had made an excellent choice, I thought, in liberating the large black vehicle; it had ample room inside for any we could rescue, and two large coolers well stocked with human blood. If we could, in truth, drag any vampires from the water, they'd be mad with hunger.

Of course, the chances of any rescue were remarkably small, but it felt right to be prepared. One should not go to one's doom without a proper effort. It was a bother that these young people, with all their short lives ahead of them, should be so willing to throw them away, but that could be said of any soldier in any war.

And we were at war. One we would inevitably lose.

I had not properly appreciated how much Morganville had changed in the past few days; I had spent too much time walled up in my office, hiding from the truth. A fight was under way between the Morganville police and a ragged band of human opponents, who were surprisingly holding their own. There were no businesses open in town, not even one. All was dark, closed, abandoned.

Dead.

Human habitations still burned lights, and I expected that inside them families huddled, terrified and waiting for some kind of rescue; morning would dawn soon, and they would prepare to go to Founder's Square, where they'd been promised what they'd always craved.

Freedom.

I would not be there to see their betrayal. I mourned the fact of it, and the necessity, but at least I would pay for it with my life. That was a kind of redemption, wasn't it?

The closer we drew to the old Civic Pool, the quieter Morganville became. Lights still burned in homes, but in many the doors were open, the inhabitants lured away, or worse. It was as if this part of the town was dead and already rotting away. Myrnin's machine produced a steady, low-level humming that was maddening in its monotony, but it did block the eerie, seductive call of the draug.

For now.

"Can you still hear it?" Claire asked me. She was sitting down on the bench seat behind us, while Myrnin had taken the passenger position to my right. "I can't. Is it still there?"

"Oh yes," I said. There were hints of sound breaking through the interference, random wails and whispers, but not enough to create a hold on us. But, I reminded myself, we were still not face-to-face with the draug, or with Magnus himself. That would make things much more dangerous. "If you begin to hear it, tell me immediately."

"We have these," Claire said, and held up a pair of blue earplugs. "They worked before."

"They might not now," Myrnin said. "The draug's call gets stronger and louder as they grow, and I can promise you, they are growing. You have silver weapons in that bag, I assume?"

"Yep," Shane said. He unzipped it and threw a fencing épée to Eve, who snatched it out of the air with the panache of someone who had seen far too many films in which the heroes lived. He took out bottles and put them in his pockets, handed more to Claire, and finally drew out silver-coated stakes. "The crossbows won't work, too much force. It goes straight through them, right? Not enough damage."

"Correct," I said. "Their substance is deceptively soft, and anything moving at high velocity, unless it spreads, will only slow them down. To stop a draug, you must cut or stab them with silver that stays in place for at least a few seconds for it to take effect. They will collapse and flee in liquid form to escape it. But don't touch them even then. In liquid form, they have tiny needles which can pierce skin."

What I did not say, and could not, was that the vampires in the pool were not submerged in water—or not wholly in it. The draug entered the water and dispersed, and fed, then emerged again. The pool would be swarming with the things, invisible and deadly.

And there was very little that could stop them that would not also kill the vampires we sought to rescue. Vampire and draug shared a common root, in the dim mists of time. We had taken very different paths, but had some vulnerabilities in common, still. Had there been no vampires in the pool, we could have poisoned it with silver; at the very least, it would have forced them out and on land, where we would have the advantage.

But this was far worse.

"How are we going to get them out?" Claire asked. "They're tied or something, down at the bottom."

"Someone will have to dive in and free them," I said.

"Guess that's me," Shane said, leaning forward. "Take a right up here. We're almost there."

"Why you?" Claire asked, frowning. "I could—"

"Swim team in high school," Shane said. "I can dive, too. I can stay down longer than you."

"Why can't you do it?" Eve asked me. "Vampires don't need to breathe."

"There are draug in the water. A vampire who goes in . . . is not likely to come out without help."

"See?" Shane said. "My job. You guys just hold them off."

It wasn't going to be so simple, but his principle was correct, and there was no reason to cast pessimism on our cause now. We were committed.

Freedom in abandoning hope, indeed.

There was one still-working streetlight here, and I parked the Bloodmobile as close as I could to the curb underneath it. Light mattered little to me or to Myrnin, but it would be important for our human friends, if we were able to emerge from this place. I turned the engine off. Even with the constant humming cycle of Myrnin's tone generator, the call of the draug was there, pulling inside me like a faint whispering shadow. I could resist it, but it stained the world around me with its desperation.

"Myrnin and I will go first," I said. "We will clear a path and hold it for you. Eve and Claire, you will hold the rear against any who try to come from outside to attack. Shane, when we clear the way to the pool, you will dive in and begin to cut the captives free. You'll have to drag them up and out of the water, one at a time. Get as many out as you can." I hesitated, then said, "You'll feel a burning sensation. That will be the draug draining you. It will weaken you quickly. Be careful."

Shane went still for a second, then nodded. I could not read his expression, but I felt the spike of adrenaline from him. Fear. A completely sensible reaction, although he had no idea what we were going to face. Not yet.

"Wait," Claire said. "Maybe we should—"

Shane took her hand, and their eyes met. He gave her a smile, and had I had a heart to be broken, that might have cracked it, a little. "Too late for that, beautiful," he said, and kissed her fingers. "We agreed, didn't we? Time to throw it all in. It's the only way we can make it."

He was right about that. I would not take a human from Morganville, not even Claire, if it came to that. They would all stay, and they would all . . .

Be given their freedom.

I could not, even now, face the terrible reality of the betrayal of that.

So instead, I opened my door, took hold of my shotgun, and said, "Go."

Myrnin had shed all hint of madness, which was a blessing; he moved with the lithe grace and speed of any vampire, and we communicated through slight gestures and looks as we took the cracked, molding steps up to the building's door. I remembered when this had been built; it seemed like such a short time ago that I'd stood on these steps with the then-mayor, shaded by a black umbrella and waving in regal boredom to a crowd of gawkers. It had been one of the last times I had appeared in public to humans, because one of them had attempted to throw silver solution on me. One of my bodyguards had been badly scarred in the assassination attempt.

I remembered the inside of this place.

It was nothing like my memories.

The ruin of the reception area was breathtaking; the carpets were mildewed and curling, the walls furred with thick, black fungus. Paint peeled from the sagging ceiling, but I could still see the lovely art deco designs beneath, like the straight bones of a rotten body.

There were no draug there to meet us.

The narrow hallway ahead was too small for Myrnin and me to enter together, so with a tiny gesture I held him back, and plunged on ahead, into a waking nightmare.

At first glance, I thought there was only one draug in the room; we could not see them, not clearly, even concentrating on them directly.

But Magnus wanted me to see him. It pleased him to show me his mask, and, behind that, his true nature. The mask was a rubbery caricature of humanity, exactly bland; the thing behind it was made of darkness and rot, and was only vaguely in a shape that mimicked our own.

"Amelie," he said. Unlike the draug's call, this was a human-like voice, one that cut through Myrnin's device cleanly. "You surprise me. I thought you'd run. You always have."

"I am happy to surprise you," I said, and pointed my shotgun at his chest. He was too far away for it to be effective, and he knew it; he smiled, a rubbery stretch of falsely human lips while the thing behind it bared teeth.

I sensed the draug rather than saw them as they emerged from the mold-encrusted walls, flooding down in pools and forming into shapes. They were all around us. I cast a lightning-fast look at Myrnin, who was slightly behind me to my right. He, too, was surrounded.

"Well," Myrnin said, in a light and oddly happy voice, "I believe it's time for a field test."

And he aimed at the wall of draug closing on him, and fired.

I spun toward mine and fired at the same instant, sending a

devastating spray of silver pellets into them. The friction of the air softened the metal and spread it, adding to the chaos of the effect, and with one shot, three draug shrieked and blew apart into liquid that rushed across the cracked tile floor toward the sparkling blue pool.

I pumped the shotgun and fired, keeping time with Myrnin's blasts. Vampire ears are sensitive, and the noise was painfully loud, but a fierce joy was on me as I saw our enemies fall. It was like the old times, the *oldest* times, riding to battle with a sword singing in my hand and a scream rising in the back of my throat, my hair flying like a banner. . . .

I heard a splash. Shane had entered the pool. I pumped another round into the shotgun and fired, and risked a glance his direction. The boy's form glided through the water, heading toward the deeper end.

I saw Oliver, face upturned and pallid. His eyes were wide and blank as a doll's, consumed with agony.

I snarled, turned back to the draug, and obliterated another line of them.

"I'm out," Myrnin said in a businesslike tone. "Reloading."

I spun to cover him and fired into the draug that were lurching toward him as he fed new shells into the shotgun, moving as calmly and carefully as if he'd been all alone on a target range. I fired my last load to protect him as he finished.

And a draug took me from behind.

I dropped my empty shotgun, drew a silver-coated knife from the sheath at my belt, and turned. I sliced it across the false skin, dragging deep. The draug collapsed against me, sticky almost-flesh, and its liquid essence flooded over my skin and stung hard.

I gagged as it tried to force its way down my nose and throat.

In the pool, Shane surfaced, sputtering and screaming with pain. He was towing a vampire toward the edge. Not Oliver.

Michael.

He shoved Michael up to flop bonelessly onto the tiles, and I saw that Shane's face was red with tiny needle-sharp stings. He was gasping and cramping with agony, but he sucked in a deep breath and submerged, again.

I had rarely admired the courage of humans, but in that moment, I loved him for it.

I clawed the draug's cold, thick liquid from my face, spit out the foul taste of it, and slashed at the next one to come at me. Behind me, Myrnin's shotgun was roaring again. I needed time to reload, but I couldn't pause. Michael was lying at my feet, vulnerable and shuddering. I was no longer fighting for just my own existence, but his.

I should have known that Claire would fail to follow orders.

She charged toward me with two bottles in her hands—some kind of water bottles, with the caps dangling free. A squeeze of her hands sent a spray of silver into the mass of draug, and the shrieks were so deafening that I felt the pull of them even through the roar of Myrnin's machine. She emptied the bottles and dropped them to grab Michael under the arms, and dragged him away, toward the hallway.

I took advantage of the temporary lull to take up my shotgun, reload with quick, sure flicks of my fingers, and begin firing again. The room stank of terror, mildew, cordite, and the rotten stench of death and draug, but against all odds, we were still alive.

Shane pushed another limp body out of the pool and went down again. I risked a fast look. Naomi. My blood-sister looked drained and very near to her final death.

She reached out toward me, and I saw the desperate terror in her eyes. I touched her hand with mine, then pumped a fresh shell and fired.

The draug kept coming. I sensed Claire coming back and dragging Naomi away, sensed Shane bringing another body out.

"Get out!" Myrnin was shouting—not to me, to the young man, who was struggling toward the shallower end of the pool. He was being pulled down, I realized. The draug, in their liquid form, had coated his body. He was too weak now to fight.

He wasn't going to make it.

"Bother," Myrnin said. He turned toward me, and flung his shotgun in my direction; I grabbed it out of the air, pumped it, and fired at both my opponents and his simultaneously, driving them back.

It was a miracle from the hands of God that we had gotten this far, I thought.

Myrnin *jumped into the pool,* grabbed Shane's shoulders, and pulled him to the steps, dumped him on the tile, and I saw the liquid that had coated Myrnin's skin during that brief immersion writhe, thicken, and squirm up his body toward his face. He scraped the worst of it off, grabbed Shane, and threw him bodily toward the door.

I looked down. There were so many more trapped there in the pool. So many of my people, my responsibilities, and I could not save them. Some I knew and loved. Some I disliked. All were precious to me, for one reason or another, even if because they were now so rare in this world.

Oliver was the last one that Shane had dragged from the pool, and he lay at my feet, limp and still.

"Myrnin!" I shouted. "Get Oliver!" I pumped and fired both shotguns again, and Myrnin ducked under the blasts to take Oliver under the shoulders. "Get him out!"

Myrnin's gun was out, and there would be no opportunity now to reload. Mine had two shells left. As Myrnin dragged Oliver for the exit, I fired them in rapid succession, dropped both weapons, and turned to go.

Magnus was in my way.

I grabbed for my knife, but he was faster. His hand went around my throat, and the singing, the *singing* . . . it crawled inside my mind and ripped apart my fury, my will, my soul.

"Not you," he said. "You don't escape, Amelie. Not this time."

He was right. There was no escape. There was nothing now but darkness, and drowning, and despair.

But I had one thing left. Just one.

I couldn't reach my knife, but I could reach the glass vial in my pocket. I crushed it in my hand and let it fall into the water in a bright rush of silver.

The silver flecks spread, and where they touched, draug glittered, turned visible, and died.

My own people would die, too, from the poison, but at least they would be at peace, and he'd be denied using them so cruelly.

"No!" Magnus flung me back, too late; it was done, and there was no undoing it. What I'd dropped into the pool was enough silver poison to kill everything in it. *"No!"*

He snarled and jumped for me, and I got my knife out, but in the end, his fangs sank deep enough in me to inject a cold, black poison, and I fell.

I heard shouts, and a confused clatter of a shotgun firing, and then . . .

. . . Then it was gone, and my last thought was one of odd satisfaction.

At last, I have stopped running.

Cold comfort, but comfort nonetheless.

NINETEEN

CLAIRE

☽

Going after Michael was sheer instinct, because Claire knew that Eve would do it in the next heartbeat, and Claire could feel the lingering, if weakened, rush of vampire blood in her own veins. It made her faster, and a little stronger, and right now, that made her the only real choice. "Stay!" she shouted at Eve, and tossed her the silver knife she'd been holding. Eve caught it and slashed at a draug—God, at least they knew what to call them now—who oozed out of the darkness at her. It screamed that awful noise and collapsed into a sticky, skin-thickened puddle.

Claire raced into the pool room.

It would have been an incredible sight, if she'd been able to stop to appreciate it; she got a blurred snapshot impression of Amelie and Myrnin, standing with their backs to each other, firing their shotguns in shattering roars that blasted apart draug in greasy black and silver splatters. Not *killing* them, really, Claire thought; she saw the sticky fluid slipping over the sides of the pool. They'd be feeding now, and gathering the strength to come back out.

Shane was in that water. It made her sick and hopeless to see him there, diving again with a kick of his feet.

Michael lay limp on the tiles, oozing a thick liquid that wasn't really water, or at least not completely.

Amelie was in trouble. Claire didn't think; she pulled the squeeze bottles that Shane had given her out of her pockets, popped the caps, and yelled as she squirted the contents at the attacking draug in two silvery arcs.

It worked, and even as it did, she was aware of Amelie methodically working in a blur, shoving shotgun shells into her weapon. By the time the bottles were empty, she was pumping the action and ready to fire.

Claire dropped the bottles and ducked as Amelie aimed and fired over her head. She grabbed Michael and immediately felt the sting of draug on her hands, but she pulled anyway, fast, for both their lives.

Eve looked at her as Claire reappeared in the hall. Claire stopped and hefted Michael up higher, braced him, and said, "I need you to keep us clear!" Eve's gaze was riveted on Michael's white, slack face, but she nodded. She slashed her silver sword across a draug that blocked the path to the door, then forced another one out of the way as Claire dragged Michael out.

The night air hit her in a rush. It was staggering how different it was from the atmosphere in that building, and Claire coughed and choked now as she bumped him down the steps. Eve ran ahead and yanked open the door of the Bloodmobile. A draug lunged out from under the vehicle, and she stabbed at him, yelping in surprise. It slithered into a drain.

Claire got Michael up and into the Bloodmobile. "Clean him off!" she told Eve, and tossed her a towel. "Blood's in the cooler! I have to get the rest of them!"

Eve, for once, was speechless. She took the towel and began wiping Michael's face clear of the thick, crawling slime as he began to spit it up in uncontrollable coughs.

His eyes were bright, bright red.

Claire plunged back into the night. Her only defense right now was speed; she couldn't carry weapons and drag victims. Luckily, the draug hadn't regrouped yet in the foyer; most of them were concentrated on Amelie and Myrnin, at the pool. She skidded into the big, open room with its glittering blue pool and foul, choking smell, just as Shane rolled another body out. Naomi.

She was easier to pull—frail, in fact—and Claire got her out without even a single draug coming for them, all the way to the Bloodmobile.

She got her in and on one of the donation chairs, and realized that Eve and Michael were no longer where she'd left them. "Eve?"

She heard a gasp, and went toward the back, where the coolers were.

Eve was lying on the floor. One of the coolers was open, and a blood bag lay fallen next to her hand.

And Michael was crouched over her, feeding.

"No!" Claire screamed. He whirled on her, snarling, and she backed up a step. "No, Michael, *stop*! She's trying to help you! *Stop!* You have to stop!"

He had blood all over his mouth, and he looked . . . savage. Desperate. The glow in his eyes was as bright as hellfire, and Eve moaned and tried to turn over.

He looked down at her, and snarled with sharp, glittering fangs fully extended.

"God," Claire whispered, and didn't really think. She just threw herself on him, locked her forearm under his chin, and pulled, hard.

It was just enough to get him away from Eve, who rolled, grabbed the blood bag, and shoved it in Michael's mouth. He bit down, and the blood squirted out. He gulped, and sucked, and drained it. Eve pulled another one out and gave him that, then a third one.

And Claire felt his body language change. It wasn't gradual—it was sudden, as if he'd been possessed or something.

Michael spat the empty blood bag out and after a second, said, "Oh my God, no . . ."

That sounded like him. Claire let go, and he collapsed backward, throwing himself *away* from Eve, who was holding her wounded neck. She looked pale and very shaky.

"Eve," he said. "Eve. No . . ."

"It's all right," she said. It wasn't. Claire could see the blood running out from under her hand, but there wasn't time—there wasn't any *time*. She grabbed the first aid kit and shoved it in Michael's limp hands.

"Help her!" she screamed at him. She grabbed a handful of blood bags and went back to Naomi; if Michael had gone nuts, Naomi would be next, and they didn't need her attacking from behind. The slender female vamp snarled at Claire when she came closer, and she threw her first blood bag to her. Naomi swiped it out of the air and bit viciously into it.

Ugh.

Claire fed her three that way and left a fourth next to her, then ran for the doors.

She reached the hallway just as Shane came sliding her way with bowling-ball velocity, and ran right into her. He was soaking wet, and he was *bleeding*—all over, as if he was sweating it. He shuddered and made little horrible sounds in the back of his throat, but he scrambled to his feet, grabbed her hand, and they ran. She'd never seen him really run like that before, like someone really in the grip of mindless fear, but she understood it.

They made it to the Bloodmobile just as Myrnin came out the door, firing a shotgun behind him and dragging Oliver with his other hand. Claire got Shane into a seat and met Myrnin at the door to pull Oliver inside. Naomi was awake and less insane now, and when Claire screamed at her to get blood, Naomi staggered to the back and came back with armloads.

"Where's Amelie?" Claire yelled at Myrnin, who was standing in the vehicle's door, still firing. He shook his head. He looked taut and desperate, and his eyes were glowing red not so much with hunger as with fear, she thought.

Amelie hadn't come out.

"We have to go back!" Claire said. Myrnin's shotgun ran dry, and he backed up into the Bloodmobile and slammed the door shut as a draug rushed forward at them.

"We can't," he said. "I'm out of shells." He sounded shaken and oddly flat, and he shoved her back when she tried to push past him. "*No.* Wait."

Magnus was standing in the doorway of the Civic Pool. He was holding Amelie, and she was limp as a doll.

Magnus held her up in silent triumph. "If you want her," he said, "come and get—"

Somebody shot him. Not Myrnin, because he was out of shells. Not Amelie, who was hanging helpless.

The shot came from a speeding pickup truck that raced by,

then screamed into a slewing 360-degree turn, and Claire recognized it. Men poured out, all armed, desperate, and *human.*

And Captain Obvious was in the lead, pumping another shell into his shotgun.

Magnus hadn't gone down, and hadn't even screamed, so whatever they were firing wasn't silver, but it was inconveniencing him, at the very least. He dropped Amelie, and she rolled limply down the steps to a crumpled heap as Magnus turned his empty, nothuman eyes on the new threat.

And laughed.

Myrnin unlocked the Bloodmobile door, lunged out, grabbed Amelie, and jumped back inside as the firing continued. "Well," he said, "it does appear that your idiot redneck friends are good for something after all. Do tell them to run, Claire." He looked down at Amelie, and stopped talking. His eyes went from red to black in a second.

Claire snapped open the window and screamed at the men in the truck. They kept firing. Well, she'd tried.

"Myrnin?" Claire asked, short of breath with fear.

He didn't look up. "Drive," he said. "Take us out of here." It was a good idea, because Captain Obvious and his friends had finished unloading their bullets into Magnus and the draug, and were piling back into the bed of their pickup, which was revving its engine. Claire jumped into the driver's seat, started the Bloodmobile, and followed the pickup as it drove away. She couldn't match its speed, but it didn't matter. The pickup was racing toward the edge of town, and she didn't intend to go that way.

She turned and headed toward Founder's Square.

"Is she alive?" Claire asked, as Myrnin sat down in the passenger seat with Amelie cradled in his arms. She looked as pale as a marble statue now. Her eyes were closed.

"For now," he said. He pulled back the collar of her black shirt, and Claire saw two giant black holes in her skin, three or four times the size of even the messiest vampire bite she'd ever seen. "There's no cure for a master draug's bite."

It was silent in Founder's Square. The cops had formed their lines again; the fight with the mob was over, just some wrecked vehicles left to mark the whole event.

The whole thing had a nightmare kind of stillness to it. Claire pulled the Bloodmobile up to the curb and parked it, and Myrnin silently stood up with Amelie in his arms.

Oliver blocked him as he turned for the door.

Oliver was still pale, and trembling, but he seemed sane, at least; he'd wiped the excess blood he'd gulped off his mouth, but there were still smears of dark red here and there. He didn't speak, but he held out his arms, and Myrnin, after a brief hesitation, handed Amelie to him.

Oliver shut his eyes for a moment, then nodded and took her outside.

Naomi followed, moving more slowly than Claire had ever seen a vampire move. Myrnin helped her out, which would have looked gallant except for his outfit, which was more like something a crazed beachcomber would wear than a knight in armor, however tarnished.

That accounted for almost all the vampires they'd rescued. Claire got up and walked toward the back. She stopped when she reached Shane, who was lying down on a donation couch. He'd wiped himself clean of the blood, but she could see bleeding pinpricks on his face and hands. He looked terrible, she thought, and wanted to cry in wild, screaming sobs. Somehow, she gulped it back.

He sat up and held out his arms, and she collapsed against him. He kissed her, and even though he still tasted like that pool, like all the nightmares, she sank into the kiss, because underneath it he was Shane, he was alive, he was *alive.*

And so was she.

He was shaking, she realized, but he was trying to comfort her with soothing strokes down her back, a gentle touch on her face.

Neither one of them tried to speak.

Michael carried Eve past them. There was a thick bandage on her neck, but the bleeding seemed to have stopped, and she seemed okay. She had her arms around him, and her head was lying in the hollow of his shoulder, and Claire thought she'd never seen a look like that on Michael's face, that complicated mixture of fierce love and fear and regret.

He looked almost as frail as Naomi had, but he carried her anyway.

"What are we going to do?" Claire whispered. "Oh God, Shane, what *can* we do?"

He shook his head and sighed, and pressed his lips against her hair in a gentle kiss. "We're going to win," he said. "That's our only choice. I don't know how, and I don't know what the cost is going to be. But we're going to win."

"Yes." The voice was raw, and quiet, but it was Oliver's. He was standing in the doorway, and Amelie was still in his arms. "There's no option now. We fight them for Morganville. All of us." He looked down at Amelie. "And the cost will be high, Mr. Collins. It will be very high indeed. Come now. It won't be safe out here for long, and the sun is coming up."

Claire didn't want to move, but she did, and helped Shane up. Oliver stared at the two of them for a moment, then shook his head.

"What?" Shane asked.

"I don't understand humans at all," he said. "Why would you do such a thing, for us?"

Shane exchanged a look with Claire, and shrugged. "Had to be done," he said. "And we needed you to stop Amelie from pulling the pin on Morganville. She was going to kill us all."

Oliver sighed. "What makes you think I won't?"

"Because you're a fighter," Shane said. "Like me. And now you're in charge."

"Oh, trust me, you won't enjoy that," Oliver said, with a touch of his old acid tone. "We haven't even begun to fight."

"Good," Shane said. "Because as far as I can tell, we're getting our asses kicked, and I'm tired of that."

Oliver gave him a slow, odd smile. "So am I," he said. He turned to go and said, in an offhand kind of way, "Thank you."

He was gone before Shane could make some kind of smart-ass remark. As, Claire could tell, he'd been about to do.

"Don't," Claire warned him, and put her finger to his lips. "Just enjoy the moment."

"I am," he said. He met her eyes, and in that moment, she could see absolutely everything in them. Everything he felt. All the fear and the anger and the horror and the determination.

And the love. So much of that.

"Sun's up," he said. She blinked and realized that outside the open door of the Bloodmobile there was a pink blush on the horizon. A new day. Maybe the last day.

He took her hand and led her out into it, and despite everything, despite the stillness and the danger and all that she knew, Claire took a deep breath of fresh, clean air and thought, *We're going to win. We have to win.*

And standing there with the sunrise washing over them, driving away the clouds, she thought that maybe, just maybe, it was possible.

"Wait," Shane said, and pulled her to a stop as she started to follow Michael, who'd already made it to the shadows, down the sidewalk toward the square. "Claire."

"We shouldn't stay out here even if the sun's up. The draug—"

He put his hands on either side of her face, looked down at her, and said, "I want you to understand something. I hate this place. I hate Morganville. I hate the vampires. But I swear to God, I will fight to my last drop of blood for Michael and Eve and *you*. Do you understand? If you want to run, if you want to go right now, I'll go. But I'm not going without you."

"If we run, what's to stop Oliver from letting everyone die?" she asked him. "From doing just what Amelie would have done?"

"God, Claire—stop thinking about them. Think about you. Just you."

"I am," she said. "I can't face being a coward. Not this time."

"Then we stay," he said. "And when we get out of this . . . and we *will* get out of this . . . I want you to promise me one thing."

"What?"

He swallowed, and shifted his weight a little uneasily, and then said, very quietly, his lips almost touching hers, "Promise me you'll marry me. Not now. Someday. Because I need to know."

Claire felt a flutter inside, like a bird trying to fly, and a rush of heat that made her dizzy. And something else, something fragile as a soap bubble, and just as beautiful. Joy, in the middle of all this horror and heartbreak.

"Yes," she whispered back. "I promise."

And she kissed him, and kissed him, and kissed him, while the sun came up and bathed Morganville in one last, shining day.

TRACK LIST

As always, I need a sound track to keep me going as I write! So here, for your listening pleasure, is a list of the songs I used on my own personal track list. Please buy the music, don't torrent it; musicians work hard to make beautiful things, and only you can make sure they can continue to do so.

"You're Going Down"	Sick Puppies
"Bullseye"	Aly & AJ
"Fighter"	Christina Aguilera
"Harder to Breathe"	Maroon 5
"Need You"	Travie McCoy
"Monster Hospital (MSTRKRFT Remix)"	Metric
"Town Called Heartbreak"	Patti Scialfa
"Don't Fear the Reaper"	Heaven 17
"I'm Gonna Make It"	Sanders Bohlke
"Land of Jail"	Gram Rabbit
"Never Underestimate a Girl"	Vanessa Hudgens
"The Hard Stuff"	Wired Desire
"Young"	Hollywood Undead

"Sail"	AWOLNATION
"99 Problems"	Hugo
"The Big Bang"	Rock Mafia
"Vicodin"	The Knifings
"In Love with You"	Jared Evan
"Play with Fire"	Hilary Duff
"Dead Girls Are Easy"	The 69 Eyes
"Black River Killer"	Blitzen Trapper
"So Bring It On"	The Cheetah Girls
"The Stone"	Ashes Divide
"Dirty Angel"	Voodoo Johnson
"Tape Loop"	Morcheeba
"My Confessions"	Onesidezero
"Voodoo Banjo"	Bonepony
"Power"	Shades of Race Cars
"Littleblood"	Division Day
"Pretty Buildings"	People in Planes
"Show Me Your Teeth"	Year Long Disaster
"Grenade"	Bruno Mars
"To Lose My Life"	White Lies
"New In Town"	Little Boots
"Chew Me Up and Spit Me Out"	Cobra Starship
"Toxic Valentine"	All Time Low
"Ready for the Floor"	Lissy Trullie
"To the Edge"	Lacuna Coil
"I Won't Tell You"	Lacuna Coil
"Spellbound"	Lacuna Coil
"What Have You Done"	Within Temptation (feat. Keith Caputo)
"Black Lung Heartache"	Joe Bonamassa
"Dream On"	Kelly Sweet

Read on for an exciting excerpt from
Rachel Caine's next Morganville Vampires novel,

Black Dawn

Coming in May 2012 from NAL

CLAIRE

It would have been better if he'd screamed.

Michael Glass didn't scream. Instead, he made a terrible keening noise in the back of his throat, arched his back, and began to flail violently inside his zipped-up sleeping bag. Fabric shredded under vampire strength, and insulation bulged out of the tears as he fought his way free, but even once it was off him he just kept . . . flailing.

Across the room, Claire Danvers bolted straight to her feet, tripped over her own sleeping bag, and managed to catch herself against a wall just before she hit the floor face-first. Her heart was slamming too fast against her ribs, and she had the sour, helpless taste of panic in her mouth.

They're here was the only coherent thought in her head. She had to be ready to fight, to run, to react, but all she could think of was how utterly scared she was just now. And how helpless.

There were things out there in the world, things that *vampires* feared, and now those things were here. She was only seconds out of a very light, fitful sleep, but she knew that the nightmares had followed her effortlessly right into the real world. *The draug.* They weren't vampires; they were something else, something that moved through water, formed out of it, dragged vampires down to a slow and awful death.

A week ago, she'd have laughed something like that off as a bad joke, but then she'd seen them come for Morganville, Texas. Come with the rains that never fell in this desert-locked, sunbaked town where the vampires had, finally, made their last stand.

Today she woke up with the blind and panicked knowledge that no matter how bad the world was with vampires in it, a world that held the draug was *vastly* worse. They'd come to Morganville, infiltrated stealthily, built their numbers until they were ready to fight . . . until they could sing their infinitely awful song that somehow, impossibly, was also beautiful and irresistible. To humans as well as to vamps.

The strongest of Morganville's vampires had gone up against it, and scored a few hits . . . but not without cost. Amelie, the ice-queen ruler of the town, had been bitten; without her, it was all going to get worse, fast.

Michael was still thrashing and making that terrible *sound,* and it came to Claire gradually that instead of cowering here while her brain caught up, she should go to him. Help him.

And then the lights brightened from dim to dazzling in the big carpeted room, and she saw her boyfriend, Shane Collins, standing in the doorway, looking first at her, then over at Michael, who was still desperately struggling against . . . nothing.

Against his nightmare.

Claire pulled in a deep breath, shut her eyes for a second, then made the OK sign to Shane; he nodded back and went to their friend's side. Michael was tangled up in the shredded remains of his sleeping bag, still flailing and, as far as Claire could tell, still dead asleep. Shane crouched down and, after a brief hesitation, reached out and put his hand on Michael's shoulder.

Michael came awake instantly—vampire speed. In one blurred second he was sitting up, one hand wrapped around Shane's wrist, eyes open and blazing red, fangs down and catching the light on razor-sharp points and edges.

Shane didn't move, though he might have rocked back on his heels just a little. That was better than Claire could have done; she'd have fallen backward at the very least, and Michael would probably have broken her wrist—not intentionally, but *sorry* didn't matter much when it came to shattered bones.

"Easy," Shane said in a low, calm voice. "Easy, man—you're safe. You're safe now. It's over. Nobody's going to hurt you here."

Michael froze. The red died down to embers in his eyes, and when he blinked it was gone, replaced by cool blue. He looked pale, but that was normal for him now. Claire saw his throat work as he swallowed, and then he shakily pulled in a breath and let go of Shane's wrist. "God," he whispered, and shook his head. "Sorry, man."

"No drama," Shane said. "Bad one, right?"

Michael didn't respond to that immediately. He was staring off in the middle distance. She didn't need to wonder what his nightmare had been about. . . . It would have been about being trapped in the Morganville Civic Pool, anchored to the bottom under that murky, poisoned water . . . being fed upon by the draug. Drained slowly, and alive, by creatures that found vampires as delicious as candy. Creatures that were, right now, invading and taking everything they could. Including every juicy vampire snack, straight to the bottom of whatever pool of filthy water they were hiding in.

There were, Claire realized, still tiny red marks all over

Michael's skin, like pinpricks . . . fading, but not quite gone. He was healing slower than usual—or he'd been hurt far more seriously than it had seemed. "Yeah," he finally said. "I was dreaming I was still in the pool, and . . ." He didn't go on, but he didn't need to; Claire had been there, seen it. Shane had not only seen but *felt* it—he'd dived in, unbelievably, to save lives. Vampire lives, but lives all the same. The draug had attacked him, too, and his skin had the reddish tint of broken capillaries to prove it.

Claire had a vivid, flashback-quality vision of the pool . . . that insanely creepy underwater garden of trapped vampires, tied down, stunned and helpless as the draug sucked away their strength and life. It had been one of the worst, most horrifying things she'd ever seen, and it had also outraged her on a very deep, primal level. *Nobody* deserved that. *Nobody.*

"It was real bad." Shane nodded in agreement with Michael. "And I wasn't in there nearly as long. You hang in there, Mikey." He reached out again and squeezed Michael's shoulder briefly, then rose to a standing position. "You feel the need to scream like a girl, let it out, dude. No judging."

Michael groaned and rubbed his hand over his face. "Screw you, Shane. Why do I keep you around, anyway?"

"Hey, you need somebody to keep you humble, rock star. Always have."

Claire smiled then, because Michael was starting to sound like his old self again. Shane could always do that, to any of them—a flip remark, a casual insult, and it was all okay again. Normal life.

Even when nothing at all was normal. Nothing.

Now that her panic was receding, she wondered what time it was—the room gave no real hint of whether it was day or night. They had evacuated to the Elders' Council building, which—like most vampire buildings—didn't much favor windows. What it *did* have was plenty of sleeping bags, a few rollaway beds, and lots of empty space; the vampires, apparently, were all about disaster planning, which didn't surprise her at all, really. They'd had thousands of years in which to learn how to anticipate trouble and what to have together to meet (or avoid) it.

Right now, she, Michael, and Shane were the only ones sleeping in the room, which could have held at least thirty without feeling crowded.

There was no sign of their fourth housemate, Michael's girlfriend, Eve. Her sleeping bag, which had been near Michael's, was kicked off to the side.

"Shane," Claire said, her fear getting another kick start. "Eve's missing."

"Yeah, I know. She's up," he said, "organizing coffee, believe it or not. You can take the barista out of the shop, but . . ."

That was, again, a tremendous feeling of relief. Shane made a profession of taking care of himself (and everybody else). Michael was a vampire, with all the fun advantages that came along with that in terms of self-defense. Claire was small, and not exactly a bodybuilder, but she defended herself pretty well . . . at least in being smart, careful, and having all the friends she could manage on her side.

Eve was . . . Well, Eve liked to live on the edge, but she wasn't exactly Buffy reincarnated. And in some ways her hard edges made her the most fragile of all of them. So Claire tended to worry at times like these. A lot.

"Coffee?" Michael asked, still rubbing his head. His hair should have looked crazy, but he was one of those people who had a natural immunity to bed-head; his blond hair just fell exactly the way it should, in careless surfer-style curls. Claire averted her eyes when he threw the sleeping bag back and reached for his shirt, because although he was always good to look at, he was seriously spoken for, and besides, Shane was standing right there.

Shane.

It came back to her in a dizzy rush, how he'd stopped her on the way into this place, in the faint dawn light. *"I want you to promise me one thing. Promise me you'll marry me. Not now. Someday."*

And she had promised, even if it was just their private little secret. She felt that shivery, fragile, butterfly-flutter feeling in her chest again. It was a fierce ball of light, a tangle of joy and terror and excitement and most of all, love.

Shane looked back at her with an intense, warm focus that made her suddenly feel like the only person in the world. She watched him walk toward her with a diffuse glow of pleasure. Michael was hot, no denying that, but Shane just . . . melted her. It was everything about him—his strength, his intensity, the off-center smile, the hunger in his eyes. There was something rare and fragile at the center of all that armor, and she felt lucky and privileged that he allowed her to see it.

"You doing all right?" Shane asked her, and she looked up at him. His dark gaze had turned serious, and it saw . . . too much. She couldn't hide how scared she was, not from him, but he was the last one to think it was a sign of weakness. He smiled a little and rested his forehead against hers for a second. "Yeah. You're doing just fine, tough girl."

She shoved the fear back, took a deep breath, and nodded. "Damn right." She ran her fingers through her tangled shoulder-length auburn hair—unlike Michael's, hers had suffered from a night on the hard pillows—and looked down at her T-shirt and jeans. At least they didn't wrinkle much . . . or if they did, it didn't much matter. They were clean, even if they weren't her own. It turned out there was a storehouse of clothing in the Elders' Council building basement, neatly packed in boxes, labeled with sizes. Some of it dated back to the Victorian age . . . hoop skirts and corsets and hats stowed carefully away in scented paper and cedar chests.

Claire wasn't sure she really wanted to know where all that clothing had come from, but she had her sinking suspicions. Sure, the older clothes looked like things the vampires themselves might have saved, but there were a lot of newer, more current styles that didn't seem to fit that explanation. Claire couldn't see Amelie, for instance, wearing a Train concert shirt, so she was trying hard not to think about whether they'd been scavenged from . . . other sources. Victim-y sources.

"Did you have nightmares, too?" she asked Shane. His arm tightened around her, just for a moment.

"Nothing I can't handle. I'm kind of an expert at this whole bad dreams thing, anyway," he said. And oh God, he really was. Claire knew only a little of how many bad things he'd seen, but even that was enough to spark a lifetime's worth of therapy. "Still, yesterday was dire, and that's not a word I bust out, generally. Maybe it'll look better this morning."

"Is it morning?" Claire peered at her watch.

"That depends on your definition. It's after noon, so I guess technically not really. We slept for about five hours, I suppose. Or you did. Eve bounced about an hour ago, and I got up because . . ." He shook his head. "Hell. This place creeps me out. I can't sleep too well here."

"It creeps you out more than what's happening out *there?*"

"Valid point," he said. Because the world out there—Morganville, anyway—was no longer the semi-safe place it had been just a few days ago. Sure, there had been vampires in charge of the town. Sure, they'd been predatory and kind of evil—a cross between old-school royalty and the Mafia—but at least they'd lived by rules. It hadn't been so much about ethics and morals as about practicality. . . . If they wanted to have a thriving blood supply, they couldn't just randomly kill people *all* the time.

Though the hunting licenses were alarming.

But now . . . now the vampires were in the food chain. They'd always been careful about human threats, but that wasn't the issue, not anymore. The *real* vampire enemy had finally shown its incredibly disturbing face: the draug. All that Claire knew about them was that they lived in water and they could call vampires (and humans) with their singing, right to their deaths. For humans, it was fairly quick . . . but not for vampires. Vampires trapped at the bottom of that cold pool could live and live and live until the draug had drained every bit of energy from them.

Live, and *know* it was happening. Eaten alive.

The draug were the one thing vampires feared, really and truly. Humans they treated with casual contempt, but their response to the draug had been immediate mass evacuation, except for the few who'd chosen to stay and try to save the vampires already being consumed.

They'd *all* tried—vampires and humans, working together. Even the rebellious human townies, who *hated* vamps, had taken a drive-by run at the draug. It had been a heart-stopping military operation of a battle, the most intense experience of Claire's life, and she still couldn't quite believe she'd survived it . . . or that *anyone* had.

Even with all that effort, they'd saved only three vampires from the mildewed, abandoned pool—Michael, the elegant (and probably deadly) Naomi, and the very *definitely* deadly Oliver. Then things had gone from terrible to awful, and they'd had to leave everyone else.

Except Amelie. They'd saved Amelie, the Founder of Morganville . . . sort of. And Claire was trying not to think about that, either.

"Hey," Shane said, and nudged her. "Coffee, remember? Eve'll be all sad emo Goth face if you don't drink some."

Again, Shane was the practical one, and Claire had to smile because he was completely right. No one needed sad, emo Goth Eve today. Especially Eve. "I could kill for a cup of coffee. If there's, you know, cream. And sugar."

"Yes and yes."

"And chocolate?"

"Don't push it."

Michael had, by this time, gotten up and joined them. He still looked pale—paler than usual—and there was something a little wild in his eyes, as if he was afraid that he was still in the pool. Drowning.

Claire took his hand. As always, it felt a little cooler than room temperature, but not *cold* . . . living flesh, but running on a much lower setting. Almost as tall as Shane, he looked down at her and smiled the rock-star smile that made all the girls melt in their shoes. She, however, was immune. Almost. She only melted a little, secretly. "What?" he asked her, and she shook her head.

"Nothing," she said. "You're not alone, Michael. We won't let that happen again. I promise."

The smile disappeared, and he studied her with a strange kind of intensity, almost as if he was seeing her for the first time. Or seeing something new in her. "I know," he said. "Hey, remember when I almost didn't let you into the house that first day you came?"

She'd shown up on his doorstep desperate, bruised, scared, and way too young to be facing Morganville. He'd been right to have his doubts. "Yep."

"Well, I was dead wrong," he said. "Maybe I never said that out loud before, but I mean it, Claire. All that's happened since . . .

we wouldn't have made it. Not me, not Shane, not Eve. Not without you."

"It's not me," Claire said, startled. "It's not! It's *us*, that's all. We're just better together. We . . . take care of each other."

He nodded again, but didn't have a chance to reply because Shane reached in, took Claire's hand from Michael's, and said—not seriously, thank God—"Stop vamping up my girl, man. She needs coffee."

"Don't we all," Michael said, and smacked Shane on the shoulder hard enough to make him stagger. "*Vamping up your girl?* Dude. That's low."

"Digging for China," Shane agreed, straight-faced. "Come on."

Claire could follow the smell of brewing caffeine all the way to Eve, like a trail of dropped coffee beans. It gave the sterile, funereal, windowless Elders' Council building a weirdly homey feel, despite the chilly marble walls and the thick, muffling carpets.

The hallway opened into a wider circular area—the hub in the wheel—that held a huge round table in the center, which was normally adorned by an equally large fresh floral arrangement . . . adding to the funeral home vibe. But that had been pushed to the side, and a giant, shiny coffee dispenser had been put in its place, along with neat little bowls of sugar, spoons, napkins, cups, and saucers. Even cream and milk pitchers.

It was surreal to Claire, as if she'd stepped out of a nightmare and into a fancy hotel without any transition. And there, emerging from another door that must have led to some sort of kitchen, came Eve, with a tray in her hands, which she slid onto the other side of the big table.

Claire stared, because although it was Eve, it didn't really *look* like her. No Goth makeup. Her hair was down, loose around her face and falling in soft black waves; even without her rice-powder coverage, her skin was creamy pale, but it looked movie-star beautiful. Natural-look Eve was *stunning,* even wearing borrowed clothes . . . though she'd found a retro fifties black pouf-skirted dress that really suited her perfectly.

She had a red scarf tied jauntily around her neck to hide the bites and bruises that Michael—starving and crazy from being dragged out of the pool—had inflicted on her.

She, and this setup, all looked a little *too* perfect. Shane and Michael exchanged a look, and Claire knew they were communicating the same thought.

Eve gave them a bright smile and said, "Good morning, campers! Coffee?"

"Hey," Michael said, in such a soft and tentative voice that Claire felt her stomach clench. "You should be resting." He reached for her, and Eve flinched. *Flinched.* Like he'd tried to hit her. His hand dropped to his side, and Claire couldn't look at his face. "Eve—"

She spoke in a rush, running right over the moment. "We have hot coffee, all the good stuff—sorry I couldn't get mocha up and running, but this place has a serious espresso deficiency . . . oh, and the croissants are hot out of the oven, have one."

"You baked?" Shane's eyebrows threatened to levitate right off his face.

"They were in one of those pop-open rolls, moron. Even I can bake those." Eve's smile wasn't so much bright, Claire thought, as it was totally breakable. "I don't think anybody ever used the kitchen in here, but at least it was stocked up. There's even fresh butter and milk. Wonder who thought of that?"

"Eve," Michael said again, and finally she looked directly at him. She didn't say anything at all, only picked up a cup, filled it with hot, dark coffee, and handed it to him. He took it as he stared at her, then sipped—not as if he really wanted it, but as if it was something he was doing to please her. "Eve, can we just—"

"No, we can't," she said. "Not right now." And then she turned and walked back to the kitchen, stiff-armed the door, and let it swing shut behind her.

The three of them stood there, only the sound of the door creaking on its hinges breaking the silence, until Shane cleared his throat, reached for a cup, and poured. "So," he said. "Aside from the five-hundred-pound gorilla in the room that we're not going to talk about, does anyone around here have half a plan on how we're going to live through the day?"

Photo © 2011 Robert Hart Studio

Rachel Caine is the *New York Times* bestselling author of more than thirty novels, including the Weather Warden series, the Outcast Season series, the Revivalist series, and the Morganville Vampires series. She was born at White Sands Missile Range, which people who know her say explains a lot. She has been an accountant, a professional musician, and an insurance investigator, and, until recently, still carried on a secret identity in the corporate world. She and her husband, fantasy artist R. Cat Conrad, live in Texas with their iguanas, Popeye and Darwin.

CONNECT ONLINE

www.rachelcaine.com
facebook.com/rachelcainefanpage
twitter.com/rachelcaine
www.rachelcaine.livejournal.com